Gorilla Black

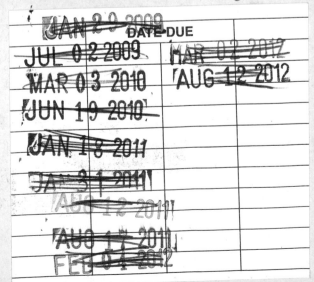

Seven

Gorilla Black

a novel

One World ▦ Ballantine Books | New York

A One World Books Trade Paperback Original

Published in the United States by One World Books, an imprint of The Random House Publishing Group, a division of Random House, Inc., New York.

ONE WORLD is a registered trademark and the One World colophon is a trademark of Random House, Inc.

LIBRARY OF CONGRESS CATALOGING-IN-PUBLICATION DATA

Seven.
Gorilla Black : a novel / Seven.
p. cm.
ISBN-13: 978-0-345-50052 6 (trade pbk.) 1. African American men—Fiction.
2. Drug dealers—Fiction. 3. Crack (Drug)—Fiction. 4. Murder—Fiction.
5. Richmond (Va.)—Fiction. I. Title.
PS3619.E95G67 2008
813'.6—dc22   2008000541

Printed in the United States of America

www.oneworldbooks.net

2 4 6 8 9 7 5 3 1

Book design by Laurie Jewell

This mad crazy thing that we call love
grows deep inside of us
Like wild flowers
Its presence demands nurturing
expects to be loved equally in return

For people are like flowers
their petals are soft and gentle to the touch
without proper care
the very essence of their being
will soon fade

break loose from their stem
then ultimately wither away

—Seven

This novel is dedicated
to children everywhere who
dare to be different.

In loving memory of
Larry, Kim, and Pat

Nikki Turner

Dear Readers,

It's here! It's really here! I can't believe I am finally launching the Nikki Turner Presents line! I can barely contain my excitement long enough to type this letter. Let me slow down and get myself together. Wheewww! Let me start, as always, by thanking you for supporting the work that I hold so dear to my heart. For my die-hard Nikki Turner fans, you know how you do it—keep those pages turning. And for those of you who are just getting on-board (better late than never), you are definitely in for a real treat!

It took a little longer than anticipated to put together the initial slate for my new line, because I didn't want to break my promise to bring my readers nothing but the cream of the crop from the Nikki Turner Presents book line. And in doing so, I wanted to be sure that I was presenting you with the authentic depiction of street life that you have grown to love and expect from my works. My team and I went through hundreds of submissions to come up with the right three bodies of work to launch the line's first full-length novels. (Thank you to everyone that submitted their work to Nikki Turner Presents!) These three endeavors were more than mere projects, books, or stories; at the end of the day I set out to develop relationships along with great books. These people showed loyalty to me, my mission, and my vision. To my authors: I respect each of you for this.

Seven, the first lady of the line, explodes on the scene with a heartwrenching, thugged-out love adventure: *Gorilla Black*. I remember when I was introduced to her via e-mail. She wanted to be a part of the *Street Chronicles* short-story collection when it was just a concept with no concrete plan on how it would be funded or published—but she still wanted in. Her persistence in convincing me that she was the next hottest thing compelled me to take a look at her work, and after reading the first pages of her story "Big Daddy" I became a fan of Seven's. I think one of the reasons I dug her so much was because I saw a lot of myself in her. But don't get it twisted; dealing with this sistah was no cakewalk. I loved her work to no end, but she challenged me about everything, and I pushed her as hard as I could. When I thought she was going to crack from the pressure and couldn't take anymore— I pushed harder. And Seven would exceed my expectations, time and time again.

Now without further ado, I would like to present to you the debut novel for Nikki Turner Presents: *Gorilla Black*.

P.S. I thank you, Seven, for allowing me to be your Lamaze coach with this book. You make me so proud, and I can't wait for the world to discover you.

"Love alters not with his brief hours and weeks,
But bears it out even to the edge of doom."

—William Shakespeare

"Things aren't always what they seem."

—Seven

Prologue

I was standing in front of the mirror reciting to myself "Let Me Not to the Marriage of True Minds," my favorite work written by my man William Shakespeare. Amanda and I had decided to recite the poem as part of our wedding vows. I stood nervously before the mirror, reciting a poem that I had learned to master by the age of seven. After tripping over my words for the last and final time, I felt it necessary to move on to another task. I circled away from the oval-shaped glass, then rotated sideways in order to get a better view of myself from all angles. With the exception of one small problem, I was impressed with what I saw. I repositioned my necktie, correcting the slight imperfection.

"If looking this good was a crime, the feds would've locked my ass up a long time ago," I boasted to my crew. My stickman Lucky, who had been down with me from day one, co-signed for me, boosting my ego even more.

"Yeah, Black, you rocking the hell out of that white tux shorty," he shot back at me.

There were more than three hundred guests waiting inside the church to witness me marry Amanda, my new love of only five months. I listened intensely as the music played and the guests were escorted to their respective seats. Fifteen minutes prior, I had been pacing back and forth, debating whether or not I was doing the right thing. See, I had just hooked up with Amanda five months ago after a disastrous break-up with the true love of my life, Starr Williams. Amanda had not only been there for me throughout my troublesome relationship with Starr, but she was also the one who had made me realize that it was time for me to hang my hat, throw down my guns, and say good-bye to the drug game. So, there I stood, patiently waiting to say "I do" to this pretty young thing who was ready to accept me, Bilal Cunningham, the largest, most notorious cocaine dealer in Richmond's Churchill, as her husband.

Ms. Cheryl stuck her head inside the private quarters. "Black, we're ready to start," she announced with a slight grin to my groomsmen and me.

I glanced down at my Rolex Yacht Master and thought to myself, *Yeah, right on time.* Then I turned to face the mirror once more. I needed just one more glimpse of myself as a single man. I checked myself up and down, making sure that my custommade tuxedo pants that had been hand delivered from D.C. were lying perfectly at my shoes. Hell, I figured if the White House employed the infamous Georges de Paris to dress the presidents of the United States, then why couldn't my staff hire him to dress me?

I brushed at the jacket, merely out of habit, because I knew that there wasn't one lint ball or piece of filth near me or my suit. I was cleaner than the Board of Health. Nawh, fuck that. On the real, I was so clean that the Environmental Protection Agency couldn't touch me. I stuck out my chest, and cleared my throat. "Let's do this!" I gazed over at my crew and motioned for them to leave with the wedding planner. Before I exited the room thoughts of Starr bombarded my mind. I worried about her and wondered what she may have been doing on this day, my wedding day, a day that she had envisioned for her and me.

I left the dressing room and halfheartedly took my stand at the altar. I scoped the chapel, taking count of those in attendance. It appeared that most of the people on my wedding list were present and accounted for. "That's what's up." I nodded to myself. Then, I focused my attention on the aisle and watched as the wedding party fell beautifully into place. Finally, the big moment came. The organist began to play "The Wedding March," and Amanda began sashaying down the aisle. I was stunned as my bride headed toward me. I don't know if I was in awe of her beauty or more in shock that I was actually getting married. I glanced over at my moms, her head hung low, deep in her lap. Then my eyes shot over to the pew where Amanda's mother and grandmother were sitting. They both wore the same solemn look on their faces. For a minute, I got lost in their eyes.

Suddenly, the doors of the church flew open and Mousey, the neighborhood gossip box, came bursting in. He looked wild and crazy, his clothes were two sizes too big, and his Chuck Taylor sneakers were dangling from his feet by threads. Mousey had a reputation for being the bearer of bad news and stormed inside the church as if his li'l ass had received an invitation. He ran center aisle, then stopped abruptly, stepping completely out of his right shoe.

"Black, come quick, something has happened to Starr!" Mousey yelled down toward the altar, half covering his mouth with his left hand. Before anyone could acknowledge his presence, he reached down, snatched up his raggedy shoe, then turned, and hauled ass out of the church.

Murmurs echoed throughout the church. Some of the guests moaned, while others leaned to the side like a stack of dominoes, whispering in the ear of the person sitting next to them. The next thing I knew, I hauled ass past Amanda and out of the church doors. Without me ever having to say a word, my crew bolted after me, because as always they were down for whatever. The crimson-colored stretch Cadillac limousine that me and my groomsmen had arrived in awaited us outside the church. We jumped in.

"Everybody strapped?" I quizzed my crew.

"Ready," all six of my niggas answered in unison as we all removed our burners from our tuxedo jackets. I tapped on the glass partition to get the chauffeur's attention. Uncle Charlie, the white chauffer who had been my driver for a minute, slid the glass down and turned his head around to me.

"Yes sir, Mr. Black?" he asked.

"To Fairfield Projects now, and don't catch any traffic lights!" I ordered him.

Gorilla Black

Chapter 1

It was a red-hot summer day. Hazy and humid. The air was so mufucking tight, I damn near couldn't breathe. It was the summer of 1980 and I had just moved to Fairfield Court Projects after my moms had gotten us evicted from our apartment in Matthew Heights. I was sitting on the front porch, reading *Negro* by Langston Hughes, when I spotted a bow-legged girl standing across the street, sucking on her thumb. She was wearing a red plastic jacket and red ballerina shoes. Her hair was rolled up in a halter top and her skinny legs were shiny, as if she had a whole bottle of petroleum jelly on them or something.

My little brother Keon, who was eight years old at the time, yelled out, "Who dat girl with the greasy legs and hot plastic on?"

Man, I laughed so hard, I almost peed on myself. The girl caught us laughing at her and from the distance I caught her rolling her eyes. I yelled out to her, "Yo, shorty girl, you better be careful, they might just pop out your head!"

She threw us an evil stare, and then dropped her stinky thumb from her mouth. "Yo, you ape looking fool; I know you ain't laughing at me with your big, black, ugly self! And my name is Starr, for your information," she shot back at me. Starr stood there rolling her neck around, with both hands placed on her imagination.

"And if I am, what you gone do about it?" I asked.

She sucked her teeth. "Call the zoo and tell him Godzilla escaped!"

"You better go take off that hot plastic jacket before you die from heat exhaustion. And if that's your imagination, you sure as heck ain't got much of one," I spat. The next thing I know, Starr spun around like she was about to bust a Michael Jackson dance move. Instead, she bent all the way over until her fingers were touching her toes, then she came up swiftly with her right hand and smacked her butt, *pow*.

"Kiss my ass, you big black gorilla!" she screamed at me.

I couldn't believe my ears; the chick had the audacity to call me a big black gorilla. I had never been called out of my name by anyone other than my moms. "Look here, shorty girl. For real, I wasn't even laughing at you, so you need to just chill out!" Starr wasn't one to back down easily, she kept the insults flowing.

"Oh, don't get scared now, with your ugly self!" she carried on, her neck spinning around like the little white chick in *The Exorcist*. I let out a huge sigh, then bit my bottom lip.

"Shorty, I ain't scared of you. I just don't want any trouble. So, don't start none, won't be none!" I warned her. Next thing I know, Starr jumped down from her porch, picked up something from the ground, and made a tight fist. I stood with my arms folded across my chest. For a minute, neither of us said a word, we just locked eyes.

Okay, I'll admit it. From where I was sitting, she was kind of cute. Truth be told, if ever there had been a beauty contest, Starr would have been named Beauty and I, the Beast. Nevertheless, I wasn't about to let that skinny, high yellow, want-to-be pageant chick from across the street know that she was indeed the shit!

Suddenly, Starr wound up her right arm as if she was about to throw a pitch in the World Series. She let go off a huge rock, almost smacking me in the head. I ducked and the rock slammed against our screen door. That did it! Enough was enough! I figured I had to say or do something to defend myself because all the little heathens on my new block were outside, and they were all pointing at me and chanting, "Gorilla-Gorilla, Gorilla-Gorilla!" They paraded back and forth.

Man, I was so mad, I had smoke coming out of my nose. With all the red she was sporting, and the temperature blazing at ninety-five degrees, I knew that I had just met the devil. I slammed my book shut and headed across the street. Yeah, I was planning to fight a girl. Keon ran after me, swinging his arms wildly, and yelled at me.

"Come back, Bilal, forget her, man!" he pleaded with me. I refused to back down from Starr so I continued in her direction. The faster I walked, the louder the chanting became.

"Gorilla, Gorilla!" some of the kids shouted, while others ran around in circles, kicking up dirt as they screamed to the top of their lungs. "It's a fight, it's a fight!" the little bastards instigated. But, like the true soldier she was, Starr didn't budge; she stood her ground on her porch. She continued talking junk, rolling her neck and pointing her fingers at me.

"I ain't scared of you, and if you come up on my porch, I'mma beat your big, black ugly tail," she threatened. As I marched over to her, I was still trying to think of a comeback, but I couldn't think of anything that could top an eleven-year-old girl's invitation to kiss her ass.

Suddenly, something stopped me dead in my tracks. To this day, I still don't know what it was. I made a tight fist with both of my hands, and then I slowly turned around to face the loud-mouth instigators that were trailing behind me. I needed to silence their heathen asses once and for all. I took in a deep breath, exhaled, then I let go of the ugliest face that I could possibly make.

"The next mutherfucker that calls me Gorilla, better call me Gorilla Black!" I yelled out.

The next thing I knew, everybody took off running as if they had seen a ghost. Later that night before we went to bed, Keon told me that when I had turned to face the crowd that I had fire in my eyes.

Chapter 2

The next morning I woke up to the sound of Momma screaming like she had gone plumb crazy. "Come on down. Time to eat!" she yelled. I grabbed Keon from the top bunk and we hurried downstairs to see what was up. I was a bit surprised when I turned the corner, only to find Momma standing at the gas stove in her nightgown. She was stirring a pot of grits with a big wooden spoon and puffing on a Salem cigarette. I grabbed a chair and sat down.

"Moms, why you fixing grits in the summertime?" I asked her.

Momma continued circling the pot of grits. "Boy, stop your goddamn complaining! You better be glad that I got up to fix you anything!" she snapped at me. "I wanted to make a big breakfast so we could celebrate being in our new place," she explained, as if moving from Matthew Heights to the projects was something to jump up and down about.

Matthew Heights was a working-class poor neighborhood,

nothing extravagant but definitely one step up from the pj's. So, I was angry with Momma for losing her job and causing us to get evicted. Momma used to be a certified nursing assistant at Retreat Hospital. She had been on the job for five years, but she kept being disciplined for showing up at work drunk. Her supervisor gave her a thousand chances, until one night Moms was supposed to be giving a patient a sponge bath, and she fell asleep drunk with her hand smacked dead between the old lady's pussy. Mom was so drunk that her hand literally had to be pried away from the old lady's coochie. Not only was she fired, but social services was called in. To make matters worse, the old lady's family threatened to sue Momma and the hospital because they claimed the old lady was traumatized and had panic attacks whenever somebody tried to wash her.

After Momma lost her job, she couldn't keep up with the rent and ended up three months behind. The landlord was willing to work with her but she wasn't putting up much effort. Instead of searching for a job, she sat at home and played loud music all day and night like some lovesick teenager. So, after being late with the rent the fourth time in less than a year, and for having a hundred-signature petition signed by our neighbors, we were thrown out on our butt like yesterday's trash. Momma couldn't understand why the neighbors filed a petition to get us evicted. The petition stated that she was too loud and ghetto, and a real nuisance to the community. They were right; over the years Momma had gotten out of control. I don't know why she acted the way she did, 'cause she was raised in the church down south and had only moved to Richmond after having me. Momma was just a naïve country bumpkin from Birmingham, Alabama, but for some odd reason she cursed like a sailor and drank like three.

"Ya'll hurry up and eat this goddamn food!" she cursed for no apparent reason. To go along with our hot grits, we had scrambled eggs with cheese, sausage, and fried apples. The eggs were running so hard, that I thought those suckers were gonna jump up off the plate and hit the back door. The sausage patties were so crumpled up that they looked like scrapple. Oh, but make no mistake about it, Momma used to be a good cook. She was a large woman; so it wasn't a secret that she liked to eat. She stood five foot five and weighed in at three hundred pounds. Her complexion was Hershey chocolate and her coal, jet-black hair extended past her shoulders. Her eyes were hazel and her smile was priceless. Momma was a big sista, she wore her weight well. That's until Melvin the Mailman stopped coming around.

Melvin the Mailman was one of her ex-boyfriends. He was Gary Coleman short, with a light complexion and a small frame. Mr. Melvin was also a deacon in our church and married with three children. At first, I thought Mom had an awful lot of mail, because Deacon used to come to Momma every day. Then he started dropping in only on Tuesdays for Bible study and they would go into her bedroom and pray together for an hour. Well, one day I was outside playing when the ice cream truck rolled through. I had forgotten that it was Tuesday, you know—Bible study night. Well, I ran inside and up to Momma's room and that's when I walked in and caught Momma humping Deacon Melvin. At first, all I could see was her ass going up and down, down and up. I thought, *Oh, my God, Momma's a freak,* because I thought she was fucking herself. Then, I spotted one of Mr. Melvin's legs. It fell from underneath hers, and I just stood there in shock. Momma spun her head around, jumped off him and yelled, "Boy, why you come busting in my room? Get your li'l black ass out of here!"

"But Mom," I whined, "can I have twenty-five cents to get a Chic-O-Stick?"

"Chic-O-Stick? If you don't get the hell out of my room, this chick gone put a stick up yo ass!" she growled.

Shortly after I barged in on them, Deacon Melvin stopped

coming over. I think Momma got depressed about it, 'cause she stopped bathing, combing her hair, or getting all dolled up. Momma smelled like Fritos and booty all rolled up into one. At times, the smell was so horrific that I would walk around and spray body cologne in the air. That solution to my problem didn't last long 'cause she got hip to what I was doing. One day I was spraying the bathroom after she had left out, and she caught me. Boy, Momma hit me in my back so hard that I fell to the floor, *Bam,* then she stood over top of me and asked, "Boy, are you trying to tell me something?"

I thought to myself, *You know you stink, so why you mad?*

"Bilal, ya'll get up from this table and go put your clothes on. I have some things I need ya'll to do today," she ordered me and Keon. We happily jumped up from the table, leaving the food right on our plates. Before heading up to our room, I noticed that Momma and her girlfriends had tried their best to make our new home as comfortable as possible. I hadn't noticed anything the night before because she had made us go straight to bed after my argument with that little heffa from across the street. Momma had strung wooden beads, which separated the kitchen from the living room. She had even purchased a canister set to separate the sugar, flour, rice, and beans. The Crisco can that use to hold recycled grease had been replaced with a forest green metallic can that read, GREASE. Two orange plastic school chairs sat positioned with our mahogany wood kitchen table, as if they belonged. I later found out that Momma's best friend, Ms. Sheila, had stolen the chairs from a nearby elementary school where she was a janitor.

In the living room, we had one couch and one love seat. The same raggedy furniture from Matthew Heights but it looked totally different with paisley furniture throws and solid colored toss pillows. Several copies of the Yellow Pages held the couch up on both ends. Momma and her friends had also stacked ten black plastic crates together to make an entertainment center. Our television, stereo player, and all of Mom's forty-fives and eight-tracks were assembled on the makeshift stand. Her favorite picture of Marvin Gaye covered the wall behind the couch. When I saw all of the changes she had made, I could no longer be angry with her for getting us evicted. I figured if Momma was happy, then I needed to be happy too. I hurried upstairs to get dressed for the day. My little brother followed behind me.

"Bilal, are you scared to live in Fairfield?" Keon asked with an unsettled look on his face.

"No, why you ask me that, Keon?"

"I don't know. I guess because of the way everybody treated us yesterday. Bilal, they acted like they didn't like us," he fretted.

"That's because we just moved around here. Don't worry, Keon, you'll make new friends," I assured him.

"But I don't want new friends. I like the ones I already have," he whined. I gave Keon a reassuring pat on the top of his head, then hugged him tight. I loved my little brother to death, and the fact that he was sad and afraid bothered me.

"Look, Keon, I'll make sure you get to visit your old friends, even if I have to take you over to Matthew Heights myself, all right?"

"Okay, Bilal," he smiled at me.

I hurried downstairs and waited patiently for Momma to give us a list of our daily chores. Momma pulled a piece of scratch paper and a pen from her purse. "Listen up, Bilal, I need you to go to the store and get a pack of bologna, a loaf of bread, two cans of corn beef hash, eight packs of Kool-aid, a gallon of milk, and a dozen eggs," she read off the grocery list. She continued on, "Oh, and ask somebody in the store to show you where you can find the seeds to plant flowers," she added.

"Huh?" I blurted out. We had just moved to the pj's. It wasn't like we had a house with a yard. I didn't understand why Momma needed flower seeds.

"You heard exactly what I said! I said to ask somebody in the store to show you where the seeds are to plant flowers. Then, I want you to get me five packs of seeds, because I'm finnid to plant some flowers in the front yard, because all that goddamn dirt out there reminds me of back home and I don't need no reminders of home! Do you hear me?" Momma growled. Momma was always overly dramatic about little shit.

"Yes ma'am. I hear you." I nodded.

Momma reached down inside her bra. "Here, take this. This should be enough," she said, handing me what appeared to be Monopoly money.

I had never seen the type of money she was handing me, so I questioned her. "What's this, Ma?" I frowned.

"Boy, it's a ten-dollar bill. It's food stamp money. Now, put it in your pocket and don't lose it!" she huffed.

"Momma, where is the store?" I wondered.

Momma stood up from the table, and stuck her pen back inside her purse. She walked over to the kitchen sink.

"Koslow's Supermarket is 'bout a mile up the road. Now you and Keon go on out there and find your way."

Before leaving, I had one more question to ask Momma. "Momma, why you got your money in your bra when you got your purse right there beside you?" I asked. Momma spun around from the sink, obviously offended by my questions.

"Bilial, don't be asking me a whole lot of damn questions. Get your black ass out of here. Just get!" she yelled. I jumped up from the table and hurried out of the kitchen. Keon had finally made it downstairs. He met up with me in the living room.

"Come on, Keon, we got to go to the store. I don't know where it is, but I'm sure we'll find it," I said as I grabbed my little brother by his hand.

. . .

We left through the back door and headed for the grocery store. I spotted one of the dudes from the day before. He was pushing an iron shopping cart, and obviously talking or singing to himself. "Hey you!" I called out to him. The dude turned and headed in our direction. "Excuse me, but which way is the store?" I asked him. He strolled over to me, pushing his shopping cart real cool, like it was a smooth ride.

"Whaaat up? Whaaat up, man?' " he struggled with his words. "My name is P-Pierre, man. What's ya'll name?" He stuttered. I realized that he had a speech problem so I tried to help him out.

"My little brother's name is Keon and I'm B—" I attempted to tell him, but before I could, he cut me off.

"Yeah, I know, your name is Black, 'cause you told us yesterday." He laughed, reminding me of my confrontation with the heathen instigators.

"You forgot Gorilla," I shot him a half smile. The dude checked me up and down.

"Man, you ugly but you ain't all that ugly." He laughed again. "Come on, if ya'll going to the store, ya'll can roll with me cause I got a whole lot of shit to get." He chuckled.

"Is that why you have your own shopping cart?" I questioned. Pierre nodded his head.

"Yeah, man, it's six of us in the house, plus Momma. I got three sisters and two brothers," he shared.

Keon jumped in; counting with his fingers, he concluded, "Three girls and three boys, just like *The Brady Bunch*."

Pierre looked Keon dead in the eye.

"Yeah, except we ain't got no daddies," he said bluntly.

Keon mumbled underneath his breath, "We ain't got no daddies either."

When we stepped into Koslow's, Pierre informed me that I

couldn't use food stamps to pay for the flower seeds. He explained to me that food stamps could only be used to purchase food and cold food at that. He suggested that I steal the seeds and keep it moving. I had never stolen anything in my life, but there was no way in hell that I was going back home without those seeds. Pierre scoped out the store while I planned my attack. He pointed out the big, fat security officer to me. He kept his eye on him while I gathered the items from the shopping list and made my way over to the flower seeds. I glanced over my shoulder to make sure the coast was clear, then I grabbed the first two packs, and read the labels silently. *Zinnias.* I shoved them into my right pocket. Then I grabbed two more, *Nasturtiums,* and shoved them in the left. Then I quickly snatched the fifth pack, *Sunflowers,* and threw them down in my underwear. I was leaving the aisle when I spotted the *Enquirer* newspaper lying on a shelf. I really enjoyed reading the *Enquirer,* so I decided, why not? I stole the newspaper too.

We paid for our groceries and just as we were about to leave, the security officer approached us. "Excuse me, young fellow." He stepped directly in front of me. I started sweating bullets. My first time stealing and I had been caught red-handed.

"Yes sir, Mr. Thompson," I read his name tag. I figured if I chumped up to him, he'd let me off the hook. He smiled politely at me.

"Oh, I see you got manners just like your little brother," he chuckled, as he walked with us toward the exit.

He patted Keon on his back and then paid him a compliment as if he had known him forever. "Keon is a nice kid; he told me that ya'll just moved to Fairfield Court Projects from Matthew Heights," he stated more so than asked. I nodded in agreement with him.

"Yes sir, we did," I answered.

"Well, you a pretty big boy for an eleven-year-old," he commented, sizing me up. "Do you play football?" he inquired.

"Well, I never really have," I answered honestly.

He looked at me and smiled. "Well, you're in luck. I'm the head coach for the Fairfield Cougars football team and we accept kids of all ages and sizes. Why don't you and Keon come out for the team?" I had always dreamed of playing football but Moms would never let me play. She said that I was too fat and that I would be too slow on the field. The thought of playing on a football team made me happy. I was excited, and it showed. I let out a huge smile.

"Tell me when. When does practice start?" I asked enthusiastically.

The security guard continued walking with us and ran off the schedule. "The Pee-wees are scheduled to practice at five thirty p.m. on Mondays and the Midgets will practice at six p.m. on Tuesdays. Practice starts next week."

"We'll both be there, Mr. Thompson. Where is practice?" I asked.

"We meet up at the Fairfield Recreation Center. I'm sure Pierre will show you where it is."

Pierre stood there with a smile on his face and nodded at Mr. Thompson. "Yeah, I'll show them," he promised.

Before disappearing into the store, Mr. Thompson turned around and yelled, "Oh, and from now on, you boys can call me Coach."

We headed back toward the projects; Pierre was pushing his cart and singing the song "Funky Town." I joined in. "Gotta make a move to a town that's right for me."

"So Pierre, what's your brothers' and sisters' names and how old are they?" Keon cut us off.

Pierre stopped singing. "I'm eleven, then my brother Paul is eight, the twins Patrick and Patricia are six, Paula is four, and my baby sister Priscilla is two," he told us.

"So, all of ya'll names starts with the letter P?" I jumped in.

"Yep," he stuttered.

"Well, what's your mom's name?" I gave him a lopsided grin. I expected him to say Elizabeth, Barbara, Mary, Veronica, or something that didn't begin with the letter P. Pierre threw his head back and broke out laughing.

"Man, my momma's name is Pearl," he laughed. Then me and Keon fell out laughing with him.

While we were walking, I came up with a new name for Pierre. "Yo Pierre, I'mma make up a new name for you, 'cause you know, everybody has a nickname," I told him. Keon jumped up and down,

"What is it, what is it?" he was dying to know.

I checked my new friend up and down, thought about the short time I had been in his presence and replied, "Putt." He looked at me half crazy and confused, then he scratched his head.

"Putt? Why Putt?" he pondered.

I had read in the dictionary that the word *putt* means to shove, to gently push as with a golf stroke made on a putting green, causing a ball to roll near or into a hole. I extended my right hand to him and looked him dead in the eye.

" 'Cause you're the push I needed."

Pierre nodded his head in agreement, and then extended his hand back to me. "A'ight then, my new name is Putt." We shook hands real tight and it was at that very moment that I knew I had made a friend for life.

We made it back to Fairfield, and as we headed down the block, Putt yelled, "Oh shit, man!" I stopped to see what had caught his attention.

"What's wrong?" I asked.

Putt didn't answer, instead he shoved me in the back. "Run, Black, run!" he screamed at me.

I shrugged my shoulders, then threw my hands up. "For what?"

" 'Cause you got on red! Now run, Black, run!" Putt yelled. The next thing I know, a big yellow dude came charging toward me like a bull at a matador.

"Take off your shirt, Black, take it off!" Putt yelled again.

I didn't know why I was being told to run, or to take my clothes off for that matter, but in any case, I ran like hell. I wasn't fast enough. The raging maniac caught up with me and tackled me to the ground.

"Leave my brother alone! Stop! Stop!" Keon cried out.

Putt screamed, "Leave 'em alone, Crazy Chris. Get off of him!" The dude ignored their cries, and he kicked and punched every ligament I owned. I didn't try to fight him back, 'cause I was holding on to Momma's bread and eggs and wad'nt no way I was going home with bread crumbs 'cause Momma hated crumbled-up bread. So, I just laid there balled up in a knot, protecting Momma's groceries at all cost. The dude beat me down like he was my daddy; but then again, I never knew what a beating from a daddy felt like.

The neighbors rushed to my rescue in an attempt to scare him off. They yelled at him, "Stop, Crazy Chris! We gone call the police!" they threatened.

"Boy, pull off the goddamn shirt!" one woman screamed.

Then I heard Keon's final plea, "I wanna go home, somebody make him stop beating my brother!" he begged.

I knew then that I had to do something to stop the beating. I wasn't sure if it would work, but I did exactly what everyone was yelling for me to do. I grabbed my shirt and raised it above my head, and threw it on the ground. Instantly, the beating stopped. I opened both of my eyes when I realized the nightmare was over. Crazy Chris stood over top of me, looked at me lopsided, then picked up my shirt and ran off. My eyes searched the crowd for Putt. I didn't see my new friend at first, then out of nowhere he came running over to me with a baseball bat gripped tight in his hands.

"Where dat, where dat crazy mutherfucker at?" he asked the crowd.

Chapter 3

In less than twenty-four hours, I had learned to cuss, steal, and had gotten my ass beat down. The thought of Crazy Chris coming back after me, and of Moms being pissed off about her eggs and her bread, threw me into an asthma attack. Putt and Keon rushed to get me home. When we got there, Keon banged on the back door real hard.

"Open the door, Mom, open up the door!" he screamed loudly. Momma took forever to open up. Finally, she swung open the back door, her face balled up in a knot.

"Why ya'll knocking at this door like a dog after you or something?" she said, with a Salem cigarette hanging from her lips.

"Momma, this man beat up Bilal for no reason and now he can't breathe." Keon jumped up and down, crying hysterically. Streams of tears flooded his face, covering his light gray eyes. Momma stood at the door with her nose turned up.

"Boy, what the hell is wrong with you? You just came from the

store, why you ain't breathe in one of those brown paper bags?"
she badgered. Keon wiped the tears from his eyes,

"But Momma, the bags we had were too big," he whined.

Momma took another pull on her cigarette, then sucked her
teeth. Putt and Keon pulled me up from the porch, and Keon
grabbed for the door handle. Momma snatched the door back.

"Uh-huh. Ya'll gone walk around to the front because I just
mopped my kitchen floor," she snapped.

Then she slammed the door in our face as if we were strangers
or would-be robbers. Putt gave me a concerned look.

"Man, is your mother crazy? You out here half dead and she
worrying about her kitchen floor!" he fumed. I shook my head at
him and fought to catch my breath.

"Man, crazy ain't the word, " I mumbled.

When we reached the front door, Momma was in the living
room slow dancing by herself to her favorite song, "When a Man
Loves a Woman." She was ticked off because we had left the groceries behind and demanded that I go back to get them. Putt vol-
unteered to go back while I changed out of my clothes that were
covered in egg yolk. Meanwhile, Momma cranked the volume up
on her stereo, switching back and forth between Marvin Gaye
and Percy Sledge. Momma loved her some Marvin Gaye, but her
favorite song was "When a Man Loves a Woman" by Percy
Sledge, so when she would get down right pissy drunk, she would
holler, "Marvin Gaye sings the hell out of that song 'When a Man
Loves a Woman'!"

Twenty minutes later, she called out for me and Keon. "Ya'll
come on downstairs, you got company." It was Putt and his little
brother Patrick.

"Black, I got the corn beef hash and the bologna for you, but
somebody stole the other stuff," he said. Momma ear hustled our
conversation.

"Hum, well, if the food is gone, then I guess ya'll ain't got shit to eat," she huffed.

"Miss, can Black, and Keon, go-go swimming with us?" Putt asked for her permission, using my new name.

"Mom, can we go, please, can we go?" Keon begged.

"Can we?" I followed up. Momma threw me an evil stare, then shook her head.

"Thirty minutes ago your ass couldn't breathe; now you wanna go swimming. Boy, I knew you was faking, that's why I didn't pay yo black ass no attention." She smirked. "Gone on. But you better watch Keon around that water, you hear me?"

"Yes ma'am, I hear you," I answered.

Before we left the house, Momma stopped Putt by pulling him by the back of his shirttail.

"By the way, little boy, my name is Ms. Joann. And tell me, just who the hell is 'Black'?" She frowned her nose up at him.

Putt wiggled away from her grip, and without ever turning around to her, he answered, "Your son."

Momma let out a sly giggle. "And Black he is!"

• • •

As soon as my feet hit the concrete, I drilled Putt about the dude who beat me up.

"Putt, what is up with Crazy Chris? Why he jump me like that?" I asked.

"Oh, yeah, Black, I almost forgot about the fight," Putt said.

"The what? Putt, it wasn't a fight, that dude beat me for no reason." I came to a complete halt, because I needed Putt to understand the difference between a fight and a beat-down. "Listen up, Putt. One person doing all the hitting is a beat-down. Two people exchanging blows is a fight," I went on to explain. "That wasn't a fight! I caught a beat-down!" I yelled. Putt, Keon, and

Patrick all laughed at me. I didn't find shit funny, so I threw them a serious look to let them know I wasn't on joke time. They all stopped laughing and I continued with my round of questioning. "Putt, why they call that dude Crazy Chris?" I carried on.

Putt began to explain. "See, people call Chris Crazy Chris 'cause they say when he was younger, his daddy used to beat his moms all the time. Until one day, his daddy gave his momma a beat-down, and she didn't get back up. Well, they say Chris was trying to wake her up and when he couldn't, he grabbed a butcher knife and stabbed his daddy in the back," Putt shared. "Black, they say when the ambulance got to his house, they found two dead bodies, Chris's mom and his dad. Chris lost his mind, and his ability to speak. To this day, the dude still can't talk. He lived at Charter Westbrook Psychiatric Hospital for years until the lady in the house across from the projects, Mrs. Irene, adopted him."

I felt sorry for Chris and was no longer mad with him for beating me down. After all, it wasn't his fault that he was crazy. "How old is Chris anyway?" I inquired.

"He's about eighteen; he just looks old because he's on all types of crazy folk medication. Mrs. Irene has about eight foster kids living there," Putt ran the facts down to me. My heart went out to Crazy Chris but I still didn't understand why he had beat me down senselessly for wearing red.

"So, Putt, what does any of that have to do with him not liking the color red?"

Putt turned to me with glossy eyes, "Because his daddy use to work at Hardee's, and every time he beat that woman down, he was wearing his red uniform shirt."

Chapter 4

Whenever you ain't looking for trouble, trouble is guaranteed to find you. The first person I spotted at the pool was the little heffa from across the street. Starr pointed me out to her friends and they began to harass me. I tried to ignore her but ignoring Starr was impossible.

"That's why you can't swim. Got your big overgrown tail over there, dangling your feet in three feet of water," she teased.

"Forget you, girl. I'm over here 'cause I got my little brother with me," I shot back at her.

"Whatever. Just make sure you don't get in, 'cause I ain't trying to swim with no sharks today," she said as she strolled by. Then Starr filled an empty sand bucket with water and threw it down my back. The ice cold water sent chills down my spine. I jumped up and gave chase. Starr ran over to the eleven feet and dove into the water. Against my better judgment, I dove in behind her.

I wasn't a good swimmer so I thought about Vladimir Salnikov.

I had just read an article on him that morning in the *Enquirer*. Vladimir had just won a gold medal in the freestyle competition in the Olympics in Moscow. I had never swum pass five feet but I put my fear of the deep water aside, and swam like my life depended on it. I pretended to be Vladimir. Just when I thought I had her, the lifeguard blew his whistle.

"Time to get out!" he yelled.

Starr jumped out of the water, pulling her fuchsia bikini bathing suit from the crack of her narrow ass; she stuck her tongue out at me and continued running off at the lip.

"If you lose some weight, you might be able to catch me the next time!" She laughed.

I pulled myself out of the water and struggled on the side of the pool. As if almost on cue, a dude wearing goggles and a swimming cap ran over to my defense.

"I got her, man, I'mma get her skinny tail!" he told me before taking off after Starr with a water gun. Starr covered her head with her hands.

"Stop, Lamont, you play too much." She ran off. I jumped up and ran in the opposite direction of them, blocking her path. Starr's instigating friends jumped in the middle of the mayhem, allowing her to wiggle her tiny butt through the crowd and clean out of the pool. I watched them closely as they disappeared up the block.

When I stepped back into the pool area, someone screamed, "He's drowning! He's drowning!" I ran over to see what all the commotion was about. It was Lamont; he had slipped and fallen into the deep end of the pool. The lifeguards pulled him from the water and tried relentlessly to save his life. I stood motionless as I watched the lifeguard place his mouth over Lamont's mouth, his eyes upon his eyes and his hands upon his hands. He stretched himself on top of Lamont, but still there was no sign of life. The man removed himself from Lamont and paced back and forth.

Putt turned to the crowd. "Somebody go and get Mrs. Barbara and Mr. Arnold," he yelled.

"Please don't let that boy die!" one of the adults screamed. Then the lifeguard attempted the hand-mouth routine again, and incredibly, it worked. Lamont sneezed seven times, and then opened his eyes. Water and snot poured from his mouth and his nose.

Before the paramedics arrived, Lamont's parents reached the pool. The odd-looking couple ran over to him. His mother kicked off her high-heeled clogs and dropped down beside him. When she realized her son was okay, she stood up and rested her head on her husband's shoulder, standing in his arms. I observed his mother closely. She was an average-looking woman in her mid-twenties. She had a phat ass and big boobs, which could be seen through her see-through nightgown. Lamont's father was an older man with salt and pepper hair. He walked with a limp and carried a walking cane. As he stood with his hand cuffed around his wife's butt, he chewed and spit tobacco in a glass jar. Seeing Lamont's very odd parents and witnessing the hand-mouth routine that the lifeguard had performed to save his life reminded me of the story of the Shu'nam mite's son in the Bible.

I remembered reading in vacation Bible school a story from II Kings. There was this young chick that they called a Shu'nam mite who married an old dude. The couple, for whatever reason, couldn't bear kids. Well, this cat named E-l'isha prophesized that she would give birth to a son at a certain time, during a certain season. Well, lo and behold, he was right 'cause the Shu'nam mite gave birth to a son. The son was born and later had some type of complications with his head. He died, and the Shu'nam mite went mad crazy. She begged and pleaded for someone to help but nobody could bring him back, not even Ge-ha'zi, the servant of E-li'sha. Well, E-li'sha was finally called to the house, 'cause I guess he was the man. He must've been a pro at reviving people, 'cause he did the bizarre hand-mouth routine to bring the kid back to life and it worked. The kid sneezed seven times and opened his eyes.

Putt walked over to me shaking his head. "Man, Lamont has more escapes than Houdini," he said as the paramedics hauled Lamont away on the gurney.

"What do you mean?" I asked.

"Black, that dude done been hit by a car, not once but twice, attacked by a pack of stray dogs, fell down three flights of stairs at the Richmond Coliseum and only broke his arm and chipped his front tooth. And, get this, when he was a baby, he survived a house fire."

The ambulance threw on its siren and sped off down Fairfield Avenue. Everyone watched in complete silence as the vehicle drove out of sight. I threw my arm around Putt 'cause he seemed worried about the dude.

"Well, Putt, I guess we should call him Lucky." I sighed.

• • •

As I approached my front yard, I noticed that Moms had dug up dirt and planted the flower seeds. She was sitting on the front porch, listening to music, and drinking a cold brewski. I hurried inside to make me and Keon a couple of ham and cheese sandwiches. When I returned to the front porch, Starr and her friends were in front of her house. They had on their black and white cheerleading bucks, short shorts and halter tops. Starr's little butt was ringleader; she led the pack of girls into a cheer.

"My back ache, my bra too tight, my booty ache from left to right, to the left, to the right, to the left, right, left," they all sang.

Momma bucked her eyes at them and sucked her teeth. "Look

at them little fast-ass girls. Don't make no sense they that damn grown!" she huffed as she headed inside the house to turn up her stereo.

Starr glanced across the street at me. When she realized she had my attention, she really began to strut her stuff. She started dancing to Momma's music. Mom was playing the song "Firecracker." Starr jerked her tiny body all the way down to the ground as she danced to the beat. It was something about the way she moved that had me hypnotized. I just couldn't seem to take my eyes off her.

Then suddenly, something strange happened. I felt my dick growing inside of my track shorts. I grabbed Momma's towel off of her empty six-pack of brewski and threw the towel across my lap to cover my erection. Then I slid my hand down my shorts, 'cause I wanted to feel my first hard-on. I placed my hand on my dick and continued to watch Starr closely as she shook her tiny ass at me. Suddenly, Momma swung open the door and snatched the towel off me.

"Boy, I know goddamn well you ain't playing with yourself!" she shouted loud enough for the whole block to hear. I jumped up and ran inside, where I continued stalking Starr from the upstairs window. It was strange; the same girl that had annoyed me had also enticed me.

When Starr noticed I was missing from my front porch, she looked up at the bedroom window to find me. When she spotted me stalking her, she gave me a pleasant smile. I could see all thirty-two of her teeth from the upstairs window. It was at that very moment that I realized there was a certain chemistry between us. Whether it was good, bad, or ugly, I wasn't exactly sure what it was. I just knew that we shared something.

Chapter 5

Momma didn't wake us up early the next morning, which was unusual for her. It was the smell of my favorite food that woke me out of my sleep. I grabbed my T-shirt and headed downstairs to eat breakfast. I was starving and dying to get my hands on some corn beef hash. I stepped into the kitchen; I was stunned when I realized that Momma was not alone. There was a stranger sitting at the table, eating breakfast. He was eating . . . corn beef hash. I had never seen the man before, and the puzzled look stretched across my face must've told him that I was uncomfortable with his presence. I pulled out a chair and joined him at the table. I examined the strange man from head to toe. He was a light-skinned brother, with jet-black, wavy hair. His eyebrows were thick and his eyelashes were long. His nose and his lips were Michael Jackson thin. He wore his hair cut close on the sides and tapered at the neck. His bare chest resembled a bird, and his nipples looked like they had a hard-on. He sat there staring at me like a topless trap in a strip joint. He was wearing one of Momma's underslips and two clothespins held the extra-large slip up to his waist. He had a distinguishing mark that stuck out like a sore thumb. He had keloids the size of the state of Delaware hanging from both of his ears. Yet and still, he was a pretty nigga, and that shit really freaked me out.

Momma turned around and faced the kitchen table with the big black skillet in her hand. My mouth watered because I just knew I was about to grub down on some corn beef hash. But Momma caught me by surprise; she slid the entire can of corn beef hash onto his plate.

"But Mom," I attempted to complain, but she cut me off.

"You and Keon gone have to eat cereal this morning, because it ain't enough hash for ya'll," she lied. "Besides, Floyd hasn't eaten since yesterday," she justified, when in fact nobody in the house had eaten since "yesterday."

"I'm just going to go ahead and send you to the store 'cause we out of orange juice, anyway. Don't wake Keon. You a big boy, you can walk to Koslow's by yourself," Momma told me. Then she reached down into her bra and handed me the food stamps. I glanced over at Pretty Boy; he circled the toast and syrup around on his plate. I stood up from the table and deliberately made myself fall over onto it. The table wobbled, causing his food to slide off his plate.

"Ooh, catch it," Momma hissed as she and the stranger grabbed at the table and plate of food. They were too slow; his delicious breakfast was now all over the floor.

"Nice to meet you," I said as I turned to exit the kitchen.

On my way out, I overheard Pretty Boy tell Momma, "Joann, I ain't for no shit out of your boy. You better check that li'l nigga."

"Oh, don't worry, baby, he ain't no problem," she assured him.

I made it to Koslow's without any problems. My Timex watch told me that I had made it there in thirteen minutes as opposed to the twenty minutes it had taken the day before. I was able to cut down on the amount of time that it took because I had mapped out a shorter route. I was very observant, and if somebody showed me something one time, I would remember it and store it in my brain forever. I had a photographic memory, and I was an avid reader. I had been reading just as long as I had been walking and talking. Momma had taken well over three hundred books from her parents' house when she moved to Richmond, and although I had never seen her read any of them, I had read them all by the age of ten.

When I was bored, I would read the dictionary, the Bible, almanac, thesaurus, and anything else I could get my hands on. I ain't gone lie, though, reading the *Enquirer* newspaper was my favorite 'cause the stories in that paper were downright hilarious. By the time I was in the third grade, I was inducted into the gifted and talented program. I tested at an IQ of 129 at age nine. The school board wanted to skip me a couple of grades, and I even received letters from Mensa because I was a few points away from being a so-called genius. My moms wouldn't allow me to be skipped a grade or, in her words, become involved with any "smart ass-organizations" such as Mensa. Momma explained that when I was two years old, I started putting together jigsaw puzzles. By the time I was three, she said, it wasn't nothing for me to put together a five-hundred-piece puzzle by myself. Momma said it took me about three days to do it, but eventually, she said, I would get it done. Momma told the folks down at the school board that I came out of her pussy brilliant, and wasn't no way in hell she was going to let no white system give credit to a textbook when it was her ass that created a genius.

I stepped inside the store and made my way toward the aisle to get the orange juice. Momma had given me a five-dollar food stamp to get the juice, but she never said anything about replacing the corn beef hash so I took it upon myself to handle my business. I grabbed the orange juice and made my way down the aisle where the canned goods were. I walked toward the counter and stood behind an old woman with a shopping cart that was running over. I glanced around to make sure no one was watching. Then I quickly sat the cans down on the floor, up close to the register and out of the way. I listened as the old woman and the cashier gossiped. I had noticed the day before that the cashier gossiped with every customer that went through her line, which was the reason why I chose *her* line to get in.

While the cashier rung up the orange juice, I conveniently made my watch fall to the floor.

"Baby, your watch fell off your arm, one of the screws is right there," the cashier said, pointing to the floor. The cashier placed the orange juice in a large brown bag and continued talking to the old woman who was at the end of the counter, trying desperately to leave. I politely grabbed the bag from the conveyor belt and sat it on the floor while I searched for my watch. I tossed my three cans of corn beef hash into the brown bag and grabbed my Timex. Then I stood up.

"I got it. Here you go, ma'am." I handed her the five-dollar food stamp.

"Thank you, young man, now you have a good day and stay out of trouble, you hear me?" she said.

When I returned home, Momma and Pretty Boy were upstairs in her bedroom. I woke up Keon and took him downstairs with me and made us breakfast.

"Keon, don't tell Mom anything about the corn beef hash because I stole it. Okay?" I needed him to promise that he wouldn't rat on me.

Keon looked worried. "What if she finds the cans, Bilal? You gone be in big trouble." He nervously bit at the tip of his fingernails. I had already stashed the cans outside way down in the bottom of our metal trash container. I took Keon to the back door and showed him where I had hid them. Keon felt better about the situation. He smiled at me.

"Thanks, Bilal, for fixing me something to eat because I was real hungry. I won't tell Momma," he chimed.

I quickly cleaned off our plates, dried them, and put them away. As soon as I finished, I heard Momma's footsteps. I grabbed my watch from the kitchen counter and the needle nose from the kitchen drawer and sat down to repair my watch. Moms walked into the kitchen, lit a cigarette on the stove, and took a pull on it. Her new man stood behind her, all up on her back.

"Don't he look nice, ya'll?" Keon and I nodded our heads yes, 'cause we knew that's what Momma wanted us to say.

Pretty Boy leaned over and kissed her on the cheek. "Baby, I'll be back as soon as church is over," he said.

"Okay, baby, I'll see you when you get home." Momma batted her eyes at him.

Pretty Boy wasn't dressed in church attire. Instead, he looked like he was on his way to a pimp convention. He had on a white suit with thin black pinstripes, which made him look like a miniature zebra. His pants gripped him tight around his butt and his too-small suit jacket stopped above his waist. He wore black and white Stacey Adams shoes with a red tassel. His shoes were leaning to the side, just like his pimp daddy hat. But the one thing that stood out the most about his attire was the *red* shirt with the large papal collar. My moms escorted her man to the front door, and I listened from the kitchen as he drove off.

Chapter 6

After I repaired my watch, I decided to go holler at Putt. I walked up the block and knocked on his front door. A tall beautiful woman opened the door. She had a pecan tan complexion and long braids that extended past her shoulders. Her eyes were light brown, and her skin was flawless; soft, and smooth like a baby's butt. For a woman with six children, Putt's mother, just like the model Bo Derek, was a perfect ten.

"Hi, Ms. Pearl, is Putt home?" I smiled at her. Ms. Pearl smiled back at me.

"Putt, oh, he told me about the name you gave him." She giggled, opening the door for me to step in.

"Yes, baby, he's here. Come on in," she invited me.

I walked into their home only to discover that Putt's house was literally a shitty mess. Clothes, shoes, and toys were scattered all over the place. Putt ran downstairs holding a shitty diaper in his hand. He walked over to me, attempting to use his available hand to slap hands with me. I backed away from him; I wasn't trying to smell his people's shit. Putt laughed when he realized that I had backed away.

"Hey, Black, hold up. I got, I got, to throw this out back in the trash can. I was changing my baby sister," he explained. I waited for Putt to throw out the shit and clean himself up.

"Ma, I'm going outside for a little while. If you need something, send somebody to come get me, okay?" Putt leaned over and kissed his mom on the lip. Ms. Pearl looked up at her son, her eyes full of love and appreciation.

"Okay, baby, thanks for helping me out this morning. I love you, baby, see you when you get back," she told him.

"Love you too, Mom," Putt responded.

The affection that Putt and his mom openly displayed was beautiful. Putt was just going outside to play for a while, but the way he and his mom carried on, you would've thought they were about to be separated from each other for a long time. Ms. Pearl stood up from the kitchen table, where she had been stitching on the sewing machine, to escort us to the front door.

"Nice meeting you, Black. Come see me again, okay?" she said, rubbing me gently on the back.

"I will," I answered as I stepped outside.

We decided to go check on Lucky, who was home from the hospital. When we approached his front yard, Lucky was sitting on the porch with his dad. His dad, Mr. Arnold, was chewing tobacco and spitting it in an old relish jar. The Richfood relish label was old and torn but it was still intact. Over the years, I had heard Momma talk about folk down South chewing and spitting tobacco but until meeting Mr. Arnold, I had never actually seen anyone do it. Richmond is in the South, but come on, folk just wasn't chewing and spitting tobacco in the hood. Mr. Arnold looked a fool, sitting in a rocking chair on the front porch, spitting that shit in a clear jar. I shook my head at him. He didn't even have the decency to cover the mess up by using a tin can. Putt spoke to Lucky and his dad as we walked up.

"Hey, Lucky. Hey, Mr. Arnold," Putt cheerfully greeted. Mr. Arnold looked at him like he had two heads.

"Who the hell you calling Lucky? That boy lives down the street!" he snapped at Putt, skeeting a mouth full of tobacco in his container. I jumped in.

"No, Mr. Arnold, I gave Lamont the nickname Lucky cause I heard Lamont's life has been spared a few times. That's all," I explained. Mr. Arnold gave me a rather disgusted look, then sat his glass jar down on the porch.

"And who the hell is you?" he said, frowning. I extended my hand to him, I figured it was the manly thing to do.

"I'm Black." I held my hand out, waiting for him to return the gesture but he didn't. Mr. Arnold checked me out from head to toe. He kicked back in the rocker, reached down and grabbed his spit can.

"Black? Boy, you better gone away from here!" he dismissed me.

Just then, Lucky jumped up from the porch, reached inside the front door, and grabbed his football.

"Yo, Dad, tell Mom I'm at the Rec Center," he said as we took off. Mr. Arnold stood up from the rocker and watched as we strolled off.

"Boy, you be careful out there, you hear me?" he yelled after his son. Lucky dismissed his father's concerns.

"Man, they be getting on my nerves with that overprotective stuff. If something is gone happen, then it's gone happen," he huffed.

The football field was packed with kids from the neighborhood. Some rode bikes, while others jumped rope or played dodge ball. There was one kid sitting on the curb alone. He was holding a football in one hand and a bat in the other. I figured we could use one more player, so I walked over to invite him in.

"Hey, you wanna play football with us?" I asked. The dude started tripping; he jumped up from the curb and started rambling.

"Man, when that mutherfucker comes back I'm gone beat his punk ass. Just wait and see," he fumed. I took two steps back from him 'cause it was obvious he couldn't control his anger.

"Whoa, calm down." I threw my hands up at him 'cause whatever he was furious about couldn't be that damn serious. Hell, we were only kids. Putt and Lucky came over, and Putt was laughing a little.

"What's up, Head? I ain't even know that was you," Putt said, slapping hands with the little angry dude.

"Head, who done made you mad this time?" Lucky asked.

Head flicked off again. He bit his bottom lip.

"That nigga name Tony. They say that mutherfucker is from New York, but I ain't scared of him. Man, I'mma beat his ass as soon as I catch him, just watch." He continued fussing, his cheeks swelled like a blowfish with every harsh word. I was curious to know what the person had done to him, because the li'l dude was serious about giving whomever it was a beat-down.

"What did he do to you?" I investigated.

"I'mma beat his ass just 'cause he's from New York, 'cause them mutherfuckers can't be coming around here thinking they bad and shit!" Head screamed.

"Okay." I nodded. If that was his reason, then that was his reason. I was not about to ask his little mean ass anything else. I checked him out, too, from head to toe. There wasn't a need for me to question why his name was Head. You would've had to be blind in one eye and couldn't see out the other to not know the answer. Head stood five feet tall, and was cock diesel for a twelve-year-old. His head was so big that it had to have taken at least two hundred stitches to sew his Momma's pussy back up after he was born. With all the trauma she endured while pushing his big-head ass out, she should've been the one paid for delivering him, not the Medical College of Virginia Hospital. That woman should have received a Golden Globe award for that delivery.

We set up our teams and were ready to play when suddenly Head spotted his target. Tony walked onto the field and Head took off after him.

"Yeah, mutherfucker, talk that shit now!" He ran after a fat kid in a New York Yankees baseball uniform. The boy was chubby but he was kinda fast; his baseball pants was all up in the crack of his behind. He pumped his hands up wildly, screaming as he tried to escape from Head.

"Leave me alone! Leave me alone!" he yelled as he wobbled off. He looked over his shoulder to see if Head was closing in on him. Head continued harassing him, even though he knew the kid didn't want a fight.

"Yeah, nigga, what you gone do! You on my turf now, so don't come around here thinking you bad 'cause I'll kick your ass every day if I have to!" Head threatened. Everybody on the field starting yelling, instigating the same way they had done with me on my first day in the neighborhood.

"It's a fight, it's a fight!" they sang their usual song.

"Come back, Head, leave him alone," Putt and Lucky yelled. Fat Tony continued to scream as he ran out of sight.

"Leave me alone. All I wanted to do was play football," he whined.

Head didn't have any sympathy at all for the dude; he continued to talk smack. "Yeah, mutherfucker, that's what I thought. I knew he was a wimp," he boasted, proud that he had scared the kid off. Putt and Lucky grabbed Head by the arms and pulled him back onto the field.

"Head, you crazy." Putt shook his head at him.

"Can we just play ball?" Lucky fretted. Head turned to me, then looked at Putt and Lucky. "Oh yeah, who is this?" he asked, pointing at me. Before Putt and Lucky had a chance to answer, I introduced myself to him.

"I'm Black," I answered. All the drama he had caused was a little too much for me. I just stood there soaking it all in.

Head nodded at me. "S'up, Black, welcome to the neighborhood." He smiled. Just that fast his entire demeanor had changed.

I let out a slight grin. "S'up," I answered.

We set up our teams and played for a couple of hours. We were leaving the football field when Fat Tony came back strong. He was stomping mad and had two other dudes with him. Head watched as the group moved toward us. It was hard to tell whether or not he was scared, there was no expression on his face.

"If they try to jump me, do ya'll have my back?" Head asked us.

"Yeah." Putt nodded.

"No doubt about it," Lucky answered.

At first, I didn't know what to say because I had never been a willing participant in a fight. However, these were my new friends and I wasn't about to let anything happen to them. Before I knew it, I blurted, "We're all in this together."

The oldest dude in the group stepped up to us, while Fat Tony and the other cat stayed back a couple of feet. "Yo, son, which one of ya'll cats got a problem with my li'l cousin?" the dude asked with bass in his voice. Since I was the biggest one out my group, I wasn't about to let them niggas punk us. I held a hard-ass look on my face with hopes of intimidating them. I wasn't sure if it would work but I tried it anyway. I stepped right up on the dude, our eyes met.

"Ain't no such thing as one of us. Around here, we are all one," I said as I held one finger up in front of his face. The dude watched my finger for a few seconds, then rubbed his face and chin. I didn' know if anything was about to go down, but within those few minutes, I had already prepared myself mentally for whatever they were ready to bring. If they wanted a fistfight, then they were about to get one.

"Look, shorty, we don't want no problems." The oldest dude backed away from me and surrendered his hands in the air. "We're just here visiting our grandma for the summer," he explained.

"So, it's true, ya'll are from New York?" I asked.

"Yeah, we're from Brooklyn," he confirmed. "I'm Skilow, this is my brother Jay and this is our li'l cousin Fat Tony," he introduced his squad. "Man, Tony is just nine years old, all he wants to do is play football," Skilow added. Fat Tony and Jay moved closer, never taking their eyes off of us. Putt, Lucky, and Head all listened in, but they let me do all the talking.

"All right, we'll be back tomorrow around the same time. I got a little brother that he can play with. I'll bring him over," I offered.

"Cool," Skilow conceded. Before he left the field, he probed us for our names.

"Yo, shorty, what they call you?" he asked. I introduced myself and my crew.

"I'm Gorilla Black, this is Putt, that's Lucky, and that's Head," I ran off our names. Then Skilow extended his right hand to me and we shook. Then everybody else clasped hands, and agreed to squash the beef.

• • •

For the first time in my life, I had finally gotten the balls to stand up for myself. It didn't matter to me that Head had started the shit for no reason; the only thing that mattered was the fact that I had represented for my team. As we approached my block, I noticed that Starr was getting out of a church van. She was wearing a long white sundress, with white plastic sandals. Her hair was in a ponytail and she was holding on to her King James Bible. Since I was already feeling confident, I decided to approach her.

"Hi, Starr," I called out to her. Starr never turned to face me; she kept walking.

"Boy, what do you want?" she asked with her back to me.

"I came over to say hi, since yesterday, well, you know." I walked fast, trying to catch up with her.

"Yesterday what?" She spun around, obviously irritated with me. Before I could say anything, she lit into me.

"Yesterday you watched me like a psycho from your window while I danced with my friends!" she snapped, rolling her eyes—again.

"But Starr, you were smiling at me when you saw me in the window," I reminded her. Starr laughed in my face, then removed her plastic slippers from her feet and headed toward the door.

"Boy, you are crazy, I wasn't smiling at you. I was smiling at my boyfriend Malcolm who lives next door to you. He was in his upstairs window too. Black, you are such a big dummy!" she insulted me. I sighed heavily and turned to walk away.

"See?" She pointed across the street, up to the window, and sure enough, there he was. My next-door neighbor sticking his head out the window. My face twitched from embarrassment. I wiped the silly look from my face and ran back across the street to join my friends.

"What she say? What she say?" they wanted to know.

I was too ashamed to tell the truth, so I lied, "Nothing. She ain't say nothing."

I glanced back up at the window to get a better look at my competition. Then I went inside to check on Keon and to tell my moms that I was going over to Head's house. Keon was upstairs watching the tube; he said he wasn't feeling well.

"Mom, I'm going over my friend name Head's house to play Pac-Man," I told her as I was leaving back out. Momma stopped me before I could get out the door.

"Oh no you ain't, 'cause I need you to help Floyd move his things in," she informed me.

"Move in?" I had a confused look on my mug.

"That's right, I said move in and don't you ask me no damn questions. Boy, I'm warning you, you better stay in a child's place!" she growled. Just then, Floyd drove up and me and my boys begrudgingly helped him remove his belongings from his car.

We were unpacking Floyd's ride when a car rolled up beside us. An old cat resembling the singer Frankie Beverly stopped by to holler at him.

"Hey Floyd, what's happening, man?" he spoke from the car. Floyd dropped the box he was holding and walked over to the driver's side window. We all stopped working and listened in on their conversation.

"Ain't nothing, playa, same suit different crease. You know how I do it. I'm still straight pimping, baby," Floyd spat. I couldn't believe my ears. Floyd's mack-daddy, played-out, want-to-be-a-pimp ass was talking real slick out the mouth.

Head laughed out loud. "Man, this dude is a clown!"

Floyd overheard him, so he shot us an evil stare and continued to shoot from the hip.

"All right, baby, I'll catch you on the flipside," he said to his friend as he strolled off. As soon as Floyd stepped foot back onto the sidewalk, Putt chuckled. Floyd gritted on us, then pimped sideways toward the house.

Putt looked up. "Oh oh, here comes Crazy Chris!" he said, before jumping out of the way. We all looked at each other, but nobody warned Floyd. Next thing I know, Crazy Chris came flying down the block, charging toward Floyd like a bowling ball at the last pin to complete a spare. One of the neighbors screamed, "You better run, man, 'cause you got on red!"

By the time Floyd realized what was happening, it was too late. Crazy Chris knocked him over into Momma's flower garden and started pounding on him. Floyd screamed like a baby in a pissy-ass diaper.

"Help me! Somebody help me!" he wailed.

Momma stormed out of the front door with a broom in her hand and started swinging.

"Get off of him. Get off my man. Somebody do something!" she begged. Momma was swinging the broom so wildly that she tripped and lost her balance. She fell over into the flower garden with Floyd, half of her body on top of his. Chris pulled at Momma, trying to get her off of her man.

Floyd cried out again. "Get off of me!" he moaned.

Momma jumped up so fast, you would've thought lightning struck her in the butt.

"Hoes up, pimps down!" Head laughed, half covering his mouth.

Momma grabbed the broom from the garden and continued swinging at Crazy Chris. Chris may have been crazy but he sure knew how to bob and weave. Momma aimed for his head with the broom but she missed him every time. Chris continued pounding on Floyd, until he finally got what he wanted. He snatched off Floyd's jacket, ripped his red shirt clean off of him, and then ran off. Momma helped her man up from the ground.

"Oh, baby, are you all right?" She held on to his left arm. Floyd snatched away from her. Like the pimp he was, he was more concerned about his looks than anything. He straightened up his hair, rubbed his face, then knocked the dirt from his clothes. He licked his lips, then sucked his teeth.

"Everything is everything, Big Momma," he said, shrugging his shoulders.

"Baby, I thought he was going to kill you," Momma exaggerated. Floyd stepped onto the porch. Realizing that he had been stripped out of his shirt and jacket, he rubbed his bird chest. He sighed heavily, then smacked Momma on her butt.

"Just hand me my hat," he told her, pointing to his pimp daddy hat that was covered in mud. Momma retrieved her man's hat from the garden. She brushed it off and handed it to him. Floyd glanced around to see who was watching. Satisfied, he placed his hat back on his head, and cocked it to the side.

"You sure you all right, baby?" Momma asked one more time. Floyd reached inside his pants pocket and pulled out a toothpick and stuck it on the side of his mouth.

"Yeah, I'm cool. It takes more than that to keep a real playa down," he boasted. Momma and her man disappeared inside the house.

Talk about a pimp in distress. If I could've captured that shit on videotape, I would have been on my way to being a rich man. I laughed so fucking hard that I peed on myself.

Chapter 7

Later that night when everyone was in bed, I crept over to Fairfield Pool with a can of black spray paint. I had a hidden obsession or talent that no one close to me even knew about. For as long as I could remember I had a deep appreciation for art. So, whenever no one was watching, I studied Leonardo da Vinci and Picasso. I loved painting and drawing but I was ashamed to let Momma know that I liked doing such things, because she would always put me down whenever I tried to be me. I kept hidden in a secret box all types of paints, brushes, and other art supplies. Tagging was a strange habit that I acquired, because no matter where I went, I would either draw a picture or scribble my initials in paint. Ever since I had gone to the place, I had a dying urge to go back and leave my permanent mark on the brick wall that surrounded the pool.

It was two o'clock in the morning when I dashed out of the house in pursuit of the pool. I wasn't sure if anything usually jumped off in the wee hours of the morning in Fairfield, but I was so desperate to leave my tag that I didn't think twice about danger. I realized at that very moment that I had changed in the last few days. I was still a quiet guy, shy and peaceful, but I had become bolder. I was now hungry. I felt like an animal. I felt . . . like a gorilla. I reached the pool, pulled the top from the can of spray paint, and began to spray. BLACK, PUTT, LUCKY, HEAD . . . BETTER KNOWN AS THE FAIRFIELD WRECKING CREW. I had no idea that we would become just that.

I sped home and tiptoed up the stairs. Just as I was about to turn the doorknob to my bedroom, I heard my mom's room door open up. It was pitch black in the house so I couldn't see who was there lurking in the dark.

"Bilal," Floyd called out to me, but I didn't answer. "Bilal, is that you?" he called my name again. I started tripping because I figured he was scared and thought an intruder had entered our home. Then I thought about Crazy Chris beating him down earlier, and I smiled at the thought.

"Boy, I see you standing over there. You better get your li'l black ass in that room before your momma wakes up!" he yelled at me. I was cold busted; my flashlights, my bright white teeth had given me away.

I took in a deep breath before responding to him. I reached for the hall light and flicked it on. There he was, standing with Momma's house robe on and a pair of her old stockings on top of his head. Wiping the smile from my face and looking deep into his eyes, I whispered to him, "You ain't my daddy, nigga! And you need to take that stocking cap off your head, looking like you got pussy on your brain." Floyd launched after me. I slammed the door shut on him, and barricaded myself in my room by placing a chair underneath the doorknob.

Fuck Floyd and feed him beans, I thought to myself.

Chapter 8

Floyd snitched on me and Momma grounded me for an entire week. I wasn't allowed to go outside nor was I allowed to have my friends over. To top it off, Momma wouldn't even let me read her *Enquirer*s. When Monday morning came, I was excited as hell when Putt knocked at the front door. It was the first day of school and he had come by to scoop me up.

"Come on down here. Your friend is here to get you," Momma called out to me. I ran downstairs and grabbed my backpack from her on the way out the door. Floyd was sitting on the front porch reading *The Richmond News Leader*. My crew waited for me at the sidewalk.

"Bye, Mom. Tell my brother when he wakes up that I said to have a good day, and I'll see him later," I told her.

"Uhm hum, see you later," she yelled from the kitchen. Floyd looked up from the newspaper, toothpick dangling from the corner of his mouth.

"You be easy, pimp juice," he smirked at me. I ignored him and stepped off. I headed down the block to the bus stop with my boys. We were so busy talking that we almost missed the bus.

"Come on, the bus is about to leave!" a thin, dark-skinned chick with a squeaky voice yelled out to us. She was wearing what appeared to be three-and-a-half-inch heels.

"Man, that's my girl Cocoa. Ain't she sweet? She's making sure her man don't miss the bus." Putt smiled.

"Putt, why your girl wearing high-heel shoes to middle school?" I questioned.

Putt poked me in the chest. "Man, don't be talking about my girl. I told Cocoa not to wear them high-heel shoes but she wouldn't listen. I don't know why her mother buys her all those grown folk clothes." Putt paused a minute, then continued. "Cocoa does look crazy in them high heels, don't she?" He laughed and so did the rest of the crew. Cocoa was having a hard time walking in her high-heeled shoes. She was walking at a snail's pace. We all ran past her and boarded the bus.

"Little girl, you gone get left if you don't hurry it up!" the bus driver yelled from the bus.

"Yeah, come on, Cocoa, speed it up!" Putt encouraged from the window.

"I'm moving as fast as I can," Cocoa insisted, her tiny body swaying from side to side as she strutted her stuff in her black and gold spiked heels.

• • •

Thompson Middle School was on the south side of town in a middle class suburban neighborhood. However, the majority of the students were bused from the east side of Richmond, mainly from the projects in Churchill. When the buses rolled up on the campus, all the chicks from the suburbs gathered around to check out the dudes from the east side of town. Head decided to show us the ropes because he was familiar with the school. It was his second year at Thompson. First, we headed to the boy's bathroom, 'cause Lucky had to take a leak.

"What up, Head?" a tall, red dude with a bad case of acne greeted us. He slapped hands with Head. The dude was rocking an expensive cream-colored silk shirt and black slacks. His black lizard shoes stuck out, not just because they were expensive but because they were about a size fourteen.

"Hey, what up, Maurice," Head shot back at him. Maurice's stick man, a dark-skinned dude in a hot, first-day-of-school brown corduroy suit, stood up against the wall. He was smoking a joint out in the open as if marijuana was legal. He threw his head back, real cool like.

"What up, Head?" he spoke, passing Head the joint. Head took it from his hand and took a hit.

"This is real good, Duke." Head gave his approval, as if he were some type of expert on weed. He took a few more hits, then he passed the joint back to Duke. Maurice and Duke offered the rest of us some, but Head declined for us.

"Nawh, man, they don't smoke," he told them. Then Head smacked hands with his boys and we left them in the smoke-filled bathroom, getting high as a kite.

"Dag, they be smoking weed like that?" Putt asked.

"Man, not only do they smoke it, but they sell it. Maurice and Duke are getting paid over Jackson Ward," Head told us.

"They look a little old to be in middle school," I said.

Head laughed hysterically. "Shit, they are old. They've been at Thompson since forever. Strange thing is, every year they continue to make the basketball team. The school don't care nothing about them boys getting an education, as long as they win the championship game, that's all that matters. Maurice and Duke sell weed, but other than that, them dudes don't know much of nothing."

We exited the building so Head could show us a spot out back. We turned the corner; a group of dudes was shooting dice behind the school. Head pointed them out.

"See them dudes right there?" He nodded in their direction. "That's G, Marvin, and Joe, and all they do is shoot dice all day," he shared. G, a chubby dude in an oversize Izod shirt, stood up when he spotted Head.

"Hey, Head. You in or what?" Before Head could answer him, the school bell rang. G and his friends snatched up their money from the ground and everybody scattered inside to make their way to class.

Chapter 9

The first day of school had been long and draining. I was exhausted and couldn't wait to get home to catch a nap before taking Keon to football practice. Keon and I had both made the football team. He was the quarterback for the Pee-wee Squad, and whenever I wasn't riding the bench, I held one of the positions as defensive lineman for the Midgets. It really didn't matter to me that I didn't get much play, I was just excited to be a part of something special. I left the building to find my bus. Putt and Lucky were waiting outside for me. Head was nowhere to be found.

"Mmm—man, did you see Head on your way out?" Putt stuttered.

"No, I haven't seen him all day," I answered.

We boarded the bus and took our seats. Just as the bus was about to leave, Head jumped on, and he seemed to be in a good mood.

"How was everybody's first day?" he asked out loud, but nobody answered. Head jolted down the aisle, making his way to his seat. When he got there, he realized someone was sitting in it.

"Baije, why you ain't save our seat?" he chastised her.

" 'Cause Portia was already sitting in it," Baije explained.

Portia, a heavyset girl with pigtails in her hair, kept talking to the person sitting in the seat across from her, as if she didn't hear her name being spoken.

"Portia!" Head screamed, trying to interrupt her conversation. Portia kept on talking, totally ignoring him.

"Portia!" he screamed her name again. This time, Portia spun her head around real fast.

"That's my name and don't you run it in the ground! I heard you the first time, do I look deaf to you?" she snapped. Head's eyes were now fiery red.

"Nawh, you don't look deaf but you sure as hell is fat!" He laughed and so did the rest of the bus.

Portia stood up as Head took the seat behind her, next to Baije.

"Head, I ain't gone have this shit out of you this year. I'll sit wherever I want to. You don't own these seats!" she told him. Head gave her an evil look; he looked like he wanted to strangle her.

"Portia, sit down before you tip the bus over!" Head's eyes were wild like they were about to pop out his head.

"Young lady, sit down!" the bus driver yelled fom the front of the bus.

Finally, Portia took her seat and the bus pulled off. It was quiet for about five minutes, so I tried to doze off. As soon as I did, Portia and Head woke me up. They were going at it again.

"Head, I know your feet can't touch the floor of the bus, but please, I'm asking you nicely to keep your tiny ass feet out of my back!" she snapped.

"Portia, shut up with your fat ass!" Head snapped at her.

Portia jumped to her feet again and swung as hard as she could at him, but she missed. There was so much force behind her swing that it spun her around and she fell over onto the floor. She scrambled to pick herself up but she was too big and not able to get up. The old saying "The bigger you are, the harder you fall" applied in this case. Portia was stuck; half of her body was lodged under the seat. A few kids on the bus hurried to her rescue, pulling her up and placing her back in the chair. Portia climbed into the seat; she was breathing heavy and worried about her hair. She patted her pigtails to make sure they were still intact. Head fell out laughing and so did I.

Portia threw us a mean look. "Oh, so you think it's funny, huh?" Portia placed her hands on her hips.

"I know you ain't laughing at me, *black boy*," she quoted me. "Yeah, I saw you spray-painting the brick wall the other night. So, ya'll call yourselves the Fairfield Wrecking Crew? And your name is Black? Black my ass, how about Fat Albert and the Gang?" She laughed. Portia was on a roll. She didn't stop there with her attack on me. "Yeah, *black boy*, you so black, you can leave your hand-print in charcoal," she joked, swaying her body from side to side. Everybody was up and out of their seats, rolling around on the bus. My own crew even laughed at the joke. I ignored Portia. One, because I wasn't a jokester, and two, because I couldn't even begin to think of a comeback.

Head jumped in. "Portia, your momma so dumb she put in an application to be the DJ for the ice cream truck," he said. Portia stopped moving; something about that particular joke had struck a nerve with her. Portia swung at Head again. For the second time, her entire body spun around. Head grabbed Portia around the neck and proceeded to choke the life out of her. She spun around in the aisle; Head's feet were flying in the air.

"Somebody get this midget off of me!" she screamed.

"Portia, I'm gone kill you, girl!" Head screamed, tightening his grip around her neck.

"Let me go, Head. You didn't have to say that about the ice cream truck. You know that man that drives the truck is supposed to be my daddy!" she said, gasping for air.

The nerdy girl who sat behind the bus driver didn't think any of it was funny; the entire scene had obviously scared her to death. She jumped out of her seat with an open milk carton in her hand and grabbed at the bus driver.

"Break it up, break it up," she cried, spilling her milk on the driver.

The bus driver pulled over to the side of the road and screamed, "I'm not a referee. I just drive the bus! Now, everybody get the hell off!" He opened the door, and ejected every single one of us.

Chapter 10

The big day had finally come: It was Saturday morning, the day of our pre-championship game. Both the Pee-wees and the Midgets had made it to the semifinals. Thanks to my little brother, the Pee-wees were undefeated. My team had lost three games, but our record was still quite impressive. We placed second in our league, and I was proud of it. Keon was nervous as we suited up for the game; the pressure to win was overwhelming.

"Bilal, do you think we're going to win today?" he asked.

"I don't know, Keon; just remember to do your best no matter what. Besides, winning ain't everything," I told him. Keon breathed heavily, then threw his football bag across his shoulder.

"I just want Mom to be proud of me," he said. I rubbed him on top of his head to ease his mind. Momma wasn't good at giving us compliments, nor did she ever praise us for a job well done. I understood exactly where Keon was coming from; on many occasions, I had tried my damnest to please her too.

"Relax, Mom is proud of you. I know she don't say it much, but I just know she is," I tried reassuring him. It was time to get to the football field. Momma called us downstairs.

"Come on before they leave ya'll. I'll meet ya'll over there. Floyd is going to bring me."

We headed to the school and boarded the bus with the other football players and cheerleaders that were waiting for us. The game was a complete sell-out. Many people came out to the game because Fairfield was playing Whitcomb Court and Whitcomb Court was undefeated. The Whitcomb Court Steelers had also won every championship game since 1975. The football field, the bleachers, and the streets were jam-packed. People both young and old came to support both teams. Seeing all of those black folks together was a beautiful sight to see. I had never seen that many black people congregated in one place in my life.

Keon held it down for his team, and sure enough, they beat the Steelers. After the game was over, Keon ran up to me, excited about his win.

"Bilal, I did it! I did it! I made us win," he said, jumping into my arms and hugging me tight around the neck.

"Yeah, you did and I'm so proud of you, Keon. I knew you could do it!" I held on to him tight and spun him around in circles. Momma ran onto the field, that nigga Floyd pimping behind her.

"Good job, Keon," she congratulated him with a light kiss on the forehead.

"Bilal, I'm sorry your team didn't win." Keon gave me a sad look.

"That's okay, Keon, as long as your team is going to the championship, that's all that matters," I responded.

Momma sucked her teeth and grabbed Floyd by the hand. "If you weren't so busy looking up on the bleachers at me and Floyd, you could've tackled that boy. You should've been concentrating on the game, not me!" she shouted. People turned in our direction, focusing their attention on Momma because she was getting loud and ghetto.

"All right, baby, see you when you get home," she told Keon, then she and Floyd strolled off. Floyd peered over his shoulder, removed his toothpick from his mouth, and mumbled to me.

I couldn't hear him but I read the nigga's lips. "See you when you get home, pimp juice, " he mouthed.

• • •

Suga Momma was the treasurer of the Fairfield Planning Committee and decided to have a party in honor of both our teams. The plan was to raise enough money to take all the football players and cheerleaders to the Virginia State Fair. It was two p.m. when we returned home, plenty of time for me to put my own master plan into action. I had decided that I needed to do something different, out of the ordinary, completely over the top if I wanted to win Starr's affection. I needed to solicit help. Putt had made it back to Fairfield before I did. He was waiting outside for me at the Rec Center. Cocoa was standing out there with him. As soon as the bus stopped, I hopped off.

"Putt, I need you to go with me to Koslow's," I asked him. Putt didn't ask any questions, he was ready to move.

"Okay. Give me fifteen minutes, I got to walk Cocoa home," he said.

"Bet, just come knock on my door when you're ready."

• • •

When I returned home from the store, Keon was upstairs in the bedroom. He said he wasn't feeling well and didn't want to play outside. I didn't know where Momma was, and I worried that she had left Keon home alone.

"Where's Moms, Keon?" I asked.

"She went to talk to the lady next door, 'cause the lady came over here banging on our door real hard," he informed me.

"Why?" I wondered.

"That lady told Momma to turn her goddamn noise down!" Keon repeated verbatim, then broke out laughing. Although I didn't know what he was laughing about, I laughed too.

"What's funny, Keon? Why you laughing so hard?" I chuckled. Keon laughed again.

"That lady asked Mom if she had any other music besides that damn 'When a Man Loves a Woman'?" He fell out laughing, then suddenly stopped. "Ooh, my head hurts, Bilal." He laid back on the bed. I turned the light off in the bedroom, then gave him my pillow off of my bed. Keon propped his head up with my pillow and his.

"Okay, Keon, get some rest. I hope you feel better; maybe you just had a long day."

"Maybe. Momma gave me an aspirin but it still hurts," he moaned.

I left the bedroom and headed to the bathroom. It was time to put my master plan to work. I locked myself in the bathroom and placed the brown paper bag in the sink. I removed the Revlon perm from the bag and the small sponge hair rollers. I read the directions carefully and then I placed the plastic gloves on my hands. If Starr liked boys who looked like Malcolm—light skin with long curly hair—then that's what she was gone get. I had to do something to straighten my shit out. That's right; I gave myself a perm, a super-strength relaxer.

I applied the chemicals, then washed my hair thoroughly with both the shampoo and conditioner, just like the directions said. I stepped out of the bathroom with the towel on my head to get the hair dryer from Mom's bedroom. I didn't want Keon to see me until my project was complete, so I jetted past our room and ran into hers. Momma caught me by surprise.

Momma was sitting on her bed, applying Vaseline to her feet. I didn't realize that the towel had fallen from my head. "Boy, what the hell have you done to you hair?" she screamed.

"Pick it up. Just pick the towel up!" she grunted. I snatched the towel from the floor and wrapped it back around my head. Momma looked at me strangely. I ignored her stare and changed the subject.

"Mom, why was you over Malcolm's house?" I quizzed.

" 'Cause that lady came over here knocking on my door like she was crazy, talking about I play my music too loud. She ain't got a damn thing to do with what goes on over here," she snapped. Momma stood up from the bed and grabbed a hair comb off her dresser.

"Come here." She gestured for me.

I sat down on the bed beside her. Momma surprised me again; she ran the hair comb through my hair.

"Hum, I told that bitch if she ever knocked on my door like that again, I was going to break my foot off in her ass. Then she had the nerve to offer me some of her old forty-fives. I told that bitch that I don't listen to no damn Otis Redding or Clarence Carter."

"Ouch!" I screamed out 'cause Momma was heavy-handed and she was killing my head. Momma didn't appreciate me complaining. She shoved me in the back and slammed the comb down on the bed.

"Well, do it yourself. I was just trying to help you out. You come flying up in my room with strands of hair standing straight up in the air. Boy, you look like a black-ass porcupine." She laughed at me and left me in her room alone.

I grabbed the hair dryer and set up shop. I placed the plastic bag on my head and sat under the dryer for twenty minutes. I attempted to grease my scalp with Momma's Vaseline, but I had left the perm in too long and my scalp was tender and hurt to the touch. After my hair dried, I parted it in small sections and rolled it up with the small sponge rollers that I had stolen along with the perm. I placed Momma's black satin cap on my head and headed to my room. I needed to be bright-eyed and bushy-tailed for the party, so I laid down to take a nap. I blasted the fan on high in order to circulate some cool air, jumped onto the bottom bunk and slid the sheet over my head. *Tonight, Starr is going to see the new me,* I mumbled to myself as I dozed off to sleep.

Chapter 11

Around six o'clock, I jumped up, took a bath, and dressed for the party. It was time to execute the second part of my master plan. I had read in a magazine about a company in Israel that was offering a free trial of skin lightening cream so I had taken the liberty of ordering it. The advertisement indicated that the results were almost instant, and although I knew that was virtually impossible, I took a chance anyway.

I gently applied the skin lightening cream to my face, removed the sponge rollers from my hair, and combed out my curls. I checked myself in the long mirror that was nailed to the back of my bedroom door. I had put a lot of work into my appearance and I was happy with the results. I snuck into Momma's room, splashed on some of Floyd's cheap cologne, and headed downstairs. I had my hair done and my skin tinted, hopefully a shade or two lighter. I stepped out on faith. I was on my way to get my girl.

I hurried downstairs. Momma and Keon were sitting at the kitchen table.

"Mom, I'm going to meet my friends, and then I'm going across the street to the party," I said.

Momma was scanning through the newspaper and Keon was putting together a jigsaw puzzle. Momma peered up at me through her reading glasses.

"That ain't no party, that's a social for grown folks," she said, removing her glasses from the tip of her nose. "You got any money to buy us a dinner?" she added. I frowned 'cause Momma knew I didn't have any money; I was eleven years old, wasn't like I had a job.

"No, ma'am." I shook my head.

"You must have some money, you bringing perms and shit in here like you got a job or something!" she snapped. "Go on, boy. I know you been stealing, so go on over there and see if you can steal me a couple of fish dinners!" She smirked. I left the kitchen; I was ashamed at what Momma knew about me. Truth was, I had become a petty thief.

"I like your hair, Bilal," Keon told me.

"Thanks Keon," I said as I exited through the front door.

I straggled up the block to find my crew. I spotted them sitting on Head's front porch. I was reluctant to join them because Portia was over there with them and I wasn't in the mood for her wise-cracks. I stepped into the yard, and forced my way into a small space toward the back of the porch. They were all talking about the football game; they continued on as if they didn't see me. Suddenly, everything got quiet. Everybody turned around and all eyes were on me.

"Black, man, what have you done to your hair?" Putt screamed at the top of his lungs. There was complete and utter silence. Everybody waited for an answer.

"I permed it," I answered bluntly, then waited for the jokes to began. I was positive that Portia and Head was gone bust on me if nobody else did.

"Man, it's boss!" Lucky jumped up from the porch and slapped five with me.

"Yeah, Black, it's gravy, man," one of the neighborhood dudes agreed. Portia stood up, and brushed the back of her trouser pants off.

"I like people who aren't afraid to be different. I bet you Starr likes it too." She smiled at me.

Head shook his head and mumbled underneath his breath. "Man, you look like a fool."

• • •

When we arrived at Suga Momma's, we were told that all the football players and cheerleaders were having pizza. The back-yard was set up with tables and chairs, and large coolers filled with juice and sodas were scattered about. Suga Momma passed out handwritten flyers and told us to go door to door to remind people that she was selling dinners. I was impressed with Suga Momma. She was a short, petite woman with broad shoulders and a short neck. She wore large bifocal eyeglasses the size of mayonnaise jars. Her hair was fully covered in gray and she wore it pinned up in a bun. Her nails and feet were freshly manicured and covered with bright orange nail polish that matched the or-ange in her floral print dress perfectly. Suga Momma had a warm and beautiful spirit. She was everything that anybody could want in a grandma. She was standing in the hot kitchen cooking, cleaning, and serving for us. Suga Momma was Starr's grand-mother.

"Ya'll boys come on in here and give me a hand," she solicited our help. "Wayne is going to pick up the pizza for ya'll in a few minutes," she added. I glanced around her home; it was the best-looking house that I had seen in the projects. A salt and pepper carpet covered the living room floor. The midnight black plush sofa and loveseat had tiny white stripes that zipped through the fabric. Yellow curtains hung at the windows, with black tie-backs. An oval-shaped glass coffee table with a clear vase that held a black, white, and yellow arrangement served as a centerpiece. The two end tables held black lamps with black and white shades. There was a glass bar on wheels, and it held her favorite taste. Vodka, gin, rum, and a gold-colored ice bucket sat center stage on the bar cart. The one thing that stood out the most was the one and only painting on the wall behind the couch. It was a beautiful replica of "The Last Supper" by one of my favorite artists, Leonardo da Vinci.

"Suga Momma, where did you get the painting from?" I asked.

"Baby, what painting are you talking about?" She stopped dicing potatoes and faced me directly. My hair caught her off guard.

"Boy, what did you do to your hair?" She gave me a surprised look.

I gave her a half smile. "I permed it."

"Ya'll kids are something else, I tell you. Ya'll come up with the craziest stuff."

"I'm talking about the painting of 'The Last Supper' by Leonardo da Vinci that you have in your living room."

Suga Momma lit a smoke and took a drag on it. "Chile, I got that original painting from a yard sale, out River Road. You know, out there where all those rich white folk live. I don't know a thing about no Leonardo ca Binci or whatever that is you saying. I like the picture 'cause its godly." She smiled.

"Well, actually, that's not the original painting. The original painting is in a church in Italy. What you have is a nice replica," I told her.

"Replica? Boy, you got one heck of a vocabulary. I like you. You pretty smart. Now get to work, your friends out there working and you in here talking to this here old lady." She laughed.

"Do you need me to do anything else inside before I leave?" I asked. Suga Momma grabbed at her foot, totally ignoring my question.

"Ooh, my feet starting to hurt already. Wayne, knock on Starr's door and tell her that I said to get her butt down here right now so she can help out!" she yelled.

A man's voice answered from upstairs. "Okay, baby, I will." On that note, I slid out the back door.

. . .

Suga Momma threw down and niggas ate like there was no tomorrow. You name it, she had it. In addition to her hot home-cooked meals, Suga Momma also sold beer and liquor. They played cards for money, and Suga Momma charged a dime per tune. If wasn't no dime dropped, then wasn't no music jumping. The older folks ate, danced, and drank until some of them had to literally be dragged home by the younger folk. Coach loaned me ten dollars, so I didn't have to steal anything like Momma had suggested. I dropped off two hot dinners for Momma and Keon. Keon was asleep, so Momma decided to eat them both.

I found a quarter for the music cup and waited my turn to play a song. Suga Momma ordered everyone to the backyard and announced, "It's *Soul Train* time!" as my song of choice, Marvin Gaye's "You Got to Give It Up," came on. The kids hurried to one side of the yard, and the adults fell into place on the other. Suga Momma and Lucky were the first to go down the line.

"Aw, work it, Momma," Suga Momma's friends teased her as the music switched over to Clarence Carter's "I Be Stroking." Lucky tried to hang in with her; his parents egged him on.

"Work it out, baby boy! Do the damn thang!" his father bragged.

We were all having a good time, when suddenly Starr came bursting through the back door. Her mouth was trembling and she was shaking like crazy.

"He put his hand under my skirt!" she yelled. Tears rolled down from her eyes heavily.

"Who, Starr?" Suga Momma ran over to her granddaughter, almost tripping over her own two feet. "Who touched you?" Starr didn't answer her grandmother, she just stood there crying.

"Turn off the godddamn music! Somebody done put their hands on Starr!" one of the adults screamed. The neighborhood cats who had been shooting dice through the cut stopped what they were doing and stormed over.

"Name the mutherfucker who touched you. Where is he? Where the mutherfucker at?!" the ringleader, a big dude named Snook, demanded to know. He had an ugly scar around his mouth and on the left side of his face. Rumor was that Snook was attacked in his sleep by a rat. He had gone to bed without properly wiping his face after eating fried chicken, leaving hot sauce around his mouth. The rat, getting a whiff of the hot sauce, attacked him, nibbling at his face and lip. Word on the street was that Snook killed the rat with his bare hands, then skinned it, boiled it in a pot, and ate the mutherfucker whole. Snook was a bad dude. He was a local thug who was well respected in the neighborhood. He would beat a nigga down in a minute. However, when it came to kids, Snook was a pushover. He never had children of his own, but he loved children and did whatever he could to protect them. He was furious and so were his boys. They demanded to know who had violated Starr.

"Yeah, where the nigga at that put his hands on this girl!" they shouted, eyes searching the outdoor crowd. Starr didn't answer them; instead, she fell into Suga Momma's arms, and explained.

"It was Wayne. Suga Momma, earlier today when you sent him

to my room to wake me up, I didn't want to tell you, but he came into my room while I was asleep and got on top of me." Starr's cries got even louder.

"What!" all of the adults at the social party screamed. Suga Momma's eyes grew larger than they already were. I thought at any minute her eyes would pop out of her head and explode, popping the frames off her oversize eyeglasses. Suga Momma snatched open the back door and rushed in; Snook and his men followed her in.

"Where he at, where he at?" the men yelled. Starr whined, sucking her right thumb. She pointed upwards with her left index finger. "He's upstairs in the bathroom."

They hurried upstairs to find him. I was scared out of my mind for Mr. Wayne. I had checked him out earlier and thought he was all right. Mr. Wayne was clean cut and well dressed. His denim blues were tight fitting, and those suckers were starched hard, with the meanest crease that I had ever seen. He was a high-waisted man, who wore his shirt tucked tight inside his pants. He rocked a small afro and wore more gold than Mr. T. The left side of his nose held a nasty pimple that needed to be popped badly. He hadn't talked much to anybody that afternoon and had pretty much stayed to himself. Mr. Wayne had presented himself in one light, but was now being exposed as the pervert he was. They dragged Mr. Wayne down the stairs; the thumping sound of his body beating the stairwell reminded me of a herd of elephants. Mr. Wayne cried out. He was no match for six angry men, so he didn't try to fight back; instead, he defended himself with his words.

"Man, I swear I didn't touch that girl. You've got to believe me!" he pleaded.

"Stop lying, you nasty mutherfucker!" Snook shouted, his faced balled up and twisted just as ugly as his lip.

"Niggah, you gone pay for that shit!" his boys followed up.

Everybody piled high on the back porch, peering into the house. We desperately tried to see what was going on.

"Get him out of my house!" Suga Momma ordered.

"Take him out front and beat him down!" Snook ordered his posse.

On that note, everybody hauled tailed around front to witness the beat-down. As soon as I turned the corner, Mr. Wayne came flying out off the house, landing on his head in the front yard. The men stood over top of him as Mr. Wayne began begging for his life.

"Help me, somebody help me!" he begged, but no one would intervene.

"Why you touch that girl? Why you put your mutherfucking hands on that child? Are you crazy, mutherfucker?" they verbally attacked him.

Mr. Wayne's eyes grew larger than Suga Momma's were. He swore on everything that he loved that he didn't touch Starr, but the men weren't buying his story. They continued to beat him down, using baseball bats, belts, sticks, whatever they could get their hands on. Conrad, who was Snook's right-hand man, even used a chain from a bicycle. There wasn't one person who dared to intervene, because folks didn't have empathy for a child molester. Mr. Wayne cried a pathetic, agonizing cry. He shed enough tears to fill up a water whale.

"Suga Momma, I swear I didn't touch her. Baby, I swear, you have to believe me," Mr. Wayne begged and pleaded but to no avail.

Suga Momma didn't care to listen to his side of the story; she just stood there watching as the men continued to beat his lifeless body to the ground. The beating reminded me of the whipping Kunta Kinte took in the movie *Roots*. The only difference between the beatings was the fact that the black men whipping his ass enjoyed every minute of it. The slave-like beating of Mr. Wayne took black-on-black crime to another level. Seeing a black man beaten down with whips and chains had me frozen in a state of shock. I stood there with the other spectators, watching but saying nothing. As I looked on, I thought to myself, *Fairfield Court Projects can't get any worse than this.* Eventually, Mr. Wayne stopped breathing. He wasn't moving at all.

"He's not breathing!" somebody yelled.

Apparently, one of the neighbors who gave a damn about Mr. Wayne called for help. As the police and rescue sirens could be heard in the distance, the men went ghost. They had beat the hell out of Mr. Wayne, then just like that they were gone. A few of them took off running up the block, while the others hid close by at one of the neighbors'. The rescue workers rushed to Mr. Wayne's aid, while the police bum-rushed the yard. They began questioning everybody about what they had seen or knew. Every single person out there, adults and children, remained silent. Everybody stuck together; there were no snitches in Fairfield. When the police realized wasn't nobody talking, they jumped back into their cruisers and drove off. The ambulance workers rushed Mr. Wayne onto a gurney and sped off.

• • •

For the next hour, we all stayed around to help clean up. I felt sorry for Starr; she was in the kitchen, still whining about what had happened to her. I moved over closer to her. I wanted her to know that I cared.

"Are you okay?" I asked in my most sincere tone. Starr glared up at me, tears forming in her eyes.

"Yeah, I'm okay," she whispered softly.

I grabbed a napkin from the table and handed it to her. "Here you go." Starr wiped the tears from her eyes, then sat the napkin on the table.

"I like your hair," she complimented me, catching me completely off guard. Starr had never said anything nice to me.

"Thank you," I finally managed to respond, and then I headed back outside to help my friends.

It was about ten p.m., and we were almost finished cleaning Suga Momma's apartment. Just as we were putting up the last of the tables and chairs, somebody yelled, "Get in the house, they shooting!" The next thing I know gunshots rang out. When I looked around, I spotted Snook and his boys, and they were all strapped. Every single one of them was packing. I didn't see anybody from my crew, so I made a dash around the corner. I tried to make it to my own house, because somebody had closed and locked Starr's back door just that fast. That's when I spotted a white van. A pitch-black man with long braids and a long trench-coat stood outside the van. He reached inside the van and came out with a rifle. Then he swung open his coat and pulled a gun. One of his boys jumped out of the van. He was packing, too. Then, just like a scene in any old gangster movie, the adversaries started blazing.

I hauled ass running. *Boom, boom, boom.* The shots were getting closer. "Awhh," people were screaming and running all over the place.

"Get the kids inside!" some lady screamed.

"Get down and stay down!" the angry men from the social party yelled. I had to get home. I refused to stop running so I ignored the warning.

"Bilal, get down!" Coach screamed at me. Just when I was about to lay down on the ground, I noticed Keon on the sidewalk. He was by himself, sitting in the orange school chair.

"Keooon," I yelled out. "Get down!" I screamed at him. I was shocked to see him sitting there because when I had taken the dinners home, he was upstairs fast asleep.

"Keon, get down!" I screamed again but he wouldn't move. I

wondered where Momma was because it didn't make sense to me that Keon was outside by himself that late at night. Keon looked petrified. His hands were folded in his lap and I could see his body shaking and trembling from across the street.

I dashed across the street. "Mom, open up the door!" I hollered for her to open up before I made it across the street. The gunfire was getting more intense. "Mom, open the door," I yelled again but Momma was nowhere to be found. Keon raised his hands and held them out for me.

"Bilal, come get me," he moaned.

"I'm coming, Keon! I'm coming," I promised him. Our house was only yards away but it seemed like I had been running a marathon. I couldn't get to my baby brotha fast enough. I ran as fast as I could. "I'm coming, Keon! I'm coming," I yelled repeatedly.

"Bilal, come get me." Keon's voice trembled.

I was about a foot away from him when a bullet hit him in the head and Keon's tiny body flipped backward in the chair. I watched my little brother's brain splatter on the sidewalk.

"Nooooo! Keon, Noooooo!" I screamed to the top of my lungs. "Momma, where are you!" I shouted.

I dropped down and crawled over to him. Keon's eyes rolled to the back of his head, blood gushed from his head and his mouth. I moved closer and hovered over top of him, still trying to protect him from the bullets that didn't have a name on them.

"Mom, help me, help me!" I cried for her. When I realized Momma wasn't coming, I took matters into my own hands. I took off my shirt and raised Keon's head; pieces of his brain fell into my hands.

"Help me, somebody help!" I screamed. Splattered pieces dropped onto the ground. I grabbed what was left of his head, and placed my shirt underneath it. "Help me, somebody help me," I begged and pleaded but there were no bright lights, no sirens, no police or rescue squads coming to help me. So, when I realized that I was on my own to care for my brotha, I did the only thing I knew to do.

I placed my mouth on top of Keon's bloody mouth, my eyes upon his eyes, and my hands upon his hands. I did what I had seen the lifeguard do to Lucky. I did what I had read about in vacation Bible school. *"Wake up, Keon, wake up!"* I screamed. I followed the Scripture exactly as it had been written and as I had understood it, but it wasn't working. Keon wasn't waking up, he wasn't moving, he wasn't coughing, he wasn't breathing, he wasn't sneezing, he wasn't coming back to me, he was gone, my little brother was gone!

Fuck the Bible and that bullshit I read in II Kings, about the Shu' nam mite's son and Elisha. This hand, eye, and mouth routine shit ain't bringing my brother back!

Blood gushed from his head. I placed my fist in the hole; I needed to make it stop. I tried, but I couldn't. The hole was just too big. I panicked; I started sweating and shaking. Urine and shit escaped me, my chest tightened and my head hurt. I thought my head was about to explode. *Maybe I'm dreaming.* I pinched myself and I didn't feel anything, *Good, I am dreaming, this is all a bad dream, this is fake blood, it's red paint.* Then I placed my hand in the red, I needed to be sure, so I touched it, then I tasted it, but this time I could feel something wet around my mouth and on my tongue; that still wasn't confirmation for me. I refused to believe that Keon was dead. My mind was playing tricks on me.

"Oh, my God, that's my baby!" That was my mother's voice. It was at that moment that I knew I wasn't dreaming. I placed my hand in the puddle of blood one more time, then I placed it on the sidewalk and there it was. My very own bloody handprint plastered on the sidewalk.

For some odd reason, in the midst of my pain, I remembered Portia's joke.

"You're so black, you can leave your handprint in charcoal."

I remembered how I had laughed to myself when she joked on me, 'cause I knew that it was impossible for anyone to leave a handprint in charcoal. Where was Portia now, I needed her to make me laugh, to tell me a funny joke, to cheer me up, to tell me the impossible. I needed somebody, anybody, to come help baby boy. I needed somebody to send me an angel. I needed the lifeguard to come save Keon for me, like he had saved Lucky.

"Somebody help me!" I screamed one last time. I glanced over at my bloody handprint again. Then I felt a strong pain in my stomach, as if someone had just knocked the wind out of me. A sharp pain zigzagged through my back, as if someone had stabbed me with a butcher knife. I couldn't breathe, but I didn't care 'cause if Keon was dead then life for me wasn't worth living. I wanted to die with my baby brotha.

Suddenly, my mom ran over to us and dropped to the ground. "Oh, my baby, help me get him inside," she cried.

Then I heard Coach's voice. "Joann, he's dead."

"Oh Lord! Oh Lord help me!" Momma cried out, the pain in her voice pierced my soul.

I threw my bloody hands up to my head. *"Whyyyy, whyyyy,"* I agonized. Then I rolled over onto my back, and everything went blank.

Chapter 12

I woke up the next morning at the Medical College of Virginia Hospital. Momma, Coach, Ms. Margaret, and Ms. Sheila were all congregated around my hospital bed. The doctor walked in holding a clipboard and pen in his hand. He glanced around at everybody, then cleared his throat.

"Morning, everyone," he spoke, then came over to the bed, dropped his clipboard and pen on the cover and proceeded to take my vitals. He nodded as if everything were all right, then turned to Momma. Picking up the clipbaoard and pen, he directed her toward the door with his hand.

"Ms. Cunningham, may I speak to you in private?" He directed Mom into the hallway.

Coach was sitting on the edge of the hospital bed, with tears in his eyes. "I'm sorry, I'm sorry," he tried apologizing but he broke down by my bedside.

Momma stepped back into the room, holding discharge papers

in her hand. She sighed. "The doctor said he's free to go. It was just another asthma attack."

When we arrived home, it was so quiet on my block that you could hear the birds chirping. Everyone was grieving over Keon's death. Coach helped me upstairs, and I changed into a fresh shirt and a pair of blue jeans. Floyd and Coach moved the bloody couch from our living room and sat it on the curb for the trash man. People packed inside the house, paying their respects. They brought over food, sodas, flowers, and cards. There was so many people in the house that there was no place for them to sit. Most of the people we didn't even know by name. Momma decided we needed more chairs, so she tried to put me to work.

"Bilal, go across the street and ask that lady that had the social if we can use some of her chairs," she suggested.

Ms. Sheila jumped in, intervening on my behalf. "I'll go. Joann, that child ain't in no position to do anything but rest," she said, rolling her eyes behind Momma's back. Ms. Sheila left the house and returned with Suga Momma and one of the neighbors. They brought over a couple of card tables and folding chairs.

"Hey, baby," Suga Momma greeted me with a warm kiss. Putt, Lucky, Head, Portia, Baije, and Cocoa came over too. They brought sympathy and get well soon cards. We all sat on the stairs, piling them high and watching as people came and went. There was silence between us. They were all sad, but as children, nobody knew the right words to say. Momma pulled out old pictures of Keon and shared them. Everybody talked about how cute Keon was as a baby, causing Momma to break down.

"I can't believe my baby is gone," she cried, as she pulled out more pictures of him. "You know, Keon has been sick for a while," she told the group. Ms. Sheila, her supposedly good girlfriend, let out a huge sigh.

"Oh really?" She frowned. Momma nodded her head, then began to explain.

"I found out a few months ago that Keon had cancer," she whimpered.

"What! And you didn't tell us!" Ms. Sheila and Ms. Margaret both exclaimed. They were furious with Momma for keeping such a big secret. After all, they were the only friends she had, and were like aunts to me and Keon. They deserved to know that their nephew had cancer.

"I just didn't want to burden anybody with it. Yeah, he had cancer. Leukemia. He was scheduled to start chemotherapy in a couple of weeks," she whined. We were all stunned by the news that had been kept quiet by one of the loudest women on the face of the earth. Usually, Momma couldn't hold water, but when it came to her own son, she kept his illness hush-hush.

"Joann, if you had told us, we could have done some things with Keon, you know, made sure he got to go to the beach, time at the park, you know, that sort of stuff. Damn, Jo!" Ms. Sheila argued. Momma sucked her teeth, totally ignoring the fact that someone else loved Keon too. Momma was selfish like that. It was no surprise to me when she quickly dismissed what her friend was saying.

"This was God's will, because Keon was going to die anyway. God just took him out of his misery sooner than later," she imagined. Pretty Boy Floyd leaned over and rubbed Momma's back, comforting her.

"It's okay, baby," he whispered softly.

Suga Momma listened as Momma spoke. From the expression on her face, it was obvious that she disagreed with Momma. She placed her liquor cup on the table and addressed Momma directly.

"Listen here, Ms. Lady. Now, I don't know you from a hill of beans, but let me tell you something," she said as she rose to her feet, serious as a heart attack. "This is not God's work, and God didn't take Keon from his misery! I'm sick and tired of people always blaming stuff on God!" she screamed loud enough to put a crack in the ceiling. Suga Momma caught us all off guard. Everybody's face was tight as she continued to rant and rave. Momma shot her an evil look, then blew snot from her nose into a tissue. She searched Suga Momma up and down, then told her what she thought she knew about God's plan for all humans.

"Ma'am, we all have a birth date and a death date. This was all in God's plan. I was raised in the church, so don't tell me about my God!" she snapped at the older woman. Suga Momma quickly snatched her eyeglasses from her face, then barked at everyone in the room.

"Let me tell all of you something." She pointed to the adults in the room. "God ain't have nothing to do with an eight-year-old boy's head getting blown off!" She began to cry. "This is the work of the devil! Okay, so we may all have a birth date and a death date, but you know what, there are times when the devil intervenes!" she snapped. "The devil comes to steal and destroy; he is after our minds and our children. The first book of Job teaches us that. The devil is forever roaming through the earth and going back and forth in it."

Suga Momma moved closer to Momma. Raising her chin, she stared directly into Momma's eyes. "Now, lady, just because your baby had cancer doesn't mean he was going to die from it. See, you had given him up even before he had a chance to live," she contended. "Hum. The devil is a liar, and we got to pray for our kids, our families, and our community," she said, wiping the light tears that were strolling down her aged face. Momma broke down crying again. Floyd continued patting her on the back. Ms. Sheila and Ms. Margaret started crying, too, as Suga Momma continued with her Bible lesson.

"Don't you know that God weeps too? God is crying about what happened to Keon. God didn't want this to happen," she said. "Now, everybody come on in this living room and I want all the adults to form a circle around these children and we gone pray for them," she ordered.

The adults formed a circle around the children and everybody held hands. Suga Momma began, "Lord, help me. I may drink a little liquor and act a fool from time to time, but I love my God," she confessed. Then she led us into prayer. "Let us all bow our heads. Heavenly father, we come to you for protection of our children. We ask for understanding." Suga Momma became Holy Ghost filled. She prayed over us and spoke in tongues.

• • •

On Sunday morning, two detectives came by to question us. One of the detectives was Floyd's friend, the Teddy Pendergrass look-alike. Momma told Detective Dotson that we didn't know anything about the men involved in the beating and shoot-out, which was true. About an hour after the detectives left, news reporters came to the door. Momma flat-out refused to speak to the press; she said she wasn't going to allow channel sixteen to editorialize Keon's murder. The next couple of days were busy for us: as soon as one person left there was somebody else banging at the door.

The City of Richmond sent a liaison over to talk to Momma. They were concerned about how she was going to pay for the funeral, so the city offered to pay all funeral expenses, and Momma gladly accepted. The city liaison explained that because Momma didn't have life insurance on him, it was the city's responsibility to bury him. The funeral was scheduled for Friday, which allowed our people from Birmingham enough time to get to Richmond. Momma hadn't seen her family in years, and she wasn't thrilled about seeing them now.

My family arrived bright and early on Friday morning, the day of the funeral. I woke up when I heard Momma crying. I hurried downstairs to console her, only to discover she wasn't alone. She was standing in the kitchen; a heavyset woman with a fancy church hat and a purple polyester suit was standing next to her. The woman's skirt was hitched up in the back. She held herself up with a walking cane as she pulled her skirt from her butt. When I entered the room, the woman was excited to see me.

"Oh, is that my grandbaby?" She spread her arms far apart to embrace me. I fell into my grandmother's arm, and she snuggled me tight. I could smell her perfume. Curious to know what she was wearing, I took a good sniff. The scent was familiar. Grandma was wearing Momma's favorite perfume, Tea Rose. She let go of me and I stepped away from her. She eyed me up and down.

"Oh, baby, I'm so sorry. I'm so sorry Grandma ain't been here for you, but we gone change all that, you hear me?" she whined. I looked into my grandmother's dark brown eyes; they appeared to be sincere.

"Yes, ma'am," I answered.

"Hey, big boy, come and give your granddaddy a hug," a voice startled me. It was my grandfather; but as I attempted to move toward him, Momma stepped directly in my path, blocking me from his view. She decided it was more important to introduce me to the other person in the room.

"Bilal, this is your aunt Sarah. She is my sister."

"Hi, Aunt Sarah," I spoke and gave her a hug.

Aunt Sarah spoke with a southern drawl. "Hey, baby. How you doing?"

"Bilal, go on and put your clothes on." Momma rushed me off.

"Fine," I answered Aunt Sarah as I headed up to my room. I needed to prepare myself mentally for the funeral. I hadn't been able to sleep and had been having nightmares ever since Keon's murder. I had never been to a funeral in my life and I dreaded going to my own brother's. I pulled out an old newspaper and began solving the questions to the daily crossword puzzle. I knew that I needed to get dressed, so I threw my clothes on, tore the crossword puzzle out of the newspaper, folded it and slid it in my back pocket. I grabbed a pen and headed back downstairs.

• • •

When we pulled up to the funeral home, the driver opened the door for me, and as soon as I stepped out, I heard someone crying. It was Paul, Putt's little brother and Keon's best friend. He was crying hysterically in Putt's arms. I locked arms with my moms and our family walked in behind us. There was only a short distance from the funeral home's entrance and where Keon's body lay in state, but it seemed as if it took forever to get to him. As I headed toward all that remained of my li'l brother, my stomach balled up in a tight knot. I looked straight ahead at the oak wood box that sat before me. I couldn't believe that the small wooden box held my brother's remains. A picture of Keon sat on top of the casket, along with a blue-and-white spray that Suga Momma had purchased on behalf of the football team. The casket remained closed because part of Keon's head had been blown off and the man from the funeral home told Momma that it would've been distasteful to show him. So I took one last look at him by way of the picture sitting on top the wooden box, then I slowly made my way to the front pew.

Paul's cry became louder; his screams bounced off the walls of the funeral home.

I cried also. It was the first time that I had cried since the night my li'l brother had been shot. I couldn't fight back my tears any longer.

"Whyyyyy?" I screamed. Then I felt a strong hand rest on my shoulder. It was Coach. He was sitting on the pew behind Momma and me. For some reason, the more I cried, the louder the organist began to play. It was like the church lady was getting a kick out of my pain, she had a silly-ass look on her face the entire time. Then a strange woman began to sing "Take Me Back to

Yonder," and that didn't help the situation at all. Everybody in the church began to cry, scream, and shout.

After the woman realized that she had the church in an uproar, she graciously took her seat and the preacher stood before those assembled.

"Bilal, do you see Floyd?" Momma whispered in my ear. I raised my head from her shoulder. I scoped the entire funeral home. No Floyd.

"No, Momma, I don't," I answered. Momma couldn't grieve her own son's death for worrying about that sorry-ass nigga. Floyd hadn't come home the night before, nor had he called. I turned back around to listen to the pastor; he was reading Psalm 23 from the Old Testament. Then he read Matthew 18:2–5 from the New Testament.

Coach's girlfriend read the acknowledgments. There were so many cards to choose from that she read only four. My cousin Alice from Birmingham read the obituary, which listed Keon's father's name as Melvin Thomas. After all those years, I had to find out at Keon's funeral that Melvin the Mailman was indeed my little brother's daddy. I sat there thinking about all the secrets that Momma had kept from me. My emotions ran high as my temperature began to boil. I was sad and angry all at the same time. To make matters worse, Momma kept peeping over her shoulders, looking for her sorry-ass man.

"Now, we will have a selection from Starrshema Williams," the pastor announced. The organist began to play "His Eyes Are on the Sparrow," and the young voice lit up the funeral home. I threw my head up from my lap to get a look at the young person who owned those vocals, 'cause whoever she was, the girl could sing. Lo and behold, it was none other than Starr, my adversary. She was wearing her blue and white cheerleader uniform. When she noticed me looking at her, she stepped away from the podium and stood in full view of everyone. Starr continued singing with the microphone in her hand, and her head tilted back so far, you could see all thirty-two teeth in her mouth. When she hit the last verse of the chorus, she poured her heart and soul into it like she was a contestant in a singing competition. Starr was very confident in what she was doing; she behaved like a pro who knew regardless of what happened that day, she was still a superstar. She pointed to her chest with her thumb, and screamed, "His eyes are on the sparrow and I know he watches meeeee!" Everyone who was seated rose to his or her feet, as Suga Momma praised God's name, shouting all the way down the aisle.

• • •

We left the funeral home and headed for the burial ground. There was complete silence in the limousine as we drove up Fairmount Avenue to put my brother into the ground. We drove about a mile until we reached Nine Mile Road. Suddenly, I noticed a cemetery on the right side of the street. I broke down again when I saw all the tombstones.

"Mom, no, I don't want to go in there," I begged.

"Boy, this ain't it!" she responded in an irritated tone, as if to shut me up.

I kept watching out of the window as the driver continued down Nine Mile Road. He drove clean past the sign that read OAKWOOD CEMETERY. I was confused.

"Mom, where we going?" I asked.

"Bilal, Oakwood is not the cemetery that the city buries people in. We got about another mile to go, so just hush for a while," she said. We drove for another mile, then the driver made a right turn on a narrow dirt road and drove the limousine onto the gravel.

"We're here," he announced.

I couldn't believe my bloody eyes. Even the dead didn't deserve to live like that. It was the most awful, godforsaken thing that I had ever seen. The grass stood about three feet tall, trash was scattered around, tombstones were broken in half, graves were sunken, and holes were left unfilled. There wasn't a visitor or one goddamn flower in sight. The graves were unmanned, unkempt, and damn right unbelievable. The cemetery wasn't fit for a dog to live in, but it was now Keon's new home.

We bailed out of the cars, and everyone gathered around my family. A strong wind blew by and the casket began to rock back and forth. I jumped up. *"Noooooo,"* I screamed. I panicked and fell over on the casket. I needed to stop Keon from falling into the six-and-a-half-foot hole. Coach and granddaddy wrestled me away from the casket and sat me back in the chair.

Momma started at it again. "Oh, God, my baby, my baby," Momma cried very little tears.

I silently wept as the pastor gave the benediction, and then he mouthed, "Ashes to ashes, dust to dust."

Folks lined up to speak to me and my moms. They gave warm hugs and kisses, and those friendly, comforting gestures during my hour of bereavement meant so much to me. I appreciated the love that I was getting.

"You're in our prayers," Putt's mother, Ms. Pearl, said as she kissed me and Momma on the cheek.

"I'm so sorry." Lucky's parents hugged the both of us.

Suga Momma hugged me and held me tight for about a minute. "Baby, it's going to be okay. You let me know if you need anything, 'cause Suga Momma loves you," she said, rubbing my face. Starr came up behind her grandmother. I waited for her to say something but she didn't. She just walked away with her hands folded across her chest.

Melvin the Mailman was the last to approach the family. The mutherfucker had a lot of nerve showing up on his lunch break. He didn't even have the decency to take the day off for his own son's funeral. He stood in front of Momma, dressed in his postal uniform. He removed his postal hat from his head as if to show respect.

"Joann, I'm so sorry. I know. I-I have to get back to work," he stuttered, then he stopped talking and walked away. When he walked past my chair, I stuck my foot out, causing him to lose his balance and stumble into the crowd. He grabbed onto one of the ladies in the crowd, trying to break the fall, but he couldn't. Deacon Melvin fell to his knees but this time he wasn't praying.

"Oh my," Grandma sighed, as some of the neighborhood men hurried to pick his sorry ass up.

After the commotion was over, the funeral home director gestured for the family to stand. It was time to say good-bye to Keon. I stood up, but when I turned to leave I was amazed at what I saw. The cheerleaders and football players from Fairfield, Whitcomb, Mosby, Creighton, and Gilpin Court Projects had formed a large K across the cemetery with their bodies. Every project on the hill represented at Keon's funeral. Suga Momma and the coach from Whitcomb's football league presented me and Momma with a plaque.

"On behalf of the Richmond Redevelopment Housing Authority, we are proud to present you with a plaque in your son's/brother's name, Keon Cunningham, for outstanding sportsmanship and being the most valuable Pee-wee player of the year," coach read. "In addition to being named the most valuable player, we are also pleased to name his team, the Fairfield Cougar Peewee Squad, as the champions of the year. We, the Whitcomb Court Steelers, hereby refuse to play in the championship against Keon's team, because he is no longer with us. However, although he is no longer with us in body, he is with us in spirit. Keon will never be forgotten, he will live in our hearts forever," he added. Then the coach turned to the children assembled on the cemetery field and nodded his head.

All the children yelled, "KEON!" in unison. The cheerleaders did a jump in the air, while the football players bowed down on one knee. Then Ms. Sheila opened a black box, and a white dove disappeared into the sky. I grabbed my moms by one hand, and Granddaddy held on to her other. We were walking back to the limousine when suddenly Momma collapsed.

Chapter 13

The doctor ordered bed rest for my moms. He said she was on the verge of having a nervous breakdown, so he prescribed her five milligrams of Valium. Momma neglected to tell the doctor that she had tripped and fallen over an uprooted casket at the old rundown pet cemetery. Our people from out of town had planned to stay for a week, but after Momma mixed Valiums with vodka and Colt 45, something happened that caused them to leave faster than anticipated.

I was in bed when I overheard Grandma tell Momma that she was sick in the head and needed help. I ran downstairs to see what was up. Grandma was standing over top of Momma, threatening to hit her with her cane. She swung the cane around loosely in the air.

"Joann, I brought you in this world and I'll take you out! Every time you get to drinking, I swear you get the devil in you!" she said, shaking her cane over top of Momma's head. Granddaddy just stood there, looking at them as if they were both crazy.

"Put the cane down, Lilly, the girl just lost her son," he said rather calmly.

Floyd showed up the same night that my people left. I crept downstairs when I heard the nigga turn his key in the door. Momma was foolishly in love; in her eyes, Floyd could do no wrong.

"Baby, where have you been? I've been worried sick about you," Momma asked, sounding pressed as hell. Floyd walked into the kitchen and laid his keys on the kitchen table.

"Baby, I'm all right. I just needed to get away to clear my head," he croaked.

"Can I get you anything? How about I fix you something to eat?" Momma pressed on.

Before Floyd could even answer, Momma was already pulling out pots and pans.

"Listen, baby, I'm tired. It's been a long day for me," Floyd chimed.

I eased down the rest of the stairs and stuck my head halfway around the wall. Floyd was sitting in the chair, with his face in his hand. My moms stood behind him, both of her hands were placed on his shoulders. I ear hustled in on their conversation. Momma began to massage her man's back.

"Baby, what happened? Why did you leave on Friday night and not return for the funeral?" Floyd sighed heavily. He didn't approve of Momma questioning him.

"Baby, don't start with me. You know I can't do them thangs." Momma continued massaging his shoulders.

"What thangs?" Momma quizzed.

"Them funerals, baby, they ain't for me," Floyd answered bluntly. I knew at that moment that he was a sorry-ass excuse for a man. If Coach was there for Mom and me, then that nigga should've been there too.

"But Floyd, I needed you so badly to be there with me. Baby, he was my son," Momma complained.

Floyd cut her off. "Joann, I'll make it up to you, baby," he promised.

Then he pushed back from the table, causing Momma's hands to fall by her side.

"Baby, I'm going on up. Bring my plate upstairs."

Before leaving the kitchen, Floyd snatched her by the back of her head, and stuck his tongue clean down her throat. Momma tongued him back real hard. After they exchanged saliva, Floyd pulled away, wiping his lips.

"Baby, I'm tired, but I ain't too tired for some of this pussy." He slid his hands underneath Momma's nightgown. Momma's eyes lit up like a Christmas tree with colored bulbs. She let out a childlike giggle.

"Stop, Floyd," she chuckled. Floyd grabbed his hat off the kitchen table.

"Baby, tighten that thang up before you come to bed 'cause you know how Floyd likes his kitty cat." He sniffed his right index finger, the one he had used to fondle her. Momma smiled at him.

"And how does Daddy like it?" she asked.

Floyd sucked his teeth. "Bald on the outside and clean enough to eat on the inside. That thing smell a little tart right now," he informed her.

"Okay, baby. As soon as I'm done, I'll be right up to tighten it up." Momma blushed.

• • •

I stayed home from school the remainder of the week. When I returned the following Monday, everybody knew that I had lost my brother. I didn't have to make up any work, because I had an A or B average in all of my classes. After Keon's death, school just wasn't the same. I didn't have any interest at all in learning. Most of the time, I just slept in class. By December, things were getting rough at home. Momma didn't go to social services to recertify her welfare case, so our food stamps and money was suspended. To top it off, social services told her that she would have to wait thirty days to reapply. They also told her that once she reapplied, her assistance would be cut back since it was just two people in the household. Momma didn't seem to worry about it, but I did. I worried day and night about how we were going to eat.

One Saturday morning, there was a rapid knock at the back door. It was Malcolm's mother; she was banging on the door like she was gone crazy. When I opened the door, she stood there with her hands covering her face. I invited her in.

"Hi, is your mother home?" she asked.

"Yes, ma'am, she is."

She dropped her hands from her face. Her grill was balled up in a tight knot. From the way she looked, it was obvious she was in excruciating pain.

"Ma'am, are you okay?" I asked her.

"Baby, call me Ms. Karen. Can you please ask your mother if she has something for a headache? B.C. powder, Bayer, something," she moaned. Ms. Karen was in desperate need of help. I ran upstairs to ask Momma for some headache medicine. Momma and Floyd were still in bed, so I barged into their bedroom.

"Momma, the lady next door told me to ask you if you had anything for a headache." I nudged her arm, trying to wake her up. Momma opened her eyes.

"Who?" she frowned.

"Ms. Karen, the lady next door." Momma wiped the coal from her eyes.

"Oh, so that's the bitch's first name." Momma sat up in the bed.

"Go over there and look in the closet on the floor and hand me that white bag." I walked into the closet, and retrieved the white bag from the floor. Momma continued with the instructions.

"Look inside and hand me one of those bottles." I slid my hand inside the bag and pulled out a bottle of pills.

"Bilal, take one of those yellow pills out of the bottle and take it to her. And tell that bitch that I said to send me three mutherfucking dollars for my Valium. Tell that bitch that I'm gone kick her ass if she don't!"

I removed one pill as I was told to do and hurried back downstairs. Ms. Karen was sitting at our kitchen table with her head down.

"Ms. Karen," I called out to her.

"Yes, baby."

"Ms. Karen, my moms said you have to pay her three dollars for this pill or else she's going to kick your ass," I said as I held my hand out with the pill on display. Ms. Karen giggled a little.

"All right, baby, I'll bring the money right back. Just wait for me at the back door." Ms. Karen snatched the pill so fast, she almost ripped the skin from the palm of my hand. Within a minute, Ms. Karen was back at the door with the three dollars.

"Here you go, baby." She handed me the money. "Tell your mom that I said thanks and I may be back for another one."

I shut the door behind her and went back upstairs to give Momma her money.

"Here is the money." I handed the three one-dollar bills. Momma never removed the covers from her head.

"Bilal, just put the money on the dresser, please," she huffed. Just as I was leaving the room, she stopped me.

"You can have one dollar for yourself," she said.

I hadn't eaten all day, so I was happy as hell to have a dollar.

Shit, a dollar could buy a lot of junk from the ice cream truck. I threw my dollar bill into my pocket and sat the other two on the dresser. Just as I was heading out the door, Floyd snatched his head from under the cover.

"Boy, shut the damn door and don't you wake us up again!" he growled at me.

• • •

So there it was. It was just that simple. I supplied the product and Ms. Karen peeled off the scratch. It was a win/win situation for all of us. With no food on the table, and a sorry-ass man lying in Momma's bed every night doing nothing but taking up space, I figured I had to do something to feed the two of us. Momma wasn't going to take all the pills anyway. So, I figured, why let them go to waste? I had just earned my first buck and I was able to eat because of it. When the ice cream truck came by later that day, I ran out and bought me two Chic-O-Sticks, a grape soda, and a bag of chips. I munched down on my junk food, and waited for Ms. Karen to get another headache. In fact, when Momma and Floyd left the house, I turned up the stereo as loud as it would go so she would catch another headache. I blasted the song "When a Man Loves a Woman" and sure enough, it worked. Ms. Karen came back; she said her head was hurting like an elephant was tap-dancing on her brain. Since Momma wasn't home to land the deal, I handled business myself.

"Oh, Ms. Karen, I'm sorry you don't feel well," I lied.

Ms. Karen said she needed two more Valiums to ease her pain and I was happy to be in the position to help her.

That was my introduction to the hustle. That was the day I started slanging them thangs!

Chapter 14

The next morning on the way to school, I supplied each of my boys with a package. I explained to them why we should sell the Valiums. We were behind Putt's building when I pulled them to the side.

"Hey, ya'll, look at what I got." I pulled out the bottle of yellow Valiums from my backpack. I handed them to Putt. He looked at me half crazy.

"Man, what's this?" he asked.

"Oh snap!" Head screamed, half covering his mouth. Head was ahead of the crew when it came to street shit, so he knew exactly what time it was.

"Man, be quiet before you get us busted! Where you get those Valiums from?" Head asked.

"I got them from my momma," I replied.

"What's up with you, are you planning to take them?" Putt asked.

"No, Putt, it's not for us to take. We're going to sell these to make us some money," I told him, plain and simple. Head was down for getting money; he approved immediately.

"Yeah, that's what I'm talking about," Head said excitedly. Wasting no time, he snatched a handkerchief from his back pocket.

"Come on, give me mine," he said impatiently.

I pulled out the aluminum foil from my book bag and handed Putt and Lucky a sheet. Head said he was good, he was gone keep his stashed in his hanky. I counted out the first ten yellow Valiums and dumped them into Putt's aluminum foil. Then I counted ten more and dumped them into Lucky's foil. They placed the Valiums in their book bags. Before I could give Head his package, he blurted out, "Man, give me more than ten. I can sell more than that, I bet you!" he boasted. We laughed at him; Head was already down for the hustle.

"Head, there's only thirty pills in each bottle," I explained.

Head looked at me as he counted. "Ten for Putt, Lucky got ten, and I got ten. Man, what you plan on selling? You didn't keep any for yourself?" he wondered.

"Yeah, I got some. I took them from another bottle," I explained. "Okay, so here's the deal. Everybody got ten pills to sell at three dollars each. That means you will make thirty dollars. Y'all get to keep one dollar for each pill you sell and two dollars will come to me. That means, after you sell all of them, you'll end up with ten dollars and I will get twenty," I continued. "So from now on, when the ice cream truck comes around, we'll be able to get what we want. Better yet, we can buy candy and stuff in school without having to ask anybody for money," I told them.

"Bet!" Putt yelled.

"Cool with me," Lucky chimed in. Head continued to walk; he didn't mouth a word. Then he blurted, "Black, why we got to give you two dollars off each pill, if we doing all the work?" he asked.

" 'Cause them my momma's pills and that's just the way it goes," I answered.

"So, Black, your Momma takes Valiums?" Lucky frowned.

"Yeah, man, your momma popping pills like that?" Putt frowned too.

Momma was a drunk, a straight-up alcoholic, but not a pill popper. "No, my moms ain't on Valiums like that. When Keon died, the doctor prescribed the Valiums to help calm her nerves, to keep her relaxed, that's all."

"Oh, so that's—so that's what these pills do. Keep—keep you calm?" Putt stuttered.

"Yeah, and they are also good for pain, like bad headaches," I answered. It was important that they had a little background on what they were going to be selling, in order for them to be good salesmen.

"Valiums make you feel real good; they make you feel like you are on top of the world," I assumed.

"All right then, let's do this." Head laughed.

We made our way down the block to the bus stop. Cocoa came strutting throught the cut. In her soft squeaky voice she yelled, "Come on, the bus is coming."

We all ran past Cocoa, who once again was walking at a snail's pace with her high-heeled shoes on. We jumped onto the bus, took our assigned seats, and watched Cocoa from the windows.

Chapter 15

The kids from the suburbs were spending mad money on my product. Since the yellow pills were such a hot commodity, I had no choice but to follow the rules of supply and demand. I raised the cost to five dollars because my supply had trickled down real low. By March, we were almost sold out of yellow Valiums but because of the demand for more, I had to step my game up. There was no way I could turn back now; having a little change in my pocket made me feel secure. I knew that even if there was no food in the house, I could always count on having a few dollars in my pocket to at least get me something to eat.

I had to think of something fast to keep the ends flowing. There were more pills in Momma's bedroom, but if I took the blue Valiums, then the bag would be left empty, which would have been a dead giveaway. Momma would have definitely known that I had been in her room stealing. I didn't want Momma to find out what I was doing, because I just knew she would kill me. Neverthless, I went for it.

The morning I snuck into Momma's bedroom to get a bottle of the blue Valiums, I rummaged through her closet and found nothing. They were gone. Not one pill in sight. The white bag was even missing. Just as I was leaving, Momma entered the room.

"What are you doing in my room?" Momma questioned.

"Oh, nothing. Just looking for my book," I lied. I hated lying to Momma, but she was the type of person that you just had to lie to.

Momma rolled her eyes to the back of her head, then poked her finger into my chest. "You think I don't know what you been doing, boy? Go to your room and wait right there!" she fumed. I nervously waited for her in my bedroom. I had stolen from Momma and shit was about to hit the fan. Momma stormed into my bedroom with her face all wrinkled up. I was petrified. I couldn't believe the next set of words that came out of her mouth.

"Since you think you know what you doing, get rid of all of them," she said, handing me the bag full of Valiums—all of them. The rest of the yellow Valiums and all of the blue. I slowly removed the bag from her hand. I couldn't believe this was happening. Momma huffed, then turned to leave the room.

"And for God's sake, please don't get caught, 'cause I ain't about to visit you in no juvenile home," she said.

"Yes, ma'am. I won't," I promised.

• • •

It was the day of the big game and school dance, and damn near the whole school was there. People walked around, styling and profiling as if they were at a fashion show. Duke and Maurice, who should have been in high school, were both stars on the basketball team. They had their own private fan club. A rack of naïve girls, who were just as old and "behind" as they were, cheered them on during the game. Folks were either styling and profiling, macking, or trying to get money.

Cocoa had a Polaroid camera, so she snapped pictures and charged two dollars a shot. Baije was the candy lady. She sold candy, chips, cookies, and Now and Laters. Me and the crew sat on the bleachers, watching the game, and waited for the kids from the suburbs to dish out their parents' hard-earned money.

"Hey Black!" Putt yelled for me.

It was halftime, and I was sitting quietly on the bleachers, waiting to check out the halftime performance. Starr was the captain of the cheering squad, and the cheerleaders had just taken over the floor. I had been dying to check her out, so when Putt called my name, I was irritated.

"What, Putt?" I frowned because he should've known not to disturb me while Starr was on the floor.

"Man, come here. Trisha needs to ask you something," he yelled over the loud noise.

"Where she at?"

"She's in the hallway."

I wasn't exactly sure what Trisha wanted because until that day she had never spoken a word to me. Trisha was very popular with the boys in school. She had the biggest ass of all the eighth grade girls. The niggas named her Big Booty Trisha. Supposedly Trisha had been giving blow jobs from as early as age nine and was fucking like a rabbit by the age of ten. I stepped around the corner to see what Big Booty Trisha's whoring ass wanted with me. I spotted her standing next to the bathroom.

"Hello, Trisha," I spoke.

Trisha stuck her chest and her butt out as if she really needed to.

"Can I speak to you in private?" she asked.

"Private? We're in school. Can't get anymore private than this," I said sarcastically.

"Well, can you just come here for a minute?" She pulled me around the corner before I had a chance to answer. Trisha started tripping real hard.

"Black, I hear you got them *feel goods,*" she said.

"Dag, Trish, you could have gotten them from one of my friends. Is that why you called me out here?"

"Well, since I don't have any money, and I hear that you are the man, I wanted to know if you could let me have two pills if I made you *feel good,*" she said, brushing her body up against mine. My mouth dropped, and my eyes bucked as Trisha grabbed my hand and pulled me into the boys' bathroom. I didn't resist.

Once in the bathroom, Trisha pushed me into a vacant stall and started grinding on me hard. Okay now, Starr was all I could think of but I was curious, so I just went along with Trisha's twisted game. She pulled my pants down to my knees, pulled my penis out, and started to play with it. It felt *real good* to me, so I let her do it until she got stupid.

"Can I kiss it?" she asked.

"What?" My eyes flew open. I couldn't believe the girl was asking to kiss my dick.

I looked down at Trisha; she was holding my dick in her hand and her lips were in the puckered-up position. She was about to kiss it when I stopped her.

"Why won't you let me?" she pondered.

"No, Trisha, why would you want to do that? That's not lady-like!" I told her.

" 'Cause I want some of those *feel goods* and I don't have any money," she answered.

Just then Putt pushed open the bathroom door and yelled in.

"Black, come on, something happened to Starr."

"Move, girl." I pulled up my pants and shoved Trisha out of my way. I ran out of the bathroom. Trisha ran behind me.

"Can I?" she continued to beg, feening for a damn Valium.

I stopped running, turned around, pulled my aluminum foil from my pocket and slid a couple of pills down the hall to her.

"Here, Trisha. You can have these. Just make sure you don't ever kiss anybody's dick for the *feel goods*," I screamed at her.

"Thanks, Black. I'll think about it," she promised.

• • •

Starr collapsed at the basketball game. I was worried sick about her and prayed that I wouldn't lose her as I had lost Keon. The doctors kept Starr in the hospital for a few days and, although she and I didn't get along, I missed having her around. I became withdrawn, isolated. I didn't want to talk or see anyone so I barricaded myself in my bedroom. Momma couldn't understand why I was feeling so sad, so she barged in on me one day and demanded that I leave my room.

"Boy, you need to get up off your ass and do something with yourself. What's wrong with you? You laid all up in bed worrying about that little fast-ass girl from across the street, ain't you?" she quizzed.

I lied, "No, Momma, I'm okay."

"Well, her grandmother told me that her li'l fast ass is coming home from the hospital tomorrow. So, you'll see the little heffa then," she added.

"Okay," I responded as if I didn't care. I was thrilled with the information that Momma shared but I wasn't about to let her know it.

It was eleven a.m. when I woke up the next morning. I jumped out of bed, threw a little water on my face, and a lot of water on my body. I was in the best mood of my life because I knew Starr was coming home from the hospital. I dressed myself in the nicest shirt and jeans that I could find, I grabbed my cash from my dresser drawer and headed downstairs. I had planned to eat, then walk over to Koslow's to buy Starr a get well soon card and a fruit basket. As I approached the kitchen I could hear Floyd's voice. I took in a deep breath before entering the room, because he was the last person that I wanted to see first thing in the morning. I turned the corner; Floyd was sitting with the chair tilted back, talking on the telephone.

I ignored his fake ass and went on about my business, fumbling around in the kitchen cabinets, searching for my last can of corn beef hash. Floyd continued talking. His voice grew louder as I slammed the kitchen cabinets shut. *Where is my corn beef hash?* I thought to myself. *Now, I know I had one can left.* Somehow, my corn beef had miraculously disappeared. I was rather annoyed because my mind was dead set on eating nothing but corn beef hash.

I damn near ransacked the whole kitchen looking for my can. I wasn't thinking about Floyd or whom he was talking to on the phone, until something he said caught my attention.

"Yeah, player, they kept me in the hospital for two days because I had a lot of bleeding," he shared with the person on the other end of the phone. He continued on. "Man, it was supposed to be an outpatient type thang. But, everything is everything. I'm all right," he bragged. I continued searching high and low for my corn beef hash; still no hash.

Floyd continued running his mouth on the phone.

"Yeah, partner. Joann gave me the money to have them nasty-ass keloids removed. Nawh, partner, she used the money from the life insurance policy that she had on her son."

What the—? I threw my hand behind my ear, and sort of like pushed it forward to be sure I heard him correctly. Floyd caught me staring. He looked me dead in the eye, and added more salt to my already open wound.

"Man, the city paid for that boy's funeral and Joann kept her insurance money," he snickered. "Yeah, man, Joann worked them mutherfuckers," he added, laughing real loud. I couldn't believe what I was hearing; a sharp pain hit me in the stomach. Then I slumped over from the pain.

"*Momma!*" I wailed. "*Momma!*"

Momma ran in to see what I was yelling about.

"Boy, what is wrong with you?" She grabbed hold of my shoulders and shook me hard, almost knocking me back to my senses.

"Momma, did you use Keon's insurance money to pay for Floyd's ear operation?" I asked her. Momma rolled her eyes, then gave Floyd a puzzled look. She didn't answer me.

"Did you, Momma? Did you?" I asked her again.

Momma still didn't answer, and Floyd sat there with a smirk on his face, pissing me off even more.

"Mom, you told them people from the city that you didn't have any insurance on Keon. Why did you lie, Momma, why did you lie?" I ranted.

POW! Momma smacked me dead in my face. "Boy, don't you ever question me or call me a liar. I ain't tell them people shit! Those people from the city came here assuming that I didn't have no insurance. So hell, since they offered to pay for the funeral, goddamnit, I let them!" she boasted. "Floyd needed to have those keloids removed, so I gave him the money to have it done!" she added.

"How could you, Mom, how could you!" I slammed my fist down on the kitchen table, knocking over a plate. I glanced down to see what I had mistakenly knocked over, and lo and behold, about a forkful of my mutherfucking corn beef hash was on the floor. My eyes shot back up to Floyd. "Nigga, you ate my last can of corn beef hash! I paid for that corn beef hash with my own money!" I snapped at him. Floyd rubbed his face with his hand, kind of cool like.

"Look here, pimp juice, you need to calm your ass down, partner!" he spat.

My moms jumped to his defense. "That's right, boy, calm your ass down! Floyd is the one who's been getting those Valiums, so if it weren't for him, you wouldn't have any money. So technically Floyd's been the one putting food in this house, and as far as I'm concerned, he can eat whatever the hell he wants, when he wants!"

I wanted to drop dead and die right there on the kitchen floor. Momma had just admitted that she allowed her son to be buried in a cheap wooden box at a pet cemetery. I instantly became sick to my stomach. I was going to vomit. I reached for the trash can and that's when I noticed that Floyd wasn't wearing any shoes. When I saw my blue and white football socks on his big feet, I flipped out. I looked up at him, then back at his feet, then at the corn beef hash on the floor. Then I thought about Keon, the man from the city, the funeral, the cemetery, Mom's deception. I was mad as hell with her and still reeling from Keon's death, and Floyd antagonizing me with his dirty looks didn't help any. I thought to myself, *This nigga done profited from Keon's death and he's wearing my socks!* Man, I lost it.

Instantly, the pain in my stomach subsided. "So, mutherfucker, you think it's funny, huh?" I yelled at him. I glanced around for an object; I spotted the needle-nose pliers sitting on the kitchen counter. I snatched it up and charged him. With the needle nose positioned sideways in my hand, I clamped it between his nostrils, and tightened the handle with all my strength. With all the rage inside me, I raised him completely out of the chair.

Momma screamed. "Oh, my God, let him go, Bilal, let him go!" she cried out. The more she cried, the harder I tightened my grip.

Blood gushed from his nose as pieces of cartilage were ripped away.

"Now, nigga, who's got the juice?" I bit my bottom lip as I spoke to him. Floyd's tiny body dangled in the air.

"Help me, somebody help," he begged, speaking through what little piece of nostril he had left.

I ignored his pitiful cry and continued with my abuse. I tossed the nigga onto the floor all the while still gripping onto the plyers. Momma ran out of the house to go get help. I continued my conversation with Floyd.

"You think I don't know what you mean when you call me pimp juice. You call me pimp juice, because you think you're the pimp and I'm your juice. You trying to say I'm your sperm. Nigga, you ain't my daddy!" I said as I got up close and personal in his ear. Floyd gazed up at me; his entire body shaking uncontrollably.

"Who's the daddy now? Answer me! Answer me. You better answer me now! " I demanded. Floyd wasn't answering my question and his disobedience really ticked me off. I danced around in a circle for a minute, then gave him a good old kick in the ass.

BAM! "Who's the daddy now?" I asked him one last time. Floyd fought hard to articulate his words; he took in a deep breath.

"You are," he finally answered, with slobber running down his mouth, and perspiration covering his face.

"All right then, pimp juice! Make sure you remember that!" I told him. Then I removed his signature toothpick from the floor and placed it back into the corner of his mouth.

"Now ask my moms to give you some more money to go and get your nose fixed!"

Just then, Momma ran back inside the house with a strange woman trailing behind her.

"Help me get him!" she ordered the four-hundred-pound woman. The fat woman had trouble getting into the kitchen, but there was no doubt about it, she and Momma were going to get me.

"Bilal, I'm calling the police on you!" Momma yelled as she and the other fat woman took off after me.

I jumped over Floyd's semiconscious body and jolted for the back door.

Chapter 16

I left home a young boy and would return a grown man. I was locked down for seven years for fucking up Floyd's nose. I didn't make any friends while I was in juvie. I pretty much stayed to myself and spent most of my time reading, studying, and counting down the days to my freedom. Over the years, Momma had only visited me about six times, which equaled less than once a year. I had grown accustomed to not getting any visits or letters from Momma, or anybody else for that matter. The only person that I ever received a letter from was my grandma Lilly. She and I had become quite close, corresponding on a regular basis. At the time, I didn't understand why none of my friends had written to me. I figured out of sight, out of mind, so I learned to live with the fact that my friends had forgotten about me.

So, after serving seven years on a trumped-up charge of attempted murder, I was free to go home. I waited patiently in front of the detention center for Moms to come scoop me up. A dark blue Chevy Chevette came flying around the corner, almost on one wheel. It was Putt and Momma, but Putt was driving the whip.

Beep, beep, beep. He blew the horn before they had a chance to reach the building.

I jogged over to the driver side. Putt jumped out of the car just as eager to see me as I was to see him.

"What up, man?" He wrestled with me.

"Man, what's up with you?" I hugged my nigga real tight. I had missed Putt terribly, but remembering his laugh and funny jokes had kept me cool during those times when I thought I was about to snap in the joint. Make no mistake about it, Lucky and Head were my niggas, but Putt—Putt was my sho' nuff nigga. Me and that nigga Putt was thick as thieves.

"Dag, man, you still look the same. I see you still ain't cut your hair, " he observed. Putt was right; I hadn't cut my hair in seven years. My hair was just as long as the day is short. Mrs. Nancy, one of the counselors at the detention center, kept it braided for me. As me and Putt caught up with each other, Momma sat in the car, not saying a word.

I walked over to the passenger side, stuck my head into the car, and kissed her on the cheek. "Hey, Momma."

"Hey, baby. Come on now, let's get this suitcase in here so we can get going," she said. Hearing Momma refer to me as baby made my heart skip a beat. Over my life, Momma had called me many things, but the word *baby* was never one of them. I smiled at her and hugged her real tight. Momma wasn't into displaying affection, so she shoved me away.

"Come on now," she said, dismissing me.

Momma got out of the car, picked up one of my bags, and placed it in the backseat. We loaded the car and were about to leave when someone stopped me.

"Come here, baby, don't you leave without giving me a hug and a kiss," the familiar voice said.

I turned toward the voice. It was Mrs. Nancy, the counselor who had kept my hair braided.

"Mrs. Nancy, I can't believe you came in on your day off to say good-bye to me!" I said excitedly. Mrs. Nancy walked over to me with her arms extended wide open.

"Baby, I had to come see you before you left. I'm going to miss you so much, baby," she said. We hugged each other for a while, then she let go of me.

"Here is my number, call me anytime." I took the phone number from her hand and Mrs. Nancy started to cry. I couldn't find the right words to comfort her, so I said what was on my heart.

"I'm going to miss you, Mrs. Nancy. Take care of yourself. I promise I will call you."

I climbed in the backseat of the Chevette and watched out the back window as Mrs. Nancy and the staff all waved good-bye to me. I buried my head in my chest and prepared for my uncomfortable ride home. *I'm really going to miss you, Mrs. Nancy,* I said to myself as we drove out of sight.

• • •

Things hadn't changed a bit in the pj's. As we drove down Fairfield Avenue past the swimming pool, I spotted my tag still spray-painted on the brick wall. Putt turned onto my street and parked the car in front of my house. I couldn't help but notice all of the flowers in our front yard.

Momma pointed to the bed full of roses and other flowers. "Bilal, do you like my flower garden?"

"Yes, ma'am, it looks real nice."

Putt jolted from the car, slamming the door shut.

"Black, I'll be right back. I'm going to see if Starr can braid your hair for you," he said, taking the initiative to get my hair cornrowed.

Momma continued bragging about her flower garden.

"You see those ones right there? They are my favorite," she said, smiling at the purple flowers that appeared to be broken from their stems.

I nodded. "They're nice."

When Momma peered over into the garden, she saw something that disturbed her so she stepped in.

"Goddamn it, Lulu! I done told you and your junky-ass friends not to throw them damn needles in my yard. Now, get them out!" she fumed.

I searched around because I wasn't sure who Momma was talking to. Our next-door neighbor ran to the door when he heard Momma shouting.

"Joann, what are you accusing me of now?" He smacked his lips.

Momma snapped at him, "Just keep this shit from over here!" she fussed.

The man stepped out onto the porch, puffing on a cigarette. "Jo, don't you start that shit with me today, 'cause I ain't in the mood for it," he said in a soft yet serious tone.

Momma shot back at him. "I don't give a damn what you ain't in the mood for. You better tell your junky-ass friends to stop leaving them damn hypodermic needles in my yard!" she repeated.

The man rolled his eyes at her, then pulled at his short denim Daisy Duke shorts. He cleared his throat.

"How you doing, Black? I heard a lot about you, nice to finally meet you," he said, all in one deep baritone. His voice didn't match his look and that shit really threw me off. I didn't want him to think it was all right to get up in my space, so I gave him a dry hello. "Hey," I spoke.

The man looked to be in his early forties. He had a couple of jailhouse tattoos on his arms, a yellow bandana wrapped around his head, and his penny loafers looked like they had been spit-shined by one of the best. Now, I'm a firm believer in the old adage "Never judge a book by its cover," but something just didn't look right with this dude, so instead of judging him or trying to figure him out, I asked him straight up.

"What's your story?" I couldn't wait to hear his answer. I would have to wait a li'l longer 'cause he ignored my question.

"Excuse me, young man, you might want to cover your ears," he warned.

"He ain't got to cover a damn thing. Whatever you got to say, you can say it in front of him," Momma raved.

"Look, Joann, you need to get you some dick, because you've been acting real shitty. Get you some gurl, then maybe you won't be so hostile," he teased.

Momma cursed him. "Fuck you, Lulu!"

Lulu swung around the banister that separated our porches and got up close and personal in Momma's face. "I already did, remember?"

Momma's eyes damn near popped out of her head. "You fucking faggot!" she screamed at him.

"Oh, Joann, but you didn't say that two years ago when I stuck your fat ass!" Lulu said, switching from his baritone voice to a soft, sexy tone. Then, in a blink of an eye, Lulu quickly disappeared into his house.

Momma grabbed my bags from the porch. "Come on."

"Who was that, Momma?" I frowned.

"Nobody but that confused ass Lulu. One minute he gay, next minute he's not!" she shouted.

• • •

Momma immediately put me to work while she took a nap. I cleaned the house from top to bottom. I couldn't help but notice the many accolades that she had received over the years from the Richmond Redevelopment and Housing Authority. Momma had a ton of awards for having the best-kept yard in Fairfield Court Projects. She was obviously more than proud of her accomplishments because she had replaced the pictures of Keon and me on her makeshift entertainment center and flooded them with awards that extended over a six-year period. The awards all read, JOANN CUNNINGHAM, WINNER OF THE BEST-KEPT YARD IN RECOGNITION OF THE YARD BEAUTIFICATION CONTEST.

I stopped cleaning when I heard a loud noise outside the door.

"Come on, Black, Starr's going to braid your hair for you," Putt yelled through the screen door.

When I stepped out, Lucky and Head bum-rushed me. They wrestled with me just as Putt had.

"What'sss up?" they both screamed, in a singsong sort of way.

Head gave me a strange look as he checked me out from head to toe.

"Damn, man, you still look the same. What's up with your hair?" He frowned.

Putt answered. "We 'bout to get that taken care of right now," Putt told him.

I spotted Cocoa standing at the end of the walkway. She was holding a little boy by the hand and a baby girl was attached to her hip. I looked over at Putt because it didn't take a rocket scientist to figure out that those children belonged to him.

"Hey, Black," Cocoa spoke, her voice still soft and squeaky as ever.

"Hey, Cocoa, what's up? Cute kids."

We headed across the street to Starr's house. Baije opened the front door and out stepped Starr. She had on a pair of black and green biker shorts and a green midriff T-shirt. Her stomach was flat as an ironing board, her ass was as plump as a chuck roast, and her thighs made Tyson chicken thighs look like wingettes. She wore her hair in an asymmetric bob. Starr reminded me of one of the chicks that I had seen on *Video Soul*. I increased my pace, admiring her beauty every step of the way. I was dying to get next to her.

"Hey, Starr," I greeted as I approached her. Starr searched me up and down almost identical to the way Head had, and at first she didn't speak a word to me. Just like old times, she ignored the heck out of me as if I weren't standing there.

"Baije, I forgot the combs and the hair grease. Can you go upstairs and get my hair bag for me?" Starr turned to her friend. After Baije turned to go inside, Starr decided to speak to me.

"Hey, Black, how are you doing?" It was just like Starr to run the show. She said and did things on her own time; she loved to be in control.

"I'm all right," I answered.

Starr reached over and ran her hands through my hair. At least she attempted to.

"Boy, this is some nappy shit right here," she said, yanking me by my bush. "Come on here, 'cause I ain't got all day!"

I flopped down on the porch and Starr grabbed a chair and sat behind me.

"Black, we gone walk to the store," Head advised.

I was reluctant to be alone with Starr because she had always acted a fool toward me. I figured if she was willing to braid my hair, then things must've been all right between us.

"All right, I'll see ya'll when ya'll get back," I responded.

Just then, Baije stormed out of the house with the bag in her hand.

"Here's the hair bag, Starr, and Head, don't be trying to leave me. I told you that I wanted to walk to the store." Baije ran after Head. Head growled at her.

"Damn, girl. Why you always gotta be following me around?" he complained as Putt, Lucky, Head and Baije all headed up the block.

Starr gathered what she needed from the bag and was about to start on my hair, but first she pulled at the back of my T-shirt.

"Boy, you got to slide back some. What's wrong with you? You think I bite or something?"

"No, I don't," I answered as I slid in closer between her legs.

"So, how do you want your hair?" she asked me. I shrugged my shoulders,

"You can braid it any way you want to," I told her.

Baby girl made a small part in the center of my head, and proceeded to braid my hair.

Chapter 17

The rain wiped out any hopes of a fun afternoon. It began to pour down as soon as Starr was finished with my hair. My crew never did come back to get me, because the thunderstorm had forced everybody to stay inside. I was dog tired and needed to rest, so I thanked Starr for her services and headed on home. I was stunned when I pushed open my room door and found a stranger lying on my mattress on the floor. I didn't want to startle him, so I kicked the mattress lightly, to wake him up.

"Dung lai! Dung lai!" the old man screamed, causing me to jump back. He sat up straight on the mattress, and rubbed his eyes.

"Hey, you must be Joann's son." He extended his right hand to me. "My name is Todd and I live here," he introduced himself.

I just looked at him. Momma hadn't told me anything about a damn boarder living with us. Being the respectful young man that I was, I reached for his hand.

"Hello, sir." I gave him a firm handshake. He pulled himself up from the mattress.

"Young man, you sure don't look anything like your pictures. Shoot, you done turned out to be an okay-looking young man." I guess that was a compliment.

"Well, thank you, sir," I responded.

Mr. Todd grabbed his blanket. "Now, you go ahead and go to bed. I'm going downstairs and make me a pallet on the floor," he said.

He turned to exit the bedroom, holding onto his back on the way out. It was obvious that his back was bothering him, so I wasn't about to let the old man sleep on the hard floor. I stopped him on the way out.

"No, Mr. Todd, you go right ahead and sleep on the mattress. I'mma be all right," I assured him.

"Are you sure about this?"

"Only a fool is for sure, and I'm positive of that," I said.

Mr. Todd laughed and tapped me on my shoulder.

"Your momma told me that you had an old soul." He chuckled. "Thanks again for letting me have the mattress, because you know what?" he asked.

"What's that, Mr. Todd?"

" 'Cause my back sure hurts like hell!" He scowled.

I exited the room, then reached my hand back inside to turn off the light.

"Please don't turn off the light. I don't sleep in the dark," he informed me.

"Okay. Good night, Mr. Todd."

"Good night, son."

Chapter 18

Between the thunderstorms and Mr. Todd snoring and talking in his sleep, I didn't sleep at all that night. Every single time there was a loud noise in the sky, he would jump out of his sleep and yell, "Enemy attack!" At one point, I ran upstairs to check on him because I heard him screaming, "Cease fire!," only to find him hiding in the corner of the room, in a cold sweat, with his eyes wide open and his body fast asleep. I shook him for a few seconds and told him that he was dreaming and to go back to bed. As soon as I returned back downstairs and drifted off, either the snoring began or the shouting. I figured my first night home I would get plenty of rest, but thanks to Mr. Todd, by the next morning, I was still dog-ass tired.

Momma walked past me in the living room. I was lying on the floor on a blanket. "Good morning, Ma."

"Hey, Bilal, you need to get on up and get your day started."

I grabbed my blanket and followed her into the kitchen.

"Hey, Ma, what's up with Mr. Todd? He had me up all night. He was snoring and running around the room like somebody was after him. He kept screaming, 'The enemies are coming,' and 'cease fire.'" Momma chuckled. What was funny—I didn't know.

"I don't pay Todd's ass no mind. After a while, you'll get used to him. I was scared when he first moved in because I thought he would zap out and kill me in my sleep. After a while, I realized that Todd ain't gone hurt a flea. He's just messed up from the Vietnam War, that's all," she said.

"So, how do you know Mr. Todd?"

Momma lit a cigarette and made herself a drink. "I met Todd at the Social Security building about three years ago when I was down there applying for disability," she said. "Todd was homeless and ain't have a place to live, but they told him that he had to give an address in order to continue getting his SSI benefits. Well, since he didn't have any family in Richmond, hell, I walked over to him and told him that he could use my address if he paid me forty dollars a month. At first he came by for about two or three months, to pick up his check and to pay me, of course. Then one day he came by pissy drunk and told me to open up his check for him so he could make sure the new increase was in it. Well, I did, and when I saw that Todd was getting 625 dollars a month from Uncle Sam, shit, I offered him your room and guaranteed him at least two hot meals a day, for four hundred dollars a month. Todd been living here with me ever since. I got turned down from Social Security and being that I don't have a job, I don't have an income, so I pay zero rent to Richmond Redevelopment Housing Authority. This arrangement with Todd works out just fine, because although I don't have to pay rent, I still have to eat and get my smokes and shit. You know," she explained.

Momma telling me that she had applied for disability worried me. I had to find out more.

"Mom, did something happen to you while I was away?"

"What do you mean?" she said, frowning.

"Well, you said that you applied for disability and that you were turned down."

"Oh, that? Boy, if every time I turn around somebody calling me an alcoholic, then I must be an alcoholic. I figure if something is wrong with me, then I'm disabled, so fuck it, I ain't ever gone work again!" she said. "Speaking of working, ain't that friend of yours supposed to get you a job?" she asked. Putt had promised to get me a job where he worked.

"Yes, ma'am, I'm waiting on him to come get me," I told her.

About ten minutes later, Putt showed up.

"Hey, Ms. Joann. What up, Black? You ready to go to work?" he asked.

I gave Putt a concerned look. "To work? I thought I was just putting in an application," I said.

"Man, I told you I was gonna get you a job. Don't worry about no application. You're already hired. You just have to bring in your birth certificate, since you don't have a photo ID," he told me. I had no idea Putt would move that fast.

"All right, let me go get ready. What time do we have to be in?" I questioned.

"Man, Church's Fried Chicken opens at twelve p.m. but we have to be in at ten a.m. so let's get moving," he said.

Putt followed me upstairs to my room. He couldn't wait to hear about me and Starr.

"So, man, what happened with you and Starr yesterday?" He was dying to hear something juicy.

"Ain't nothing happen. She just braided my hair, that's all."

"Man, we left you alone with her for a long time and you mean to tell me ain't nothing happen?" Putt found it hard to believe. "Why you ain't try to hook up with her?" He frowned.

"Man, she was busy braiding my hair and listening to music. That girl sang every song that came on the radio, and she kept popping gum in my ear," I fumed.

Putt laughed at me. "Man, we didn't mean to take so long, but by the time I talked to my manager about you, it started raining real hard. Plus, Head and Baije started fighting on the way back, and me and Lucky had to keep pulling Head off her."

Yeah, it was raining hard and thundering bad, but the whole time the sun was still shining, I recalled. Then I remembered something Starr had said. "Man, Starr kept saying some junk about the devil beating his wife." Putt fell out laughing at me.

"Man, when we were young, people used to say that if the sun is out while there's a thunderstorm, that it meant the devil was beating his wife." I shook my head because the old saying was ridiculous and had no merit.

"Speaking of beating his wife, did I hear you say that Head and Baije were fighting?" I backtracked to Putt's earlier statement.

"Yeah, that's what I was trying to tell you, but you started tripping about Starr."

"For real. Head be whipping her?" I didn't want to believe it.

"Man, Head be whipping Baije's ass all the time," Putt informed me.

"When did that start?"

"Well, the first time he beat her up was at the prom. Me and Luck try to talk some sense into him, but he says Baije be getting on his nerves."

"Does Baije's mother know about this?"

"Man, she gotta know, 'cause Baije's prom dress was all bloody and everybody 'round here was talking about it," Putt said, shaking his head in disapproval.

"Does Head's mother know that he is beating down a girl?" I

gave Putt a concerned look 'cause in my eyes this was serious shit.

When I was younger, I had thought about whipping Starr's little ass on a number of occasions, but those were thoughts and a thought without action really don't mean a thing.

"Man, Head's mom ain't never home." Putt reminded me of what I already knew.

"Yeah, that's his problem. He's taking his frustration out on Baije, 'cause he's mad with his own mother. For real, Putt, I think Head has parental alienation syndrome."

"What is that?" Putt frowned.

"Well, it's really not a medical diagnosis, but my therapist said that there has been talk of research on this subject. I think it has to do with feelings of loss, anger, and/or feelings of betrayal for having parents who either abandon or reject you. I'm not sure, so don't quote me on that." I shared what little I knew on the topic. "Anyway, I think Head got something going on in his head that he really needs to get out."

Putt was quiet for a minute and then he said, "You could be right. His mom ain't never home, and the man he thought was his daddy just decided one day that his sperm didn't make boys so he stopped visiting Head cold turkey."

"Oh yeah, what's the man's name?" I asked. Putt rolled the man's name right off of his tongue.

"Lloyd 'Slot Machine' Pittman, and he's an old legend in this town. He told Head's mother that he only made girls and that Head couldn't possibly be his son. He said he had a few babies floating around Richmond, but hell if Head was one of them."

"So, who did Starr go to the prom with?" I flipped the conversation because I felt uncomfortable talking about Head behind the nigga's back.

"She ain't go to the prom. Starr told everybody that she didn't go to the prom because the guy she wanted to go with lived out of town and couldn't make it."

I pressed for more information. "So, Starr's boyfriend lives out of town?"

"Man, I guess so, but then again, who knows. Starr says so many different things that we don't know what to believe. One minute she says she's from New York, and then she says she's from Florida. One day, Suga Momma is her mother, then the next month, Suga Momma is her grandmother," Putt chimed. "Bottom line is, who really gives a fuck about who, what, where?"

I jumped to Starr's defense. "Man, hold up. Now, you know that a lot of folk from the South done lied about being from New York, am I right?" I threw my hands up. "And we all know that Lucky is the only person around here that has ever lived out of town. And Putt, you also know that most people call their grandma their mom. That doesn't make it a lie, now does it?"

"Whatever, man, you gone defend her anyway 'cause that's your girl." He shrugged.

I hurried to the bathroom, bathed quickly, and threw on the blue denim jeans and shirt that the state had purchased for me. I hadn't seen my hair 'cause Starr had wrapped it up and put a satin cap over it. I removed the cap and then the scarf, and lo and behold, I was amazed at what I saw. I stormed out of the bathroom, mad as hell.

"Man, what the hell did she do to my hair?" I screamed at Putt, as if he had something to do with it.

"Calm down, Black, ain't nothing wrong with your hair. Why you bugging?" he hollered. Once again, Starr had sat me up.

"What is this shit?" I pointed to my head, then I ran back into the bathroom to look at myself in the mirror. Putt threw his hands up in the air.

"Man, one minute you defending the girl, and the next minute you mad as hell with her. On the real, Black, your hair is fly!" he exclaimed. I did a double-take in the mirror, checking the sides, the top, and the back of my hair.

"Man, this is whack!" I exploded.

Putt stood there looking at me, as if my hair problem was no big deal.

"So, if you don't like it, just take it out. Ain't no need of complaining about it," he huffed.

"Man, Starr tricked me. She told me that she was starting from the center of my head, when clearly she started from the bottom around my neck, to get my hair like this," I snapped. "I mean, what kind of hairstyle is this when your hair is braided all the way around in a circle until one braid ends up at the top center of your head?" Putt shook his head at me again.

"Man, you done been away so long that you don't even know what's fly. Man, that shit right there is called the Coliseum, because it goes around and around in a circle just like the Richmond Coliseum does. Man, Starr used to have all the chicks coming to her for that hairstyle; she's the one who created it. It's a throwback hairstyle. She brought it back just for you," he exaggerated.

I stopped complaining and looked Putt dead in the eye.

"Do I look like a girl to you?" I asked sarcastically.

"Nawh, you don't, and you didn't look like one when you put that goddamn perm in your hair back in the day, but you did it anyway, didn't you?" he joked.

I thought about the perm, and how I was the only dude in school with one and I fell out laughing. Putt was right; there was no difference between the perm and the Coliseum braids.

"Man, Starr knows you are a trendsetter, that's why she chose you to be the first dude to give it to. Man, if I was you, I would rock the hell out of that hairstyle, and I guarantee you, before long, niggas gone be biting!" Putt said.

I thought short and hard about what Putt said to me.

"All right, I'mma keep it like this," I told him. So, for the next few weeks, I rocked the hell out of my Richmond Coliseum braids!

Chapter 19

Before reaching Church's Chicken, I had one very important stop to make. I had waited seven years to thank the people who had helped me out on the day of my arrest. I walked into the Chinese restaurant; the Kims were standing behind the glass.

"Hey, Mr. Kim, Mrs. Kim." I smiled as I spoke to them.

At first, they both just looked at me like I was any old nigga from around the way. Then they remembered me.

"You all grown up now, but I remember yo face," Mr. Kim said, as he came from behind the glass that separated him from his customers. I was happy to see the Kims; they were genuinely good people. On the day that I had attacked Floyd, the Kims had hid me out in their restaurant. They fed me for free and offered to let me stay there overnight.

"You got a nice place here, Mr. Kim," I told him.

"Yeah, thank you. So, how's yo motha? Is she still wit dat man?" Mrs. Kim asked.

I was surprised that they remembered my story, 'cause in fact I had told them the whole truth.

"No, Mrs. Kim, she ain't with him no more," I answered.

"So, what are you doing wit yo'self?" Mr. Kim asked, sweeping the front of his store.

Putt interrupted, "Black, it's time to go." He checked his arm watch against the one the Kims had on the wall. I answered Mr. Kim's question before leaving.

"I'm going to be working right across the street from y'all. Right over there at Church's Fried Chicken. I just came by to thank y'all for what you did for me," I told them. Then I blew Mrs. Kim a kiss and shook Mr. Kim's hand.

"What's yo name again?" Mrs. Kim yelled from behind the glass.

"My name is Black, Mrs. Kim. Just call me Black." I turned to her and let out a huge smile.

"Okay, see ya later, Blat." She waved.

The Kims watched out the window as I crossed the street.

Putt gave me a look of disgust.

"Black, do you see how fat Ms. Kim is? Man, I ain't ever in my life seen a fat Chinese lady. I didn't know rice made you fat?" Putt questioned.

"Man, leave them people alone; the Kims are all right with me."

• • •

Church's Chicken was just a hop, skip, and a jump from the Chinese restaurant. I was eager to start my first day of work. We walked in and sat at an empty booth and waited for the manager. The manager was sitting with her back to our table, interviewing another applicant. I couldn't help but overhear the conversation she was having 'cause she was talking loud and fast as if the man she was talking to was deaf and slow. Not only was the voice familiar to me, but the apple-shaped head, with the stringy hair, was one that I couldn't forget.

"Putt, is that what's-her-name?" I snapped my fingers, trying to put a name to the lady's voice and back of her head.

Before I could get the question out, the woman and the man stood up.

"Like I said, we ain't hiring right now, but I will keep your application on file, and as soon as something becomes available, I'll be sure to give you a call," the fast-talking woman promised. She escorted the man toward the door, and held it open for him to exit.

"Then again, you should call and check with me at least once a week, 'cause you never know when I might need somebody, 'cause these kids come through here and roll out like it ain't nothing," she said. The man was halfway out the door and she was still yapping.

"Bilal Cunningham!" She turned to me as she screamed my birth name. The manager of Church's Chicken was Gurdy, Coach's old yapping girlfriend who used to be a cashier at Koslow's.

"Hey, Mrs. Gurdy, how you been?" I stood up to greet her.

Putt covered his mouth and laughed. "We got you!" He laughed.

"Hum, I knew that if Putt told you that I was the manager that you wouldn't take the job. I know ya'll kids say that I talk too much. I don't talk too much; I just love to talk. See, that's what's wrong with ya'll kids today, you ain't got nobody at home to talk to you, let alone take up time with you, so you get it twisted when I try to show you love," she rambled.

"Hey, Mrs. Gurdy, are you still dating Coach?" I asked.

Mrs. Gurdy turned away from me, "Nawh, baby, I ain't with him. We got married right after you went away and became legally separated a year ago. Hum, you know, he got all involved in that Jehovah Witness religion and started getting crazy on me. I damn near died in a car accident and he refused to let the hospital give me a blood transfusion, talking about it was against his religion. After the accident, I started having a lot of medical problems and instead of him being there to support me, he started running around on me, chasing women, big old fat ones at that." She turned up her nose.

Putt excused himself to go change into his uniform.

"Y'all go head with that religion stuff. I'm going to get changed so I can help train you, Black." He laughed.

"Mrs. Gurdy, I'm sorry things didn't work out for you and Coach, but maybe one day the two of you will get back together," I encouraged.

Mrs. Gurdy's eyes welled up with tears. "Listen, baby, he left me," she said, pointing to her chest. "Forget it. I don't want to talk about this anymore. Just make sure you bring in your birth certificate and a picture ID by next week," she said.

Chapter 20

Over the next two months, I worked like a slave. With such a hectic schedule, I had very little time to socialize. The only time that I saw Starr was when she was braiding my hair. We were short-staffed at work, so Putt and I had to work six days a week most of the time. Most of my paycheck went to Momma; so when I was able to have a little free time, I didn't have any money to do anything. So, when I heard that the Tougher Than Leather/Run's House tour was coming to Richmond, I knew I had to be in it to win it. I asked Gurdy to put me on double shifts so I could earn some extra money. Putt was strapped for some extra ends, so he worked double shifts with me.

We were at work one night when Gurdy suddenly fell ill and could no longer work the cash register. She hurried to the back of the store, her arms wrapped around her belly. Storming behind her to see if she was okay, I attempted to enter her office, but the door was locked. I was worried sick about her because she had started acting strange a few days prior.

I knocked on the door. "Mrs. Gurdy, are you okay?" I hollered through the door. I didn't get a response from her, but I could hear her talking to someone on the phone.

"Yo Black, is she all right?" Putt was concerned as well.

Just then, I heard Mrs. Gurdy tell the person on the phone, "Okay, I'll see you when you get here."

Then she cracked open the door to the office and peeped out at me.

"I'll be okay. I just have an upset stomach, that's all. Can you and Putt hold it down for me?" she asked.

"Yeah, Mrs. Gurdy, you know we got you. Don't worry, I can work the cash register."

"Oh, by the way, when my cousin gets here, send him to the back. He's bringing me something for my stomach pains," she said.

When I returned to the front of the store, there were two chicks standing with their backs to the counter. They were looking out the window at a group of guys in front of the Chinese restaurant.

"Man, look at that ass right there! Shorty is phat as duck butter," Putt said, biting down on his bottom lip so hard, he damn near broke the skin. I couldn't help but notice the chick in the red jean denim suit was phat to death. Phat as duck butter just like Putt said.

I tried to be calm about it, though. "Her butt is nice," I said plainly. "Did you take their orders?"

"Not yet," Putt answered, never taking his eyes off the girls' behinds.

"May I take ya'lls order?" I interrupted them.

The girls spun around quickly. The chick in the red denim

jeans was ugly as all outdoors. Putt jumped back and shoved me on the shoulder.

"What the—?" He frowned up his nose at her. The not-so-attractive girl batted her eyes.

"I'll take a number one," she said, sure of herself. Her gold teeth lit up the restaurant when she smiled. The not-so-attractive girl had two gold teeth up top and two at the bottom. Her skin was as bumpy as a country road, her face full of acne and grease. She was not lovely, so the greasy shine on her face didn't help her at all. To top it off, she had two yellow sponge rollers hanging from the side of her head and a large nose with a diamond-studded earring pierced on the left side of it. I shook my head at the chick. She was more than a hot mess.

"Next." I turned to take her friend's order.

"I'll have a number two, and throw in an apple pie, please," she said.

Her friend was a thin girl with a short crop haircut. She had about five holes in her right ear, with small diamonds in each hole. Her left ear had two holes and she wore small hoop earrings in that ear. She was an average-looking girl, sort of petite. Something about her reminded me of Cocoa. Apparently, Putt thought so too.

" 'Sup, shorty. What's your name?" Putt asked her.

"I'm Jennifer, but everybody calls me Jen. And yours?"

"I'm Putt." He smiled at her.

I figured it wouldn't hurt to talk to her friend; after all ugly chicks needed love too.

"And what's your name?" I asked the ugly girl who was working the hell out of the red denim jeans.

The girl blushed. "I'm Chelle." She smiled from ear to ear. Her gold teeth glistened as she circled her tongue with her lips. "What ya'll getting into tonight? 'Cause we trying to have some fun," she added.

I ignored the question, but Putt felt the need to entertain her. "What ya'll want us to be getting into?" he asked.

Chelle turned directly to me and licked her lips. "You trying to fuck or what?" she asked me, straight up with no chaser. The chick was as brave as a white man on an Indian reservation. It was obvious Chelle wasn't afraid of shit. She batted her eyes again, then rolled her tongue around.

"Want to take a ride?" she asked boldly.

"Nope, my momma told me to never get in the car with strangers," I shot back at her.

Putt and Jenny both laughed. "Gad day, shorty, you don't waste any time, do you?" Putt asked Chelle.

"Shit, we ain't got a whole lot of time. Life ain't promised to-morrow, so why not live it up while you can," Jenny jumped in, snapping her fingers and throwing her tiny hips around.

"Oh, it's like that, huh?" Putt flirted.

"It's like that," the girls said in unison.

"All right. Give us ya'll home phone and pager numbers, and when we're ready to live it up, we will call." Putt smiled, handing the girls a napkin so they could jot down their phone numbers.

Before leaving, Chelle turned to me and looked me dead in my eyes. Before she could say anything, Putt cut her off.

"Yo, Chelle. I hope you don't mind me asking, but did you get all four gold teeth put in at the same time?"

Chelle continued to stare at me while answering his question. "Nawh, I got them at different times. I'm about to get four more. Two more at the top and two more at the bottom." She smiled. When Chelle threw her body on the counter, trying to get up in my face again, I backed away from her. She licked her lips a second time.

"Nigga, what you scared or something? Look, check it right: I've been seeing you in here for a minute now, and I like what I see. Just so you know, I want to fuck you and suck you like you're my king. I want you to sit your dick right here in this pot of gold. So, be my king and sit your dick on my throne." She winked at me, then stepped off.

We watched as the girls exited the store. When Chelle walked, her ass shook like a bowl of Jell-O. There was no question in my mind that she should've been the spokesperson for Jell-O and not Bill Cosby. Chelle was indeed one foul-mouth chick, but she was the sexiest gorilla I had ever seen.

"Gad day! Did you hear that? She wants you to be her king! Black, I don't mean no harm, but that bitch is phat to death. If I was you, I would fuck her. Just make sure to put a bag over her head." Putt laughed.

About thirty minutes had passed and not one single customer had entered the restaurant. All the long days and nights that I had put in were starting to take their toll on me. My eyes were getting heavy, so I decided to read to keep from falling asleep. I grabbed the stool from the drive-thru and sat down on it. I reached under the counter and grabbed the book that I had been reading. Putt threw his face into my book searching for the title.

"Man, what you reading?" he asked, after not finding it on his own.

"I'm reading *The Flying Boy* by John Lee," I told him.

"Who? Who the fuck is John Lee? Did the Kims give you that shit?" Putt frowned his nose up. "Man, let me find out you reading a karate book. You mess around and be in this mutherfuckers like you Bruce Lee and shit," he joked.

I shook my head at Putt, then answered seriously. "Nawh, this book is about the codependent child of an alcoholic father, and no, I didn't get it from the Kims; I got it from my therapist when I was in juvie. She gave me the book because I was diagnosed with being codependent," I shared with him.

Putt had no idea what I was talking about. He looked at me, confused.

"What does that mean?" he questioned.

"Codependent people go out of their way to please other people. We tend to seek the approval of other people and do things to appease others even when what we are asked to do is uncomfortable for us. My therapist says that codependent people are people pleasers. We have trouble saying no to folk and seek approval from others. At the same time, we have high expectations of others, because we are sometimes perfectionists so we become irritated when people don't meet our expectations. My therapist says that I am codependent with my mother."

Putt frowned his nose up at me again. "Man, that ain't you. Don't listen to everything those white folk tell you." He smirked.

"Anyway, enough about me. I'm tired of talking about that," I said, abruptly changing the subject. I marked my page with my book cover, then closed my book shut. "Man, whatever happened to Crazy Chris? Where is he?"

"Chris is all right, he's still around. About a week before you came home, they say Chris flipped out and Mrs. Irene had him sent to the psych hospital for ninety days for evaluation."

"What do you mean, he flipped out?" I snickered a little.

Putt continued, "I don't know exactly what happened, but he should be getting out real soon. Matter of fact, what day did you come home from juvie?" he asked, trying to remember a day that I would never in my life be able to forget.

"June seventeenth," I answered.

"Okay, then I believe Chris flipped out around June tenth, it was the ninth or the tenth. Something like that. Either way, he should be coming home soon," Putt said, almost sure of himself.

I stood to my feet as a rush of customers suddenly entered the restaurant. Putt slid over toward the grill.

"May I take your order?" I asked the dude that stood before me.

He turned to the two guys with him. "Yo, son, do you remember him?" he asked his boys. The dude stood there grinning with a big Kool-aid smile on his face. I didn't know why the dude was smiling so hard at me, so I grilled him and his boys up and down. We all eyeballed each other for a minute. I stepped back from the cash register to get a better look. The dude was excited, he bounced around the restaurant, then slid back over to the counter.

"Yo, son, s'up?" He slammed his hands on the counter as if to say, *ain't this a mutherfucker.* I suddenly recognized the face, but I just couldn't put a name with it. He threw his right hand up and pounded hard on his chest.

"It's me B. Skilow from New York. Shorty, remember me?"

I couldn't believe it was Skilow. I hadn't seen him since the incident at the football field all those years ago. Skilow damn near had more ice on his hands than the ice machine that stood behind me. He extended his hand out to me and the glare from the ring on his middle finger almost blinded me. Talk about being nice on the ice and designer down from head to toe; Skilow was the epitome of fresh to death.

"S'up?" I smacked hands with him.

"How you be, son?" He held my hand for a few seconds before letting go of it.

I nodded. "I'm good, I'm good."

I glanced over at his boys. They just stood there looking at us, all quiet as mice.

"Yo, Tony, this is Gorilla Black, son," Skilow said, jogging Tony's memory.

I checked Tony out again; he looked good too. He wasn't Fat Tony anymore; he had thinned out a great deal.

"Yeah, son, I remember you now," Tony, said reaching across the counter to smack hands with me. Fat Tony had more ice around his neck than I had teeth in my mouth. His diamond-cut necklace spelled TONY, of course.

"Damn, shorty, good to see you still around; we hear niggas been dropping like mosquitoes in Richmond. Whatever happened to Richmond being slow?" Jay jumped in. Jay wasn't flashy like Skilow and Tony. He wasn't rocking any jewelry or fly gear at all. He was dressed like a normal dude. Immediately I liked his style 'cause Jay was a normal nigga like me. He wasn't about all that bling-bling type shit.

"Shit, man, we just came from over Highland Park. Them niggas over there is serious about getting paper, ain't they?" Skilow stated, not really looking for an answer, but rather voicing his opinion.

In a weird sort of way, I was somewhat glad to see them because they reminded me of how bold and daring I used to be.

"Yo, Putt, do you remember when we met them on the football field in front of the school, way back in the day?" I jogged Putt's easily forgotten memory.

Putt nodded his head. "Oh yeah, man, I remember that. That was the day when Head was fucking with the fat kid?" Putt laughed.

"Well, I'm the fat kid. Tell that little nigga ain't nothing fat about me now but my pockets," Fat Tony boasted, patting his side pockets.

Just then, someone walked in, interrupting the reunion.

"Excuse me, dawg. Is Gurdy in the back?" the man said. Putt recognized the dude, but I didn't.

"Yo, what's up, Maurice? Yeah, go on back, Gurdy is back there," Putt told him. Before the dude disappeared to the back, Putt stopped him.

"Yo, Maurice, this is Black. I know you haven't seen him since he's been home."

Maurice spun his entire body around. "Damn, shorty. I was 'bout to walk right pass you. What's up, Black?" He dragged his words. "What's up, players?" he spoke to the New York boys.

" 'Sup," they all spoke, never taking their eyes off of him as if they knew Maurice wasn't to be trusted. Maurice continued on. Obviously their stares didn't faze him. Maurice was from the Ward; the only thing that could scare a nigga from the Ward was God himself. The people from the Ward didn't fear a darn thing. Maurice looked at the three out of towners one last time, then turned his back on them.

"Damn, Black, it's good to see you, man. Glad you're home." He cracked a smile. When he smiled, I noticed his left front tooth was black and cracked. He had an old raggedy stocking cap on his head that was full of snags. It was amazing to me that the same dude that was once best dressed in middle school and star of the basketball team now looked a shitty mess.

"Man, for a minute, I ain't think you was gone ever get out. I heard you fucked up old dude some kind of nasty," Maurice said, eyes rolling to the back of his head. "Hey, Black, let me ask you something, man, 'cause I done heard all kinds of shit about that situation." He scratched his head, as if he was puzzled.

"Shoot," I said, waiting for his question.

"Did you fuck that dude up for fucking with your momma?" Maurice asked, body swaying from side to side. "Did he beat her down or something?"

"Nawh, Shorty, I fucked that nigga up cause he ate my corn beef hash," I told him bluntly.

Maurice's eyes widened and his body stopped rocking. "Oh, that's all I needed to know. I just had to hear it straight from the horse's mouth. Niggas told me that you fucked that dude up over some food, but I ain't want to believe it," he said, eyes rolling around in his head again. Maurice was high as helium. "You know what, Black? Niggas say you crazy as shit! Man, are you still selling them Valiums or what?" he asked, as if his ass needed anything else.

"Nawh. I don't mess with that stuff at all," I told him. Maurice reared way back and then rubbed his face.

"My man, Black, you my nigga if you don't get no bigger." He chuckled.

Then Maurice headed toward the back to find Mrs. Gurdy.

"Damn, son. I see niggas got mad respect for you around these parts," Skilow noticed. "Yo, B, you might be in the wrong profession," he added. "No disrespect, son, but while you in this mutherfucker's flipping bird, you could be getting some real paper, yo. Shit, if niggas on to you like that, you could use that shit to your advantage and fuck around and be king round this mutherfucker!" Skilow talked and everyone listened. "See, I knew it was something about you that I fucked with when I first met you. The way you stepped up for your team told me back then that you had heart. Damn, who would've ever thought, all these years later, I would run into you at Church's Fried Chicken. Yo, B, on the real, this here shit ain't for you. I'm telling you, man, you got the potential to do great things. You's a mufucking leader, a ruler, you can run shit, I'm telling you, son." Skilow spat.

At that moment, the floor belonged to Skilow and he did one hell of a good job trying to sell me the fast life. I stood there silently as Skilow tried relentlessly to boost my ego and his boys gave me my props too. They nodded their heads as if what Skilow felt or believed was the Bible. I checked around for Putt; coincidentally, he was nodding his head too. I waited for a moment because I wanted to make sure the right words escaped my mouth. I had been through too much, seen too much and had no thoughts of getting into any more trouble. There was no way in hell I was going to jeopardize my freedom. Being home felt too good, and I wasn't going to let anybody take my freedom away. I didn't need him to spell it out for me. I knew exactly what the fuck Skilow was trying to sell me.

I took in a deep breath. "Nawh, shorty, the fast life ain't for me. I got my GED while I was locked up, and now I'm trying to go to college. Man, I'm trying to do something positive with my life, you dig?" I was trying to talk just as cool as he had. I continued with my own spill. "Come on, y'all know that fast money means fast death, and a nigga like me ain't trying to die young!" I added, giving them a serious look. I was talking to three niggas who was already getting paper, and obviously not afraid to die.

Skilow sucked his teeth, then nodded his head at me. "I feel you, son, much love and respect." He patted his chest with a balled fist. "Just remember, though, hustling is what you make it." Then he leaned over the counter and grabbed the pen that Jenny and Chelle had used to jot their number down. He grabbed a menu from the counter and wrote his home and pager number on it. "B, if you change your mine, give me a call. I come thru a lot 'cause I got peoples down in Virginia Beach that I have to take care of," he added.

Then Skilow and his boys left the restaurant. We watched as they jumped into a black 1988 Ford Explorer. Just when the truck was about to pull off, Fat Tony jumped from the backseat and ran back in.

" 'Sup?" I asked.

"Yo, Black, Skilow told me to leave this with you." He glanced around, and then reached into his back pocket. "He said he wants you to find a real cokehead, a veteran, a mutherfucking coke connoisseur and let them test this product and then have them to tell you what they think. He said if they tell you that it's just okay, then he won't ever bother and try to convince you about getting paper again. He said don't even call him with the report. But, he said when that veteran comes back begging and pleading for more, when that expert witness comes to you and tells you that it's the best coke to ever hit Richmond, then he said to call him collect 'cause he'll be on standby, waiting to accept your call."

The cats from New York had mad game. The way they hustled their words, you would have thought they had taken a persuasive speech class. Fat Tony stepped to the back of the restaurant and handed me a small bag of cocaine. I held it tight in my hand.

He grabbed onto my balled fist, and whispered, "Man, this here is Brooklyn's finest. It's recompressed cocaine. It's about eighty-nine percent pure, so make sure you get a veteran, and I emphasize the word *veteran*, to try this shit out!" he added. I didn't want the niggas to think that I was soft so, against my better judgment, I slid it in my pocket. Although I had no intentions of letting anyone try it out.

"All right, Tony, tell Skilow that I said, one love."

Tony walked smoothly out of the restaurant and jumped back into the truck. As they were pulling off, Maurice came from the back of the store.

"All right, Black, a'ight Putt. I'll holler at y'all niggas later," he said, scratching his head.

Chapter 21

It was closing time and Mrs. Gurdy was still in the back office dealing with an upset stomach. Putt and I cleaned the place up and closed down the restaurant. Mrs. Gurdy was supposed to give us a ride home but she was taking too long. It was raining like cats and dogs but I didn't want to miss my hair appointment with Starr, so we decided to make a run for it. I threw my apron over my head and dashed on home to Fairfield.

It was midnight when we arrived at Starr's house. I knocked on the door real hard. I wanted to be sure to wake her if she was asleep. Starr opened the door with attitude.

"Why you got to be knocking so hard?" she barked. Her complaining reminded me of Momma.

"Man, can you just let us in? I got to pee," Putt said, shoving his way past Starr.

I followed Starr into the kitchen. She wasn't alone. Baije, one other chick, and a couple dudes were sitting at the kitchen table.

I glanced over at the two dudes. One of the dudes at the table was my old neighbor and competitor. It was Malcolm and he sat there with the same simple-ass look on his face that he had as a child.

"What's up, man?" I spoke to him out of politeness. Truth was, I never cared for his meek ass, and his being around Starr made me dislike him more.

" 'Sup," Malcolm and his friend spoke back.

Putt had been upstairs using the bathroom, and within minutes he returned downstairs and brought with him a big appetite.

"Yo, Starr, you got anything to eat? Any fish? Dag, man, I'm hungry," Putt said, rubbing his stomach as if he hadn't eaten all day. For a slim guy, Putt loved to eat and seafood was his favorite. Putt didn't eat red meat at all, but anything else was fair game. He had just eaten a whole bucket of chicken during our shift, yet he was ready to throw down again on some grub.

Starr was working hard to finish Baije's hair, and Putt's begging annoyed her. "Dag, boy, all you do is eat all day, it's a wonder you ain't fat! Go ahead, Putt, and fix you something. Suga Momma made some chicken and dumplings, cornbread, and peach cobbler before she left. You can have some. The food is in the refrigerator and the cornbread is over there on the counter."

Putt eased his way inside the refrigerator. I didn't know if he was just desperate for food or straight up ignoring the rest of the people in the house. In any event, Putt didn't speak a word to anyone else until he retrieved the pots and pans from the fridge. He sat the pots down on the stove, then offered Suga Momma's food to everyone as if he had a right to.

"Hey, ya'll niggas want some or what?" He turned to Malcolm, his partner, and the other chick. "Baije, you want something, Boo?" he asked Baije directly.

"We good," Malcolm and his boy replied.

"No thanks, Putt." Baije smiled.

"I'll take a little bit," the sneaky girl who was waiting to get her hair done accepted Putt's offer. The girl had been sitting quietly while she watched every move that everybody made. I don't know how long she had been at Starr's house, but her eyes were wandering around the room as if she had just gotten there. She was checking out the place and everyone in it. I had never seen the girl before but there was something about her that just didn't sit well with me. I didn't trust her, so I kept my eyes on the little sneaky heffa.

"All right, Barbette, I got you!" Putt said, calling the girl's name.

"Hey, Starr, can I use the phone to call my girl? I need to make sure she got back into the dorm okay." Cocoa was away in college, away from her children, away from her man, and Putt often worried about her. Starr rolled her eyes at Putt, then shot me a funny look.

"He sure is asking for a lot, ain't he? Go ahead, Putt, you can use the phone but you gone pay me for that long-distance call." Starr snickered.

Putt placed the pot on the stove and hurried upstairs, where he could talk to his girl in private. Putt was a very private dude. He never really spoke much about his relationship with Cocoa, but he loved the girl more than life itself. Cocoa had just started another semester at James Madison University. Together they had two beautiful children: a little girl, CoShonda, and boy, Pierre Jr. While Cocoa was away at JMU, the children lived with Putt and his mother in the same three-bedroom apartment that he had grown up in with his five siblings. Putt's mom helped to raise his children while Putt worked hard as a dog at Church's Chicken to support his entire family.

"Tell Cocoa we said hello, and ask her if she's still coming up for the concert tomorrow," Baije yelled after him.

"All right, I will," Putt hollered back downstairs.

A few minutes later, Starr let out a huge sigh and stretched her arms high into the air. From the dead look on her face, it was obvious she was beat.

"Ya'll, I'm getting tired. I need something to keep me up 'cause after I finish up Barbette's hair, I still got to do Black's," she said, stretching and yawning with her mouth wide open, showing all thirty-two of her perfect teeth. She dropped her arms to her waist and turned to Malcolm.

"Malcolm, fire up another joint for me," she urged her boyfriend.

Malcolm stood up with a simple grin on his face, reached inside his front right pocket, and pulled out a bag of weed.

"Tom, you got any paper left?" he asked his partner, who hadn't spoke a word. Tom's eyes were already bloodshot red and they were barely opened. He set down the pack of strawberry cookies that he had been munching on like a cow and stood up from the table. Tom patted himself down like 5-0 did a nigga in a police raid. I shook my head at him because he was a bit dramatic and the rolling paper was just that—rolling paper. It wasn't that serious, yet he felt the need to perform. He finally opened his mouth to speak.

"I ain't got no more paper. We gone have to go and get some more," he said, sounding dumb as fuck. He patted his pockets again as if the paper were going to miraculously appear. I laughed out loud at him because I figured if he was wearing his own pants, he should have at least known what was in his pockets.

Starr shook her head at her half-ass friends, then directed Malcolm to her purse.

"I got some, it's upstairs in my purse. Malcolm, can you go get it for me?"

Malcolm dotted for the stairs, but Starr stopped him in his tracks. "Never mind, I'll go get it myself. Baije, give me a minute, girl, I'm almost done." She smacked her lips and headed upstairs to get the rolling paper.

Starr came back with the E-Z Wilder paper and handed it to Malcolm. He grabbed a handful of weed from his plastic bag and laid it out on the table. He licked the paper, laid the weed inside the E-Z, then rolled the joint. When he was done preparing the marijuana stick, he passed it to Starr. She sat the marijuana stick between her lips and lit fire to the tip. Starr hit the weed like a professional pothead. It was the first time I'd seen her puff.

"You smoking?" Malcolm rolled another joint and raised it up at me.

I declined. "Nawh, I don't smoke."

Everybody at the table started smoking, so it didn't take long before Malcolm's sack of weed was gone. Suddenly, there was a knock at the back door.

"Get the door, it's Head; he just called on the phone," Putt yelled downstairs for someone to open up.

"It's me, shorty, open up," Head yelled from the other side of the door.

When I opened the door, Head stepped in with a mean look on his face. He immediately jumped at Baije and got right up in her face.

"Why the fuck you in here getting high with these niggas?" he yelled at her. "Man, I smelt the shit as soon as you opened the door. Baije, come the fuck on!" he snapped again.

Starr snapped back at him, waving the hair comb in front of his face. "Head, don't come up in here disrespecting my house and blowing our high. I'm finished with her hair anyway." Starr rolled her eyes at him. Baije didn't mouth a word back to Head. She looked at him, stood up from the chair, grabbed her purse and her jacket and let out a light sigh.

"I'll see you tomorrow, Starr. Good seeing you, Barbette." She waved good-bye.

"Nice seeing you too." Barbette waved back, checking Baije and Head from head to toe as they exited.

"All right, Black, I'll get up with ya'll niggas tomorrow." Head frowned, gritting on Malcolm and his boy. He hunched his shoulders toward them. "Fuck ya'll niggas looking at?" he asked them. Malcolm and his boy continued to sit quietly, high as a kite off of weed. They looked stupid in the face and knew better than to respond.

"All right, Head, see you tomorrow." I laughed as I shut the door behind him and Baije and locked it.

Barbette was dying to get her hair done, and she quickly jumped into the make-believe salon chair.

"So, how do you want your hair?" Starr asked as she removed the hat from Barbette's head. Starr's mouth dropped to the floor when she saw what little she had to work with. "Damn, girl, what happened to you?" Starr rubbed her hand through Barbette's bald scalp.

Barbette stuck her own hand in her head and played with her scalp. She began to explain why her hair was gone.

"Girl, I let this lady at a shop downtown perm my hair, come to find out she wasn't the stylist, she was the damn shampoo girl." Barbette sucked her teeth.

"Whaaaat!" Starr exclaimed.

"Yeah, girl, my cousin Victoria referred me to the so-called Dominican shop. Girl, when my hair started falling out, I went over to Victoria's house because I was going to beat her ass!" Barbette snapped, her eyeballs bulging with rage as she told the story.

Starr questioned further, "Oh, so, you went looking for the shampoo girl over Victoria's house?"

"No, I went to Victoria's house to beat Victoria's ass! That bitch knew what she was doing when she sent me downtown to that little-ass rinky-dink shop. Bitch told me, 'Girl, those Dominican women can do the hell out of some hair,' when she knew all along that them bitches can only work with natural hair. Those whores don't know shit about perming," Barbette fumed.

Starr found her story hard to believe. "Barbette, why do you think Victoria would intentionally set you up?"

Barbette slid to the side of the chair so she could look at Starr. " 'Cause Victoria let the same Dominican perm her hair the month before, and her shit fell out. That's why her fat ass is gone natural. She's running around telling people that she cut her hair off beause she wanted the natural Nubian look, which is far from the truth. Girl, Victoria's fat ass be lying!" Barbette rolled her eyes and neck.

"So, did you and Victoria ever fight?" Starr asked as she continued to cut the dead ends from Barbette's hair.

Barbette stomped her feet on the kitchen floor a few times, then smacked her fist together. The thought of the fight had apparently pissed her off.

"Did we fight? I ain't gone lie to you, Starr—Victoria beat my ass, but you best believe that I gave that fat bitch a run for her money!"

Starr shook her head in disbelief, "Girl, that's crazy. I still don't understand why your own cousin would set you up. But if she did set you up, then that's messed up!" Starr concluded.

Barbette sat all the way back in the chair so Starr could continue working on her hair. She pulled out a fingernail file from her purse and proceeded to shape her nails. "She probably set me up because she found out that I slept with her man when she left me in her house to go to the grocery store," she said nonchalantly, like it was no big deal.

Starr snatched the back of Barbette's head real hard and pulled her to the sink. "Damn, Barbette, you slept with your cousin's man? You are one scandalous-ass whore. I'mma be sure to keep you from around my man." Starr flipped on the water, shoved her in her back, and pushed her head down into the kitchen sick.

"Black, can you go upstairs and check on Putt 'cause he's been up there for a while," Starr noticed. Before I could make it upstairs, Putt came down, smiling from ear to ear. He rubbed his hands together.

"All right now. I'm good to go since I talked to my girl, now I'm ready to eat!" he said. "I hope ya'll didn't let my food burn."

Putt walked over to the stove and lifted the top from the pot.

"Man, I don't believe this shit!" Putt screamed.

"What, Putt, what's wrong?" Starr stopped what she was doing long enough to peep over in the pot.

"Man, you mean to tell me that I didn't turn the pot on? I don't believe this, now I don't have anything to eat!" Putt was infuriated. He slammed the lid back onto the pot. Nobody said anything because Putt was hungry and stone mad and we all knew better than to mess with a man who didn't have any food.

Apparently Barbette thought it was funny. Ten seconds later, she broke out laughing.

"You stupid," she laughed out loud.

"What the fuck is so funny and who you calling stupid?" Putt asked her.

Barbette stuck her fingernail file back into her purse and answered him. "Fuck you, Putt. You're stupid, that's who," she spoke rather calmly, still giggling.

"Fuck me? Barbette, I wouldn't fuck you with another nigga's dick, you stank hoe." Putt balled his face up at her.

I intervened because Putt knew better than to disrespect a female. All the women in his life, disrespecting a female should have been the furthest thing from his mind. "Come on now, Putt, don't disrespect the girl like that."

"Her bald-headed ass disrespected me first," Putt said, angrily putting the pots and pans back into the refrigerator.

Barbette turned her head in my direction, putting me in the middle of something I had no involvement in. I was trying to help her out, and she thanked me by being disrespectful. "You shut up 'cause you ain't got shit to do with this," she spat at me.

Before I could say anything, Starr intervened, putting an end to the back and forth bickering. "That's it! Everybody get the fuck out except Black, 'cause I'm still going to do his hair. The rest of ya'll leave now!" Starr insisted.

Barbette's big old tough ass started whining, "But you ain't finish my hair." She patted the top of her head again.

"And I ain't gone finish it. Now try me like you did Victoria and watch and see just what the fuck I do to you. Girl, you better get the fuck out my house, running off at your mouth like you're bad. Black ain't say shit to you but you gone disrespect him? You better get out of here now!" Starr let her have it.

Malcolm and his boy rose up from the table. "All right, Starr, we'll get with you later," they said.

Putt started in with Barbette; he just wouldn't let it die. "Now, that's why you ain't getting your bald head done, Skeezer!" he teased her.

Barbette rolled her eyes at him, but said nothing.

"All right, Black, be ready at ten a.m. so we can go to the mall," Putt said as he exited through the back door.

Starr gathered up Barbette's belongings and handed them to her. Barbette couldn't believe that Starr was putting her out; she really believed that it was a joke. "Girl, you gone leave me with my hair like this, knowing the concert is tomorrow?" she worried.

"Look, Barbette, I don't care about your hair or the show. You shouldn't have been in here disrespecting my house or my friends. Like I said, Black ain't say shit to you. I don't know who you think you are, but that acting like you bad shit don't cut it with me. Besides, I don't know if I want your sneaky ass around me after you just admitted to me that you screwed your own cousin's man. See, it's bitches like you who make it hard for women like me. If I were Victoria, I would have cut your ass too short to shit for messing with my man. Barbette, I heard that you was like that, but I didn't want to believe it, 'cause it's not my place to judge anybody. But when you lay all your cards out on the table, then I have no choice but to play my hand, and the one game I don't play is messing with other people's men." Starr broke Barbette down to pieces.

Barbette wrapped her scarf back on her head, and then threw her hat on top.

"That's all right, I'll find somebody else to fix my shit," she hissed.

"Then do that, bitch!" Starr told her, then escorted her out the front door, almost closing her foot in the door as she locked it.

Starr tidied up the kitchen and asked me to join her upstairs. She said she was tired and wanted to get comfortable before braiding my hair. We went up to her bedroom. She turned the radio to 97.5 Slow Jams.

"Black, I'm going to take a quick bath because I feel yucky from doing hair all day. You can turn the TV on if you want. I'll be right back," she said.

I don't know how long I had been asleep, but Starr shook me hard to wake me up. "Wake up, Black. Boy, I thought you were up 'cause your eyes were wide open. I've been trying to wake you up for a few minutes." Starr laughed. "I've never seen anybody sleep with their eyes open," she added.

I woke up only to find Starr standing before me in a pair of skintight leather pants and a black leather top.

"Do you like this outfit, 'cause this is what I'm wearing to the Run's House concert?" She spun around so I could get a full view of her attire. I was surprised that she thought enough of me to ask my opinion. I smiled when I realized that my opinion mattered to her.

"Yeah, you look good," I answered honestly.

"Now all I got to do is find the right pair of shoes," she thought out loud. "Black, can you go downstairs and get me a wine cooler out of the refrigerator? You can have one too," she offered.

"Starr, I don't drink or smoke, but I'll go and get you a cooler." I stood up from her plush recliner chair and made my way downstairs.

When I returned, Starr was sitting on the bed in an oversize T-shirt. "Black, can you turn the radio up just a little for me?" She took the open bottle from my hand and took a sip from it. "Hum, that's my girl right there!" She snapped her fingers to the tune on the radio. It was the sexy songstress Sade. Star sang along to the lyrics of "Tar Baby." Something about the song had always made me uncomfortable, so whenever I would hear it on the radio, I would turn it off. Nevertheless, I didn't say anything about it to Starr; I just took a seat and listened to her sing the entire song.

When the song ended, I watched Starr take a sip from the cooler and lick her lips.

"Boy, you are crazy. Why you looking at me like that?" She laughed. She had caught me staring at her and found it to be rather amusing.

I didn't say anything, I just kept staring at her as she continued to sing the songs on the radio. I enjoyed listening to her sing. Starr's voice was beautiful. The song "Let's Wait a While" by Janet Jackson came on next. Star slid down on the bed and sat the wine cooler on the nightstand.

"Woo, I'm tired. I'm going to have to do your hair in the morning," she said while yawning.

"It's already morning." I laughed, pointing to her clock radio.

"So, you might as well just stay here, so we can get up early and get it done before you go shopping," she offered. "Turn the light off. You can sleep in here, just don't try anything," she added.

Within minutes, Starr was fast asleep. I stayed awake for a few minutes, trying to figure out how I had ended up in bed with her. I don't know exactly when I fell off to sleep, but around three a.m., I woke up when I felt something laying against my chest. It was Starr; she was laying on my chest, looking up at me.

"Girl, you scared me." I threw my head back so I could look into her beautiful brown eyes. Starr sat up in the bed, rolled over onto her knees, and then removed her T-shirt. She tossed it onto the floor.

"Take this off," she said, grabbing at my Church's Chicken shirt.

I sat up in the bed and did exactly what she requested. Starr moved closer to me and reached for my pants. She began to un-buckle them, but I stopped her when I remembered the cocaine in my pants pocket.

"Hold up a minute." I backed off the bed. I stood up, removed the cocaine from my pants, and shoved it down inside the pocket of my Church's Chicken apron. Then I took my pants completely off and got back on the bed with her.

"Come here, Black," Starr said, reaching out to me, her eyes leaving me to believe that she had been longing for me.

I slid on the bed next to her, she laid me on my back and got on top of me. Everything happened so fast, it was almost as if she had planned it. Starr straddled my waist and began making slow circular moves. I started breathing heavy. I had never in my life been this close to a woman's nectar. She grabbed my hands and placed them on her breasts. I was still a virgin, had never been with a girl in my life, and boy was I nervous. I was just as nervous as a porcupine in a balloon factory. I thought at any minute I would bust open.

Following her lead, I moved to the beat of her drum. We con-tinued humping each other slowly as the song "Two People" by Tina Turner played softly in the background. Starr started suck-ing on my chest, and that shit really felt good. I raised her off me, laid her on her back, placed my mouth on her breast, and sucked both of her titties.

Starr moaned, "Oh Black, that feels good." Then she took my hand and slid it between her thighs. Although I had never been with a chick before, I knew exactly what she wanted. Hell, I had seen my fair share of porno flicks while I was in juvie, so I knew what to do with my finger. I gently slid my index finger inside of her, and she squirmed as I stroked her clit.

"Do you have a rubber?" I breathed heavily in her ear.

"No, I don't. I don't want you to put it in, I just want to feel you up against me," she said as she ran her fingers through my unbraided hair.

Next, Starr grabbed my penis and massaged it in her hand. My body shivered. Starr kept playing with my penis, until it grew at least a good twelve inches.

"Damn, Black, it's big," she said, sizing me up.

Then she laid me back down and started humping me again. I humped her back, fast and erratically. I was so excited to be with her that I was losing control.

"Slow down, Black," she warned me.

I tried to pump my brakes, but after about three minutes of bumping and grinding, my left leg started to shake uncontrollably. My dick tingled and I felt like I was about to explode. I screamed aloud.

"Oh shit, Starr, I'm about to cum?" I guessed.

Starr sat up in the middle of the bed and grabbed my dick and began to beat it. Before I knew it, I had lost complete control of myself. I felt so damn good, that I was moaning uncontrollably.

"Ooh, awh, ooh, awh." I shook, I jerked, and I shivered.

Like the good cheerleader she was, Starr cheered me on.

"Yeah, Black, make it happen. Make it happen, Boo," she said, still jerking my dick for me.

I was oohing and aahing; it wouldn't be much longer.

"Yeah, Boo, yeah, Boo," Starr chanted, then she grabbed her T-shirt from the floor and held it out for me as I busted my first nut.

"There it is!" I shot my cum all over her T-shirt. I collapsed on the bed as Starr wiped my semen from my penis with her shirt.

"Is Suga Momma coming home early?" I asked because I didn't want her to catch us in bed together.

"No, Boo, Suga Momma stays with her boyfriend on the weekends so I have the house all to myself," she told me.

"Word?" was all I managed to say.

"Yeah, she stays with him, 'cause she stopped bringing men home ever since—" then Starr cut her sentence short.

"Ever since what, baby?" I asked.

"Well, you know. Ever since. You remember what Mr. Wayne did to me, don't you?" Starr asked, sadness written across her face. I knew what she was trying to say but like Starr, I didn't want any memories of Wayne or the incident surrounding my brother's death. I hated thinking about it; whenever I did, it made me sick.

"Baby, let's not talk about that," I said, stroking her hair and snuggling her in my arms. Starr turned and looked up at me, then kissed me on the lip.

"Okay, Boo," she agreed, then turned back around, positioning herself back in my arms. I kissed her on the top of her head.

"Thanks, Starr," I told her.

"Thanks for what?" she asked, never turning around to face me.

"Thanks for your support. Girl, you are one heck of a cheerleader!" I praised her.

Starr laughed at me. "Boy, you are so crazy. Good night. I'm going to sleep." Starr shoved her right thumb into her mouth and rolled over to her side.

"Good night, Starr." I smiled.

Chapter 22

Starr finished my hair around two p.m. I went home to check on Momma and to get my money to go to the shopping mall. Momma and Mr. Todd were sitting at the kitchen table, enjoying their favorite beverage. They were drunk as two skunks early in the day. Usually when Momma drank, she used the small-size bathroom cups to hold her liquor, the kind that people used to gargle their mouth with mouthwash. Several of the empty cups sat on the table. The nasty smell of Salem cigarettes filled the air. Momma and Mr. Todd must have smoked a whole carton because cigarette butts filled the ashtray and ashes were all on the table. From the looks of things, it was possible that the two of them had been partying all night. One unattended cigarette lay burning in the ashtray.

"Hey, Mom, Mr. Todd," I spoke to them, as I smashed out the burning cigarette nub in the ashtray.

Momma snapped at me, smacking the back of my hand. "Boy,

don't you touch my smoke! You think you grown, don't you? First you stay out all night, over there with that li'l fast-ass girl, and then you think you can come up in here messing with shit!" she chastised. "You really are starting to smell yourself, huh? Well, if you sniff real good, you'll realize that your big ass stink!" she growled.

Mr. Todd just looked up at me. He was too messed up to say anything. I ignored Momma and made my way to the pantry to use the phone.

"I'm about to call Grandma," I said, not really asking for permission, but kind of seeking it. I dialed the telephone number; Grandma picked up on the first ring.

Momma yelled out in the background. "And don't be running up my phone bill calling your so-called ass grandma. I don't know what you keep calling her for anyway," she complained. Ignoring Momma again, I didn't respond to her comment.

"Hello, baby, hello?" Grandma answered, not acknowledging whether or not she heard Momma's complaining in the background.

"Hey, Grandma. How are you feeling today?" I smiled at her through the phone.

Grandma sighed heavily. "Baby, I'm doing just fine. How about you?" she cared enough to ask. I loved talking to Grandma; her kind words always made me feel special.

"I'm okay, Grandma. How's Granddaddy and Auntie?" I asked.

"Daddy's fine, Auntie's fine. Everybody doing okay," she assured me.

I wanted to tell Grandma about the concert, but I was afraid that she wouldn't understand. Grandmother was a devout Christian, loved the Lord, and praised him day and night. I figured Grandma of all people wouldn't judge me, so I decided to tell her anyway.

"Grandma, I'm going to a concert tonight."

"What kind of concert, baby? Is it one of those rap concerts?" she wanted to know.

"Yes ma'am, it is." I drew my face tight, as if Grandma could see me through the phone. She let out a disappointed sigh; I could imagine she was shaking her head on the other end of the line.

"Now, Bilal. I done told you to be careful about what you listen to. That rap music ain't nothing but devil music. I know you young people like listening to that stuff, but like I told you before, that kind of music ain't no good for your spirit or for your soul. Eventually, if you keep listening to that stuff, you're going to start believing in it, speaking it, and living it. The Bible says to keep a tight rein on your tongue, which means you have to watch what you say and for that matter, baby, you have to watch what you listen to!" she said. Grandma paused momentarily to catch her breath.

"Now, if you love the Lord and say you're a Christian, you gotta act like a Christian at all times. You can't be a Christian when it's convenient for you. Now, I know you're young, but in due season you will learn. Bilal, promise me you will keep reading your Bible. Baby, I have heard the lyrics to some of that rap music. That's shoot 'em up, bang, bang music. I know all about that group, what's the name of that group out in California, what they call themselves, NWA?" she asked. I laughed to myself because Grandma was on a roll.

"Yes, ma'am, but that's not the group I'm going to see."

"Don't matter. They all the same," she mustered.

Grandma continued. "Have you been reading your Bible?" she asked me.

"Yes, ma'am, I have," I kind of lied. Truth was I hadn't read the Bible in three weeks.

"Have you been going to church?" she quizzed on.

"No, ma'am, I haven't had time because I've been working so

much," I made an excuse for myself. Grandma sighed again, then continued to break me down.

"Well, I'm going to tell you again. It's okay to read the Bible at home but you have to go to church to fellowship amongst saints. You got to fellowship with other believers. Baby, I want you to read Acts two, forty to forty-four; the Bible will tell you the same. You hear me?"

"Yes, ma'am, I promise I will." I had only called to check on her, but Grandma was giving me a much-needed Bible lesson.

"You have to go to church and to Bible study so you can get proper instruction and direction from a minister, or someone that's trained to explain the Bible to you. You see, people sit at home and read the Bible by themselves and misinterpret things that they have read, and when they do, they aren't getting the proper understanding. Then they take certain Scriptures and things out of context and end up causing a lot of trouble for everybody. I wish your momma had of—" Grandma was about to finish her lecture, but Momma so rudely interrupted my phone call.

"Bilal, get your ass off my phone. You've been on that phone with her long enough!"

Grandma overheard Momma cursing me. She smacked her lips. "Baby, like I said, I wish your momma would have—"

Momma screamed my name again. I then cut Grandma off.

"Grandma, I'm sorry but I have to go now," I told her.

"All right then, but don't you get into any trouble at the rap concert, you hear me? Be good," she reminded me.

I stood up because Momma was peeping around the corner, looking at me half crazy.

"Okay, Grandma. I'll call you later," I promised.

"Okay, baby, and by the way. I got that money order that you sent me. You don't have that much yet you are so willing to share. Bless your heart. Love you baby, bye," she thanked me, her smile shining through the telephone.

"Bye, Grandma," I said, and then I placed the phone back in the cradle. I hurried upstairs to the bathroom, took a quick bath, and changed my clothes. I grabbed my money that I had stashed away in a sock. On my way downstairs I overheard my crew. They were outside waiting for me in Mr. Arnold's pickup truck.

"Come on, Black!" they yelled for me. I jumped down the remaining stairs, hurried out the door, and on to the back of the flat-bed with the crew. Mr. Todd was standing at the driver side window, kicking it with Mr. Arnold.

"All right then, butterfly." He waved good-bye to his new friend.

On that note, we drove off.

Chapter 23

We were excited as hell when we reached the Richmond Coliseum. The joint was packed to its maximum capacity. We met up with Starr and Baije, who told us that Cocoa had caught a flat tire and wouldn't be able to join us. Starr was looking like her usual diva self. She was rocking her skin-tight leather pants and form-fitting leather halter top. She wore big bamboo earrings with her name cut into them. Her hair was pinned up in a bun, and she had on sexy black leather heels. Starr was definetly on point. There wasn't one chick in the coliseum that could touch her.

Baije looked good too. She wore tight-fitting jeans and a form-fitting T-shirt that showed off her hourglass figure. Baije's ass wasn't nothing to play with either. She had a banging body, but truth be known, she wasn't the swiftest deer in the forest. Baije, like her mother, father, aunts, and everybody else on both sides of her family, had dropped out of school. In the pj's her family had earned a rep as the Eighth Squad, 'cause it was a known fact that none of them mutherfuckers ever made it past the eighth grade. Baije may have been dumb as a brick, but the girl had a reputation for dropping chicks like hot potatoes. She was usually quiet and stayed to herself, but if anybody messed with Starr, you best believe she would track them down and beat the breaks off them. If Baije didn't leave a chick bleeding, then to her that meant she didn't win the fight. So, if she had to, she would beat the same chick over and over until they shed blood. Word on the street was that if you fought one person in her family, you had to fight all nine hundred of them. While Baije and her family had a rep for being bad, I never understood why they allowed Head to knock her upside her head whenever he felt like it.

As we gathered around to take a group picture, a rack of loud-mouth niggas looked on as the photographer snapped a couple of shots of me and the crew. One of the onlookers was rocking the same leather Adidas sweat suit that I had on. I had spent my last dime on that suit and was somewhat embarrassed to see another nigga wearing it. I didn't have enough money to buy new sneakers, so I rocked the same ones that I had been wearing while I was in juvie. I ain't gone lie, my sneakers were tore up from the floor up, but I said fuck it, I rocked them with the leather Adidas suit anyway.

We finished taking pictures and were about to go inside the corridors when suddenly a loud voice came over the intercom.

"Will everybody listen up? Pay attention. I need everyone to quiet down in here. I have an important announcement to make." A man's voice bounced off the walls of the coliseum. Everything got so quiet, you could hear a pin drop.

"We hate to inform you, but tonight's show, the Tougher than Leather Concert featuring Run-DMC has been canceled due to technical difficulties." The announcer's voice was loud and clear and disappointing to the crowd. Man, people went bananas; the Tougher Than Leather Concert being canceled was like the world coming to an end. Folks damn near lost their minds.

"What the fuck you mean the show's been canceled due to technical difficulties?" they shouted as they turned over trash cans and shit. They acted like complete fools. The voice came back over the intercom again, addressing the crowd's concerns.

"All ticket holders will be able to get a full refund." Before the man could finish explaining the return policy, people started pushing and shoving to get to the box office. "Refunds will be issued on Monday morning," the voice echoed throughout the coliseum, even louder. The next thing I know, a gunshot rang out in the coliseum and people hauled ass for cover. I grabbed Starr by the hand and we all ran to the nearest exit.

"Man, that's why I hate coming to this raggedy-ass coliseum. I'm not ever coming here again. From now on, we're going to start going to the concerts in Hampton," one girl cried on her way out the door.

Lucky phoned his dad to come scoop us up, but he wasn't home. We were all dead broke and couldn't afford a taxicab, so we started hiking across the Martin Luther King Bridge. Cars were riding past us on the bridge, blowing horns and yelling out of windows at us as if we were tramps on a hoe stroll. Starr complained about getting tired, so we stopped for a minute so she could get herself together. We started walking again, when suddenly she began gasping for air.

"I can't breathe." Starr fought for breath, grabbing hold of the guardrail. Baije reacted to her best friend right away, locking arms with her to keep her from falling.

"Starr, just calm down and take it easy. Breathe slowly." Baije remained calm while coaching Starr, who was now in panic mode.

"What's wrong? What's happening to her?" I worried as I held her up by the other arm. Baije didn't bother to answer; she was busy tending to her friend. Putt jumped in, trying his best to explain what none of us really knew.

"Man, I don't know. Starr has problems with her heart or something. Remember when we were in middle school and she passed out at the basketball game?" Putt flashbacked, trying to get me to remember Starr's past problem.

Starr's breathing intensified and she began to cry even more.

"I want to go home. Just take me home," she cried softly.

I couldn't stand the sight of seeing her in pain or the sound of her begging to get home but there was nothing I could do to get her home any faster. I was dead broke and taxi rides weren't free. I had to think of something to get her off of her feet.

"Get on my back. I'll carry you home on my back." I bent over, offering her a free ride. Just then, a car pulled up alongside the guardrail. I stood up to see who was in the car that had slowed down beside us.

"Hey man, is she all right?" the dude in the passenger seat hollered at us. I recognized his face; it was one of the niggas from the picture stand. The driver, the dude in the Adidas suit, stuck his head around him.

"Yo, man, if she sick I can drive her across the bridge to MCV or give ya'll a ride home. It'll be kind of tight back there with all of ya'll, though," he said, offereing all of us a ride when he knew there was no way in hell all of us could fit into his whip.

Lucky was the first to speak. "We good, but you can give the ladies a ride," he suggested. Then Lucky turned to me, Putt, and Head for our approval. He didn't want us to feel uncomfortable with letting the girls ride home with the dudes, so he explained how he knew the cats.

"Man, I know the driver. That's that nigga Earl from the Holiday Club. He ain't gone fuck with them," Lucky said. Earl overheard him. He stretched his neck out farther to get a glimpse at who had spoken his name.

"Yo, who dat?" He leaned forward. "Oh, what's up, Lucky?" He acknowledged that he knew who Lucky was too.

Putt thought it was a great idea; however he thought it would be even better if I agreed to take the free ride home with the ladies so he added in his own suggestion.

"Black, why don't you go 'head and ride with Starr and Baije? You can't let her ride by herself. Them niggas might be all right, but we ain't gone take no chances with them niggas for real," he told me. Starr was beginning to look faint, so I made a decision quickly.

"All right, I'mma take you up on that ride," I said, accepting the ride from the stranger named Earl. I grabbed on to Starr, picked her up off her feet, and stepped over the guardrail with her in my arms. Baije attempted to follow but Head stopped her from getting in the car.

"Where the fuck you think you going? You ain't riding with them niggas. Black can take care of Starr, so you get your ass back over here," he told his girl, while gritting on Earl and his boy. Sure enough, Baije did exactly what Head told her to do. She stepped back over the guardrail and stood beside her man with a pitiful look on her face.

"Starr, I'll be over as soon as I make it home," she promised.

The passenger jumped out of the front seat and I placed Starr in the seat and buckled her in. I hopped in the backseat with the nigga and we took off. On the way to the pj's Earl's boy irritated the hell out of me. Earl had boom box speakers in the trunk of his ride, and he blasted the song "A Bitch is a Bitch" by NWA. His boy knew every single word to the song, and I had to listen to the punk sing all the way to Fairfield. The fake rapper dude got on my nerves and by the time we made it to our destination, I had a throbbing headache.

When we pulled up in front of Starr's house Earl turned the music down and said to me, "Take care of Ms. Lady." He smiled, showing his gold teeth. I marveled at the dollar sign that he had cut into his tooth. Since I had returned home from juvie, I had seen more gold tooth in the hood than I had seen baby daddies but never had I seen anybody flossing like Earl.

Before I knew it, I blurted out, "Man, that's straight!"

Earl looked at me and then smiled even harder.

Starr stepped out of the car and I climbed from the back. "Ai'ght, man," I thanked him for the ride. His boy happily jumped from the backseat and plopped back down in the passenger seat. Earl passed something to his boy, then his boy handed it to me. Starr was walking up the sidewalk and she almost fell. Focusing only on her, I never opened my hand to see what the dude had dropped in it.

"Man, let me get her," I told them as I turned my back to them and ran off after Starr.

"All right, playa," Earl yelled, before driving off slowly.

I jogged up the walkway to assist Starr with opening her front door. I needed my extra hand to help her, so I opened up my balled fist. I was surprised when I realized what Earl and his boy had left with me. *Ain't this something. This dude done drop twenty dollars in my hand.* I spun around and hauled ass running after the car, 'cause I didn't need the nigga's money.

"Yo, wait up!" I chased after the car, screaming for the nigga to stop.

His boy threw his head out the window; he was smiling hard and laughing even harder.

"Yo, Earl said keep that in your pocket, 'cause you never know when you might need it." He laughed, then threw his head back inside the car. I could see the back of Earl's head; he was laughing too. I continued to chase the car down the block.

"Hey, come back, come back!" I screamed to the top of my lungs.

When I realized they weren't going to stop, I stopped chasing and watched them drive out of sight. I headed back toward Starr's house but she had long gone inside. I opened my fist and glanced down at the money again. I spun around quickly when I heard the sound of a car engine 'cause I thought the whack-ass dudes had come back. I stood there for a minute trying to figure out why Earl had given me twenty dollars. Then I realized the obvious. I had accepted a ride home from a stranger, so Earl knew that I didn't have any money to get Starr home in a taxicab. To make matters worse for myself, I had complimented the nigga's tooth; some shit that a girl would do. I stood in the middle of the sidewalk with the twenty-dollar bill in my hand, scratching my head, trying to figure out what was wrong with the picture. Then, it finally hit me. *I got punked!*

Chapter 24

Starr was pissed off and flat-out refused to speak to me. I knocked on the door; she opened it up, visibly upset about having to accept a ride from a stranger.

"Black, what the fuck do you want? I'm not messing with your ass. You couldn't even pay for me to get home in a cab!" she ranted.

"Starr, I'm sorry but I don't have any more money. I had to give my moms my paycheck and I used the money I had saved up to buy this outfit. You know I need clothes," I tried rationalizing with her. Starr braided hair on a regular basis, so I didn't understand why she was just as broke as I was.

"What about the money you made from doing hair?"

Starr didn't approve of my question. She threw me a psychotic stare, "I know you ain't just ask me what the fuck I think you did. You know what, Black? Get out of my face, and leave me the hell alone. I don't want you anyway. I was high last night, that's the only reason I was with your black ass!" she cursed me out, cutting me up with every word.

"But Starr, why you acting like that?"

" 'Cause Black, you are one selfish mutherfucker. You always have been and always will be. Just like when I wrote your ass them letters, you ain't never write me back 'cause all you ever think about is yourself!" she yelled in my face, spit flying out of her mouth and landing on my lips. Starr shoved me away from the door and then slammed the door shut in my face.

I hit the door as hard as I could with my hand, trying to get her to open up.

"Starr, what letters? What are you talking about?" I yelled.

"Don't play dumb with me, boy. I know your momma gave you my letters 'cause she told me she did. Just get the hell away from my door!" Starr fumed.

I banged on the door a few more minutes, then decided it was time to just go home. Thirty minutes later, I was watching out the living room window when I spotted Starr getting into a car with a strange dude. Momma walked into the living room, catching me by surprise. I dropped the curtain from the window.

"Hum, I done told you to leave that li'l fast-ass girl alone," Momma said. Apparently she had seen Starr leaving with the guy too. "Listen, Bilal, me and Todd are going out for a while so be sure to lock up my house if you leave back out."

"Yes, ma'am, I won't forget."

As soon as Momma and Mr. Todd were out of the house, I ran up to her bedroom to locate the letters as well as my birth certificate. I still hadn't turned in a copy of my birth certificate because whenever I asked Momma for it she claimed to be too busy to give it to me. I rambled through Momma's junk box and discovered Keon's birth certificate and his death certificate. I also found the papers from Omaha Life Insurance. I couldn't believe it. Momma had cashed out a ten-thousand-dollar policy on Keon, all of which she spent on Floyd.

I also found old pictures of Momma, Deacon Melvin, and his wife at a church retreat. There were also pictures of Momma and Floyd after I had fucked up his nose, which confirmed my suspicion that she was still involved with him after I had been sent to juvie. Then I stumbled across the letters that my friends had written to me. They were unopened and wrapped up in a thick rubber band. The letters were from Putt, Lucky, Head, Coach, Portia, Jeffrey, and even Malcolm. I tossed the letters to the side and anxiously searched for more. I was relieved when I saw a stack of letters addressed to me, and the return name and address label read Starrshema Williams. For some odd reason, Momma had kept Starr's letters separate from the others. I ripped open the first envelope and began to read.

Dear Black,

I am writing you this letter, for the 3rd time. So, if I don't hear back from you, then I'm not going to even worry about it because I'm not going to keep writing you and you don't write me back. Well, anyway. Putt told me that you wanted to go with me. Is this true? Well, if it is, my answer is yes. I don't have a boyfriend anyway, and for your information, Malcolm is not my boyfriend. He is my best friend, just like Baije. FYI—I told Malcolm to act like he was my boyfriend cause I wanted to make you jealous, so he played along with me. So, if you still like me, let me know or check the box (like we use to do in elementary school, ha, ha). If I don't get your answer in a week, then I will assume that you changed your mind and that your answer is NO. OK, bye.

*P.S. Tell your moms she better stop being mean, cause God
don't like ugly, and Suga Momma says that he ain't all that crazy
about beauty either.*

Xxoooxxxoooxxxoooxxxoooxxxooo Forever a lady,
Starrshema Williams

Starr had spoken the truth. She had been trying to get with me
over the years. I examined the box for more letters. I had a gut
feeling that I would find more of Momma's well-kept secrets.
Then I discovered my birth certificate. *Finally,* I thought to my-
self. I began to scan the birth certificate, in no particular order.
Child's name: Bilal Moab Cunningham. D.O.B.: April 16, 1969.
Birthplace: Birmingham, Alabama. Weight: 8 pounds, 15 ounces.
Mother's name: Joann Sharonda Cunningham. Father's name—
*Well, ain't this something? Why is his name on my birth certificate?
I can't believe that the Vital Statistics Department would make such
a mistake on such an important document. Momma should have
told me. We can easily get this fixed,* I thought to myself. I placed
everything back in the box the way it was, with the exception of
Starr's lovely letters and my birth certificate. I closed the door to
Momma's bedroom, headed back downstairs to the couch, and
watched CNN until I dozed off.

Chapter 25

It was around three p.m. when I woke up the next day. I jumped up when I heard Lucky's voice coming from the kitchen. I cleared the coal from my eyes and headed in.

"What's up, Black? Sorry we ain't come back for you last night, but Head and Baije got into it on the bridge and the police came and took all of us to the police station," he told me.

"Man, that mess with Head and Baije is getting old. He needs to cut that mess out," I said, disapproving of Head's abuse of his girl. Lucky's dad, Mr. Arnold, and Mr. Todd were chilling at the kitchen table. The old cats were drinking gin straight with no chaser. I struck up a conversation with the old cats.

"Hey, did you know that twenty million people lost their homes after the flood in Bangladesh?" I made small talk with them.

"Well, I heard about the flood but I didn't know that it was that many people. Lord have mercy!" Mr. Todd said, unable to stomach the truth.

"Who told you that?" Mr. Arnold asked, verifying my source.

"I saw it on CNN last night. Man, that shit is sad. They say about four hundred people died in the flood too," I added. Both men shook their head. The tragedy was just too hard for them to believe.

"Yeah, the U.S. government probably had something to do with that damn flooding," Mr. Todd accused Uncle Sam. He petitioned the opinion of his old buddy. "What you think about that, Cheap Charlie?" He turned to Mr. Arnold.

Mr. Arnold shrugged his shoulders. "Don't know, could be, who knows," he answered.

Mr. Todd stood up from the table and took his last shot of gin straight to the head. He sat the cup down and let out a nasty burp.

"Boy, I got to get me some chop-chop, or else I'm gone get sick, drinking this Seagram early in the morning." He twisted his face. Mr. Todd smelt like shit on a stick but his personal hygiene was the last thing on his mind. He ransacked the refrigerator searching for food.

"Dad, let me ask you something. What's up with all that slick talk you and Mr. Todd be talking?" Lucky asked his father.

I jumped in. "Yeah, Mr. Todd, what's with all that slick talk you be putting out there? Why do you and Mr. Arnold talk in riddles?" I asked.

Mr. Todd, or Uncle Todd as I preferred to call him, continued fumbling around in the fridge.

"Ain't no chicken, ain't no pork, ain't no beef, no lamb, turkey, nothing!" He slammed the refrigerator door shut. "It ain't a living ass in there to eat!" he growled, kicking the bottom of the refrigerator with his foot. "What's that you say, son?" He spun around to me, his demeanor switching from pissed off to meek and calm.

"Uncle Todd, I want to know why you and Mr. A talk in codes," I repeated.

"You hear that, Cheap Charlie? They say we talk in codes."
Uncle Todd turned to Mr. Arnold and they both chuckled.

"Boys, that's Vietnam talk; I understand exactly what Todd is
saying." Mr. Arnold laughed.

Lucky tapped his dad on the shoulder. "Dad, that's because
you were in Vietnam too," he reminded him and we all broke out
laughing.

I reminded Uncle Todd of the first night when I met him and
how he was running around and talking in his sleep, yelling,
"Dung lai." Uncle Todd began to break the codes down for me.

"Boy, dung lai means 'halt' or 'stop,' " Uncle Todd told us.

I nodded. "Okay, so what about when you were yelling, 'Incoming'?" I questioned.

Mr. Arnold jumped in. "Incoming means hit the dirt!" he
shared.

"Okay and what is a Cheap Charlie? 'Cause Uncle Todd, you
just referred to Mr. Arnold as a Cheap Charlie a few minutes ago.
Mr. Arnold proudly accepted the title of Cheap Charlie."

"Hey, 'cause that's exactly what I am." Mr. Arnold laughed,
then Uncle Todd broke down the definition of a Cheap Charlie.

"Over in Vietnam, a Cheap Charlie was a U.S. serviceman
who didn't waste his money," he said.

"Man, ya'll are funny." Lucky smiled at the two Vietnam vets.

Uncle Todd and Mr. Arnold decided to give us more than what
we had asked for. They began to break down more vet jargon.

"Let's see, what else can I tell you boys. Okay, I got one. A butterfly is a playboy, so that would be me." Uncle Todd pointed to
himself. "And a flower seeker is a man in search of a prostitute,"
he continued on.

Mr. Arnold jumped in. "And that would be you too, Todd," he
labeled his friend. Uncle Todd gave Mr. Arnold a funny look.

"I'll be damn if I'm a flower seeker; you was the one out looking for pussy last night. Had me riding with your crooked leg ass

up and down, down and up Second and Broad Street, looking for prostitutes!" Uncle Todd rolled his eyes at his buddy.

Lucky gave his dad a strange look. "Oh, so you was out tricking again last night, Dad? Man, I'm telling you, you better not bring anything home to Mom." Lucky smirked. Mr. Arnold was embarrassed that his son found out that he had been out tricking again on the hoe stroll. He dropped his head in his chest and didn't utter a word.

"Don't worry, Lucky; your father ain't going to give your mother a disease, cause none of the hookers on the hoe stroll would trick with him. They said Mr. A is too cheap and doesn't want to pay the price for good hoe pussy," Uncle Todd told Lucky, putting his dad's business all out in the open.

Mr. Arnold sat quietly, then suddenly he snapped. "Now wait a minute here!" He slammed down on the table with an open hand. "Ain't no damn way I'm a Cheap Charlie and a goddamn flower seeker. You can't be both!" he shot back.

"Exactly. 'Cause if you know you're tight with your money, you shouldn't be on the hoe stroll trying to buy pussy. Don't you know pussy ain't cheap no more, Mr. A?" Uncle Todd joked. Then Uncle Todd added, "By the way, boys, chop-chop means food— something to eat—and we ain't ever got any of that around here," he griped.

Lucky and I laughed hysterically, until Uncle Todd shot us a mean look.

"Now that I'm thinking about it, what is Joann doing with my goddamn money? Joann, get your ass up, girl, and find me something to eat! I'm paying to eat around here, now ain't I?" he shouted up at the kitchen ceiling, hoping and praying Momma would hear him from her bedroom.

The two old gizzards left to go and get something to eat. About an hour later, Mr. Arnold's pickup truck came flying around the corner on two wheels. The old men bailed out of the truck, leaving the doors of the truck open. Uncle Todd ran into the yard, holding his bloody head in his hand, crying for help. Mr. Arnold wobbled up the sidewalk behind him; his limp leg wouldn't allow him to move but so fast.

"Help, help, we got robbed, we got robbed!" they both screamed. Me and Lucky jumped up from the porch to help the old cats. I grabbed on to Uncle Todd, and Lucky grabbed a hold of his dad. Momma jumped up from the chair and ran inside to get a towel for Uncle Todd's bloody head.

"What happened?" Both men were out of breath; it took them a minute to gain their composure, so they didn't answer us right away.

"Dad, who robbed ya'll? Are you okay?" Lucky said, worried about his father. Lulu overheard the commotion, so he ran outside to help.

"Black, you sit Uncle Todd down in the chair, and Lucky, you sit your dad down on the porch. Everybody stay calm, everything will be okay," Lulu said, jumping in and taking control of the situation. Lulu had a way of calming people's nerves.

"Dad, where were ya'll and what did the guys have on?" Lucky asked. Mr. Arnold took in a deep breath but before he could answer his son, Uncle Todd jumped in.

"We were over on Twenty-fifth Street at Triangles Restaurant and it wasn't no 'they,' it was only one sucker who robbed us. It was a black man in his late thirties. He was riding a girl's five-speed purple and lavender bicycle and wearing a white jacket with a red and black dragon on the back. He had on black jeans and navy blue and white sneakers. See, we had just paid for our food and were about to leave, then *bam*, out of nowhere, that son of a bitch hit me in the head with the butt of the gun," Uncle Todd recalled, illustrating how the robber had banged him on the head with the gun.

Mr. Arnold nodded in the positive, agreeing with most of what Uncle Todd had just described. Mr. Arnold added to the story, giving his version of what happened. He jumped up from the porch and gave us a visual demonstration.

"But first he yelled, 'This is a stick-up!' So I threw my hands in the air," Mr. Arnold said, using his fingers as a gun, pointing at us just as the robber had pointed the gun at them. He continued on, "But Todd—Todd wasn't going out without a fight. So, he pretended that he had a gun too. Todd put his hand underneath his shirt, made an impression of a gun, pointed at the man and yelled, *Dung lai*! The man didn't understand him and he felt threatened, so he snatched Todd's hand from underneath his shirt and then clucked him upside his head with his gun. Boy, he hit him so hard, I felt the barrel of the gun myself," Mr. Arnold dramatized. He sat back on the porch and slid his right foot out of his shoe.

"I'm surprised that Todd is still alive; 'cause as hard as he hit him, he could have killed him. Are you okay, buddy?" Mr. Arnold asked Uncle Todd.

"I'll be all right," Uncle Todd nodded.

Just then, Momma came out of the house with towels, a bowl of ice, alcohol, peroxide, and cotton balls. Momma sat the items on the small table on the porch and Lulu cleaned the small gash in Uncle Todd's head.

Lucky jumped up. "Come on, Black, let's go find the nigga who robbed them." We headed to his dad's truck.

Mr. Arnold yelled after his son, "Be careful, son, there are some fools out there on the road. Drive carefully." While he warned his son about road safety, he didn't warn him about how dangerous it could be to go searching for a man with a gun. I followed Lucky to the truck. We jumped into Mr. Arnold's raggedy ride and sped off.

We drove to 25th Street looking for the dude that had unleashed the dragon on Uncle Todd. We searched high and low for him but didn't see anybody who fit the description. Finally, we met up with a dude on the corner; he was nodding hard and wiping his face with a dirty face towel.

"Yo, Pete, did you see anybody wearing a dragon jacket 'cause the nigga just robbed my pops," Lucky hollered out of the window at the dude. The dude dropped his dirty towel from his face.

"Yeah man, that nigga Dope Dick David just robbed those two old dudes. Man, that nigga David is larceny," Pete said, rocking back and forth, talking slow as molasses. Lucky pulled the truck over to the curb so we could talk to Pete.

"Tell that nigga when I see him, I'mma make him eat his gun," Lucky said, biting down on his bottom lip. Pete nodded forward, then scratched his chest and stood up tall.

"Man, ain't no need of wasting your time with that nigga David, 'cause he damn near dead anyway. And as far as I know, that nigga ain't got no gun, man. Trust me, if that nigga ever gets his hand on a gun, it would be good as sold," he said. Pete's eyes closed completely shut. Then he rocked forward again, then he leaned back, almost tipping himself over. He caught himself from falling, opened his eyes up real fast, then looked around as if someone had pushed him or something. Immediately, he went right back into his trance.

"Yo Pete, is that nigga David from Churchill?" Lucky asked.

Pete rocked over again but this time he remained leaning in the forward position for about a good twenty seconds. We waited patiently for him to raise back up.

"Man, that nigga David is from all over. After he took the money from the old dudes, he said he was on his way to Whitcomb Court to get a pill of dope. You know them niggas over Whitcomb Court got some good ass dope!" Pete said, testifying to what he knew. Before we pulled off, Lucky had one more question for Pete.

"So, Pete, why do they call that nigga Dope Dick David?" Lucky inquired.

Pete let out a slight chuckle. "Man, they call that nigga Dope Dick David 'cause he done shot up so much mutherfucking dope, that the only good vein he got left is in his dick, so that's where he shoot up at. Man, they say the nigga dick swells up so fucking big that he needs help just to pull that mutherfucker out of his draws," Pete told us. Then he added, "That's why the nigga go around robbing mufuckers on his daughter's five-speed bicycle, he can't ride his son's bike, 'cause the handlebars get in the way of his dick."

"All right, shorty, thanks for the info." Lucky thanked him and was about to pull off but Pete stopped us.

"Hey, hold up. Between the two of ya'll, I know I can get two or three dollars," he begged. I checked my pockets knowing good and well I was flat broke.

"I don't have any money," I told him.

"Yeah, we ain't got it right now, Pete," Lucky answered.

"A'ight, but next time ya'll niggas see me, look out for me," Pete said, then stashed his dirty face towel in his back pocket and headed down 25th Street.

"Man, who was that dude?" I asked Lucky.

"Man, that was Sneaky Pete. Niggas call him Sneaky Pete, 'cause he will steal the draws off your ass, your clotheslines, or from wherever and then, if you ain't paying attention, he'll try to sell the shit right back to you. Man, one time my dad was giving the nigga a ride but Dad needed to stop off at the store first, so he went inside the store and left Sneaky Pete in the car with it running. Well, when Dad came out, the car was turned off, so he tried to start the car back up. When he couldn't get the car to start back up, he popped the hood of the car. Man, don't you know the battery was missing from the car and so was Pete? That nigga Sneaky Pete had stolen Dad's battery and fled the scene." Lucky laughed.

"And he got the nerve to call somebody else larceny." I laughed with him.

• • •

We drove around Whitcomb but nobody had seen Dope Dick David. We decided to call off the search so we headed back to Fairfield. When we approached my block, we noticed a gang of people congregated in the middle of the street. We parked the car and bailed out. A young dude from 'round the way ran up to us.

"Man, ya'll just miss the fight of the century! Man, Lulu just smoked that junky," the young boy bragged.

Just then, Momma, Lulu, and the two old vets walked out onto the front porch. From Lulu's appearance, it was obvious he had given somebody a beat-down. His signature yellow headscarf had fallen and was wrapped around his neck, and small droplets of blood were on his shirt.

"That damn junky made me break a nail!" Lulu fussed, holding a nail clipper in his hand.

"What happened?" Lucky and I asked.

Lulu explained the incident in full gory detail. "The dude who robbed them came rolling through here on a bicycle. Yep, he rode right past the house and Mr. Arnold spotted him. So, I ran behind his ass, and bitch-snatched him off the bike and tried to beat him down to a puff. How did he think he was going to rob somebody from Fairfield then bring his stupid ass over here? I tried to kill that mutherfucker for robbing Mr. A and Mr. T. Sheed, fuck that! We are all family around here, and I'm not going to let anybody come through this mutherfuckers trying to snatch ass. Hum, what the fuck do I look like? A mutherfucking punk?" Lulu carried on.

"Niggas must have me confused with being a punk bitch. They got the game all fucked up if they believe that shit! I'm Lou by day and Lulu by night, don't get it twisted. I'll fuck a nigga up if I have to but I ain't gone lie, though. When I picked David up and off the bike, I grabbed him between his legs, and oh, my, when I felt that nigga's dick, I thought about dragging his country ass to my house, tying his feet and hands to a chair, and then spreading my ass on top of him and riding his dick all night long, 'cause oh my God, David has a dick like an elephant's." Lulu fanned himself because the memory of Dope Dick David had him all hot and bothered.

Momma frowned. "A'ight, Lu, watch your damn mouth," she snapped at him.

"Which way did he go?" Lucky asked.

"Hell if I know, but I took his bike so he probably ain't gone but so far." Lulu laughed.

"Where's his gun? Did you get his gun too?" Momma asked.

"Gun, what gun? Are you talking about this old silly thing right here?" Lulu reached into his pocket, and pulled out a silver-plated imitation of a 25-caliber weapon. It was a cigarette lighter. We were all surprised. Dope Dick David had robbed Uncle Todd and Mr. Arnold with a cigarette lighter. The two old men had been robbed blind, in broad daylight, without a gun.

"Chile, this thing can't hurt a flea. I can't believe big dick is riding around robbing people with it. Listen up, Black and Lucky, let me tell you boys one thing. Don't ever pull a gun out on a nigga if you ain't planning to use it. If you pull a gun on a nigga, you better pop the nigga and make sure he's dead while you're at it. 'Cause if you don't, trust me, a real street nigga will be back to get you," Lulu said, sharing his knowledge of the streets. He continued, clipping his broken nail. " I can't believe that junky pulled this fake-ass cigarette lighter out on me. I tried to make his ass eat it, I bet his throat hurts from me shoving this shit in his mouth!" Lulu chuckled. "Joann, let me get a smoke from you, 'cause I'm going in now. I'm tired and I have to get up at five o'clock tomorrow morning," he said, twisting his body all around.

Momma reached inside her bra, pulled out her pack of Salems and handed them to Lulu. He took a few cigarettes, then returned the pack to her.

"All right then, I'll see ya'll tomorrow." LuLu waved good-bye.

"Lulu, you gone pay me for my cigarettes," Momma said, looking inside the pack.

"Pay your ass shit," he mumbled, then closed his front door.

Chapter 26

It was Monday morning. Time to get back on the grind. I walked into work dead tired from the weekend.

"Hey, Mrs. Gurdy," I spoke to the boss lady.

"Hey baby," she spoke to me and kept on about her work.

I noticed a new girl standing behind the counter. She was wiping down the countertop and loudly popping gum.

"How are you?" I asked.

The girl looked at me shyly. "I'm okay," she replied.

I went toward the back of the restaurant. The delivery truck was there, and the driver was unloading a freight of chicken and other restaurant supplies.

"Hey, tell him to leave a few of the chicken boxes by the back door," Mrs. Gurdy said. I assisted the driver with unloading the truck, and per the boss lady's instructions, I stacked three boxes of chicken and left them by the back door.

Around two p.m., Putt rolled in. He and the kids had been away at JMU for the weekend visiting Cocoa.

"What's up?" I smacked hands with him. Putt spoke back, but something wasn't right with him. He wasn't smiling, which was unusual for him.

"Everything all right?" I asked him.

Putt threw his head sideways and sat down. His eyes welled up with tears.

"Man, Cocoa is leaving me and the kids, " he said, his voice real low so no one could hear him.

"What are you talking about?" I exclaimed.

"Black, she called me down there to tell me that she was in love with somebody else. Cocoa is in love with a white dude that she met in school last year," he said, then dropped his head on the table. He continued talking, unable to look me in the face. Putt kept his head down on the table as he continued to talk.

"The white boy that she is messing with already graduated and is now in medical school in Spain, or some goddamn where, and he wants Cocoa to drop out of school and marry him. Believe it or not, her little ass is going to do it," he shared. "And on top of that, she gave her mom temporary custody of my kids," Putt went on to say.

I couldn't believe that Cocoa was taking my boy through this type of torture. Putt was a good dad, he did the best he could to take care of his children, and his mother was one hell of a grandmother. I encouraged him to fight for his.

"Man, you have to fight for your kids. Don't let her take them. I'll do whatever I can to help you. We can start saving up money to get you a good lawyer," I suggested.

"Man, Cocoa's moms got money; we can't go up against her. You know she married one of those bigwigs at Philip Morris to-bacco company, that's how she was able to get out of the pj's," he huffed. I didn't care about how much money Cocoa or her mother had, I was willing to go up against them if my nigga was willing to. I remained positive; it was the only way to keep Putt in good spirits.

"Man, don't think like that. Just keep doing what you're supposed to for your kids and God will work it out. He'll give you favor," I said. Putt raised his head up from the table, looked me in the eye, and nodded his head.

"Thanks, man, you always know the right thing to say." He stood up and prepared himself for work. "Hey, ain't that Chiquita behind the register?" he asked me.

I shrugged my shoulders. "I think that's her name."

• • •

On my break, I stepped out back to get some fresh air. I caught Mrs. Gurdy standing out back, holding a torn-off piece of paper up to her nose. She jumped when she spotted me. I glanced up at her; a beige substance surrounded the area between her nose and her lips. She quickly brushed the substance away.

"Mrs. Gurdy, what are you doing?" I asked, as if I had a right to.

Mrs. Gurdy dropped the torn sheet of paper to the ground and turned her back to me. A small pickup truck backed up to the back of the restaurant. The driver got out. "My man Black, you my nigga if you don't get any bigger." Maurice spoke to me, as he stepped around to the back of the truck. "Yo, Black, do you remember Duke from Thompson Middle? That nigga Duke is in the truck." He pointed.

I stepped over to the passenger side; Duke was in a serious nod, his head damn near on the dashboard.

"Duke," I called his name. He looked up at me, eyes rolling around in his head.

"Damn, Black, good to see you. Man, you gone have to forgive me but I'm high as a kite," he apologized, then lowered his head to his chest. I stepped away from the truck. Duke raised his head and stuck it out the window.

"Come on, Reese, hurry up and load them boxes, man!" Duke encouraged Maurice to hurry it up. Mrs. Gurdy and Maurice began to load the boxes of chicken onto the flatbed. I thought to myself, *Are they doing what I think they are doing?*

"What are ya'll doing?" I stuck my nose in their business. The boxes were too heavy for Mrs. Gurdy, so she soliticed my help.

"Black, can you and Reese load the rest of those boxes onto the truck?" She had the nerve to ask me to help them steal.

"Mrs. Gurdy, I'm sorry but I can't do that. That's stealing and I stopped stealing seven years ago. Mrs. Gurdy, why are you stealing these people's stuff anyway? Are you on crack? Do you need money to support a drug habit or something?" Mrs. Gurdy's eyes grew wild, and she was obviously offended by my question.

"Boy, you need to mind your own business. Hell no, I'm not on crack. If you must know, I snort dope if it means anything to you!" she snapped.

Maurice and Duke fell out laughing at her. I didn't see shit funny, so I continued with my questions. "So, a drug is a drug. What's the difference?" I asked sarcastically.

Mrs. Gurdy rolled her eyes around in her head for a minute, then looked at Maurice and Duke, who was still inside the truck falling out laughing.

"Dope will make you steal from the white man but crack— well, crack will make you steal from your own damn momma." She frowned.

"You got that right!" Maurice agreed, giving her a high five.

"A'ight, Reese, nigga come on," Duke yelled from the truck.

After finding out Mrs. Gurdy was a dopehead, I spent the rest of my break around the side of the building trying to clear my head. I admired Mrs. Gurdy and was disappointed to discover that she used drugs. My break ended abruptly when I overheard Putt and Mrs. Gurdy arguing. They were going at it hard. I ran inside to see what all the noise was about.

"No, you need to get your shit and get up out of here. You, too, Chiquita!" Mrs. Gurdy fumed.

"What's going on?" I asked all of them. Gurdy took her apron off and slung it on the counter. She tapped her feet on the floor a few times before she began to explain. Mrs. Gurdy was mad as hell. Her medium-brown complexion had turned stone cold red. She was on fire. I had never seen her that angry before.

"I came up front and the lobby was packed with customers and neither Putt nor Chiquita could be found. I look around and find them in the ladies' rest room. Putt was sitting on the toilet and Chiquita was squatting over top of him about to sit on his dick. I caught them just in the nick of time because them two fools was about to have sex on the job, in a nasty-ass bathroom. Here it is the busiest time of the day and they're in the back trying to fuck!" she fumed.

The customers inside the restaurant all covered their mouths in dismay. They were appalled to be inside an establishment were people fucked and fried chicken at the same time.

"Ooh, gosh, that's nasty!" some of them screamed. A dude that was dressed to kill in his Sunday's best grabbed his lady by the hand. "Come on, baby, let's bounce up out of this nasty place. I'm going to take you to Omar's for dinner," he insisted. Omar's was a top-of-the-line restaurant in Richmond. I figured if the dude had bread like that to spend, he should not have been standing in line at Church's anyway. I didn't care one way or the other about his business. I definitely didn't try to stop them from leaving.

Mrs. Gurdy panicked when her customers all started walking out.

"Oh my God, we are losing business. Get out, Putt and

Chiquita, get out now!" Mrs. Gurdy yelled, but Putt and Chiquita didn't move; they both just stood there looking at her with their arms folded. Mrs. Gurdy grabbed the telephone from the wall.

"That's all right, since ya'll are refusing to leave, I'm calling the police," she threatened.

"Calling them for what? What you gone do, tell them somebody was trying to get some ass in the bathroom? Getting ass is not illegal but what your ass has been out back doing is," Putt defended himself. "Go ahead and call the police, so I can call corporate on your ass and tell them you've been stealing from the company. Go ahead, make the call," Putt called her bluff.

Mrs. Gurdy placed the phone back inside the cradle and spun around the floor trying to figure out her next move.

"You know what? All of ya'll hoodlum mutherfuckers is fired. Get out!" she yelled.

"But Mrs. Gurdy, you can't fire us, we ain't do nothing," I pleaded, trying to save our jobs.

Mrs. Gurdy looked at me half crazy. "Boy, I've been waiting on your birth certificate and picture ID and you still haven't brought it in, so your little ass is fired too. Get the fuck out!" She directed us all to the door.

"That's what I get for hiring a bunch of raggedy-ass project kids," she insulted us.

Mrs. Gurdy's comment didn't sit right with any of us. At the exact same time, I, Putt, and Chiquita yelled, "Fuck you!" in unision.

Mrs. Gurdy grabbed the phone and started punching down on the numbers. "Fuck it, I'm calling the police on ya'll anyway!" she said. We all grabbed our belongings and bounced.

"Come on, Putt, we'll find another job. Church's Chicken ain't worth all this," I told him as we left the restaurant. Mrs. Gurdy kept running off at the mouth. She followed us to the door, still talking shit.

"Make sure ya'll don't bring your poor, raggedy asses back to my spot!" she shouted behind us. Chiquita turned to go back. She was ready to light into Mrs. Gurdy's ass.

"Fuck you, bitch! When I see you on the street, I'm gonna kick your ass," she yelled.

"That's why your husband left your junky ass!" Putt retaliated.

"You crackhead!" I shouted at her.

We were way across the street when Mrs. Gurdy felt brave enough to step outside the door.

"Fuck all of ya'll, and Black, you are a stupid mutherfucker 'cause Mrs. Gurdy snorts dope, not crack. Mrs. Gurdy got too much class for that!" she retaliated.

We dotted across Mechanicsville Turnpike before 5-0 showed up. Suddenly, Putt stopped running and turned to Chiquita.

"Chiquita, where you going?" he asked her. Chiquita batted her eyes at him, giving him her sexy look.

"I was wondering if I could go home with you so we could finish where we left off," she said. Putt cleared his throat, preparing himself for what he needed to tell her.

"Look, Chiquita, you a nice girl and all, but I don't mean no harm—" Chiquita cut him off.

"Oh, you got a girlfriend?" she asked, obviously disappointed.

"Nawh, baby. That's not it at all. Listen, I'm going to tell you the truth straight up, 'cause I think it's important that you know this for future reference. Baby girl, when we were in the bathroom and you pulled your underwear down, well, baby, I don't know how to tell you this, but your ass was funky. Chiquita baby, you smell just like fish. I love fish and I'm telling you, that was lake trout I smelled. I love eating fish, but hell, I ain't trying to hit no pussy that smells like it. So, I hate to tell you this, but I'm going to have to pass on the pussy. Maybe another time, you know, when things are a little better for you," Putt told the girl with a straight face.

Chiquita appeared somewhat embarrassed, her jaw dropped. "Oh, I did have a bacteria infection, but I thought it cleared up. I took all the pills," she explained.

Putt shook his head and rested his hand on her shoulder. "Baby, you might want to call your doctor back, because he may need to prescribe something else for it. Tell him the pills didn't work or something," Putt suggested.

Chiquita scratched her head, considering what Putt had said. "Yeah, you're probably right. Okay, I'll catch up with you another time," she agreed. "Nice meeting you, Black," she said, then Chiquita took off running in the opposite direction, across Mechanicsville Turnpike.

We increased our pace, trying to get home as fast as we could. Putt jumped right into another conversation, but I was still laughing at his conversation with Chiquita. Putt was brutally honest and said things that I wouldn't dare say.

"Anyway, man, stop laughing, ain't shit funny. What happened when you called Starr on your break?" he asked.

"Man, from this day on, I'm not thinking about her. I called her house, she answered and as soon as I said hello, she hung up on me. I don't even want to think about that girl," I said, then quickly changed the subject. "Putt, I'm worried that Mrs. Gurdy gone kill herself by snorting that dope," I commented.

"Man, I don't know about all that. I don't know if snorting dope can kill her, but I sure as hell know that she can overdose from shooting it up. I've seen that shit a thousand and one times myself. Like this one time, this dude shot up some bad shit and they tried to bring him back by putting ice between his legs. Well, when that didn't work, they drug him outside, laid him in the cut, and let his ass die. The nigga's own sister did that shit to him."

"What. His own sister?" I questioned.

"Yep. She ain't call for help 'cause she had bench warrants out on her. Man, when they found that dude through the cut, he was naked, his eyes were wide open, and his body was frozen like an iceberg," Putt shared.

"What do you mean frozen like an iceberg?" I wanted more information.

"Man, this shit happened in January, the dead of winter. It was the coldest winter ever. It had snowed for seven days and seven nights and everybody had been stuck in the house but somehow them junkies was able to get out to score," he told me.

"Man, I'm sorry you had to witness something so horrific. So, I guess you saw him when they finally came to remove the body?" I assumed. Putt shook his head, then rubbed his face.

"Black, I might as well tell you. I'm the one who found him. The man I'm talking about was my mother's boyfriend. He was the twins' daddy. He and Momma had gotten back together after he got out of jail. He was doing good, had started working and everything. So after he did his time at the halfway house, Momma let him move in with us. Well, when he didn't come home two days into the blizzard, Momma sent me over to his sister's house to look for him. Man, when I found him laying in the cut, I screamed nonstop for about an hour for somebody to come help me. By the time somebody came, I couldn't stop screaming. Momma said I cried and screamed all night long. I even cried and screamed in my sleep. I ended up losing my voice and couldn't talk for a few days. Black, man, when I finally started talking again, the stuttering was gone. My speech was normal like everyone else's. The doctors couldn't figure the shit out, but Momma says that sometimes it takes a horrible thing to happen to scare the shit out of us. I guess that right there scared the shit out of me. After finding the twins' daddy dead, I swore to God that I would never use drugs."

I didn't understand why Putt had kept something so important from me. After all, we told each other everything.

"Putt, how come you never told me about that?" I asked him.

"I wrote you a letter telling you about it, but when you never wrote me back, I just decided to never talk about it again. 'Cause man, sometimes it's best to not talk about certain things; it helps you to get over it faster."

"Actually, man, that's not true. In fact, if you don't talk about things and keep things bottled up inside, the pain gets manifested so deep that it will affect you in many different ways. Ways that you don't understand or can't possibly imagine. So, it's better to talk about your feelings and deal with whatever issues you may have," I told him. "And by the way, I never got that letter; you know I would have written you back," I added.

"Black, who told you that shit about stuff getting manifested? Man, where do you get all that stuff from?" Putt laughed at me.

" 'Cause I read all the time, watch the important shit on TV, and some things I just know. Don't ask me how I know what I know, I just do," I answered honestly.

"Black, you smart as hell but I do have one question. How come you got all this book sense, but no street sense?" Putt said as he opened up his front door to let us in.

"What you mean?" I asked, kind of offended by Putt's question.

"Like, man, you don't know the difference between coke and dope. Mrs. Gurdy is on dope, heroin, man. You kept saying that she was on cocaine." He laughed.

"Coke, dope, drugs are drugs, don't make me no difference." I laughed.

"Hey, Black, do you think I should've brought Chiquita home with me and put her ass in the bathtub? 'Cause man, I'm horny as hell."

"Putt, you and Cocoa just broke up. It's only been one day and you're ready to screw somebody else already. I can't believe you were trying to get some in a nasty bathroom."

"Yeah, we've been broken up for one day, but she ain't gave me no pussy in six months, and I am feening right now," he responded while picking up the telephone.

"And anywhere is better than nowhere when it comes to getting pussy. So, let me handle my business, please!"

I turned on the television, and kicked back on the oversize sectional couch. Putt punched the seven digits on the telephone. "Yo Black," he whispered, covering the phone with his hand. "You were born smart and I was born to fuck!" He nodded at me. Then the person on the other end picked up. "Hello, Jenny. What's up? This is Putt." He smiled.

Chapter 27

Jenny invited us out to her home in Henrico County and told us to bring along a couple of our friends. Head drove his mother's whip, and we arrived at her house around eleven p.m. Jenny's home was beautiful. She lived in a three-bedroom ranch that sat on two and a half acres of land. The closest neighbor was about a mile down the road. When we walked in, the first person I spotted was Chelle. She strolled over to me, wearing a tight-fitting T-shirt that read I'M MY NIGGA'S BITCH.

There were a few other chicks in one of the back bedrooms. You could hear the music blasting as they listened to "A Bitch Is a Bitch" by N.W.A. I made my way into the den, and Chelle followed behind me. Putt and Jenny didn't waste any time barricading themselves in her bedroom. Lucky and Head kicked it with two other chicks. I flopped down on the navy blue sectional sofa. Chelle sat down beside me.

"You want a beer?" she offered.

"No, thank you. I don't drink," I answered plainly. We hadn't been there for ten minutes and already Chelle was invading my space. I pretended I had to go to the bathroom just to get away from her.

When I returned to the den, there was a girl sitting in the corner by herself. She had on a burgundy and gray Virginia Union University sweat suit. She sat with her legs crossed Indian style, and her face buried in a literature book.

"So what are you reading?" I asked her. She looked up at me, as if I had disturbed her.

"And your name is?" she asked sarcastically.

"Oh, I'm sorry. My name is Black," I replied.

The girl sucked her teeth and poked her lip out. "Is that your real name or street name?"

"You know, I thought about my answer after I had given it to you. My name is Bilal, and yes, Black is my street name." I laughed.

"That's better. My name is Amanda. Nice to meet you. I'm reading for a paper that I have due on Wednesday. I'm just getting started."

Just then, Chelle interrupted our conversation. "Black, do you want a beer?" she blurted out. I had already told her once that I didn't drink.

"Yes, Chelle, I will take one," I answered to shut her up. Chelle left the room to go get the beer and I continued talking with the girl.

"May I see your book?" I asked.

Amanda handed me the book, and I sat back on the couch and skimmed through the pages.

"So, who or what are you going to write your paper on?" I wondered.

Amanda let out a huge, disappointing sigh. It was obvious she wasn't looking forward to the assignment.

"I don't have a choice; my professor assigned me William Shakespeare," she huffed. "I know he's supposed to be the best, but I just can't get into his writing," she huffed again.

I closed her book shut and offered her some words of encouragement. "That's because you're thinking about it too hard. Just try to read with understanding," I told her.

She raised her brow. "What does that mean?"

"When you read, you have to listen with an open mind. Don't try to change the words by making them something that they aren't. Remove any inhibitions you may have, be free and ready to explore whatever path the writer takes you on," I said.

Amanda turned to face me. "What school do you go to?" she wanted to know.

"Oh, I'm not in school," I said.

"Shucks, I was going to ask you to be my tutor or something 'cause you kind of deep." She chuckled. "Do you know any of Shakespeare's poems?" She smiled at me.

"Well, actually I do."

Just then, Chelle pranced back into the room. "Here you go." She sat the beer can down in front of me, then squatted next to the sofa that Amanda and I were sitting on.

"Okay, then shoot. Chelle, be quiet, because he's about to recite a poem," Amanda announced.

Normally, I was shy around people I didn't know, but whenever I was reciting Shakespeare, I felt comfortable and in my element. I cleared my throat. "Okay, here we go. This is called "Let Me Not to the Marriage of True Minds" by my man, the infamous William Shakespeare."

Let me not to the marriage of true minds
Admit impediments, Love is not love

Which alters when it alteration finds,
Or bends with the remover to remove:
O, no; it is an ever-fixed mark,
That looks on tempests and is never shaken:
It is the star to every wandering bark,
Whose worth's unknown, although his height be taken.
Love's not Time's fool, though rosy lips and cheeks
Within his bending sickle's compass come;
Love alters not with his brief hours and weeks,
But bears it out even to the edge of doom,
If this be error and upon me proved,
I never writ, nor no man ever loved.

I felt a rush of adrenaline after reciting Shakespeare. I let out a huge sigh to release the anxiety. Amanda stood to her feet and started clapping.

"Bravo, bravo," she cheered.

Chelle stood up with her hands on her hips. "Who was that? Is that a rap song that you tried to make into a poem?" she asked.

"No, crazy girl. That's Shakespeare. Dang, were you listening? He said that in the beginning," Amanda reminded her.

Chelle rolled her eyes. She could care less about Shakepseare, or anything else important for that matter. "No, I didn't hear him. I got a buzz going on right now," she claimed.

"So, Bilal, what's your interpretation of the poem?" Amanda smiled at me.

"See, now you trying to get me to do your homework," I teased her.

Amanda play-hit me with her hand, punching me on the arm. "No, I'm not," she giggled.

"For me, it means to accept your lover for whom he is without trying to change him. For love takes time." At that moment, Starr quickly came to mind.

Amanda gathered her things to leave. She threw her book inside her backpack and headed out. "Well, Bilal, it's been a pleasure meeting you." She extended her hand for me to shake it. Instead, I kissed her on the back of her hand.

"Nice meeting you too, Amanda. Good luck with your studies," I smiled.

"Lock the door behind me and tell my cousin that I'll call her in the morning," Amanda said to Chelle, who then escorted her to the front door.

I sat on the couch, wallowing in self-pity. Thinking of Starr made me depressed. Chelle walked back in holding a bottle of Mad Dog 20/20 in her hand.

"You want some?" She held the bottle up to my face. Then she opened the bottle and poured me a cup, almost forcing me to drink it. I drank cup after cup until the entire bottle was gone. I had a buzz so when Chelle pulled me into the bedroom, I didn't refuse.

Once in the bedroom, Chelle threw the double lock on, pushed me back, and hopped on top of me. She straddled my waist and began to tug at my pants, trying desperately to pull them off.

"Wait a minute. Do you have a bag? I mean a condom?" I blurted out.

"Yeah, there's a condom right there on the nightstand. Black, just lay back and relax," she told me. Then Chelle removed my dick from my pants and played with it for a minute. She massaged my balls and wasted no time putting my dick in her mouth. She sucked it slowly.

"Damn, girl," I moaned.

I pumped in and out of her mouth, fucking her mouth hard as I could. At one point, Chelle snatched her head back, and then slid an enormous amount of saliva onto my dick. Then she tossed it right back into her mouth, slurping her saliva as she sucked me off. The shit felt better than good, it felt great, but for some reason, my dick wouldn't rise to the occasion.

"Black, I want you to fuck me so bad." Chelle looked up at me with them big-ass scary eyes. I couldn't stand the sight of her, so I turned my head in the opposite direction.

"Suck my titty," she said, then tried shoving her left breast in my mouth. I jerked my head away from her. There was no way in hell I was going to put my mouth on her breast. Just no way.

"Chelle, can you just play with my dick?" I asked.

Chelle was happy to oblige. She threw her head back down and proceeded to slob on my knob. The more saliva she worked up, the better it felt. Still, my dick wouldn't budge. All the pulling and sucking on my dick was making me tired.

"Chelle, that's enough." I stopped her.

Chelle raised her head up and used the pit of her arm to wipe the slob from around her mouth.

"I guess that beer has you messed up," she assumed.

"I guess so," I lied. Truth was, I didn't know what was up with my dick, or down with it, for that matter.

Just then, the song "Two People" came on the radio and instantly I thought about the night that I had made out with Starr. I was in a love trance, and didn't realize that Chelle had dropped back down to my dick. She forced her mouth back around my penis and began to suck it again. I imagined being with Starr, and this time my dick didn't waste any time rising to the occasion. I figured while I had an erection, I better act quickly.

I turned Chelle's phat ass over onto her stomach and she backed that thang up for me. She got on her knees in the doggy-style position. I grabbed the condom from the nightstand, slapped it on my dick, and thrust my dick as hard as I could into her pussy from the back door. I pumped a few times, and Chelle enjoyed every second of it.

"Oh Black, don't stop, don't stop," she moaned.

Chelle turned her head around and looked up at me, and immediately my dick went soft. Boy, was she so unattractive.

"Oh Black, don't stop, don't stop," she moaned again.

I thought to myself, *I'll be damn if I'm not.*

I rolled off of her and jumped clean off the bed. Putt knocked on the door, saving me in the nick of time.

"Black, come on. We're ready to leave," he yelled for me.

"I gotta go." I pulled up my pants and hauled ass out of the room. Chelle fumbled around in the bedroom, trying to get her stuff together so she could chase after me.

Jenny escorted me and the crew to the front door. When we stepped outside, two dudes approached her front yard. I recognized them immediately. It was Gold Tooth Earl and his boy.

" 'Sup." The niggas had the audacity to speak to me. I ignored them and shoved my way past. Chelle stepped onto the porch, more than likely to hunt me down, but to her surprise, she had guests.

"Bitch, I know you heard your mutherfucking pager going off!" Gold Tooth Earl broke bad with her. Chelle sucked her teeth, looking past him and straight at me.

"Boy, I didn't hear no damn pager," she shot back at him.

Earl stepped up onto the porch, then shoved her into the house. The storm door closed tight behind him. He didn't realize that we could hear his conversation so he started talking shit.

"So what, Chelle, are you fucking with one of those broke-ass Church's Fried Chicken niggas?" he asked her.

Putt was closer to the front door than I was. He snatched the door handle and ran back inside. "You got a problem, mufucker? Who in the fuck are you talking slick about?" Putt bucked at him.

His boy ran inside to his aid, throwing his hands up in the air like he was about it. "What's up?" He gritted like he was Billy bad ass. "What's up?"

I was tired, my dick was sore from Gold Tooth Earl's ugly-ass girlfriend sucking on it, and I wanted to go home to wash my dick off. So I squashed the beef real quick.

Before I knew it, I ran inside, snatched Gold Tooth Earl around his neck, and picked him clean up from the floor.

"Nigga, I will break your fucking neck!" I said as I grabbed hold of the storm door with my other hand and tossed that nigga out onto the porch. Lucky and Head heard the commotion and jumped out of the car and ran over to the house. Putt ran outside, and so did Earl's homeboy, Mr. Billy bad ass.

"Nigga, I wish you would jump in it. Let 'em fight, nigga," Head dared Billy bad ass.

I bent over, picked Earl up from the porch, and threw the nigga into the yard. Then I hit a wrestling move on him. I hit him with a Ricky Steamboat elbow drop. I jumped up, and then landed on him with all my weight. My elbow landed in the pit of his stomach, and he gasped for air. The nigga tried to roll from underneath me, but I jumped up from the ground and grabbed him by the tail of his jacket with both of my hands. Fuck the nigga thought he was going? I wasn't about to let the nigga go nowhere.

"Break it up. Break it up," the girls screamed.

Lucky and Head both yelled, "We ain't breaking up shit! Kick that nigga ass, B!"

I snatched Earl's punk ass up from the ground, and then I let him go. I had overpowered him so quickly that it didn't seem fair. I wanted to give the nigga a fighting chance. I threw my hands up and backed away, still holding my position.

"Chelle, go to the car and get my shit!" Earl yelled at her.

"Oh, nigga, so you got a gun. So what, nigga, you don't know how to use these?" I spat, throwing my hands up in the nigga's face. He tried to get away from me, but I bounced around him, blocking his path. "Nigga, I'mma fuck you up just for thinking about a gun," I promised him. Then I jabbed him in the face, *bop, bop, bop*. He fell back, and then started swinging wildly at me like a Catholic school girl in a street brawl. The nigga was no competiton for me. I punched him a few more times in his grill, then I jabbed him in his jugular and he fell down.

I continued talking to him. "I'm sick and tired of all ya'll punk-ass niggas. Everybody shooting mufuckers over dumb shit. Whatever happened to throwing these niggas?" I bounced around, waiting for him to get at me.

Earl wasn't trying to do shit; he just laid there.

"Get up and fight, nigga!" I demanded. I backed away, allowing him to make a move.

Earl rolled over to his side and staggered to get up. Then he yelled that same old punk shit again. "Chelle, go get my gun! Get my shit out the car or else I'mma beat your ass when this is over!" he threatened.

That did it for me. It was the last time that I was gone let the nigga threaten me with a gun. I gave him a minute to gain his composure, and when he stood up, I jabbed him again. He rushed me and tried to hold onto me. I threw his hands off me, and then I smashed both of his ears with my hands, distorting his balance and causing him to tumble to the ground.

When he fell, I dropped down on top of him and pounded his face with my hand. I must've hit him a thousand times before I heard something crack and felt the wetness of blood splattering in my face. I glanced down at my fist, and Gold Tooth Earl's gold tooth with the money sign engraved in it was stuck to my knuckle. I held it in my hand and examined it carefully.

"Hey, Putt," I called out to him. Putt gave me an odd look, as if he didn't know who I was. "Man, look at this. This nigga got the nerve to be calling us broke, when he's sporting a cheap-ass gold cap. Look at this shit." I held up the gold cap for Putt's inspection.

Then I walked back over to Earl. I squatted down beside him. He squirmed around on the ground. I told him, "Oh, no, don't try to get up, I don't think you want to do that." Everybody was quiet, so I glanced around to see what they were up to. They all had these crazy looks on their faces as if something was wrong with me. I didn't know what the fuck their problem was, so I continued my conversation with Earl.

"Hey, Earl. Let me ask you something: How you gone call me broke, when you rocking this fake-ass gold cap? Now, Earl, you know that niggas in Richmond don't wear gold caps; niggas in Richmond get their shit glued on permanently. Only niggas from New York wear gold caps. Okay, so what, you from New York now?" I tortured him.

Earl didn't answer me, so I repeated myself. "Earl, I asked you, where are you from? Are you from New York?"

Earl looked up at me, covering his face with his hand. He answered with the little bit of air he had left in his body. "No, man, I'm from Central Gardens. Right here in Richmond," he said. He softly called out to his girl, "Chelle, come help me."

I picked up Earl's Kangol from the ground, examined it, and decided that I liked it. So I figured we would trade. I removed my Church's Chicken hat from my back pocket and placed it on top of Earl's head. Then I placed his Kangol on top of mine.

"So Earl, tell me, who's the chicken now?" I laughed out loud.

Then, I reached into my front side pocket, pulled out a twenty-dollar bill, and threw it on top of him.

"Here's the money you gave me. You may need it to go toward replacing your gold cap." I laughed, and then I hurled up a wad of spit in my mouth and sprayed it on his ass. "Now nigga, give this spit back to your girl for me, 'cause she lost a lot of saliva tonight when she was slobbing on my knob," I gritted on him. That's when I turned to my crew.

"Come on ya'll, let's roll."

Chapter 28

For the first five minutes in the car, nobody spoke a word. Head was terribly upset about the entire ordeal. He felt that things could have turned out differently and we weren't prepared because we weren't strapped. Head was right—it was 1988 and the small town of Richmond, Virginia, was the murder capital of the world. Just about everybody was packing, 'cause wasn't nobody fighting anymore, and even when they did fight, they didn't fight fair. The drug market was on the up and up and everybody was getting paper, and although there was enough money to go around, at times niggas was just plain greedy and unwilling to share.

There were just too many dope boys on the streets, and because of that, jealousy and envy were inevitable. The idea from niggas up north, thinking that brothas from the south were soft and country was a myth, at least when it came to Richmond niggas anyway. Back then, a nigga from Richmond would drop you for something as small as mispronouncing his name. Niggas in Richmond were hard core, ruthless gangstas. For the most part, they felt they had to be.

Head parked in front of my house and we wiped down his mother's ride with soapy water. Blood had dripped on both the inside and outside of her whip. I noticed a downstairs light on in Starr's house, so when my crew left, I decided that it was time that Starr and me have a heart-to-heart talk. I called her.

"Hello," she answered in a sleepy tone.

"Starr, it's me, Black. Don't hang up," I told her.

"Boy, what do you want?" she raised her voice at me. "I am asleep!"

"Look, Starr, I really need to talk to you. I'll be over there in a minute, so meet me on the back porch," I said, not giving her a chance to respond. I grabbed the scroll from the makeshift entertainment center, dashed out of the house, and over to Starr's. When I turned the corner, she was waiting for me on the back porch. It was late, so I didn't waste any time. I jumped straight to the point.

"Listen. I never did get any of your letters. For some reason, my moms kept all the letters that everybody gave her to give to me. Now, Starr quit playing these games with me. You know that I like you and that I want to be with you. I was surprised when I read your letter; never in a million years would I have imagined that you liked me too," I said, managing to give her a slight smile.

Starr looked me in the eye, then lit a cigarette. "Black, that letter is old and so are we. There can never be an us," she said, blowing smoke circles into the air, then fanning the smoke away with her hands.

I wasn't about to let her slip away from me again, so I pulled out my deck of cards and tried my hand. Win, lose, or draw, I wasn't going out without a fight. I called her bluff.

"Listen. This letter is not old. As far as I'm concerned, you wrote it six days ago, and you told me in the letter that I have a week to let you know whether or not I wanted to go with you." I sat down in the chair next to her. I flipped the letter open and handed it to her. Starr examined the letter carefully but failed to see my point. She handed the letter back to me.

"Boy, what are you talking about?" she hissed.

"Starr, I got you on a technicality," I said seriously.

Then I stood up and shoved the letter back in her face.

"Starr, look at this. Your letter does not have a date on it. So, as far as I'm concerned, I still have time to give you my answer. Your letter in your own words says to let you know within a week. A week could have been six years ago, six months ago, but to me, it was only six days ago. So, today is the seventh day, and my answer is yes!"

Starr laughed so hard, she almost fell out of the chair. She threw her cigarette down and smashed it out with her foot. Then she slid out of her chair and landed on my lap.

"Oh my goodness, Black, you are so crazy! But that's what I like about you. You do some crazy stuff." She chuckled even harder. "Tell me, Black, what is it about me that you like? All these years have passed and you still like me?" she questioned.

I couldn't believe that Starr needed to question why I or any other dude for that matter liked her. Starr was the baddest chick in Richmond, hands down, plain and simple.

"Starr, you are everything a man could want in a woman: You are beautiful, smart, talented, feisty, classy, hood, all rolled into one. Girl, you are my everywoman!" I confessed.

Starr kissed me lightly on the lips. Then she spoke the magic words. Words that I had longed to hear. "Black, I like you too. From the first day you moved to Fairfield, I liked you, but you and Keon was being mean to me," she reminded me. "Black, I'll admit, aside from you being smart, funny, and your own man, you know what else I liked about you and I still do, to this day?" She moved her head away from me and looked deep into my eyes.

"What's that, Starr?" I waited to hear.

"Your teeth, Black. Your teeth are so bright. They're beautiful and on many occasions, your smile has brightened my day," she said, causing me to blush. Man, if I were butter, I would've melted at that exact moment.

"Oh, but one more thing. What I don't like is your temper. You need to calm down. I still can't believe you fucked Mr. Floyd up over a can of corn beef hash. Black, you can't be messing people up over food." Starr shook her head.

I had to assure her that just because I assaulted him, I would never, ever do anything to hurt her.

"Baby, trust me, there was more to it than just a can of corn beef hash. Starr, I will never do anything to hurt you," I promised her. Starr poked me in my chest, "Oh, I'm not worrying about that, 'cause if you so much as try to hurt me, I'll cut your ass too short to shit!" She laughed.

"Okay, so now, do we go together?" I smiled at her.

Starr rolled her eyes to the back of her head and smacked her lips. "Black, ain't nobody saying go together no more. From this day forward, I'm your woman and you're my man. Simple as that. Bet?" she asked.

"Bet." I smiled.

Then Starr kissed me softly on the lip and we sealed the deal. There was something else that I needed to know because it had been on my mind.

"Oh, by the way, who was that dude I saw you leaving with in the old raggedy Cadillac? You know, the one you left with the same day of the concert when we caught the ride home from Earl," I asked.

Starr laughed at me and hugged me around my neck. "That was my cousin. He lives in Fredericksburg. I knew you were watching out the window, so I hugged him before I got into the car just to make you jealous."

"Yeah, you used him to try and make me jealous just like you did Malcolm," I laughed.

"Black, I just be messing with you. I don't want nobody else." Starr assured me by following up her statement with a few kisses around my neck. I reached inside my back pocket and pulled out the gift that I had for her.

"Here, baby, I made this for you while I was locked up." I smiled, handing her the gift. I hoped and prayed that she would like it because I had put a lot of thought into the painting.

Starr opened the scroll, and her eyes lit up like firecrackers on the Fourth of July.

"Ooh, my God! Thank you so much. I like it, Black. Nobody has ever done anything like this for me. Did you paint this yourself?" she asked.

"I sure did," I answered. I had hand-painted a picture of the Last Supper. It was an original piece that I had named "The Gorilla Black Version." The painting included me, Keon, Putt, Lucky, Head, Starr, Cocoa, and Baije.

"Well, it's getting late and I know you need your beauty rest, so I'll leave you be." I stood to leave.

"Okay, Boo. Do you think we can go to the movies this weekend?" Starr asked.

"Sure. What do you want to see? " I answered without thinking.

"Can we go to see *School Daze,* since you were locked up when it came out earlier this year? It's playing for ninety-nine cents over at the Westover Theatre," Starr asked.

"Yeah, I'll love to go see *School Daze* with you."

Starr gave me another light peck on the lip, and I went home a happy man. As soon as I stepped foot into the house, the phone rang. I ran to the kitchen and snatched it from the wall.

"Hello?" I wondered who could be calling so late.

It was Starr. "Boo, I forgot to tell you that somebody called me tonight and told me that you beat up Gold Tooth Earl in Henrico. Is that true?" she asked.

Starr had just talked about my quick temper, so I was reluctant to tell her the truth but I wasn't about to start our relationship off on the wrong foot by telling lies, so I answered honestly.

"Yes, I did."

"Okay, I just wanted to know whether or not it was true. Black, I just want you to know that I don't want any of these dudes out here in the street. Like I told you tonight, from now on, it's me and you," she promised.

"All right, Starr. One love, baby." I gave her a big smile through the telephone.

"One love, Boo." She smiled back.

Finally, I was in a committed relationship with Starr. I wasn't sure if Gold Tooth Earl was going to try and come back, but in any event, I wasn't sweating his punk ass. I sat up for a while, trying to think of the best way to tell Momma that I had lost my job. I knew eventually that I would also have to tell Starr. I had made plans to take her to the movies, and although the movie was only ninety-nine cents, I didn't have one copper penny. I had borrowed twenty dollars the day before from Lulu 'cause I needed something in my pocket until payday, and I had just given that twenty to Gold Tooth Earl, which left me broker than a broke dick dog. The only thing left in my pockets were lint and lint balls, and lint and lint balls, damn sure, couldn't pay our way into the theater. I got up to get me something to drink from the refrigerator. Momma's footsteps startled me.

"Hey, Mom." I spoke to her as she walked into the kitchen.

Momma held both hands on her hips. She jumped straight to the point.

"I heard you earlier when you came in with your loud-ass friends, but I was too tired to get up. Look, I'm going to make this easy for you, 'cause I know you been trying all night to figure out how you was going to tell me. I called your job looking for you and Gurdy told me that she had to fire you and Putt because ya'll have been acting a fool at work."

"Momma, that's not true," I attempted to tell her.

"Boy, don't you interrupt me when I'm talking to you. Let me tell you this, you can't stay here for free. So, you better do whatever you have to do to get some money because I still want my goddamn money every two weeks. You grown now and I'll be damn if I'm going to take care of your black ass. So, if you got to get out there and sell your ass, then that's what the fuck you better do!" she yelled, stormed out of the kitchen, and headed back up to her room.

I mumbled underneath my breath, *I got fired because I didn't take in the birth certificate.*

Momma yelled back downstairs as if she had read my mind. "And if you keep talking back, I'll throw your ass out of here right now!" she growled.

I left the kitchen and flopped back down on the couch. I turned the tube to CNN. The only way we had cable television was because I was paying for it. I sat there, scared, lost, and confused and not knowing what to do. I was afraid that Momma would carry out her threat and throw me out on my ass. I remembered what it felt like when we had been evicted from Matthew Heights. Having all of my personal belongings thrown out for all the neighbors to see was one of the most humiliating things that I had ever endured. There was no way in hell that I was going to let that happen to me again.

I had made up my mind that I was going to start looking for

work immediately. I figured I'd put in an application at McDonald's. I even thought about applying to the Virginia Laundry, where Lulu worked. I grew tired, so I stood up to change out of my work pants and into my night shorts. I cleared my pockets; flipping them inside out, I laid the contents from my pockets on the table. As I was clearing my pockets, I spotted the torn-off piece of paper that Skilow had written his numbers on. With no job, no money for the movie, and Momma riding my back, the idea of looking for a job quickly went out the window. Desperate times called for desperate measures. I would have to put in applications, then wait to be called for an interview. I figured I could hook up with Skilow and make a few dollars until I could get back on my feet. I ran into the kitchen, grabbed the phone off the wall, and stretched it into the pantry. I tried him at his home in New York first. A dude answered the phone and told me to page him. I paged the number and waited patiently by the phone. Within two minutes, the phone rang back.

"Yeah," I spoke into the receiver.

"Who dis?" the voice on the other end asked.

"It's Black, from Richmond, Fairfield Court, man," I answered.

"My man B. You called. No need to say another word. Where are you calling me from?" he inquired.

"I'm at home," I told him.

"You ready?" Skilow questioned.

"As I'm gone be," I shot back at him. I had to be just as cool as them niggas from up north.

"Check it, B. I'll be that way around four p.m. today," he said.

I glanced around the wall, checking the clock in the kitchen. It was already 1:30 in the morning. "Nawh, Low, it's still light out around that time. What about ten o'clock?" I suggested, already thinking ahead of the game.

"Okay, that's cool. Where should I meet you?" he asked.

"Behind the Cool Lane Bowling Alley," I told him.

"Bet," he agreed.

I was about to end my conversation with him when he said, "Yo, B, don't bring a gang of niggas with you, man, 'cause that ain't how I do business. Bring your stick man, Putt. I like him; that nigga right there got your back. So, stick with him," Skilow said, telling me shit about Putt that I already knew.

"I hear you, Low."

"A'ight, B. Later," he said.

"One love," I countered, and then I placed the receiver in the cradle and returned to the couch. I laid down, resting my head on the pillow, and I felt a little better knowing that I was in the process of resolving my money problems.

Chapter 29

It only took a couple of years for a nigga to come up. I was running shit over Fairfield and had the entire city of Richmond's cocaine market on lockdown. I started out as a nickel-and-dime hustler, but once I proved that I knew how to get money, Skilow stepped me up by trusting me with small amounts of weight. Not being one to hustle for another nigga, I let Skilow know how I felt about it. I ended my commitment to him, and he and I became business partners. Skilow wasn't a jealous type dude, so he had no problem with the new arrangement. He turned me on to all of his connects, and soon my pockets stretched just as long as his did. My crew was loyal and stuck it out with me while I was trying to build up, so of course I kept them all on the payroll.

I ran my operation in a professional manner. I attribute much of my success to the customer-service principles that I had learned from working at Church's Chicken. I knew from first-hand experience how critical customer satisfaction was to a successful business. I knew that a good-quality product, trustworthy employees, and access to service were the most crucial components for any business. So I made sure that my product was always on point. I hired testers, professional cokeheads who got freebies for trying out my product before it hit the street. I hired the best employees—loyal niggas with no drug habits—so I didn't have to worry about anybody taking from me. And in order for my customers to have access to my product at all times, I produced work schedules. I had corner hustlers who worked around the clock, so there was access to my product twenty-four hours a day, seven days a week, 365 days year. On weekend and holidays, my people worked even harder, because the demand for cocaine was greater during those times. Back then, it was a tradition for people to get gassed up on weekends and holidays; and because getting fucked up had become the American way of life, I respected the needs of the American people.

My corner hustlers were the type of dudes who sold drugs for a living and had no hopes or dreams of doing anything else with their life except making fast money. They liked nice clothes, drove fast cars, and had plenty of women; but at the end of the day, they weren't millionaires, simply because many of them didn't have millionaire potential, or because they were just fine being exactly where they were—on the corner. I had no problem with their lack of aspiration, because after all, big dreams ain't for everybody.

Me, on the other hand, I aspired to be a millionaire. So, two years later, I had a cool half a million stashed away and me and my girl were living the American dream. The first big piece of money that I made, I used to have Keon's body exhumed from the old pet cemetery. I reburied him at Oakwood Cemetery, which was the resting place of most folks from Richmond's Churchill. I visited Keon on a regular basis and kept fresh-cut flowers on his grave, and when I couldn't pay him a visit, Starr was responsible to take care of things.

Starr and I had weathered our fair share of ups and downs but for the most part our relationship was good. I gave her anything and everything she wanted and then some. She stayed laced in the latest fashions. She drove a brand new 1989 midnight black Cadillac, with custom-made all-white leather seats. Her seats were trimmed in black leather and the word STARR was cut into the headrest. The emblem of a star was embossed into the seats.

Starr stood by my side when I was on the come-up. She would hide coke in her pussy when we traveled or stash my product in places that nobody but her knew about. Starr was the Bonnie of all Bonnies, my needle in a haystack, my eyes behind my back. Starr was without a doubt my ride or die chick.

While my girl stayed dressed fresh to death in the latest clothes, jewels, and furs, I kept it simple. I rocked blue or khaki Dickey uniforms every single day except when we were stepping out to a concert or party. The only thing that I spent any real money on was shoes. I wore a different pair of kicks every day; you rarely ever saw me wear the same pair twice. I drove an army green Range Rover—well, at least everybody else drove it for me because I didn't have a driver's license.

Starr and I lived in a mini-mansion in a rural area on the outskirts of Richmond. The closest neighbor was about three miles away, and that was just the way I liked and needed it to be. Keeping a low profile had kept me out of trouble and people out of my business. In the two years that I had been hustling, I had never had any hiccups with the law. At that point in my life, life was fantastic. I had been dealt a good hand and I had absolutely no regrets.

• • •

We were out on the strip one day when Big Booty Trisha and Portia came balling down the block. Portia had spent several years away in the military. When she returned, she decided that she liked women. Portia and Trisha were a hot item. They did everything together: lived together, hustled together, even tricked together. They hurried over to me, increasing their pace.

"Yo, Black, can you tell one of your people to look out for us, because I'm broke. I'll get you straight tomorrow," Portia begged, patting at her pockets for a more dramatic effect.

Head jumped in. He couldn't stand beggars; regardless of how much money they had spent with him, Head didn't give anybody shit for free. "Don't give them shit, Black. When them niggas got money, they go everywhere else and spend it, but as soon as they broke, they come over here expecting you to look out for them," he griped.

"Ain't nobody talking to you." Portia frowned.

Head laughed in Portia's face. "Yo, Portia, if your girl sucks my dick, I'll give ya'll enough coke-em-up to last the rest of the week." He grabbed his crotch.

Trisha covered her mouth and whispered to Portia, "Baby, I'll do it," with a look of desperation on her face. Then Trisha looked over at me. "Hey, Black, come on. Let me get some of them feel goods," Trisha begged.

"Trisha, I ain't got no mutherfucking feel goods, and you better not let me find out that you out here sucking dick for you and Portia to get high. Portia, what the fuck is wrong with you, got that girl selling her ass and slobbing on knobs for you?" I snapped.

Portia threw her hands up. "Black, that was her idea," she said.

"Yeah, but you ain't straighten that shit out either. If she is willing to trick, you know you're going to let her do it, and that shit ain't right, Portia!" I fumed.

Just then, Starr returned with my can of corn beef hash and a grape Shasta soda. She sat it on the hood of somebody's parked car. Trisha stood there shaking like she was about to pee on herself.

"Starr, take Trisha in the house to use the bathroom before she pees on herself and then throw on your sneakers, baby," I added.

"Throw on my sneakers for what, Boo?" Starr tossed me a confused look.

" 'Cause we're about to see if Trisha can outrun you," I told her, initiating a race between Starr and Trisha. If Trisha wanted to get high, then I was going to make her ass work for it honestly.

Starr laughed. "Outrun who? Baby, those Huguenot High School track days are over. Trisha's ass can't outrun me." She laughed, then hugged Trisha around the neck. Starr was cool like that; although Trisha and Portia was cokeheads and stayed gassed up most of the time, Starr never treated them any differently. In fact, she enjoyed seeing them whenever they came into the neighborhood.

Head insulted Trisha again. "Yeah, Trisha can't outrun Starr, 'cause Trisha is a mutherfucking crack star, not a track star," he joked.

Trisha rolled her eyes at Head. "Forget you," she mumbled underneath her breath and Starr carried her off to the bathroom.

I was sick of listening to Head disrespect Trisha and I blamed Portia for not defending her girl. "See, Portia, that's what I'm talking about. How you gone let a nigga disrespect your girl? Portia, if you gone act like a nigga, then act like a nigga. You come back from the army acting like you a starch butch. Portia, you ain't no butch for real. What your ass need to do is take lessons from Dyke Demetria from Nine Mile Road," I told her.

"Who is Dyke Demetria?" Portia asked.

Portia had obviously missed out on a lot because everybody in the city knew Dyke Demetria. Man, woman, animal, or child.

Dyke Dee was a young legend in the town. I explained to Portia who the person was that she needed to take butch lessons from.

"Dyke Dee is the baddest butch that ever walked the streets of Richmond. Dyke Dee is so bad that some people call her Big Daddy. One time, she beat a nigga's ass down to the ground just because the nigga corrected her when she referred to a twenty-dollar bill as a dove and not a dub. Man, them niggas fought for hours; they even stopped in between rounds to take a break."

Putt laughed. "Yep, Dyke Demetria beat that nigga's ass for the right to call a twenty-dollar bill a dove," he backed the story up.

"Dee swore to God that a twenty-dollar bill was referred to as a dove, because she said that back in the 1800s, there was a picture of a bird imprinted in the face of the bill. She was wrong, but she was close. In all actuality, the twenty-dollar bill in 1800 had a vignette of an eagle in the face. She may have been wrong about the type of bird that was printed on old money, but at least her ass knew a little something about history, particularly when it came to scratch," I added.

Putt and Lucky fell out laughing. They had often referred to the beat-down as the fight of the century. Portia stood there listening intensely. I continued, "The funny thing about the whole incident was that the dude she beat had no idea why a twenty-dollar bill was called a dub. He was fighting about some shit that he knew nothing about. He heard everybody else calling a twenty a dub, so like everybody else, he started saying it too."

"Man, you should have seen it. Dyke Dee beat the hell out of the nigga," Lucky said as he fell all over a parked car laughing.

Head stood there but said nothing. Then, despite everything I had just said, he interjected. "Shit, don't nobody know why it's called a dub. Ain't nobody trying to figure out where slang comes from. Slang is just a part of street life or living in the hood," he complained. I finished off the can of hash and sat it down on the hood of the car.

"Man, I read somewhere that the nickname dub originated back in the nineteenth century during the Confederacy. A double sawbuck comes from the wooden legs of a sawhorse, which form an X, and X is the Roman number for ten. Since X twice equals twenty, that's how they came up with dub, which actually means double." I shared what I knew.

"Man, what the fuck does a double sawbuck or whatever the fuck you just said have to do with money?" Head griped.

I looked at him. "Fuck if I know. I ain't finish reading that part yet. All I know is that somewhere, somehow, our black asses starting calling rims and twenty-dollar bills dubs, when we don't have a clue. I even tried to look up the word dub in the slang dictionary and that shit ain't even in there." Everybody fell out laughing.

"Damn, man," they mused.

"Anyway, the moral of the story, Portia, is that if you gone be a nigga, then act like a nigga," Head interjected again, quoting what I had said to Portia minutes before.

"Dyke Dee might have been wrong, but her ass fought for those bragging rights. After that fight right there, Demetria was the only nigga in the city that was allowed to call a twenty-dollar bill a mutherfucking dove," Putt spat.

Portia shook her head. "Man, you mean to tell me that somebody was fighting over something as stupid as that?" she asked.

We all nodded our heads.

"Damn, man, Richmond niggas be fighting over some dumb shit," Portia commented.

I grabbed my drink and finished it off in one gulp. "Ain't got nothing to do with Richmond. Niggas all over the world are fighting over dumb shit," I spat.

Starr and Trisha returned, but Starr wasn't wearing her sneakers.

"Wait a minute, baby. Where are your tennis shoes?" I asked.

"Tennis shoes? If we gone do this, let's do it the right way. This is going to be a sho'nuff throw-down project race. We're about to run right here, barefooted, in the middle of the street, on the hot-ass blacktop!"

The crowd went wild. "Ooh shit! It's on!" they screamed.

"Hold up, hold up one minute now!" Portia said. "What's in this for Trisha if she wins?" The talk we had given her about Dyke Dee and how she needed to toughen up had already started to work on her.

I responded, "If Trisha wins, I will supply ya'll with fifty dollars' worth a coke a day, for the next thirty days. If Starr wins, then ya'll don't get shit, plain and simple."

The idea of free coke for thirty days was music to Portia's ears. She got up close and personal in Trisha's ear. "Girl, you better win this mutherfucking race!" she growled, letting Big Booty Trisha know that losing wasn't an option.

Starr and Trisha took their positions. Putt yelled, "On your mark, get ready, get set, go!" and the girls took off running. Within seconds, Starr left a smoke trail behind Trisha as she took the lead. Trisha tried relentlessly to catch up to her, her booty bouncing on her back as she ran.

Suddenly, Starr began to slow down as Trisha increased her speed. Trisha ran past Starr so fast, she looked like Jackie Joyner-Kersey on crack. Starr stopped running dead in her tracks, then fell over, collapsing in the middle of the street. I ran over to her.

"Starr! Starr!" I called out to her but she wasn't responding. I dropped to the ground beside her, snatched my T-shirt off, and placed it under her head. Starr gazed up at me. Her eyes were open and her lips were moving, but nothing was coming out. "Help me get her into the house," I told Putt.

I lifted Starr in my arms and carried her to Suga Momma's house. Putt helped me inside and I placed my baby on the couch. Starr began to cry, more worried about me than herself.

"Boo, I just made you lose fifteen hundred dollars," she worried.

"Nawh, baby, don't worry about that." I rubbed her head, trying to comfort her with my every stroke. "Putt, I need a cold washcloth," I told my righthand man.

Starr's breathing was sporadic, but she desperately tried to talk. "I don't know what happened. I felt a sharp pain in my chest, then I couldn't catch my breath. I'm sick and tired of this happening to me," she whined.

Putt came back and handed me the cold washcloth, and I dampened her face with it.

"She will be all right," I told Putt, who was just as concerned as I was.

"Ai'ght, man. Call me if you need something else. I'm going back up top to make sure niggas doing what they're supposed to be doing," he said.

"Thanks, Putt." Starr managed a weak smile.

Putt leaned over and kissed Starr on her forehead. "Ai'ght, li'l sis, take it easy."

I propped my baby's head and feet up with pillows and headed into the kitchen to get her a cold glass of water. I was coming out of the kitchen when I heard a loud screeching sound, then a loud bang. I ran to the front door to see what was up.

"Black, Crazy Chris just got hit by a car!" the neighborhood gossip box, Mousey, yelled. I turned to Starr. I hated to leave her but I needed to see what was happening on my block. If somebody had gotten hurt, then that meant 5-0 would be coming any minute. I needed to clear my team from the streets.

"You gone be okay, baby?" I asked her.

"Yeah, Boo, go ahead. You need to see what's going on out there," she said, understanding my need to be gone for a minute. I hurried back up the block, only to find Crazy Chris lying in a puddle of blood.

"What happened to him? Who hit him!" I demanded.

Mousey was the first to start talking. "Crazy Chris was chasing Big Booty Trisha across the street because she got on red shorts and the man over there hit him!" he rambled, talking fast as he pointed to the car on the sidewalk with the man still slouched over in it.

I glanced over my shoulder at the crowd and realized that half of the people on the strip were wearing red. I didn't think it was fair that Crazy Chris had to be subjected to the color red if it provoked him. I didn't think it was right for him to live captive in his own neighborhood; constantly being reminded of his past because mutherfuckers insisted on wearing the fire color. Chris may have been crazy but he was human, and as Thomas Jefferson once said, he was entitled to life, liberty, and the pursuit of happiness. I knew that I had to put a stop to the madness before somebody else was seriously hurt. Chris beating a nigga down was one thing, but him being hit by a car was a horse of another color.

I took in a deep breath and turned to face the crowd. "From now on the color red is prohibited, and if anybody is caught wearing red in Fairfield Court, they will have to answer to me!" I broadcasted loud enough for the whole neighborhood to hear. The mother of one little boy snatched her son out of his little red wagon and ordered him inside to change his red shirt.

Apparently, the serious look on my face told everybody that I was not on joke time because those that were wearing red hurried inside to change out of their clothing. From then on, the color red was prohibited in my hood.

Just like that, I shut it down!

Chapter 30

Ms. Irene phoned from MCV Hospital insisting that Starr get to the ER right away. When we arrived, we were escorted to a waiting area where the hospital chaplain prayed with Ms. Irene and Suga Momma. We joined them in a prayer circle, and with all heads bowed, the chaplain read from the book of John, chapter 8, verse 2 to 11. *He that is without sin, let him cast the first stone.* Starr and I had no idea why she had been called to the hospital, until Suga Momma broke her years of silence, deciding at the moment that it was time that Starr learned the truth.

"Starr, we need to talk to you," Suga Momma said, sliding over next to Starr on the hospital sofa chair. The expression on Suga Momma's face was so tight, not one of the wrinkles from her aging skin could be seen. By the way she looked, I knew then that whatever it was she needed to tell Starr had to be serious. The hospital chaplain gave Starr a comforting pat on the shoulder, then he left the room. Ms. Irene joined Suga Momma and Starr on the sofa chair, tears forming in her eyes before she broke down crying.

"Baby, what we have to tell you is not going to be easy," Ms. Irene jumped in, not allowing Suga Momma the opportunity to take charge of the conversation with her granddaughter. Ms. Irene was terribly upset.

Suga Momma's face soon filled up with tears but she was still strong enough and wanted to be the one to break the news to Starr, so she did just that. "Irene, please let me," she insisted.

Ms. Irene turned her head in the opposite direction and gave a confirming nod. Starr glanced back and forth at the two of them; she was annoyed with the long wait.

"Dang, what is it?" Starr frowned at the two old ladies.

"Well, Starr, Chris is your brother," Suga Momma said flatly, her voice never changing in range.

I looked at Starr to read the expression on her face because I was surprised at what I had just heard. As far as Starr knew, she had been an only child, so I wasn't sure how she would take news of a brother. I didn't want to see her upset over this secret. I squatted down beside her and rested my hand on her knee.

Starr's nose flared up and I knew then that she was angry. "How is that?" Starr asked, nose still turned up in the air.

Suga Momma began to explain. "Well, baby, my son, your father, Christoff St. John Williams, fathered a son with Irene's daughter Trudy. I hate to tell you this, but Chris is that son. Chris is really Irene's grandson, not a foster child," Suga Momma said matter of factly, obviously tired of holding on to the secret and just ready to put it all out on the table. Suga Momma was a caring person, and I knew that she loved Starr with all her heart, but the way she spit out the news lacked compassion. I brushed it off as to her being nervous and ashamed.

Starr smacked her lips and shook her head. She was getting more pissed off by the minute. "So I'm not an only child. Is that what ya'll are telling me?" She sucked her teeth, looking back and forth between the two women. Before Suga Momma or Ms. Irene could answer, Starr kept on talking.

"Better yet, what ya'll are telling me is that my father was a cheater because after all, he was married to my mother," she said, her voice full of anger and disgust.

Suga Momma wiped her tears, and responded, "Yeah, baby, he cheated on your mother. You and Chris are seven years apart."

"So your daughter knew my dad was married but she fucked him anyway!" Starr snapped, getting close and personal in Ms. Irene's face, sending her spit flying across the room.

Ms. Irene broke down crying all over again.

It was one thing for Starr to be upset, but to be rude and disrespectful to Ms. Irene was unacceptable. Suga Momma jumped in, correcting Starr right away.

"Now, Starr, you know better! I know you are upset but you need to watch your mouth. Don't you talk like that to Irene; you know you better respect your elders!" Suga Momma interjected, snapping back at Starr while shaking her finger in Starr's face.

Starr sighed heavily, then moved her head away from Suga Momma's finger but she dared not talk back to her grandmother.

Ms. Irene calmed herself down, blew her nose, then tried talking to Starr. "Baby, my daughter Trudy made a bad decision when she got involved with your father," Ms. Irene agreed.

Starr nodded in agreement, then huffed and puffed.

"Why are ya'll telling me this now? What does any of this have to do with me?" she said, fuming.

" 'Cause, baby, the hospital doesn't have any type O blood nor does the Virginia blood bank and your brother needs a blood transfusion ASAP or else he might die," Suga Momma told her.

Starr jumped up off the couch and stood to her feet. "Then why are we all sitting around here for?" she growled. Starr took off running into the hallway, yelling and screaming like a mad woman, "Nurse, get me a doctor. I need a doctor now!"

• • •

Starr fainted while giving blood, which caused her to be admitted into the hospital. It was then that doctors discovered that she had pericarditis, inflammation of the pericardium, the thin sac that surrounds the heart. Upon learning of Starr's medical condition, Suga Momma disclosed that Starr's mother, Jasmine, had heart problems, too. Starr didn't know much about her parents. She had been told since childhood that she and her parents were in a car accident and that both of her parents died and that she was the only survivor.

Starr's mother, Jasmine, was a runaway from Memphis who fled to Richmond to escape the physical abuse she endured from her stepfather after her mother died. Suga Momma found the young girl sleeping outside in a Dumpster next to the hotel where Suga Momma worked as a cook. Instead of calling the police or child protective services, Suga Momma took her home to live with her. Suga Momma had always wanted a daughter and planned to raise Jasmine as her own, but her plan backfired when Jasmine and Suga Momma's only child, Christoff, became lovers. The two later married, and Starr was the product of that union.

Over the next few weeks, Starr and I spent a lot of time with Crazy Chris. We took him shopping, bought him new glasses, got his hair cut, and made him look normal. For his birthday, we rounded up all the kids from the neighborhood, rented four coach buses and a few shuttle vans, and headed to the Washington Zoo. Starr enjoyed her time spent with Chris, and although

Chris couldn't verbally express his appreciation, it was obvious that he enjoyed his time spent with her because whenever she came around, he lit up like a Christmas tree. Chris's issue with the color red still existed, but Starr could wear whatever color she wanted around him.

Chapter 31

Somewhere between Richmond and D.C., Starr must have lost her damn mind. While we were at the Washington Zoo celebrating Chris's birthday, Starr accused me of staring at a D.C. chick with a long weave down her back, fake eyelashes, and tight-fitting Parasuco jeans. I swore on everything that I wasn't checking the chick, but Starr didn't believe me. As we boarded the bus to leave the zoo, she made it clear that I was not to sit next to her. She refused to talk to me on the bus ride home and as soon as we made it to Fairfield, Starr jumped off the bus and headed to her car. Baije followed behind her. I walked over to the Caddy and stuck my head in the driver-side window.

"Starr, why you acting like that? You need to stop tripping; you know I wasn't looking at that girl like that." Starr just smacked her lips and rolled her eyes at me. Honestly, I was looking at the girl, not because I thought she was attractive but because I wa checking out her jeans. Chicks in Richmond weren't rocki

Parasuco jeans and I wanted to ask the girl where I could get a few pairs because I thought my girl would look good in them. Starr didn't want to hear a word that I had to say. She started up the engine and put the car in drive.

"Starr, where are you going?" I asked.

Baije said, "Black, we're going to the mall to buy us an outfit. You know the Beast from the East is at the Showplace Arena tonight," she said.

Starr just sat there staring out of the window. Starr was spoiled and stubborn as hell at times. I knew that she needed time to calm down, so I just backed away from the car.

"All right, I'm not gone hold ya'll up. Do ya'll have enough money?" I asked, pulling a wad of money from my front pocket. I handed the roll of money to Starr, but she wouldn't take it.

"Give that shit to the trick in D.C.!" she shot at me and sped off.

. . .

My attitude was messed up the rest of the evening. I couldn't wait for the show to end because I was planning to bite off a few choice words to Starr once we met up at home. I was outside on the strip with my corner hustler niggas when Shelton came speedballing through the cut. He was sweating bullets and walking crackhead-ass fast.

"Yo, Black. Man, where Frankie at? I'm trying to get some of that good-ass crack you got him working with. Man, where are all your workers? I don't see any of them out here, what's happening, man?" Shelton yelled out loud, straight up disrespecting me and lying at the same time. My workers were out on the block, his crackhead ass just hadn't looked for them. I was already having a bad day and the sight of Shelton pissed me off even further so I tepped to him.

"Nigga, what the fuck is your problem? Why you screaming

my mutherfucking name like you crazy?" I grabbed his raggedy ass and shook him. Just as I was about to go upside his head, Shelton covered his head and ducked.

"Go 'head, Black. I'm just trying to get high, man. You got anything on you?" he asked, then looked at me dumbfounded 'cause he already knew the answer to his stupid-ass question.

Putt stepped in, trying to save Shelton from a beat-down. "Go 'head, Shelton, man. Get from around here 'cause he ain't in the mood for your bullshit tonight." Putt slightly shoved him in the back. Shelton resisted and refused to walk away. He didn't heed the warning that my right hand man had given him. Instead of getting the hell off my block, the nigga screamed my name again.

"Black, if you give me a couple of rocks tonight, I'll look out for you tomorrow. I'mma be boosting all day tomorrow at Chesterfield Mall, and I'll be sure to pick up some fly shit for Starr," he said, begging and bartering with me. I checked Shelton up and down and let out a slight chuckle because he was a pitiful sight. See, Shelton used to be a high roller back in the day. He had plenty of women, nice cars, fly clothes—the whole nine, but he violated the number one rule for hustlers, which is *never get high on your own supply*. Shelton went from living in a hundred-thousand-dollar home, which was a lot of cheddar back then for a home in Richmond, to living on the street.

I watched him closely as he bounced around on the sidewalk, begging and trying to barter with me. I remembered the first time that I had actually seen Shelton. It was the night that Mrs. Gurdy had fired me, Putt, and Chiquita from Church's Fried Chicken. Shelton was the high roller in the lobby that boasted about leaving Church's and taking his girl to Omar's for dinner. He was the same dude who made a comment about Putt being nasty for trying to have sex in the restroom. Now, years later, the dude who used to be sharp as a tack and clean as a tick was shitting and pissing behind buildings and washing his ass whenever he could in service station bathrooms. I laughed to myself when I thought about how he had fallen off. I headed across the street to stand by myself because one more word out of Shelton and I knew I was going to explode. I stepped across the street and stood next to a tree. Putt continued talking to Shelton. He warned him again to leave.

"Black, let me talk to you for a second," Shelton screamed again. Then he had the balls to cross the street behind me. Shelton had just violated two major rules. Disrespecting my name and broadcasting my business in public. On top of it, he wasn't even addressing me correctly.

"Black, Black, let me talk to you, man," he repeated himself like a broken record.

I waited on the sidewalk and as soon as he stepped foot in front of me, I grabbed a Coca-Cola bottle from the ground and cracked him upside his head. I hit him so hard he fell to the ground and blood gushed from his head. I stood over him and kicked him a couple of times.

"What's my mutherfucker name?!" I yelled at him.

Shelton squirmed around on the ground, blood racing from his head.

"Help me, somebody help. I'll look out for a nigga, just help me," he begged.

"What's my mutherfucking name? Say my name, nigga, and say it right! " I shouted at him over and over again.

Putt and a few members from the crew ran over and pulled me away from him.

Putt tried to help his dumb ass out. "Shelton, you ain't from around here. You know the rules, man. What's his mutherfucker name?" he shouted at him.

Shelton laid there on the ground. He knew better than to try to get up. He looked up at us; we had him surrounded in a circle.

"What's my mutherfucking name? Say my name, nigga, and say it right!" I gave him one more chance. Shelton wasn't answering me fast enough so I kicked him in the ass again.

Shelton screamed out loud. "Ah, please stop," he whined. "It's Gorilla Black. Your name is Gorilla Black. Now please, just let me go. I'll make it up to you," he begged.

I nodded for my crew to get him out of Fairfield.

"Get the fuck from around here!" Putt ordered as one of my corner hustlers helped him up from the ground. Shelton took off running through the cut. As Shelton ran clean out of sight, I told my crew what I suspected.

"I need everybody to keep an eye on him. I think Shelton is 5-0."

"Why you say that?" Putt wondered.

"The way that nigga was screaming my name, it's almost like he was recording me or something," I answered.

• • •

Around midnight, my pager went off with code 9-1-1. I dashed to the corner pay phone and dialed the number back. It was Baije and she was out of breath.

"Baby girl, what's wrong?" I questioned.

Baije didn't waste any time explaining. "Black, we were dancing, when all of a sudden, this dude walked up to Starr and said something to her. Then, the next thing I know, he smashed her in the face." As she told the story, her voice trembled one minute, and fire raged in her voice the next.

"Who is the nigga? Where he at?" I demanded.

My crew overheard me. They rushed over to the pay phone and stood beside me while Baije continued.

"I don't know who he was, but the half-white-looking dude he was with came and took him away. Black, ask Head if he remembers the albino dude that use to hang at skateland over Southside, because that's who he is with."

I turned to Head and asked, "Do you know of an albino dude that use to hang at the skateland over Southside?"

Head nodded and snapped his finger, trying to remember the albino's name. "Yeah, I remember the nigga. They call him Whiteboy. Why, what's up with that nigga? He did something to my girl?" Head asked, as he tried getting the phone from me.

I snatched the phone back from him.

"Baije, pass the phone to Starr!" I told her.

"She doesn't want to talk to you, Black," Baije said.

"Just ask her if she's a'ight and if she knows the nigga's name."

"B, man, what the fuck is going on? Starr and Baije all right?" Head asked. I didn't answer right away because I was trying to gather as much information as I could.

I heard loud background noises, the phone drop and Baije's voice fade away.

"Baije!" I called out to her, but she didn't answer. "Baije! Starr!"

"Man, she dropped the phone!" I yelled.

Just then, Baije came back to the line. "Black, I stepped away from the phone to talk to this dude 'cause he said he knew who hit Starr," she huffed.

"Who is he? Who the fuck is the nigga that put his hands on something that belongs to me!" I screamed.

"Yeah, who is the nigga?" some members of the crew said.

"Black, the dude's name is Dice and he is from Southside-Afton Apartments," she told me.

"Dice? Did you say Dice? Baije, are you sure that's the nigga's name?" I needed to be certain that I was going after the right ınk.

"Yeah, Black. They say his name is Dice, 'cause he likes to roll them mutherfuckers!"

I ordered Baije to take Starr home and stay there with her. I slammed the phone down and ordered a couple of my loyal workers to go to my house to watch over the ladies. I turned to my crew, filled with anger.

"Take me to the crap house on Chimbarozo Boulevard," I ordered. "A nigga named Dice from Southside just put his hands on Starr. They say he likes gambling, and since he's been partying on this side of town tonight, I'm sure that's where he gone be."

Chapter 32

We jumped in the car and headed toward Chimbarozo Boulevard, where every major gambler in Churchill did their thang. Since Head liked gambling, he was familiar with the crowd that frequented the place. Head was well known for having a mean streak, so whenever he showed up the owner of the house would have security pat him down. Head handed me his nine-millimeter as we were about to enter, and I hid it underneath my shirt.

The best of the best could be found at this after-hours spot. There were old school heads—professional career gamblers who never worked a day in their life, young bucks who gambled for extra income, and drug boys who already had money but gambled out of gluttony. We stepped inside the hot spot. Cigarette smoke and weed filled the air. A few tricks were scattered throughout the joint, waiting to be picked up by a nigga and taken to the hood, where he'd hit her off with a couple hundred dollars.

The chicks who hung out at the after-hours spots were not the same type of chicks that you would see in the regular nightclubs. These were straight hood chicks; they loved money, knew the game inside and out, and only fucked with well-known, money-getting niggas. Whether it was alcohol, weed, shopping sprees, cocaine, or dope, the chicks that hung in the after-hours spot had some need that only an after-hours-spot nigga could fill. These chicks were not about to waste their time going to a regular club. It just wasn't worth their time. The possibility of them finding a moneymaking nigga at a regular nightclub in Richmond, by their measurement, was slim to none.

We made our way through the crowd, asking a few dudes if they had seen or heard of Dice. A few cats had heard of him, but nobody had seen him. I ran into G, one of the oldest gambling heads I knew. G had been gambling since Thompson Middle School. G's money stretched just as long as the day was short. Funny thing about it was, he never sold drugs a day in his life. All he ever did was shoot craps and run numbers, yet he damn near was a self-made millionare.

"Yo, G, you know a nigga named Dice or an albino dude name Whiteboy from Southside?" I asked him.

G hurried to get inside the bathroom; he was next in line. "Yeah, man, them niggas out back. Hold up, Black, I got to take a leak." He hurried into the restroom to release himself.

I hurried through the crowd and made my way outside. One half-white looking dude with long dreadlocks to his butt looked out of place. It was the albino brother, Whiteboy. I couldn't figure out who he was with so I focused my attention on the crap game. There were four guys shooting dice, and they had raised the stakes to five hundred dollars a shot. Putt, Lucky, and Head fell into the crowd, trying to help me weed out the infamous Dice. There was one dude flossing real hard. He was a dark-skinned brother, slender build, with a low tapered haircut. He was losing money big time, but it seemed as if the more money he lost, the more shit he talked. The dude rolled the dice and continued talking cash shit.

"Scared money don't make money!" He tried his best to intimidate the other crap shooters.

"Yeah, that's what I'm talking about, roll them mutherfuckers, D," Whiteboy encouraged.

Bingo, I said to myself. I knew then that I had my target.

"Yo, Dice," I called his name as if we had been introduced before.

Dice glanced over both of his shoulders to determine where the voice was coming from. He appeared irritated when he couldn't figure it out. I stepped in front of him, stepping over the other dudes, the money, the dice, all that shit. I looked him dead in the eye and nodded at him to let him know that it was I calling his mutherfucking name.

"Man, who the fuck is this interrupting the mufucking crap game? Nigga, what you, 5-0 or something?" He eyed me up and down, the same way dudes check out the new kid on the block or on their tier in the clinker. It was apparent to me that Dice had balls; because if I was 5-0, he wasn't even showing them respect.

"Nawh, Nigga, ain't no mutherfucking 5-0. My name is Black, nigga, Gorilla Black, and I'm going to give you a chance to explain to me why the fuck you put your hand on my girl. And, I'm only giving you a chance to explain for the sake of being fair. Then, after I get your answer, I'mma beat your punk ass anyway, 'cause for real, your answer doesn't matter to me," I said.

Dice balled his face up in a knot and glanced around at the crowd. "Man, who the fuck is this nigga?" he asked, but nobody answered.

"Nigga, I just told you my name. What, nigga, you deaf and dumb?"

Dice snatched his pocket change up from the ground and tucked it away in his saggy pants. This caused all of the other dudes to scramble to get their loot from the ground. Dice gave me a lopsided stare, then gritted his teeth and said, "Man, fuck you and your lying-ass bitch!" he screamed at me, loud enough for everybody inside and outside the after-hours spot to hear him.

All the niggas outside scattered to get out of the way. It was like a scene from a western, when the most gangster dude in town showed up at a bar and everybody cleared the floor in preparation for a showdown. The only exception was, I wasn't a dude from the west. I was Gorilla Black from Churchill, the Eastside of Richmond. I was from mutherfucking Fairfield Court Projects and I was about to let the nigga know that I wasn't no bullshit-ass dude.

Before I knew it, I jabbed Dice in the face, not one but three times repetitively, *bop, bop, bop*. He struggled to keep his balance. Whiteboy ran over, and my crew stopped him dead in his tracks.

"Back up, mufucker," Head told him. "Back up!"

Dice wasn't going out like a punk so he threw his hands up. I backed away from him, and when the nigga rushed toward me, I walked the dog on the nigga's ass! I threw my elbow at him as hard as I could, striking him in the temple. He staggered about half a yard and fell up on the fence.

"Bet nobody jump in this, mutherfucker!" Head and Lucky warned the crowd.

Putt followed up. "That's right; I dare a mutherfucker to jump in this shit. Beat that nigga ass, B," Putt said, egging me on.

Suddenly, Whiteboy pulled a gun from his shirt. "Nawh, ya'll niggas back the fuck up," he said, pointing the gun at the crew.

"What, nigga? You gone shoot us because your boy getting his ass kicked? Nigga, I'll make your bitch ass eat that mutherfucking gun," Lucky shouted.

With all the commotion going on, Dice was able to grab the gun from Whiteboy and he fired it into the air. *POW, POW.* Niggas hurried out of the backyard, but my crew didn't budge. Dice pointed the gun back and forth at us and it was obvious that being in control made him happy. He was smiling as if the shit that was going down was funny.

"Fuck ya'll gone do now, huh, huh?" Dice bounced around the yard, talking cash shit. From the look in his eye, I could tell he didn't know his next move. I realized then that he wasn't happy but nervous as hell. I gave him a minute to figure out what he was gone do, but after he danced around the yard with the gun in his hand for about three minutes, I figured he wasn't going to do a damn thing except smile and talk shit.

I charged him, and we tussled for the gun. The gun fell, and Whiteboy picked it up from the ground and pulled the trigger. As close as he was to me, he missed.

"Go to the car!" I yelled to my boys.

Head and Lucky scurried away, but Putt wouldn't move. He stood there, refusing to leave me.

"Yeah, nigga, who's the punk now?" Whiteboy bit his bottom lip. As he moved in closer, he pointed the gun directly in my face. I backed away from him and tripped over a small tree stump in the ground. When I fell onto my back, he stood over top of me and cocked the barrel of the gun. Just as he was about to pull the trigger, I felt something rub against my stomach. It was Head's nine-millimeter. I pulled it from my waistband, and *boom.* I let off one round, hitting Whiteboy in the torso. He fell over from the shot and hit the ground. His .357 Magnum fell out of his hand. The nigga probably could have had me, but he waited too long to blast off.

I scooted away from him and tried to pull myself up. Dice grabbed Whiteboy's gun from the ground and started after Putt. I sprung up from the ground, like Bruce Lee in an action flick, and yanked Dice by the tail of his shirt with my left hand. Dice spun around and with his finger on the trigger, he tried to pop me, but he wasn't fast enough. I let off two rounds in his chest, *boom, boom*. I dropped his punk ass too, dead on the spot.

"Let's go." Putt grabbed me and we ran from around back. We passed Lucky and Head on the way out.

"Nigga dead," Putt told them. "Let's move it!"

Lucky and Head ran with their burners by their side. Head stopped and turned around to the crowd. He pointed the burner and said, "Ain't nobody see nothing, right? Right?"

Niggas threw their hands up as if to say, *We ain't got nothing to do with it.*

We hurried to the car. Head jumped into the driver seat, and Lucky and Putt threw me into the back. I was still holding onto the gun until Putt snatched it from me.

"Drive across the bridge," Putt yelled to Head.

"They both dead?" Head queried.

"I don't know about Whiteboy, 'cause that nigga was still moving. But that nigga Dice is a goner," Putt told him.

I rocked back and forth as the car sped off. The sound of Lulu's voice was ringing in my ears. *If you ever pull a gun on a mutherfucker you better use it, because he will be back for you if you don't.* I didn't need a mutherfucker to be coming back for me, so I ordered Head to go back.

"If he ain't dead, then I need to go back. Turn around, I have to go back and finish the nigga!" I said as I tried to open the door while the car was moving.

"Nawh, B, we can't go back. Not now, anyway. The block is hot!" Lucky jumped in, trying to calm me down.

The realization that I had just shot two mutherfuckers finally hit me, and the fact that it was possible that I killed one of them hit me even harder. I vomited everything that I had eaten that day and maybe even the day before. Head pulled over to the side of the road and let me out. Never in a million years would I have imagined myself committing murder.

"You all right?" Putt worried.

"Yeah, I'm all right."

Lucky handed me the grape soda that I had in the back seat from early that day and I gargled with it, cleaning the vomit from my mouth.

"Fuck, man, you got vomit all in the car and all on my flavs," Head complained.

"Man, just drive to the bridge so we can toss the gun," Putt said, dismissing Head's arrogance. There we were, in the midst of a murder, trying to figure out our next plan of action, and all Head was worrying about was his ride and his Nike sneakers.

"A'ight, man, which bridge?" Head asked in an irritated tone.

Lucky answered for all of us. "The James River, of course."

We drove to the bridge and Putt tossed the gun. Then we headed to Petersburg, where we checked into a hotel. We called Starr and Baije and asked them to meet us. I knew that the niggas at the after-hours spot wouldn't snitch because the majority of them was from Churchill, so I knew that they had my back. I sat quietly in a chair near the window thinking and rethinking about the events that had transpired. I had just shot two mutherfuckers and possibly killed one of them. Except for the vomit all over my shirt, I was jive a'ight. I never once felt sorry for the dudes that I had shot. Hell, I mean, they asked for it, so they got it. I sure as hell didn't sign on for that shit. I was a drug dealer, a hustler, that's it, that's all. All I ever wanted to do was make money so I could feed my mother and my girl. I never signed on to be a murderer, but when life comes at you fast, sometimes you have to flip the script and break your own rules.

Chapter 33

Dice didn't survive his gunshot wounds, and Whiteboy was left wearing a piss bag. Rumor was that his brother Li'l Wayne and the boys from Afton were planning to come back hard, so I ordered Fairfield Projects on lockdown. No man, woman, or child was to be outside after dark.

Two weeks after the murder, we were at Suga Momma's. Starr refused to talk about what happened with her and Dice at the Showplace Arena, so I still didn't know all the details.

"Starr, did you know that the boy who was killed up Churchill at the after-hours spot was Wayne Jennings' nephew?" Suga Momma asked. She was reading the newspaper and there was an article on the front page about the double shooting and murder.

What she said startled me. "Who?" I inquired.

"Wayne Jennings. Black, you remember Mr. Wayne, don't you? That old pervert that I use to date years ago. The one who tried to molest Starr when ya'll were kids," she added.

"Oh, yeah, I remember him. How could I forget, he's the reason Keon is dead!" I exclaimed. "Didn't Mr. Wayne die a few years after that?" I asked.

"Yeah, he did," Suga Momma said.

I glanced over at Starr, who had never answered her grandmother's question.

"Starr, did you know that the boy that died was Mr. Wayne's nephew?" Suga Momma repeated.

Starr got up from the chair and and sat her empty glass in the sink.

"Yeah, I heard. Come on, Black, I'm ready to go to the mall," Starr responded.

"Yeah, Starr, I know you remember him because Mr. Wayne used to bring his nephews over the house to play with you," Suga Momma said. Starr ignored her; she was ready to go shopping and had no interest in what Suga Momma was talking about.

"Come on, Black, let's get to the mall before they close," she said, all of a sudden in a rush.

Starr was acting weird, so as soon as we left the house and jumped into the car, I asked her, "Starr, how long have you known that Dice was Mr. Wayne's nephew?"

"Please, Black, don't start asking me a lot of questions about that damn boy. Shit, he's dead now anyway, so what difference does it make?" Starr snapped.

"I'm not asking you a lot of questions, Starr. All I want to know is when did you find out that he was Wayne's nephew and why didn't you tell me?" I griped.

"Black, if you gone talk about this all the way to the mall, then maybe we shouldn't go," she said, frowning. I shook my head at her. I didn't have time for Starr's attitude so I let it go.

. . .

Starr shopped for three hours. When we returned to Fairfield, Rosetta Street was blocked off and yellow tape, police, and paramedics surrounded the street. We jumped out of the car and ran over toward the crowd. Mousey ran up to me shaking uncontrollably.

"What happened?" I asked him. Mousey's mouth was trembling so bad that he couldn't speak. He just stood there shaking and crying. I knew then that something terrible had happened, because there was nothing in the world that could shut Mousey up.

I hadn't noticed that everybody on the block was in tears until Starr started screaming to the top of her lungs. I turned around and looked into the crowd. Everyone was crying, even some of the hustlers on the corners.

"Where's Putt, Lucky, and Head?" I yelled. "Where my boys at?"

"Black, calm down, They are okay. They're in your mother's house," Mr. Arnold said, resting his hand on my shoulder.

"Why the cops out here and what's up with the yellow tape?" I asked.

This time, Mousey was able to speak. "Mr. Black. They came through here and killed Lulu and shot your uncle Todd," he cried.

"What!?" I growled.

"Yeah, Mr. Black. You know the dude that got killed named Dice? Well, they say it was his brother Li'l Wayne from Southside. Him and his boys from Afton came through blazing," Mousey managed to tell me.

I glanced around for Starr and noticed through the cut her standing with the rest of the crowd. I ran over, and that's when I spotted Lulu's penny loafer hanging from underneath a bloody sheet.

One of my corner hustlers walked over to me with rage in his eyes. "Man, they ain't have to shoot Lu and Uncle Todd, man.

They ain't have nothing to do with it. We gone get them niggas for this. Don't worry, boss, we gone get 'em," he said while gritting his teeth.

I stood there in silence, thinking back on some of the conversations that Lulu and I had shared. It was Lulu who told me that if you ever pulled a gun on a nigga, that you better use it and make sure the nigga was dead or else he'll be back for you. It was Lulu who told me that after you commit your first murder, you will more than likely vomit or shit on yourself. I, of course, later found one of those acts to be true. Lulu may have lived his life as a gay man, but make no mistake about it; he was one of the toughest men I knew. There wasn't anything about the streets that Lulu couldn't school you on and I loved the nigga for always keeping it real with me.

Lulu would often kick it with me and the crew. He often reminded us to stay loyal to each other, to not let anyone or anything come between us, and although he had a monstrous dope habit, he constantly preached about not getting high off of your own supply. Lulu's favorite saying was, *Re-up but don't gas up*.

I paced back and forth trying to understand how the Afton boys could've gotten through. Then I realized that after we had returned from the mall, we were able to roll through just as easy. It was customary for one of my men to wait for me on the corner so they could get all guns out of any vehicle that I was riding in. But, for some reason, on that day it didn't happen.

"Those mutherfuckers want war, I'll give them war!" I yelled.

I ran three houses down and stashed my burner in the house of one of my loyal customers. I ordered everybody that worked for me to get in position. I ordered Starr to go inside Suga Momma's and to wait for me to come and get her. I dashed across the street. Putt was coming from around back and met up with me.

"Man, where in the fuck is Mattlock? That nigga was suppose

to cover that corner. He was suppose to be on lookout," I said angrily.

Mattlock was one of my lookout kids. And I named him that because he didn't miss a beat. "Putt, how the fuck did those niggas get on this block? Where was Mattlock?" I was mad as hell and unless his mother had died and gone to hell, Mattlock needed one heck of an alibi to get him off the hook.

Putt shook his head. "Man, he said he had just stepped inside to take a leak," Putt said, repeating Mattlock's pitiful excuse.

I couldn't believe what I was hearing. This nigga was inside the house pissing while my people were outside getting gunned down.

"Man, I'mma beat the breaks off of him!" I shouted. "Where the fuck he at?"

"Black, let him go. He already feels bad enough. He's inside your mother's house with Lucky and Head. I got Murk covering his corner," Putt said.

Just then, 5-0 rolled up on me and Putt. A fat cop hung his head out of the passenger-side window. "Hey, Black, can we talk to you for a minute?" he yelled out the window at me.

I turned around and looked his fat ass square in the eye. "Man, I just got here so you ain't got shit to talk to me about!"

"What's that you say, *boy*?" he said.

Putt shoved me away to save me from getting myself into trouble and we disappeared through the cut.

"Fuck you, you fat-ass mutherfucker!" I mumbled underneath my breath.

I spoke to Mattlock about his not being in the right place at the right time. I reminded him that God had made him a boy and gave him a penis for the sole purpose of being able to whip it out and use it outdoors and that while on duty all potty breaks needed to take place outside. Momma informed me that since Uncle

Todd was hospitalized at the VA Hospital and wouldn't be coming back, that I would have to increase her weekly allowance in order to replace the money that she was getting from him.

Lu's family didn't have any money to bury him so I took care of the funeral and burial expenses. I buried him near Keon at Oakwood Cemetery. We were at the burial ground, standing around talking and telling funny stories about Lulu, when Dope Dick David showed up. David took Lulu's death very hard. David and Lu had been having a sexual relationship, which started right after Lulu had given Dope Dick David a beat-down for robbing Uncle Todd and Mr. Arnold. Dope Dick David was crying his heart out at the cemetery, and some people questioned whether or not he was crying so hard because of his lover or the loss of free dope.

Later that evening we rode over to the VA Hospital, which happened to be on the Southside, to check on Uncle Todd. Uncle Todd had no memory of any of us. We were told because of his physical injuries and the post-traumatic stress disorder that he suffered because of the Vietnam War that he would not be leaving the VA Hospital. Momma hadn't gone to see him and she refused to sign any paperwork, so I listed Starr and me as his next of kin.

When darkness fell, we left the VA Hospital and drove around Southside, searching for the boys from Afton. We had heard that they hung out at a reggae club on the corner of Hull Street. We spotted members of the Afton crew in the parking lot of the reggae club. The parking lot was packed with club-goers, and because I didn't believe in doing drive-bys, I ordered Lucky and Head, who were ready to open fire, to chill out. We drove away from the scene, unnoticed and unrecognized.

Chapter 34

Head disobeyed my orders. He rounded up a few other cats and they did a drive-by when the reggae club was closing. An innocent little girl who was riding in a car nearby was shot when they opened fire. When I heard of this, I called an emergency meeting with the leaders of the crew. It was eight o'clock on Sunday morning when we met up. Head jumped out of the car, irritated that he had to get up so early. Baije waited for him inside the rental car.

"What's up?" Head spoke, wiping coal from his eyes. Starr was with me, so I politely asked her to excuse herself. She went over and got inside the rental car with Baije.

"Man, what happened this morning? I hear you and Frankie took it upon yourselves to go back and do a drive-by?" Head looked at me as if I had two heads. He hurled up spit, and shot it on the ground.

"Man, ya'll make me leave the hotel early for this shit! Fuck, man, I'm tired as hell," he grunted. "Shit, Frankie over there. Fuck wrong with his mouth? Why he ain't tell you what happened?" Head griped.

"Hold up, Head, Frankie ain't a mutherfucking leader in the crew. He don't make no decisions. You were in charge, so I'm trying to understand why you took part or allowed that shit to happen," I shot back at him. Head lit a cigarette and leaned back on the car. Just then, Starr opened the passenger-side door of the rental and got out. Baije attempted to get out with her.

"Bitch, didn't I tell you to stay in the mufucking car?" Head chastised her as if she were a toddler in time out being told not to get out of the playpen. Baije quickly got back inside the car and closed the driver-side door.

Starr jumped to Baije's defense. "Girl, if you want to get out of the car, then get out of the car. Baije, he's your man, not your daddy!" she interjected.

Head threw his cigarette to the ground in frustration. "Hold up, Starr, you ain't got shit to do with this, so mind your own mutherfucking business," he yelled, disrespecting my lady.

"Head, you better slow the fuck down. You way out of line now, don't you ever disrespect Starr!" I said. "Besides, Starr is right, you need to stop talking to Baije the way you do. Man, why would you call your own girl a bitch, better yet, why would you call any female a bitch?" I asked him.

"B man, you kill me what that righteous shit. You act like you ain't ever call a girl a bitch or like you ain't ever curse at Starr. Man, you be tripping hard," he said.

Putt and Lucky intervened, because they knew at times me and Head bumped heads and they didn't want things to get out of hand.

"Man, ya'll need to just chill out for a minute," Putt said.

"Let's get back to why we're out here," Lucky added.

I ignored Putt and Lucky because I needed to straighten out the little smart-ass nigga that was standing before me.

"Head, you have never heard me call a woman a bitch and you never will. If you ever do, it'll be the day I'm on my deathbed. I can't stand to hear a man disrespect a woman. It ain't got shit to do with being righteous. It has everything to do with being a man."

Head stepped away from the car. "So, you saying I ain't a man?" he asked as he shrugged his shoulders.

"Come on now, Head, you taking this shit a little too far. That's not what I'm saying," I told him.

"That's what it sounds like to me," Head shot back at me.

"Listen, Head, I'm not going to stand out here and go back and forth with you, arguing like two little-ass girls and shit. I called a meeting to find out why you took it upon yourself to do a mufucking drive-by. I hope you know a little girl was shot because of your decision!"

Head pulled his jeans up 'cause they were falling from his waist. He hurled up more spit and shot it through his teeth. "Black, I'm a grown mufucking man. Yeah, I took it upon myself to go back over there. Fuck them niggas. Them niggas probably thought we were punks or something 'cause we hadn't blast back yet," he said.

"Fuck what them niggas think!" Putt interjected.

"Man, everybody know ain't no mufucking punks over here. Head, timing is everything. That little girl could've been killed," Lucky jumped in.

"So what the fuck? Them niggas killed Lulu and fucked Uncle Todd all up and shit," Head said.

"Yeah, man, and we gone handle that shit when the time is right," I said.

"Black, the time is now! Fuck we waiting on, Christmas?" Head asked sarcastically.

At that point, I knew that Head wasn't on the same type of time like everybody else but I tried rationalizing with him anyway.

"Man, I got this," I told him.

"Whatever, man," he mumbled.

Head was really playing himself that morning. He was getting on my nerves with his smart-ass mouth and all the nasty spitting, so I shot him down quickly.

"Well, too mufucking bad if you don't like the way I'm handling shit. I make the decisions for the crew and if you don't like the way I run my shit, then get the fuck out and leave your mutherfucking badge on the way out the door! That goes for you and anybody else," I snapped.

Starr jumped in front of me; she knew that I was hotter than a chick on her menstrual cycle, and the more Head talked the hotter I got.

Head lit another smoke and continued to run off at the mouth. He just didn't know when to shut the hell up. "Man, sometimes your decisions ain't always the best decisions," he continued, blowing smoke up at the sky.

"Head, the niggas know that we ain't scared. Trust me, when you don't react right away, that is when you have niggas on their toes, 'cause they don't know what you're thinking. Niggas ain't coming for you, or gunning for you, when they have no idea what they might run into," I told him.

"See, Black, you think you know everything, and that shit be getting on my nerves. B, I was on the streets while you was locked up. I know how niggas think, and right now, we look like a bunch of pussies to them Southside boys. You don't have all the answers, and I'm tired of you acting like you do," he blurted out, flexing his shoulders as he talked.

"Keep talking, Head, just keep running off at the mouth. I'm listening," I told him as I sat back on the car and allowed him to talk himself right out of a job.

"All I'm saying, Black, is that I'm tired of you acting like you know more than us. Always reciting Shakespeare, quoting the Bible. Just like the day when we was out here on the strip and Big Booty Trisha and Portia rolled through. We were out here having a good time kicking it, when you wanted to talk about dubs, doves, and vignettes and shit. You out on the strip trying to give niggas a lesson on eagles, sawbucks, and shit. Ain't nobody want to hear that, man, " he ran off at the mouth. His words were coming full force but did not mean a damn thing to me. Head laughed. "Then on top of it, you couldn't finish the conversation, because you ain't got all the facts yourself." He smirked.

I allowed him to finish making a mockery of himself, and then I replied. "Yeah, I remember the day clearly. I remember exactly why I stopped talking about it. It was because you were standing there looking at me like you were crazy with yo big-ass head. Nigga, you were jealous of me then, and you're jealous of me now. Head, just 'cause I know more than you don't mean I think I'm better than you, you little punk-ass mutherfucker!" I shot at him, my words so sharp they could have cut him up in pieces.

"Man, Black, fuck all that shit you saying. Like I said, you think you know everything," he repeated himself. "You want to blame me for that little girl getting shot, blame Starr's ass. I heard she made up the whole thing about what happened at the Showplace anyway," he said, disrespecting my lady for the last time.

Starr attempted to speak, but I cut her off. "Oh, you calling my girl a liar?" I jumped at him, his head meeting me at the waist. Putt and Lucky pulled me away.

"Black, ya'll niggas cut it out!" they begged.

"I ain't call her shit, the streets are talking," Head mused.

"Head, come ooon," Baije called out to him.

"Bitch, stop calling me!" he screamed at her. "Shut the fuck up!"

"See, you know what your problem is, Head? You got the short man's complex. Mutherfucking Napoleon Bonaparte complex. Beating and disrespecting your girl makes you feel like a man. Knocking another nigga makes you feel even better. You need some mutherfucking therapy, nigga. That's what's up." I smirked.

"Oh, like you don't, nigga? You smart as hell, just like the dad you never knew," he came back at me.

"Nigga, you keep talking that 'daddy' shit as if that shit's gone hurt me. Nigga, I can't miss what I never had. But you, on the other hand, you knew your dad. So tell us, Head, how does it feel knowing that your father walked away from you?"

Head's face filled with rage, and he grabbed his keys from the ground. "Man, fuck this. Ya'll niggas ain't got no love for me. I'm out. Give my spot to another nigga." He turned and strolled off.

"Head, come back, man! Stop tripping, man," Putt yelled after him.

"Come on, Black, don't let the nigga leave," Lucky pleaded with me. Head jumped into the rental, handed Baije the keys, and she started up the car.

"Baije, call me," Starr said as they drove off.

Head never looked at us again.

"Come on, Black, don't let the nigga leave the crew," Putt said with a sigh.

"Putt, when somebody walks away from you, it's best to just let 'em go," I told him.

I hopped in the passenger side of the Rover and Starr opened the driver-side door.

"Yo Starr, call around and see if you can find out the little girl's name and what hospital she's in. Then send some flowers and some money to her room. And I don't mean a little bit of money. I'm talking about some real scratch," I told her.

"Okay, Boo," Starr said as she cranked up the Rover and drove us home.

Chapter 35

We were one man down, but it was business as usual. Head stayed away from Fairfield, and although I missed the nigga dearly, I refused to call him first. Things had been quiet for two weeks, until one morning a man's body was discovered in the Gilpin Court Housing Project. Putt called me, barely able to speak.

"Turn to channel sixteen news on the TV, Black." He struggled to get the words out, then hung up the phone.

I grabbed the remote control and turned on the tube. A news reporter was live on the scene of a murder. She reported that a black man, Hezekeil "Head" Watson, had been found murdered, his body stuffed down a manhole. Head's money green Lincoln was up on the curb, the driver-side door still open. A young woman dressed in a nightgown and hair rollers was being interviewed by the reporter.

"Yeah, I know him. He was just at my house last night. He left about two a.m. 'cause he said he had to pick his girlfriend up from her uncle's house. I can't believe somebody would do this to Head, he was such a nice guy," the chicken head whined.

The news reporter seemed more interested in the relationship of the deceased and the young lady than she was about a possible motive or who the killer may have been.

"I notice you said he was with you until he had to leave to pick up his girlfriend?" the news reporter questioned. "Well, exactly what is your relationship to the deceased? How did you meet him? Were you two lovers?" she asked.

The chick, whose name was Valencia, looked the reporter dead in the eye. "Damn, bitch, you nosey as hell. The damn man is dead, and you out here worrying about whether or not I was fucking him. Bitch, you work for channel sixteen, not me, so don't start asking me a whole lot of questions. I don't get paid to snitch, you do!" She snapped at the reporter, gathered up her three kids, and switched off.

The news reporter stood there in disbelief as everybody on Calhoun Street broke out in laughter. The reporter turned away from the crowd and said, "This is Allison Bassadi reporting live. Back to you, Megan."

I jumped up from the bed, grabbed the phone, and called Putt back.

He answered on half of a ring. "Yeah?"

"It's time. Not another mutherfucking day is going by," I decided.

"This is the day I've been waiting for. Meet me at the spot in an hour," he told me.

I sat on the side of the bed. Starr passed me my sneakers and I threw them on.

"Baby, I got business to take care of. I'll be back." I kissed her on the lips and rolled out.

• • •

We waited until one a.m. before heading to Southside. We knew that the boys from Afton hung out on Hull Street. We parked and laid low in a U-Haul truck. It was around 2:30 when we spotted Whiteboy leaving in a black Pathfinder by himself. We followed him. He pulled in a parking space and got out with a small brown paper bag in his hand. We bum-rushed him so fast that he never knew what hit him. We gagged him, threw him in the U-Haul, and took his truck. We drove him to Foresthill Park, where we knew we wouldn't be caught. Once we got him there, we threw the nigga out of the U-Haul and removed the rag from his mouth.

"Please don't kill me. I got two kids," Whiteboy begged.

"Oh, mutherfucker, you got children now? You should've thought about your children when you killed my boy!" I said as I punched him in the face.

"Man, I didn't do it. I'm not the one who pulled the trigger on him," he cried. "Please, man, my little girl's birthday is tomorrow. Please don't kill me. I'll do anything you want me to do," he begged.

I noticed the piss bag on his side. I had always wondered how a piss bag worked, so I came up with a marvelous idea.

"Well, there is one thing he can do for us, right, Putt?" I turned to Putt. Putt stood with his arms crossed, not having a clue as to what I was talking about it. He nodded his head, agreeing with me anyway.

"Yep," he answered.

"What is it?" Whiteboy cried out.

"Man, I want you to cauterize yourself, or whatever that shit is you have to do when you use the bathroom," I told him.

"What?" Whiteboy frowned.

"Oh, nigga, so you got a problem with that. Untie the nigga, so he can get to work." I chuckled. We picked him up from the ground and stood him up at the back of his truck. He was trembling and shaking,

"But I don't have to pee," he whimpered. Whiteboy wasn't as big and bad as he made himself out to be. The night the nigga pulled the gun on us at the after-hours spot, he was Big Bad Billy Bad Ass; now without a gun, the rabbit wasn't having any fun. Whiteboy was scared as a mutherfucker, so I knew he would tell me whatever I wanted to know. I interrogated him.

"Who pulled the trigger on my boy?" I grabbed him by the chin and looked him square in the eye.

"Man, it wasn't me, it was Li'l Wayne and Happy Shooter," he snitched.

I didn't care what type of pressure a nigga was under; snitching on your niggas was a no-no in my book. I decided at that moment that I *really* didn't like his ass.

"Nigga, you're supposed to be down for your nigga, die before you rat on your niggas. You know what, Whiteboy, I don't like your style. Fuck it; I want you to drink your piss!" I snapped at him. Whiteboy started crying like a baby with a bad-ass diaper rash in need of some Desitin ointment.

"Come on, man, please don't make me do that," he begged.

"Do it now!" Putt shouted. Lucky and Frankie stood guard. They were laughing the entire time.

Whiteboy turned away from us, made a couple of moves with his bodily organs, and with the bag and shit, and then turned back around with the piss bag.

"I'm finished," he said, handing me the bag, for what I don't know.

"Drink that shit!" I shouted in his face.

Whiteboy turned the bag up to his face and gulped down his own urine. Lucky laughed so hard, I thought he was going to need stitches. Whiteboy did exactly what I ordered him to do. I was still planning to pop him, but I needed to know one more thing before I did.

"So, Whiteboy, tell me what was the last thing my nigga said before ya'll killed him."

Whiteboy used the pit of his arm to wipe the wet urine from around his mouth. "The last thing that Head said to us was, 'Tell my niggas that I loved them. Fairfield Wrecking Crew for life! Now suck my dick, you punk mutherfuckers!' "

Water formed in Lucky's eyes. Putt snatched Whiteboy by his dreadlocks and cut off a chunk of his hair. Frankie gave me a wild look.

"Want me to finish him off?" Frankie said, pointing his thirty-eight directly at Whiteboy's temple.

"Please don't shoot me. My little girl's birthday is tomorrow," Whiteboy pleaded again.

I shook my head at Frankie. "Nawh, I got this one," I said, raising my burner from my side.

"Too late!" Putt jumped in. He came up quickly with his .357, shooting Whiteboy in the chest, sending him headfirst to the ground.

We pulled him up from the ground and sat him back in the driver seat of his truck. Putt grabbed the small brown paper bag from the front seat and looked inside. Inside the bag there was a birthday card for his little girl, a bag of barrettes, and a yellow and white birthday candle. The white candle was trimmed in yellow and the candle itself was in the shape of the number 7.

"Guess he won't be needing any of that. All right, let's wipe down and get out of here!" I told my boys.

Chapter 36

It would've been a cold day in hell before I allowed those niggas to get away with killing Head. Not only did they shoot him twice in the back, but they stashed my man's body in a nasty manhole. Two days after Whiteboy's murder, Vice rolled up on the strip and took us all in for questioning. Once they had me in the interrogation room, they played a tape with my voice on it. It was a tape of the conversation that I had with Shelton the day that I demanded that he call me Gorilla Black.

"So, Mr. Cunningham. I see you can get pretty nasty when things don't go your way," the detective said, referring to the recorded conversation. The detective reared back in his chair and puffed on a cigar, purposely trying to piss me off by blowing smoke in my face. I refused to let him upset me and I sure as hell wasn't about to say anything without having legal representation, so I played dumb.

"Man, I don't know what you're talking about. When do I get my one free phone call? Because until I talk to my lawyer, I ain't got nothing to say to ya'll," I told him.

Just then, a white officer, the same fat cop that rolled up on me and Putt the day that Lulu was killed, walked into the interrogation room. A half second later, Floyd's buddy, the Frankie Beverly look-alike, came in behind him. Until that day, I had no idea that he was a cop, let alone a homicide detective on the Richmond Police Force. He walked into the interrogation room holding a folder about three inches thick in his hand. He flashed his badge and introduced himself.

"Detective Dotson. Homicide," was all he said.

He acted as if he didn't know me. Detective Dotson took a seat at the table and the fat cop stood by the door, blocking it as if I were going to try to make a run for it. I was stuck in the room with two detectives and one fat-ass cop. With nowhere to run or hide, I had no choice but to hold my own. I laid back in the chair and threw my hands behind my head. I wanted them to know that there was nothing they could say or do to break me down.

"So, I see we finally dragged the Fairfield Wrecking Crew in for questioning," the fat cop said to detective number one, who was still puffing on the cigar. Dotson looked me over, flipped through his folder, and stood up from the table with a smirk on his face.

"Yeah, we have them all in for questioning in the most recent Southside murder at Foresthill Park and for the murder that took place at the after-hours spot in Churchill," he briefed the fat cop. "I even have yours truly on tape assaulting a man because the man didn't call him Gorilla Black," he continued. "The funny thing about all of this is we can't get anybody to talk and honestly, this tape is not enough to bring him up on any charges. I mean, hell, what are we going to charge him with? Cracking a crackhead upside the head?" Detective Dotson said, amusing his peers with a little comedy. The fat officer laughed at him, his big belly rolling every time he did.

"Good point, detective. I guess for now, you got to at least let G-u-e-r-i-l-l-a Black and his friends go." He laughed hysterically. Detective Dotson opened the door and slid to the side for me to pass through.

"I guess you're right. Get out of here!" he told me. On my way out the door, I turned around to the fat robo cop and said, "That's G-o-r-i-l-l-a Black, you got it buddy?" I smirked.

The fat cop jumped up and threw back his fist as if he wanted to hit me. Detective Dotson shoved him back.

"Go ahead, man, go ahead and hit me so I can sue the city. I can use a little extra change anyway," I said.

"You better watch yourself, son. It's just a matter of time before we get you," the fat cop threatened.

• • •

The Crew was ready to hunt Shelton down like the snake he was and rip his head off, but I persuaded them not to. If anybody was going to be doing jail time, it needed to be time well spent, and Shelton's crackhead behind wasn't worth a nigga going to the clinker. Besides, as often as he was hitting the pipe, it was just a matter of time before he was dead anyway.

We returned to Fairfield and were out on the strip talking about our visit to the police station. We were tripping about it while listening to music, our guns stashed in bushes, under cars, in junkie's houses, when suddenly loud thumping invaded the neighborhood. It was Brother Shakim and his men. The Muslims headed down the block, all of them marching in perfect unison. Minister Shakim approached the crew.

"Good day, my brothers," he spoke, as he removed his jet-black eyeglasses from his deep dark eyes. His men stood proudly as they continued to march in place.

" 'Sup," we acknowledged him and his men.

Whenever the Muslims came through, we showed them the utmost respect, because for the most part, most of them had been there and done most of the same shit we were doing. We mentally prepared ourselves for another black-on-black crime lecture. It was customary for the Muslims to show up to preach to us about it.

"Mr. Black, I'd like to speak to you in private, if you will," Minister Shakim asked of me.

"No problem," I agreed, stepping away with him and leaving my group.

I was certain that Minister Shakim and his men had paid us a visit because they had heard about the recent murders and the beef between the Crew and the boys from Afton. I folded my arms and waited for his lecture to begin. Minister Shakim rubbed his hands together; licking his lips, he was ready to speak.

"Brother Black, I hate to interrupt you on such a beautiful day but I wanted to speak to you about the recent rash of crime in the area." He stopped talking and pulled a handkerchief from his long, black trench overcoat. I don't care what the temperature was like outside, the Muslims were always dressed to impress and most of the time overdressed. I wondered if they even knew what short sleeves and bowties looked like. I mean really, *by any means* is a suit jacket really that *necessary?* I shook my head at him and thought to myself, *Is the dress code really that serious?*

"What about the recent rash of crime?" I wondered.

"Well, Brother Black, yesterday, while one of my men was parked in the parking lot of Schwartz Supermarket, somebody stole a case of bean pies out of the backseat of his car. Brother Black, we are out here today paving the streets because we want to find the fool who was brave enough to steal from Brother Sadiki. When he stole those bean pies, he didn't just steal from Brother Sadiki, he stole from the entire Nation of Islam," he said.

I wasn't a stick-up kid nor was I a thief—anymore—so I didn't understand why Minister Shakim was bringing that foolishness to my attention. I just looked at him, then unfolded my arms.

"No, bro, I don't know anything about that. Ain't nobody been through here selling no pies, but if anybody does come through, I'll be sure to call you. You can leave your number with me," I told him. Minister Shakim wrote his number down and handed it to me.

"I sure do appreciate this. You know, it ain't all about the bean pies, it's about the principle. There are principalities in this!" he exclaimed.

"I feel you, my man." I nodded at him, not totally agreeing with how far he was willing to go for a box of bean pies.

While I certainly understood the principle behind it, and I definitely believed that some things were worth fighting for, at the same time I believed in picking and choosing your battles, and I wasn't actually sure if I would have been out paving the street, trying to hunt a nigga down over some pies. I started to just offer Minister Shakim the money to replace the missing items but to do so would have been disrespectful to him and the Nation of Islam. They were men of high standards and principles and although I was raised as a Christian, I respected what they stood for. It wasn't my place to knock theirs or anybody else's religion or beliefs.

"Later," Minister Shakim said, and then he jumped in front of his men, who were all standing at attention. At Minister Shakim's demand, they did an about-face turn and headed back up the block, all marching in perfect unison.

"Man, what did he want? What's up, B, what he talking about?" my boys eagerly asked. I turned to my crew with a confused look on my face.

"Man, they are out here trying to find out who stole a case of bean pies from Brother Sadiki," I told them with a straight face.

"They what!" Putt hollered.

The next thing I know, everybody out on the strip was running back and forth, up and down the block and falling all over the ground, laughing.

"Now, that's some serious shit right there!" I hollered.

• • •

We buried Head in a mausoleum over the Northside of Richmond, because it was Head's wish to never be lowered into the ground. Not too many people attended Head's funeral, because his reputation as a quick-tempered bad boy had cost him a lot of friends over the years. There were no outsiders at his funeral service, just the crew, the team, and a rack of old people from Fairfield Court that had known him practically his entire life. We were standing outside the mausoleum quarters, waiting for the service to end, when Valencia and a few of her girlfriends showed up. Baije was holding up pretty good, until Valencia started in with her Oscar-worthy performance.

"Whyyy, whyyy did they have to kill my baby? Head, I love you, please don't leave me, please don't go," she cried, falling all over her friends as if she was Head's main girl. She was doing a whole lot of crying, but not one teardrop fell from her eye.

The fact that Head had cheated on her, and the idea that the girl had the nerve to show up at the funeral, infuriated Baije to no end. Before I knew it, she was beating Valencia down to the ground. After Valencia picked herself up, Starr demanded that she and her friends leave. When they didn't leave fast enough, Starr and Baije jumped the four girls and although the ratio was two to four they single-handedly beat them senseless. Some of the old ladies from Fairfield even jumped in, swinging and hitting the unwanted guests with their purses. I wanted to break up the fight, but the crew advised me not to. Starr and Baije were raging mad and needed to blow off some steam, so I sat back with the rest of the team and let them kick the girls' butts. The funeral home director was appalled at the ladies' behavior. He jumped into his hearse and left us all standing at the mausoleum. Ms. Cheryl, Head's mother, wept as the driver pulled off.

"But he didn't even get to say 'Ashes to ashes, dust to dust,'" Ms. Cheryl wept.

Chapter 37

Over the next few weeks the beef between the Fairfield Wrecking Crew and the boys from Afton escalated. More and more people were getting involved, and life in Richmond was being altered by the minute. Niggas from Southside couldn't travel to Churchill and vice versa without some type of physical altercation taking place. Innocent people who had nothing to do with the beef were being victimized, shot at, beat down, or threatened. Whenever we stepped out we had to ride deep, and from what we knew, the niggas from Southside was carrying it the same way. There was fighting at the malls by teenagers from both hoods; girls gritting on each other in the hair and nails salon, and shootouts at nightclubs. The freedom to live, work, and play anywhere in the city was taking its toll on innocent people. We were at war in the city, we were at war with each other, but more important, we were at war with ourselves.

The effects of all the drama started to take its toll on Starr. I came home one day after a brief encounter with a group of dudes from Southside. I was at Regency Square Mall with the crew and a couple other members of my team, when we ran into a group of dudes from Afton. It was ironic that we ran into them there because Regency Square Mall wasn't in either of our neck of the woods. It didn't matter how many times we battled with them, that nigga Li'l Wayne was never around. I had never seen Li'l Wayne in my life, but I was just dying to meet him. I wanted him so bad, I could taste his blood. The crazy thing about it was that for the most part we didn't know what they looked like and they didn't know us from Adam. It was strange, but wherever we went, we could just smell the niggas we had a beef with. It was something about the look in their eyes that told us they were from Southside.

I went home after a shoot-out in the mall's parking lot, disappointed that we didn't drop any of them niggas. I decided to go home and relax a little before getting back on the grind. I straggled up to the third floor and headed into the bedroom. I pushed open the door to our bedroom. Starr jumped up from the bed and to her feet with a startled look on her face.

"Why you ain't call me on the intercom to let me know you were downstairs?" she asked defensively. Starr was blocking my view of the bed, and her eyes held a suspicious look. I slid my neck around her; I could tell something was up. I spotted a small saucer with at least an eight ball of coke and a cut-up straw laying in the plate. I couldn't believe it; Starr had been snorting coke.

I grabbed the saucer and held it up to her face. "What the hell are you doing? So, you getting high now?" I fumed. It wasn't a secret that Starr loved smoking weed or cigarettes, but cocaine? Nah, I wasn't about to put up with that.

"Boo, please don't be mad at me but I . . . With all this stuff happening, people dying, Head dying, everybody in the crew getting crazy, I just can't take it anymore. I needed something to relax me," she whined.

"Starr, if you need to relax then take a warm bubble bath. Damn, Starr! I can't believe you going out like this. Where did you get the coke from? Who sold it to you, because whoever sold it to you got a problem with me now."

Starr just looked at me and sat down on the bed. I was already vexed about the shoot-out, and my adrenaline was still pumping, so I tried calming myself because I didn't want to take my frustration out on Starr. The longer she sat there saying nothing, the more upset I became. She grabbed me by the arm and pulled me down on the bed with her.

"Boo, calm down. The person who sold it to me didn't know that I was the one buying. I got Malcolm to score for me. It was Malcolm." She sighed. I bit my bottom lip, and snatched my arm away from her. I was sick of Malcolm and the relationship he had with my girl.

"You still messing with Malcolm's punk ass." I sighed.

"Boo, next to Baije, Malcolm is my best friend and I trust him. He won't tell anybody that I'm getting high," she fussed.

"I know he won't 'cause getting high is a thing of the past for you. You know your doctor told you to never use drugs because of your heart condition. Yet, you running around behind my back snorting coke? Starr, make it your last time. Don't ever let me hear about you getting high again," I said. "Understand me?"

Starr gave me a sad face, then buried her head in her chest. She was either upset because I was disappointed with her or upset that she had been caught red-handed. Whatever the reason was for her puppy dog look, she didn't answer me either way.

"Starr, do you hear me talking to you? I'm serious, baby, leave that shit alone. It's not a game, that coke will kill you, baby girl." I hugged around her neck to let her know that I wasn't mad with her. Starr slid into my arms and raised her head from her chest.

"Okay, Boo, I won't do it again," she promised.

I stood up from the bed, and dropped the plate on the bed.

"Starr, I have something to ask you." I knelt down in front of her and took her right hand.

"What is it, Boo?" She raised a brow.

"Starr, you know that I love you with all my heart and soul, don't you?" I began.

"Uhm, hum." Starr smiled, her smile melting my heart.

"Well, today I went to the mall to get something for you." I pulled the ten-carat diamond engagement ring from my back pocket and popped open the box. Starr's eyes grew larger than her entire body. I gazed up at her and looked deeply into her eyes.

"Starr, will you marry me?" I caught her completely by surprise. Starr jumped up from the bed and started running around the bedroom.

"Yes, yes," she screamed to the top of the roof. "I will marry you!" She ran back over to me and hugged me real tight. Then she dropped down to her knees and unbuckled my khaki pants. They fell to the floor.

"Hold up, I'll be right back, don't pull your pants up yet, " she yelled while running out the room.

When she came back, she had an ice bucket, full of ice. She laid me down on the bed and began massaging my entire body. She began to trace my naked body with ice cubes. The ice was cold, causing my dick to grew rock hard and stiff.

"Damn, Boo, where did you get this idea with the ice?" I moaned as she played with my manhood. Starr licked her sexy lips, turning me on even more.

"Boo, you know I love Spike Lee movies. I got this idea from *Do the Right Thing*. Remember the scene with Spike Lee and Rosie Perez?" she reminded me.

"Yeah. I remember. Just make sure you do the right thing and leave that coke alone," I said. Starr jumped on top of me, and started grinning.

"I just did the right thing. I got rid of all of the coke I had, 'cause I just put the last li'l bit on your dick. That's why it's harder than a brick!" She laughed. Starr slid her pussy onto my dick and rode me like a cowgirl in a rodeo show.

I woke up an hour later, showered, dressed, and left Starr in bed asleep. I headed to the projects to check on things and to also get my birth certificate. I knew that I would need my birth certificate in order to get a marriage license. It was a typical day on the block, children were outside playing, and everybody from the team was posted up. I headed into Mom's house.

"Hey, Mom," I called out to her as I stepped inside.

"I'm back here in the kitchen."

Momma had gotten spoiled, and although I had offered many times to buy her a house, she refused the offer. She said she wanted to stay where she was because she felt comfortable in the environment. So, instead of moving into a house, she fixed her place up like it was one. I paid to have the apartment redecorated twice in one year. Momma's apartment was laid and there wasn't anything that she didn't ask me for that I eventually didn't get her. She would buy something one day, and then the next day decide she didn't want it. Instead of returning the items, she would sell the new shit I had just bought her and ask me to give her money to get more. Momma was the only person in the project with wall-to-wall carpet. She even had carpet going up and down the stairs.

Despite the fact that I took good care of her, Momma was jealous of my relationship with Suga Momma. She argued with me whenever she found out that I did something for Suga Momma. I couldn't tell her that not only was she getting five hundred dollars a week from me, but Suga Momma was getting the same allowance. The only difference between the two was that Suga Momma kept hot cooked meals ready for me and the crew. If anybody was ever hungry, all they had to do was go to Suga Momma's house to eat. Momma, on the other hand, didn't do anything to deserve what she was getting. Momma was getting five hundred a week just for being Momma.

"What's up, Mom?" I stepped into the kitchen, leaned over and attempted to kiss her on the cheek. She turned sideways, avoiding my kiss. "Mom, your hair looks nice," I complimented her. She didn't thank me for the compliment; instead she found something to complain about.

"Yeah, I'm still going down to that girl on Main Street, but I think that bitch is charging me too much because she knows I'm your momma. Don't make no damn sense how people try to get over on me because I'm your momma. Like I'm rich or something. You're the one with the damn money, not me!" Momma fussed. "Why can't Starr fix my hair, anyway? Hell, ain't that what she do?" she carried on. Then Momma stood up and opened the refrigerator and grabbed a small can of grapefruit juice. She mixed the grapefruit juice with her Seagram's gin.

"Bilal, I need some money," she stated bluntly. Momma was always begging for money, even when she didn't need any. It was just her way of controlling me.

"How much?" I asked. Momma thought about her answer seriously. She used her hands and fingers to count.

"Let's see, Ten West Leigh Club tonight, a couple drinks at the club, loan Bob two hundred till payday. Four hundred will be perfect," she said.

"Okay, Mom, but all I have on me is three hundred. Give me a minute and I'll have some more money bought over to you," I told her. Momma rolled her eyes at me. She was impatient and wanted her money right then and there.

"Why I always got to wait when I ask your ass for something?" She smirked.

"Oh Mom, by the way, I need my birth certificate 'cause I'm planning to marry Starr." I came straight out with it because I knew she would object.

"Oh yeah?" Momma doubted, her eyebrows raised up, reaching her forehead.

"Yeah, Mom, me and Starr are getting married, so we need to get my birth certificate corrected, okay?" I told her. Momma sucked her teeth.

"Are you going to call somebody to bring that hundred dollars over here or what? 'Cause I'm going to need the money before you get the birth certifcate," she hounded.

"I'm calling them now. If you can go and get the birth certificate I would really appreciate it," I egged her on. It never failed with Momma; she always made me feel like nothing was for free with her. It was a shame that I had to beg and barter for my own birth certificate. I should have taken the birth cerficate when I took the letters but I didn't because I figured if Momma would miss anything from her box, it would be the birth certificate, since I had been asking for it and she had refused to give it up.

Momma took another hit of her drink and then moseyed upstairs. She came back with the box that contained all of her important papers. She sat the box down on the table.

"Find it yourself," she said as she slid the box in front of me.

I began looking through the stacks of paper. I ran across an insurance policy. When Momma turned her back to fix another drink, I opened up the policy and briefly scanned the policies and its provisions. My moms had made a couple of changes to the life insurance policy that she had originally taken out on me. I kept searching until I ran across the birth certificate.

"Here it is," I said, handing the birth certificate to Momma.

"See, right there. Why do they have granddaddy listed as my father? I don't know how they made a mistake like that but we need to get it fixed." I shook my head in dismay.

Instantly, Momma began to cry. "Oh, Bilal, this here ain't no mistake. Your granddaddy is your daddy," she cried out.

"What!" I yelled. I jumped up from the table, knocking over Momma's drink. "Momma, what do you mean? Your own daddy raped you? Why didn't that nigga go to jail?" I shouted. I threw my hands up to my head. I couldn't believe what I was being told. I was in shock. "Mom, you mean to tell me that your own daddy had sex with you?" I frowned at the thought. It was the most disgusting thing I had ever heard of. How could a man sleep with his own daughter? I wanted to go to Alabama, find Grandaddy, and cut his dick off. *Sick bastard,* I thought to myself.

"Yes, Bilal, he did," she confirmed. My eyes grew big and my heart began to thump like thunder.

"Oh my God, Mom. I'm so sorry for you. I had no idea that you've been through all of this," I agonized with her. I grabbed her by the top of her hair and kissed her on the top of her French roll. "Mom, I love you so much. You will always be my queen. I'm so sorry, I didn't know." Momma got up to fix herself another drink but I stopped her. "I got it, Mom, just relax, and here, I got six hundred dollars for you. If you don't like your hair, go get it done over," I told her.

Momma grabbed the tiny cup of liquor from my hand and the money. She took a sip from the cup.

"Why did you tell me you only had three hundred on you? See, your black ass be lying to me all the time." She turned the cup back up to her mouth, and in just one gulp, she demolished the whole cup of gin and juice.

I ignored her, and asked my own question. "Who is Bob?"

Momma stood from the table and staggered toward the living room floor. Just then, the phone rang.

"Get that for me. If it's Bob, tell him I said to hurry," she yelled. I snatched the phone from the wall.

"Who is Bob?" I asked again.

"That's my new man. I met him down at the Ten West Leigh Night Club. Just answer the damn phone!" she screamed.

"Hello," I spoke into the phone.

"Hey, baby, how's my grandson doing?" It was Grandma, calling from Alabama.

"I guess you can call me grandson, or stepson, now ain't that right, Grandma!" I growled at her.

"Ooh, Bilal. What did your mother tell you?" she asked, surprised at what I knew.

"She told me that her daddy had sex with her and that's how I was conceived. All these years I thought Momma was just crazy for the sake of being crazy, when all along you and granddaddy made her the way she is. Stop calling here, I don't ever want to speak to ya'll again!" I told her.

"Bilal, things aren't always what they seem. Please give me a chance to explain," she begged. I didn't want to hear shit Grandma had to say. I refused to listen to her excuses. Granddaddy had committed, in my eyes, the worst sin known to man. Having sex with his own daughter was the most despicable thing I could fathom.

"Ain't nothing you can say to me to make me understand that! There is no excuse for a man molesting his own daughter. Now I don't want to be rude to you, Grandma, but I'm hanging up!" I warned her.

Momma listened in from the living room and jumped in. "Yeah, hang up on her ass!" Momma countered from the other room.

Grandma continued talking, trying desperately to get me to listen. "Bilal, if you want the real answers about how and why you were conceived, look in the book of Genesis. There you will find all of the answers," Grandma said.

"Grandma, stop putting religion into everything. Everything ain't about God!" I slammed the phone down and joined Momma in the living room.

"Are you okay?" I asked Momma.

Momma was peeping out the window, her too-short skirt up her butt. "Yeah, I'm fine. I'm looking for Bob. I'm waiting on him to pick me up," she said.

I didn't know who Bob was and I worried that Momma could get hooked up with the wrong man. With the beef escalating the way it was, I didn't trust anybody. For all I knew, Momma could have been dating one of my enemy's fathers. I just didn't want to take any chances with my moms. I needed her to be safe no matter who she was with.

"Mom, I hope this dude is okay. Then again, he can't be. What kind of man would borrow money from a lady he just met? He got a car, so he ought to have a job."

Momma hissed, then turned away from the window and walked past me into the kitchen. "Actually he don't have a car, he's driving mine. You know, the one you bought me that I can do whatever the hell I want to do with. You need to mind your own business. You didn't notice that my car wasn't parked outside? Your little black ass notices everything else, so how did you miss that? Boy, you ain't as smart as you think." Momma laughed under her breath.

"No, I didn't notice your car was gone. Mom, just be careful about who you date, okay? You've lived through enough already. I'll call you later to check on you," I told her before leaving.

I stepped onto the porch and headed down the block. I needed to be by myself in order to clear my head. The news that my own granddaddy was my father had me speechless. I didn't know what to think, how to react, or what to do. I walked over to John F. Kennedy High School's football field and took a seat on the bleachers. I was sitting alone for about a minute when out of nowhere, Baije pops up.

"Hey, Black, I see you over here by yourself too," she said. I looked at her. Baije looked a mess. Her hair was all over her head and she still had coal in her eyes.

"Baije, what's up? What are you doing out here?"

"I just need to be by myself. I'm waiting on Starr to come get me, but I wanted to come clear my head first. Black, I think I'm going crazy. I can't believe Head is gone. I miss him so much that I don't know what to do." She sat down beside me on the bleachers and dropped her head in her hands. I threw my arm around her to comfort her.

"Baije, I know it's hard. No matter what Head did, we all know that he loved you," I told her.

"Yep, Black. No matter what, I know Head loved me. You know, Black, I don't know if you know this, but I really can't even read or write. Head did everything for me and took care of everything, all the bills, everything. He could have left me a long time ago 'cause I was illiterate, but he didn't. Did you know that Head was teaching me how to read and write? He also wanted me to get my GED. Every day he would talk about that. I told him I would, but I never signed up to take the classes at the Adult Learning Center. But now that he's gone, I'm going to do it. I owe Head that much." A stream of tears covered Baije's face.

"Baije, that's a smart decision," I said, proud that she had decided to take control of her own life. I rubbed the top of her messy head.

Suddenly, Starr ran up on the bleachers and starting swinging.

"Oh, so ya'll mufuckers creeping out on me, huh?" she accused us.

"What are you talking about, Starr?" I asked.

"Nigga, I've been paging you and you ain't call me back!" Before I knew it, Starr smacked her best friend so hard that Baije fell down one flight off the bleachers. "What the fuck are you and Baije doing over here in the pitch dark all cuddled up and shit!" she screamed.

"Starr, what are you doing? Calm down. Starr, you're the only friend I have. You know I wouldn't do that to you. Please calm down, Starr!" Baije begged.

"Nah, you fucking with my man, Baije. Bitch, I can't believe you backstabbed me!" Starr continued with her accusations. She was going ballistic, not listening or hearing anything we were saying to her.

"Starr, me and Baije was over here talking about Head. I was over here clearing my head and Baije just happened to be over here doing the same thing," I tried explaining.

Starr began to lose her breath, so she sat down on the bleachers to calm her nerves. She took in a deep breath and began to relax a little.

"Baije, go move the car out of the street and wait for me. I'm coming," she said, huffing and puffing. Despite being smacked all around by her best friend, Baije did what she was asked to do. Baije ran to the street and moved the car. She got in and waited.

"Baby, what is wrong with you? You know I would never cheat on you and I would never disrespect you or Head. Come on now, Starr, you know me better than that. Baby, I don't need this right now, I just found out some terrible news and now I'm not sure if you would want to marry me," I told her, then I flopped back down on the bleacher and wallowed in my own self-pity.

Starr stood between my legs. "I'm sorry, it's just that when I saw you with my best friend I went crazy. I thought ya'll were deceiving me," she huffed. "What's wrong, Boo? You don't look right," she said to me. I pulled her down and placed her on my lap in order to break the news to her.

"Starr, I just found out who my daddy is." I sighed.

"Who is he; do I know him or something?" Starr questioned.

"Baby, I just found out that my granddaddy is my daddy. Momma's own daddy had sex with her and she got pregnant with me." I told her all that I knew.

Starr jumped to her feet, almost falling off the bleachers. "What the—? Are you okay?" she asked, worried.

"Yeah, I'm okay. I just don't know what will happen if I have children. They could be deaf, dumb, crippled, blind, or crazy."

"Boo, don't even think like that. Our children will be fine. Then again, if something is wrong with them, we'll just love their retarded asses the way they are." Starr laughed, then kissed me gently on the lips. "Damn, Boo, I guess that explains why your mom is so crazy." She frowned.

I chuckled. "Yeah, Momma is crazy as all outdoors. I guess she can't help it."

"Well, Boo, I still want to marry you. As a matter of fact, I was thinking about the date when I woke up and that's why I was paging you."

"Oh, really. Baby, I'm sorry but I left the pager in the house. You had my mind so messed up after that bomb sex session that I couldn't think straight when I left the house." I laughed.

"Well, I want to get married on June tenth next year," she said.

"June tenth? On your birthday?" I repeated.

"Yep. Let's get married on my birthday." She smiled.

I stood up and pulled my baby up with me. "Okay, baby," I agreed. "June tenth next year it is."

"We can get Head's mom to do all the planning. Shit, make her work for the money you putting out for her," Starr hissed.

We crossed the street and got inside the car with Baije. Starr apologized to her best friend.

"Baije, I'm sorry I went off on you. I don't know what got into me. Girl, I was tripping. I think I must've had some type of flashback or something." Starr giggled.

Baije happily accepted her best friend's apology. "That's all right, girl. Good thing my hair wasn't fixed 'cause you would've messed it all up," Baije joked.

"Oh yeah, about that hair—I'm taking you to get that mess fixed tomorrow. We can't have you running around looking simple. You still have a reputation to uphold." Starr chuckled.

Baije smiled, and the two were happy being best friends again.

Chapter 38

"Black, Black, wake up, wake up!" Starr shook me hard, waking me from a deep sleep. "Lucky's been shot!" she screamed.

I jumped out of bed, grabbed my burner, and headed out the door. A couple of my workers had stayed over that night, so they strapped up and followed me. When we arrived at MCV Hospital, Putt and a few of the members from the team were already there. They were standing in the hallway, pacing back and forth, and from the looks on their faces, they were ready to kill.

"Man, what happened?" I rushed over to them.

"Man, them niggas tried to kill Luck last night when he went to take shorty girl home over the West End. They say the Z flipped over three or four times and pinned his legs underneath the steering wheel. The doctors are in there working on him. He ain't dead, but they say he may be paralyzed." Putt punched the hospital wall. "I'm getting tired of those niggas, man," he fumed. "Those mutherfuckers think we are playing with them."

"Man, fuck them niggas. It's on!" Frankie, one of the members of the Crew, charged.

Lucky's parents walked up, and the looks on their faces said that they had been up crying all morning long.

We all spoke to them, then we each gave Luck's mom a reassuring hug. Mr. A was livid about what happened to his son. He voiced his concerns out loud in the hallway.

"You know, this shit is getting out of hand now. My boy don't deserve this, he ain't ever hurt a flea, and now he may not be able to walk. If I could get those son of a bitches myself, I would. Oh, they better be lucky my Vietnam days are behind me. I'd catch them mutherfuckers and use they asses for target practice. I'd gun them all down!" Lucky's dad yelled. I hugged Mr. Arnold around his neck and pulled him aside.

"Mr. A, Lucky is a fighter," I told him. "He fights with all his heart, so he will come through just fine, just watch and see."

"They say my baby was pinned inside that car and couldn't get out. Some city workers rode by and saw him and pulled him from the car in the nick of time. As soon as they got him out, the car went up in flames. My baby is lucky to be alive," Lucky's mom said, sobbing.

The more Lucky's parents talked, the angrier the Crew became. They began making threats and using obscenities in the hospital hallway.

"I need everybody to just chill for a minute while we're here at the hospital, but as soon as we leave, we got some business to handle," I assured them.

A minute later, Putt spotted Victoria, who was asking a nurse about Lucky's family. The nurse pointed down the hallway to us and Victoria headed in our direction. Victoria was Lucky's on-and-off girlfriend and Barbette's first cousin. Victoria was a deep sista. She was full figured, well grounded, smart, and sophisticated, but at the same time, she would drop the next sista's ass in a New

York minute. Victoria strolled down the hallway in her fight-the-power gear. Her hair was wrapped in an African print turban, and her Afrocentric jewelry and bangles dangled all over the place, making noises as she walked. Victoria headed toward us; her red, green, yellow, and black T-shirt hugged her tight and so did her jeans. She was swinging a colored crocheted bag that matched her T-shirt perfectly. I could tell by the look on her face, Victoria wanted answers.

"What happed to Lucky? Where is he? I heard he got shot?" she pressed. Victoria had a strong presence, so whenever she spoke, most listened. The entire hallway fell silent.

Frankie gave her the hush signal. "Vicky, calm down."

Victoria shot Frankie a crooked look. "My name is Victoria, not Vicky, so don't be shortening my shit unless I give you permission to, okay sweetie?" she snapped at him. Then she hugged Lucky's parents. "Ya'll okay?" she asked, kissing them both lightly on the cheek. "Let me know if ya'll need anything. You got my numbers?" Then Victoria turned to me. "Where's Starr?" she inquired.

I told her, "She's gone to get everybody something to eat." Victoria placed her hands on her curvaceous hips and let out a huge sigh.

"Okay, so is Lucky going to be all right?"

"We think so," Putt answered, unsure of the answer he gave. Truth was, we really didn't know what the future was going to hold for Lucky.

"This mess with ya'll and the boys from Southside is getting out of hand. This mess is stupid!" she said, looking at each and every one of us as she spoke.

Putt jumped in. "Victoria, I will never disrespect you 'cause you're Lucky's girl, but you are way out of line right now," he told her.

Victoria rolled her neck from side to side, dropped her hands from her hips and pointed at Putt with her index finger.

"First of all, I'm not his girl, I'm his friend. If I was his girl, I would've been with him at ya'll's little party last night and not that chick from the West End. So, let's not try to play me for weak. Okay? I know what time it is. All I want to know is, what are ya'll beefing about?" she asked all of us. We ignored her question, so she asked again. "I said, what are ya'll beefing with the boys from Southside about?" she demanded to know.

" 'Cause we don't like them niggas, that's why!" Frankie answered.

"Word," Dread cosigned for him.

Victoria shook her head, then pulled a tissue from her crocheted bag. One small tear fell from underneath her right eye. She slowly wiped it away.

"Tell Luck when he pulls through that I said to get at me." Victoria left the message with no one in particular. Then she strolled off, heading back up the hallway. Before she disappeared completely out of sight, she turned around and yelled, "Yo, Frankie, Dread, I really need ya'll to think about the answer to my question." And just like that, Victoria was gone.

• • •

The doctors came out after operating on Lucky for several hours. They stated that Lucky was going to be okay but he would never be able to walk again. I gathered my Crew in a huddle outside the emergency room. It was time to step things up a notch.

"Listen up. From now on, we ain't sleeping on these niggas. Whenever they come at us, we gone get at them the same day. I don't give a fuck if ya'll at church and you run into one of them niggas, you better start blazing in the sanctuary!" I told them, meaning every word that I said.

My men all nodded in agreement.

"Now, let's go get our gear and go handle this shit!"

• • •

Later that evening, we headed to the storage unit where we kept our arsenal of weapons and military clothes. Around eleven p.m., we headed to Southside in search of our prey. I had paid an informant to give me the 411 on all of their hangouts. We scoped out every corner, crap house, and trick house on the Southside, to no avail. We couldn't locate our enemies. We were traveling back to Churchill when we decided to check for them in Blackwell. We spotted a few cats on the corner near the courthouse, so we jumped out and bum-rushed them.

"Anybody seen Li'l Wayne, Happy Shooter, or any of them niggas from Afton?" We surrounded the group. Some of us had our burners raised up, some of our burners laid low by our sides. The Blackwell cats didn't waste any time getting their hands up. They knew what time it was.

"Nawh, them niggas don't hang over here. This is Blackwell. Them niggas don't run shit over here," one of the cats voiced, obviously turned off by our invasion of their block.

I kicked around their money, which was lying on the ground. I wasn't planning on robbing them; I just needed them to know that I could have if I wanted to. They were out shooting craps under a bright-ass street light and neither one of them had the sense enough to know that they needed to be protecting their shit. One of the dudes showed his nervousness.

"Man, don't rob us. We ain't got shit to do with them niggas' beef," he explained.

"We ain't gone rob ya'll niggas, we don't need ya'll chump change." Putt laughed.

The dude relaxed a little. "A'ight, man. But, like I said, we ain't got nothing to do with them niggas' beef," he repeated himself. One of his boys spoke up; he was much bolder than his friend.

"Man, ya'll got beef with them niggas. Why bring the heat over here? Li'l Wayne runs Afton, that nigga don't run shit over here! That nigga don't run this part of Southside," he fumed.

I didn't particularly care for his attitude, but I wasn't about to drop him just because he spoke up. Besides, I liked a bit of cockiness in other niggas.

I shot back at him, raising my gun next to his face. I got up close and personal and whispered in his ear. "Southside is Southside, now ain't it," I said in a sinister tone, scaring the shit out of him. The dude threw his hands up to his face, and I laughed at him. "Man, if you say ya'll ain't got nothing to do with it, then I'll take your word. Just tell them mutherfuckers if ya'll see them that Gorilla Black been through looking for them."

Just then, Frankie, who was the time watcher, yelled, "Time's up!"

We backed away from the group and jumped into the truck. Before we pulled off, I overheard the third dude who had never spoke a word tell his boys, "That was that nigga they call Gorilla Black from Fairfield. I wish we could have seen his face." We drove off slowly down Hull Street and removed our masks from our faces and our bulletproof gear.

We were disappointed that we couldn't locate our prey.

Chapter 39

In an effort to stop the violence, a task force was assigned to both neighborhoods. The police came through, rounded up the Crew again, and took us back down for questioning. Richmond's finest couldn't find any witnesses to any of the murders or shoot-outs. If there were any witnesses, they just weren't talking. With fifty thousand cops on the corner a day, I couldn't stand the heat. I started going to Virginia Commonwealth University's library to read, study, and clear my head. The library was the only place in town where I could find peace and not have to worry about bumping into my enemies.

I was there one afternoon researching Lucky's medical condition. Victoria had suggested holistic healing for him, and I wanted to see if that was a known cure for quadriplegics. I was sitting at a table in the library when I accidentally bumped into Amanda.

"Excuse me, ma'am, but can you tell me where I can find some literature on Adolf Hitler?" The familiar voice got my attention.

"You may want to check over in that section," the librarian responded.

I never looked up from the book I was reading, until five minutes later when the familiar voice returned.

"Okay, I'm going to check these books out. Can you hand me a card to fill out? Oh, goodness, what is today's date?" the voice asked.

"Today is Thursday, March 22, 1991," I answered before the librarian had a chance, never looking up from my book.

"Well, thank you very much. Bilal?" the girl called my government name. I looked up and that's when I realized it was Amanda. I stood up from the table to properly greet her.

"Hey, last time I saw you, you were dressed in Virginia Union gear. What's up with the VCU attire?" I laughed. Amanda walked over to my table and sat down. I sat back down with her.

"Hey, Bilal, it's good to see you. I transferred from VUU to VCU. I've been going here for a while."

"Do you like it here?" I asked.

"Uhm hum, much better. VCU is more diverse. Do you go to school here? Did you ever go back to get your GED?" she asked.

"Nawh, ain't much change with me. I just come here to study, that's all," I answered modestly.

"Oh, okay, I see. Well, the last time I spoke to my cousin Jenny, she told me you were doing real well," she said.

"Yeah, things couldn't be any better. As a matter of fact, I'm getting married in June," I shared. Amanda stood up from her seat and reached over to hug me.

"Oh, Bilal, that's great. Congratulations." She hugged me as if we were really and truly old friends. I barely knew the chick and I felt a little uneasy with her all up on me like that. I backed up off of her breasts, which she had thrown all over me.

"Well, I don't talk to my cousin that often. I mean, don't get me wrong, I love her, but we just don't have the same interests. You will probably see her before I do, so tell her that I said hello." Amanda turned and headed back to the check-out counter to retrieve her books.

"Hold up, girl, you can't carry all that stuff by yourself. Let me help you. How far do you have to go?" I insisted on helping her.

"Oh, a little ways from here. I'm parked across the street, over by the Dailey Planet Homeless Shelter," she told me.

"All right, I'll carry your books to your car for you. I was about to leave anyway."

We left the library and headed across the street to Amanda's car. There was a large field that separated the college from the street. The field was packed with homeless men and vagrants begging for food, and people sleeping on benches. Amanda and I made small talk as we walked. When we reached her car, there was a loud commotion coming from across the street at the shelter. I turned to see what all the havoc was about and found two men arguing over the last free meal that had been dropped off by a meals on wheels van. Amanda sucked her teeth and pointed.

"Just look at them. They act just like heathens. There's nothing wrong with them anyway, they are homeless because they want to be homeless." Amanda rolled her eyes, judging the men she didn't know.

"It ain't that simple, Amanda. I doubt if anybody wants to be homeless," I responded.

"What do you mean it ain't that simple? They are lazy and just need to get a job. McDonald's is right down the street and they are always hiring." Amanda opened her car door.

"Believe it or not, Amanda, there are a lot of hardworking people who are homeless. There are intelligent men and women who are homeless, and people with mental and physical disabilities as well that make up the homeless population. People can become homeless because they lack resources; don't assume that all homeless people lack motivation or drive. That's a myth," I interjected. Amanda ignored everything that I had just said. She pointed across the street at the men.

"Look, just look at them, fighting over cold lunches. Ooh, I can't stand to look at them." She frowned. I turned and focused my attention on the two men.

"Floyd?" I blurted out.

"What? Do you know one of them?" Amanda asked me with a look of disgust on her face. I was embarrassed to see Floyd out-side the shelter fighting over food. It brought back memories of my confrontation with him. All those years later, the man was still hungry and having to fight just to get something to eat.

"Nawh, I thought he was somebody that I knew, but that's not him," I lied.

"Hum, I was going to say, from over here, it looks like that man's nose is fucked up!" Amanda cursed.

"Girl, I didn't think you had a curse word in you," I joked with her, trying to get her stiff ass to lighten up.

"Ha, ha, don't let the sweet taste fool you." She laughed. I put her books in the backseat and closed her door shut.

"All right now, Amanda, you take care."

"Okay, Bilal, good seeing you. You take it easy and stay out of trouble," she said, before driving off in her Ford Escort, her brakes making a grinding sound as she sped off down the road.

I hurried home because I had plans to take Starr out for din-ner. When I approached my house, I noticed a strange car parked in the driveway. Starr and Malcolm were sitting at the kitchen table; Crazy Chris was staring at the TV in the den.

"Hey, Boo." Starr greeted me with a kiss when I stepped in.

"Hey, Black, what's up?" Malcolm spoke.

"Man, you need to move your car from my driveway," I told him.

"Man, my bad, I didn't think you would be coming home any-time soon," Malcolm apologized. He jumped up and hurried out the door. Starr jumped up from the table with a plate in her hand; she sat the plate in the sink and turned the water on.

"Starr, come here," I called out to her.

"What, Boo, let me wash these dishes first," she replied, trying to cover up her mess again.

I moved in closer to her and turned the water off.

"Nawh, Starr, don't play with me. You've been in here getting high again, haven't you?" I fumed.

"What? Why you say that?" she asked.

" 'Cause you got the evidence under your nose." I wiped the coke from the area between her nose and upper lip. Immediately, she took offense.

"Why you always got to come home and start shit!" she yelled.

"Starr, don't try that reverse psychology mess with me. Look at this. Coke is still on the plate." I removed the saucer from the sink and showed her the residue of cocaine that she hadn't snorted. Malcolm walked back into the kitchen, catching the tail end of the conversation.

"Nigga, why you keep coming over here getting Starr high?" I jumped in his face. Starr got in between us.

"Black, please stop. Malcolm can't make me do nothing I don't want to do. Besides, he don't even snort coke," she yelled.

"Leave, Malcolm. Get the fuck out of my house, man, and don't come back over here unless you want your fucking neck broke!" I told him. His punk ass was lucky that I let him go without incident.

Malcolm grabbed his bag of M&M's chocolate candies from the table.

"Black, man, I don't want any problems. I would never do anything to hurt Starr," he said.

"Malcolm! Shut the fuck up and get the fuck out of my house!" I gave him one more chance. At the sound of my voice, Malcolm's entire body shook, and he hauled tail out of the house.

"Starr, I'll talk to you later. Let me take this ride back to the city." He ran out and jumped into his car.

I sat down at the kitchen table, disappointed that I was having the same conversation again with Starr.

"Starr, why are you in here getting high with Chris?" I said. "That's disrespectful not only to yourself but to our relationship and your brother too."

"Ain't like he knows what's going on anyway. Hell yeah, I'm still getting high. I got to do something to keep my sanity. Everybody dying and shit; this is just too much for me," she complained. Starr stomped out of the kitchen and ran into the den with Chris. I followed her.

"Starr, let me talk to you," I begged. Starr plopped down on the couch next to her brother, grabbed the remote control, and flipped throught the channels. Chris rocked back and forth in front of the television, smiling and giggling to himself.

"Starr, he's watching TV, don't change his channel," I told her.

"Black, I do not feel like talking about this. I'm tired of arguing with you." She smacked her lips, then changed the TV back to the program Crazy Chris had been watching.

"Starr, what are you talking about? You act like we argue all the time. This is the only thing we've ever really argued about," I said.

"Well, I'm sick and tired of arguing anyway, and I'm not going to marry any man who thinks he's my daddy and likes to argue with me all the time!" she screamed at me. Starr was getting loud, and Chris had started rocking faster.

"Starr, calm down, you are upsetting Chris," I said calmly. "All of this screaming is not necessary."

"There you go again, telling me what's not necessary. You know what, Black, you need to decide if I'm the one you want to marry, 'cause obviously you got too many complaints about me," she said.

"Baby, all I'm saying is you need to stop getting high. I can get you some drug counseling if you like. If you don't want to do it here in Richmond, I'll send you away. There's a good rehab program in Arizona," I said, trying to get Starr to listen and understand where I was coming from.

"Arizona? Arizona? Now you trying to send me away. Why, so you can fuck around while I'm gone? You know what, Black, it's over. I'm not marrying you." Starr snatched her car keys off the coffee table and grabbed Chris by the hand. I let out a huge sigh. Her continually calling off the wedding was getting old.

"There you go again calling off the wedding. Starr, you can't keep doing this every time you get mad about trivial stuff." I followed behind her and Chris.

"Ain't nothing trivial about your man calling you a cokehead!" she shouted at me. "Arizona. Ain't no black people in the desert, but you trying to send my ass out there? You know what, Black, you are good and crazy!" She stomped through the house. Starr was being irrational; I could see there was no use in trying to talk to her anymore.

"Starr, if you need more time that's fine. We can postpone the wedding. But if you don't marry me by this Christmas, it's over. I love you to death, Starr, but I can't keep going through this." I sighed.

Starr spun around and looked at me like I was half crazy, and then screamed: "Mutherfucking Arizona! Nigga, you have lost your mind!" Then she and Crazy Chris left the house.

• • •

Starr didn't take me seriously. She continued getting high and became so bold that she started sniffing cocaine right in front of me. It hurt me dearly to see Starr's cocaine habit spiraling out of control, yet I refused to contribute to her drug use. Starr wouldn't reveal who her supplier was; she just assured me that my drugs were not reaching her hands, or her nose for that matter. Meanwhile, I continued going to the library, where I would meet Amanda and tutor her. Her world history class was studying the life and times of Adolf Hitler, and since I had studied the ruthless leader in my spare time, I was more than happy to assist.

Chapter 40

Two weeks before Christmas Starr called off the wedding again. I came home only to find her and all of her belongings missing. I couldn't understand why Starr didn't want to marry me. I was good to her and gave her the world, but obviously the world wasn't good enough. I needed to do something to clear my head, so I headed over to VCU to the Christmas play being sponsored by their arts and humanities department. Most of the student body was gone home for Christmas, but there was a small group of students who lagged behind. I was leaving the student union when Amanda approached me.

"Hey, Bilal, did you enjoy the play?" She stopped me before I exited the building.

"Hey, Amanda, I didn't know you were here." I pretended to be surprised. I had actually noticed her from afar but really didn't feel like being bothered with her.

"Yeah, the play was real nice. I wish I had tried out for a part. Are you by yourself?" she asked, looking over her shoulders.

"I'm always solo when I come up here. You know that, Amanda." I half smiled. Amanda chuckled a little.

"Well, what are you about to do? I'm about to get something to eat, would you like to join me? My treat," she offered.

I smiled at the invitation. "Amanda, you know that I'm not about to let a lady pay for anything. If you want something to eat, I'll get you something to eat. No problem." I nodded.

"Okay, cool. There's this nice place around the corner that everybody is heading to. We can just go there." She motioned for me to follow her.

Before we exited the student union, Amanda turned to me and asked, "Are you sure your fiancé wouldn't mind?"

"Don't have a fiancé anymore," I confessed. "She called off the wedding—again."

"Oh my God, Bilal, I am so sorry. It's Christmastime. You shouldn't have to go through this alone. I'm so sorry for you." Amanda apologized over and over again, as if she were the one who had broke it off with me.

Amanda and I dipped into the cold air and headed toward the Fan District. The Fan District was an area near the university where students, vagrants, musicians, punk rockers, and just plain old everyday weirdos hung out. I wasn't worried about running into anybody that I knew. A black person from the hood hanging in the Fan District was like a Jehovah's Witness at a Christmas concert. It just wasn't happening.

We settled in a nice cozy spot where jazz musicians played and couples sat and fed each other. Since I wasn't on that type of time with Amanda, I felt uncomfortable in the environment, but after a few bottles of champagne, I began to loosen up.

"Bilal, do you remember how you helped me ace my essay on Hitler and my final history exam?"

"Yeah, how could I forget? I thought you would never catch on," I joked. Amanda reached across the table and smacked me on the arm.

"Boy, don't be funny. I tried very hard and did my best." She laughed. "Thank you very much."

"Just joking, girl. It's the champagne messing with me. You know I don't drink," I told her. Amanda never removed her hand from my arm; she began to stroke my arm up and down.

"Bilal, this band really sounds good. You think?"

"They're all right," I answered, not really caring about the music one way or the other.

"Come on, let's dance. Everybody else is dancing." She pulled at me. I snatched my arm back.

"Nawh, Amanda, I don't get down like that." I sat up straight in the chair, making sure the champagne wasn't getting the best of me.

"You what?" She frowned.

"I don't dance," I told her.

"Excuse me, waiter, can we get another bottle of champagne and an order of buffalo wings?"

"Sure," the waiter said, taking down the order. Five minutes later, the waiter returned with the order.

"Now you know ain't no way they cooked those wings that fast!" I laughed. "I'm not eating them."

Amanda examined the wings carefully. "You're right. When we finish this last bottle of champagne, let's just leave. I know where we can get some buffalo wings that are so good, they'll make you want to smack your momma," Amanda joked. We finished the bottle of champagne and left the cozy spot, leaving the half-cooked wings right on the table.

"So where are we going?" I asked.

"To my apartment so I can make you some of those smack-your-momma wings," she stated.

I was reluctant to go home with Amanda because Starr was heavy on my mind, but before I could say no, I said, "Yes."

"Okay, I live not too far from here on Monument Avenue. Do you want to leave your car at the school and ride with me?" she asked.

"I'm in a hoopty tonight, so it really doesn't matter," I responded.

"A what?" she huffed. "Bilal, you have got to talk so I can understand you. I don't understand all that slang talk."

"All right, Ms. Amanda, I can respect that. Let's just walk back to the school and get your car, then you can take me to get mine and I'll follow you home. How's that?" I joked with her.

Amanda rolled her eyes at me playfully. "Much better," she smiled.

"I've got to make a phone call first," I said. I stepped over to the corner pay phone to call Putt, who answered on the first ring. "Man, I'm glad you're home. Listen up. I'm about to go over Amanda's house. Hey, Amanda, what is your address and home telephone number?" I yelled out to her. She gave me the information and I repeated it to Putt, who chuckled through the phone.

"Amanda who, man?" he questioned.

I laughed with him. "Amanda, your girl Jenny's distant cousin. Shorty is trying to kidnap me, talking about how she gone make me some buffalo wings. You know good food is the way to my heart, so I'm going with her." I laughed.

Putt let out a huge squeal. "Man, I don't blame you, I know you love Starr to death, but life goes on. Oh, and by the way, man, we need to step our shit up a little and get us some car phones, man. It don't make sense that we still using pay phones and shit. If them white mufuckers can ride around with car phones in bags and shit, so can we. Get Head's mother to handle that shit after the holidays," Putt said. "All right, nigga, holler at you later."

"A'ight, man, just call me at this chick's house or page me if anything hops off," I told him before Amanda and I strolled down the block and jumped into her car.

We weren't at Amanda's house five minutes before she was jumping out of her clothes. Amanda took a shower while I sat and watched TV in her living room. As soon as she was finished, she came out into the living room, stepped in front of me, and dropped her beach towel.

"Make love to me, Bilal," she said in a sexy voice. She leaned over and kissed me on my neck. I was there for buffalo wings, not pussy, so I tried to get her up off me.

"Amanda, no." I attempted to reject her, but before I could, she was all over me like a dog in heat.

She wrestled with my pants and unbuckled my belt. The next thing I know she had my penis in her mouth and she was swallowing my balls. Everything happened so fast that before I knew it, Amanda was dragging me down the hallway to her bedroom. She laid me down on her full-size bed and jumped on top of me, dropped her head down to my pole and sucking me some more. I pumped hard into her mouth, trying to get my dick on the hard. I was feeling good; my eyes had rolled to the back of my head.

"Don't stop," I moaned. "Damn, Amanda."

Amanda slid a mouthful of saliva onto my dick and that shit drove me crazy. She raised her head up, and I looked down at her to see why she had stopped.

"Eat me," she said.

"What!" I sat up straight on the bed.

"Eat me, Bilal. Eat my pussy," she said. The same girl who just thirty minutes ago was as proper as a Catholic school girl was begging me to eat her out.

"Baby, I'm sorry, but I don't eat anything that can get up and walk away from me," I told her honestly.

Amanda must've been out of her damn mind. I barely even knew her; how dare she ask me to eat her pussy.

"Whatever, I bet you ate your fiancé's pussy," she said, over-stepping her boundaries. Since she was pussyfooting around in my business, I figured why not tell her the truth.

"Actually, I never have," I said bluntly. I had never eaten Starr's pussy or any other pussy a day in my life and I sure as hell wasn't about to eat out a chick that sucked my dick just because I had tutored her in world history. Amanda was bugging. She was a girl gone wild. She was young, hot, and ready to be fucked.

"Bilal, I am so horny. I haven't had any in a while. Fuck me, Bilal," she begged. Amanda rolled over to her stomach and arched her ass in the air. She reached over to the nightstand and handed me a condom. I strapped it on. Just as I slid my dick in, Amanda reached over again to the nightstand. This time, she turned on the radio. The song "Two People" by Tina Turner came on. That song always made me think of Starr. Immediately, my dick went soft. I rolled over to my back, and Amanda dropped down, trying to slob on my knob again.

"Nawh, just stop, Amanda. It must be the champagne," I said, shoving her away. Amanda's pussy was on fire and she wanted so badly to be fucked.

"Oh God, I'm so horny!" she shouted, bringing God's name into her horny little world. It wasn't the time or place for her to be calling his name, but she did.

"Oh God, I'm so horny," she repeated. "I've got to get this cum out of me!" she screamed.

Then Amanda opened the drawer to her nightstand, pulled out a pink toy vibrator with circulating balls, checked the batteries to make sure they were in, and then she cocked her legs wide open.

"Bilal, you want to see me get off?" she asked me.

"Why not," I answered. I propped myself up with my elbows and watched. Amanda massaged her own clit with her middle fin-ger, and then she swirled her ass around as she played with her-self. By the look on her face, it was obvious that her finger felt good on her clit. She licked her lips, grabbed hold of her breasts, and played with them. Amanda was getting hotter by the minute. Her eyes rolled to the back of her head as she humped up and down on the bed. Suddenly, she stopped pleasuring herself with her hands. She grabbed the vibrator, hit the switch and shoved it into her pussy.

"Ooh, aah, ooh, aah, ooa, aah, this feels so good," she moaned. "I'm cumming, oh God, I'm cumming!" she screamed, pleasuring and releasing herself.

After Amanda busted her nut, she reached deep into her pussy and pulled out the condom that had come off of my dick. She tossed the condom onto the floor and threw the toy dick onto the recliner chair.

"Hum, hum, hum, now that was good," she exclaimed.

Afterward, she wrapped her legs around me and fell off fast asleep.

• • •

Starr refused to get back with me. She straight up ignored me whenever I saw her. When I wasn't working, I spent my time over Amanda's house. I really missed Starr and wasn't exactly crazy about Amanda, but she gave me the attention that I so desired. Starr and Amanda were like night and day. Amanda wasn't domesticated at all; the only thing she did know how to cook was buffalo wings, so we ate a lot of carry-out. I never asked Amanda to be my lady, but after spending so much time with her, she gave us the title of "couple."

There was one little problem in the relationship. I just couldn't keep a hard-on with her. The sex with Amanda wasn't all that great. In fact she was probably what some would call a dry fuck. Her pussy dried up easily, and, at times, trying to get my dick inside of her dry pussy would leave my dick sore and scabbed up. However, Amanda's head game was on a thousand. Amanda could suck a dick until the roosters came home; yet and still, there were times that my penis wouldn't rise to the occasion. I went to the doctor, believing that I had erectile dysfunction. After several tests, it was concluded that there wasn't a thing wrong with my penis. The doctor told me that my inability to keep an erection was more mental than anything else.

Chapter 41

It was New Year's Eve, and G was throwing the biggest, most talked-about party in town. Somehow he had managed to get the Jewish owners of the Cool Lane Bowling Alley to reopen the building just for him. The building had been shut down for years, but G made them an offer they couldn't refuse.

Putt decided to take Jenny along with him. They had been together ever since their first night together and two years later, Jenny was pregnant with Putt's baby boy. Putt never did get custody of the two children that he had with Cocoa, but he was allowed visitation and was able to get his children on some weekends and most holidays. Putt was a proud father. He looked forward to having his third child and loved Jenny to death for carrying his seed. Amanda learned about the party and knew that Putt was taking Jenny so she asked me to take her and I agreed. As soon as we stepped into the party, Dread approached me right away.

"What's up, boss, Putt, ladies? Boss, let me holler at you for a minute." Dread pulled me to the side.

"Yeah, what's up, Dread?" I wondered.

"Look, man, I'm not trying to be all in your business but why did you bring shorty girl here? Man, don't you know that Starr is here?" he questioned. "You should've known Starr was gone be here." He shook his head, 'cause he figured I had set myself up for trouble.

"No, actually, I didn't think Starr would be here because we normally step out together, and besides, Starr has been acting crazy since she's been falling off," I said as I cased the joint, hoping and praying that Starr wouldn't catch me out with Amanda.

By my estimate, there was already about four hundred people in the joint. I figured if I laid low that it was possible that me and Starr wouldn't bump into each other.

"A'ight, good looking out," I said to Dread.

We decided to take our place in the VIP room. The ladies chilled out on a sofa, and me and Putt sat in the corner tripping off the clowns in the VIP. I couldn't understand for the life of me how half the people back there thought they were *very important people*. There were more than a few tricks scattered about, broke dudes, and a sprinkle of real niggas with real money. We later found out that G had charged the not-so-VIP folks fifty dollars for a pass.

We were in the back kicking it with the crowd, when Dread came in.

"B, Putt, come here for a minute." He motioned for us.

We excused ourselves from the ladies and stepped outside the VIP room to see what was up. Dread pointed to the dance floor. A crowd was gathered around a small table.

"Oh my God, what the—?" I exclaimed. My mouth dropped to the floor.

It was Starr, and she was jamming on top of a table. Starr was always a good dancer, and over the years, cheerleading and track had done her body good. Although she looked a little rough around the edges at times because of her new coke addiction, Starr's body was just as tight as a virgin's pussy. She was still a perfect size three. Starr was on top of the table, dropping it like it was hot. All eyes were on her as she backed that tiny thing up. I couldn't believe that Starr was showing out like that. I stood there for a few minutes watching her like everybody else.

"Man, she's been up there for at least ten minutes, dancing nonstop. B man, Starr is high as a kite." Dread gave me an embarrassed look. He pointed to the crowd, "Man, you see Frankie and Baije, they've been trying to get her down, but she won't stop dancing." Dread worried about her.

I zoomed in closer to get a better look at my ex. Starr looked damn good. She was wearing a long red fitted dress that dipped low in the back and the front. Her red stiletto heels made her look about two inches taller than she was, and she had dyed her hair auburn and pinned it up in a bun. Starr may have been tripping off of the coke, but you best believe when I tell you, she was still the baddest chick in the bowling alley.

I shoved my way through the crowd and headed down front. When Starr noticed me, she danced even harder. Baije turned to me as I approached.

"Black, she won't get down," Baije whined. "Please help us get her down."

"Starr, get down!" I snatched a few chairs out of the way and demanded that she get off the table. "Come on now. Get down. Don't make a fool out of yourself in front of all these people." I reached for her, trying to talk some sense into her head. Starr broke out laughing,

"Me make a fool out of myself? I don't think so. I'm still the baddest chick in town. Why you think all these hoes are crowded around this table checking me out! *Whores!*" she screamed at them. All the girls around the table who were watching her every move turned their heads for a minute, but then they turned right back around and continued watching. They couldn't help it; Starr was the shit and she knew how to throw down.

"Anyway, don't worry about me, you need to worry about that country-ass girl you got with you. Her country ass got on a black and green sweater skirt set. That shit was played out in the late eighties, but you wouldn't know that 'cause your black ass was locked up or were you?" Starr ran off at the mouth, still dancing, throwing her hands up and shaking her butt at the same time. "Now get away from me," Starr fumed.

"Excuse me but who are you calling country?" Amanda's voice startled me. She had followed me out of the VIP and had been standing there watching the entire time. Before I could say anything, Baije jumped at Amanda.

"She's talking about you! And what? You want to do something about it?" she bucked in Amanda's face. Starr continued dancing on the tabletop; her back was turned, so she was oblivious to what was going on around her. I tried to calm Baije down.

"Come on, Baije, this girl ain't about that," I jumped in.

"Black, you know damn well you should not have brought this girl with you to the party. You wrong for that!" Baije rolled her eyes at me.

Amanda pulled at my shirt. "Baby, can we go home, because this party is just too ghetto for me. I don't have time for this," she said.

Baije overheard Amanda and she snapped. "See, ho, you think you're cute but you're not. Look at you, and look at my girl. You can't touch Starr with a ten-foot pole!" Baije argued, causing a bigger scene than the one we already had.

"Baije, chill out!" Putt demanded.

"I'm not chilling shit. This stank ho come up in here thinking she all that, calling this party ghetto and gritting on my girl. Fuck her, I'm about to beat the—"

Before I knew it, Baije had grabbed Amanda, put her in a headlock, and pounded her in the face. Me and Putt pulled Baije off of her, but not before Baije had knocked Amanda's earring off, sending the oversize hoop flying clean across the room. Amanda and Jenny may have been cousins, but Jenny wasn't crazy enough to intervene in the fight. She didn't risk having her unborn child injured, so she stayed clear and let them fight. The old saying *Blood is thicker than water* didn't apply in this case. Jenny yelled for help and that's basically all she did.

"Stop, ya'll stop! Baije, stop, you gone kill that girl!" she hollered from a distance.

Just as soon as we had Baije and Amanda separated, Starr kicked off her stilettos, jumped off of the table, and ran over and stole Amanda in the jaw. *Pow.* Amanda held her face in her hand but didn't try to fight back. I guess she figured she couldn't handle the *ghetto* girls.

"Come on, you trick, you want some of me?" Starr bounced around, holding her red gown up with her hands because it was dragging the floor. Then, she let go of her gown and threw her hands up in front of her face and invited Amanda to bring it.

"Come on, show me what you got, bitch!" Starr said, bobbing and weaving like a professional female boxer. I picked her little behind up and carried her toward the front door.

"Put me down, put me down." Starr kicked and screamed. "You better get your country-ass girlfriend. Don't touch me!" she shouted on the way to the front door.

"Black, get her out of here. We're right behind you. We got them," Putt, Frankie and Dread shouted, following me out.

"Stay back, Boo, before you get hurt," Putt yelled to Jenny, who was trying to keep up with all of us.

The crowd parted and made room for us to get by. On the way out I spotted Barbette out of the corner of my eye. Ever since I had been getting money, the bald-headed chick had been trying to get at me.

"Hey, Black," she giggled, as if the entire scene was funny.

Starr stopped kicking long enough to see who had spoken to me. When she realized it was Barbette, she kicked her foot hard one time in the air, catching Barbette in the face, sending her bald-headed behind flying to the ground. Barbette screamed in pain.

" I'mma get you, Starr," she wept from the floor.

"Bring it! I told you, bitch, one time before not to ever fuck with my man," Starr screamed at Barbette. The fact that she was still referring to me as her man surprised me.

Baije fought to get away. She wanted a piece of bald-headed Barbette too.

"Let me go, I'mma kick that bitch ass too!" she yelled.

Finally, we made it to the front door with the screaming ladies still fighting and kicking. G and his security opened the door to let us out. I turned to him and apologized for the disruption that I had obviously caused.

"Man, I'm sorry about this. I owe you one, man. Get at me tomorrow,"

G smiled, then let out a slight chuckle. "No problem, Black. The more shit that happens at a party, the more memorable the party is. Ya'll just made my night. Niggas gone be talking about this for days," he said, laughing.

We separated the girls in the parking lot and tried to get them to calm down. Starr and Baije picked up empty beer bottles and started throwing them at Amanda. I shoved Amanda into the car. I wanted to talk to Starr, but I had to get Amanda out of harm's way. I had no choice but to leave with her.

"Ya'll make sure they get home okay. Don't let Starr drive because she is too messed up," I told my Crew.

They nodded. "We got them man, just go home."

I started up the Range Rover, and Amanda and I drove off to my house. It was the first time that I had ever taken Amanda to my home. I allowed her to shower and she changed into one of my T-shirts. I felt sorry for Amanda because Starr and Baije had done a number on her. Her face was bruised, and she had a bloody nose. We spent the rest of the evening flipping channels, waiting on the countdown to the New Year. Someone called the house a few times, but whenever I answered they hung up. I suspected it was Starr, so I ended up taking the phone off the hook. Although I was angry with Starr for causing a scene, I just couldn't get the picture of her in that red dress out of my mind.

I grabbed a pillow and rested my head. Within minutes, I dozed off to sleep and was dreaming about the day that I had asked Starr to marry me.

The next thing I know, Amanda was screaming, "Yes, Yes, I'll marry you! Oh, Bilal, it was so nice of you to propose when the clock struck twelve-oh-one!" She ran around shouting, happy about the proposal. I sat up straight on the couch and rubbed my eyes. That's when it hit me. Amanda wasn't aware that I sometimes slept with my eyes open. I had been talking in my sleep, apparently asking Starr to marry me. I thought to myself, *Lord, what have I gotten myself into?*

Around two a.m., I jumped up to check my voice mail messages. I figured if Starr was the one playing on the phone, she had more than likely left a few obscene messages. There was one message waiting. I listened to the message in its entirety.

"Hello, Bilal, I'm calling to wish you a happy New Year. I love you and I hope that you will find it in your heart to speak to me soon because there are some things you need to know. If you don't want to talk to me, then please, look for answers in the book of Genesis." I erased Grandma's message from the phone and crawled into bed with Amanda, who was fast asleep in my oversize T-shirt.

Chapter 42

Amanda and I were engaged under false pretenses. I just couldn't bring myself to tell her that I was proposing to Starr in my sleep and not to her. I didn't want to hurt her feelings, so I went along with the wedding plans that she and her family had started to make. Besides, I was ready to settle down and although I wasn't in love with Amanda, I figured I could learn to love her. I started going to church with Amanda, which by coincidence just happened to be only minutes away from Fairfield.

By March, rumor of my plans to marry Amanda were circulating. When Starr heard of the wedding, she slashed all of the tires and broke out all of the windows on my Range Rover. Whenever I would see her, she would yell obscenities at me or not say anything to me at all. One day I was out on the strip when Starr called me over to Suga Momma's. I was surprised that she wanted to speak to me. I hurried over to Suga Momma's porch.

"Hey, Starr, what's up?' I asked, trying to keep cool. I kep neutral look on my face because there was just no telling with Starr. I had no idea what she was up to.

"Black, can you please go and check on the Kims because I just heard that people have been threatening them all day since the verdict was read in the Latasha Harlins case," Starr informed me.

Latasha Harlins was a black teenager who had been shot over a bottle of orange juice by a Korean store owner in California. I had been keeping up with the case because the senseless murder of Latasha had outraged me.

"For real?" I frowned. I had to get to the Kims right away. I couldn't let anything happen to them because they had looked out for me in my time of need.

"Yeah, somebody just called to tell me that Mrs. Kim was crying and yelling for people to leave them alone." Starr knew how much I liked the Kims.

"Thanks, Starr, for letting me know. I'm going up there right now." I thanked her.

It was the first time since our breakup that Starr and I had a civilized conversation so I took advantage of the opportunity. If Starr was willing to take me back, I would have dropped Amanda quick, fast, and in a hurry.

"Starr, come on now. It shouldn't be like this. You walk around acting like you don't know me. We've been through a lot together and I can't stand not being friends with you. If you don't want me at least be my friend. Damn, Starr, you know how I feel about you, girl," I rambled, trying to get it all out as fast and efficient as I could.

"I'm going in now. It's kind of chilly out here. I hope everything is okay with the Kims. I know how you feel about them, so I thought you should know." Starr straight up ignored everything that I said, then she closed the door shut on me. I left the porch and headed up the block.

"Yo, I need a ride to the Chinese restaurant," I yelled at no one in particular.

"Damn, Black, didn't you just finish eating corn beef hash?" Putt laughed.

"Man, I ain't hungry. Starr just told me that niggas been wilding out on the Kims ever since the verdict in the Latasha Harlins case came out today."

"Who in the hell is Latasha Harlins?" Frankie asked.

"That's the little girl that was killed last year by the Korean woman over a bottle of orange juice in California," I informed him.

"Oh, I ain't know nothing about that. So why are people messing with the Chinese folks if a Korean lady was the one who killed the little girl?" Frankie inquired. Dread blew out a deep sigh.

"Nigga, you stupid as hell. You asked some dumb-ass questions. Frankie, what do you know?!" Dread teased.

"I know how to make money," Frankie bragged.

"Yeah, nigga, you know how to make money, but what good is it to you if you don't know how to count it," Dread shot back at him.

"Frankie, Chinese and Koreans are all of Asian descent. That's why," I answered his question.

"That's why what?" Frankie looked at me stupid. He had forgotten that fast that he had asked a question. I jumped into the car with Putt and Dread. Everybody laughed at Frankie, who for the most part was dumb as a brick but knew how to stack paper.

The Kims were scared out of their minds. Teenagers from nearby neighborhoods had come through and vandalized their building, breaking windows and verbally threatening them. I gave the Kims all of my contact numbers to reach me, then I had Head's mother meet with them to deliver twenty thousand dollars. The Kims had a sick daughter back in China and worried that if they closed down for a month that they would lose mo and ultimately their business. I was happy to give them a little cash to tide them over until the race riots subsided.

It had been a long, disappointing day for me. I hurried home with hopes of going straight to bed. When I got there, Amanda was waiting for me, and she appeared to be pretty upset.

"Bilal, can I please speak to you for a minute?" she said as she followed me into the bedroom.

"Yes, what is it?" Amanda was always pressing me about something as soon as I stepped into the door. That really pissed me off about her; she didn't know how important it was for me to relax. Amanda was always up in my space. Unlike Starr, she never allowed a nigga time to breathe.

"I know that you gave those Chinese people some money, and I'm just trying to understand how you think we are going to continue to live comfortably if you keep giving our money away. You need to be a little more thrifty," she had the nerve to form her mouth to say.

After all of my blood, sweat, and tears, I couldn't believe that Amanda had the audacity to say "our money." It was Starr who had looked out for me and helped me build my empire, so what the fuck was Amanda talking about? She was definitely on some bullshit and I had to check her on the spot.

"Our money? Listen, Amanda, as long as you and I are together, don't you ever question me about what I do with my money. Starr never did that," I told her. Amanda frowned.

"There you go again, always talking about Starr. If she loved you, Bilal, she would be here with you and not in the streets chasing drugs. She chose drugs over you."

Amanda was way out of line and I needed to put an end to her attacks on Starr once and for all.

"Amanda, I've asked you before not to talk about Starr in a disheartening manner. You don't know her, so I would appreciate it if you keep her name from your mouth. Besides, you're pushing your luck," I told her straight up. Amanda had only one leg left to stand on, and she was about to lose that one.

"Well, you're the one who mentioned her." Amanda plopped down on the bed.

I wasn't in the mood to argue with Amanda, but it seemed like she was asking for a fight. She continued running off at the mouth.

"I mean, what have those Chinese people done for you to make you want to give them twenty thousand dollars," she continued.

"Listen, I'll do whatever I want to do with my hard-earned money. This is all my shit, and twenty G's ain't no money anyway. One other thing, I'm going to straighten out Head's mother for putting you all in my business."

Head's mother was my personal assistant; she and Amanda had become pretty close, because for the most part they were just alike. Stuck up, bourgeois broads who really didn't have much of anything, yet they thought they were better than everybody else. Amanda and Head's mother were two peas in a pod. Neither one of them had any other girlfriends, so they depended on each other's company.

"Twenty thousand dollars, that's a lot of money!" Amanda fumed.

"Yeah, keep talking and I'll send them some more," I told her as I left the bedroom. I took my shirt off and headed for the shower. Before I could get into the shower, the phone rang. I stepped back and picked it up. It was Starr, and she was crying.

"Black, I'm sorry to call your house. I'm not trying to start trouble with you and your girl," Starr whined.

"Starr, you ain't causing no trouble, what's wrong?" I snapped.

"Black, Li'l Wayne and his boys threw me into a car and dr

me around the block for thirty minutes and wouldn't let me get out of the car. I thought they were going to kill me. Black, I was so scared," Starr cried hysterically.

"Starr, where are you now and where were you when this happened?" My blood pressure was boiling over.

Starr took in a deep breath and began to explain. "I was in Blackwell," she answered.

"Starr, what were you doing over Southside? You know Southside is off limits for you because you're my girl. I mean, you were my girl," I corrected myself.

"Black, I never lied to you before and I'm not going to lie to you now. I was over Southside looking for some coke because I can't get anybody to sell me shit 'cause you got everybody in Churchill scared of you. Malcolm won't even score for me," she fussed.

"That's right, Starr; I dare a nigga to sell you anything. That's the word I put on the street. You need to stop getting high 'cause that shit is bringing you down and with your heart problems, if you keep it up, that shit is gone kill you. You know what the doctor told you. Anyway, are you okay? Did them niggas hurt you in any way at all?" I asked as I pulled my shirt back over my head.

Amanda sat on the bed, looking at me like I was crazy. If looks could kill, her eyes would have murdered me a thousand times over. I turned my head in the opposite direction.

"No, they didn't hurt me, but he told me to tell you that he was going to kill you. Black, that little dude is crazy. Li'l Wayne is ugly and crazy so be careful," she warned me.

"Fuck that nigga. When have you ever known me to be scared of a nigga? That nigga is a punk and I'm going to handle this shit. I'm letting you know right now that you will have around-the-clock security from now on. I'm not going to let anything happen you," I promised.

"Black, you can't have people following me around everywhere I have my own life to live," she fussed.

"Just watch and see. Keep your little tail in the house. I'll get up with you later, and Starr, you better answer the phone if I call," I told her, and then I slammed down the phone.

Amanda stood there watching me with her hands on her hips. "So whenever she calls, you jump. Is that how it's going to be?" she huffed.

I grabbed my keys. "Amanda, you knew what you were getting yourself into when you hooked up with me. It ain't like I had a job when I met you, so you need to understand that all of this right here comes with the territory. Starr is my ex, but I'm not going to let a nigga abduct her and then threaten me. So, you are either down with me and all that comes along with it or you're not. And oh, by the way, you need to stop lying to your family, telling them I'm in school to be a doctor and that my house and cars were left to me in an inheritance. Hell, they are going to find out sooner or later anyway," I told her.

Amanda moved in close and wrapped her arms around me. "Baby, what about your plans to get out of the drug game and go back to school? I thought you told me you were tired of this life," she said.

"I am tired of this life, but right now, I'm in too deep. It will happen. I'll get out in due time. Don't wait up for me; I'll be back in the morning. Lock up, set the alarm system, and remember that there's a thirty-eight-caliber handgun under my pillow and, Amanda, you better use that mutherfucker if you have to!" I said as I stepped into the night air.

Chapter 43

We drove around Southside all night long searching for Li'l Wayne and his boys. Once again, they were nowhere to be found, and the streets they were known to hang on were like ghost towns. We knew that it was just a matter of time before we crossed paths with them, so we waited patiently for the time to come. The ongoing beef was too serious for any one of us to slip up, so we planned carefully and waited to catch them and end this once and for all.

A few days after Starr's abduction, Putt and Jenny came by the house to pick up Amanda. Jenny and Amanda were going on a bus trip to Atlantic City, and Putt had agreed to drop them off. He rang the doorbell a few times to let me know he was outside. hurried downstairs to let them in. I was excited to be seeing my lson, John Paul. I opened the door and grabbed the baby car-'rom Jenny. Putt shoved his way past me and headed straight fridge. Baby John Paul was fast asleep in his carrier, so I kissed him lightly on the forehead, and Jenny headed upstairs with the baby to check on Amanda.

"You get any sleep last night?" Putt asked me, head stuck all up in my refrigerator. He helped himself to a bottle of orange juice and grabbed a handful of grapes.

"Nawh, man, actually I didn't get any sleep 'cause Manda was all over me, kicking me in my head and shit. Man, she either sleeps too wild, or she likes to sleep right under me. Either way, I can't rest when I sleep in the bed with her, so sometimes I just sleep on the leather couch in the room," I answered.

Putt shook his head at me and grabbed one of Amanda's bananas off of the kitchen counter.

"Man, stop complaining. That girl loves the hell out of you, man," he said, peeling the banana and taking a big chomp out of it. Putt was one greedy dude. He hadn't been in the house five minutes and already he had eaten grapes, swallowed a bottle of juice, and was on his way to demolishing the banana. He jumped up and stuck his head back into the refrigerator and pulled out a pack of turkey meat and grabbed a loaf of bread from the bread box. Putt slapped two slices of meat in between the Wonder bread and bit into his dry sandwich. I just looked at him.

"Yeah, man, I know she loves me, but still." I shook my head at him.

"Still what? Man, you still not over Starr," he stated as a matter of fact. "B, man, you need to get over Starr and move on with your life," Putt continued, voicing an opinion that he had for some time. Putt caught me completely off guard with his comment, because if nobody else knew how I felt about Starr, Putt did. He was my righthand man. He practically knew everything about me and besides that, we talked about Starr all the time, so I didn't understand why he was telling me to forget the one chick that he knew I truly cared for. Putt was tripping and for what? I didn't know.

"Man, I'm marrying Amanda in a month. Call it what you want," I shot back at him. Putt stood up from the table, cleaned up his mess, then fixed himself a glass of ice water.

"By the way, B, I have something to tell you about Starr, but first you got to promise not to flip out," he said, shaking the ice around in the glass.

"What is it?" I asked. Something about Putt's tone that morning wasn't sitting right with me. In all of our years of friendship, it was the first time that I felt uneasy with him. Putt pushed back from the table and sat the empty glass down.

"Man, word on the street is that Starr was fucking with the nigga Dice and that she went over Southside to apologize to Li'l Wayne for Dice being killed. B, Li'l Wayne and Dice are first cousins, they're not brothers. Dice's mother and Li'l Wayne's mother are the sisters of Mr. Wayne, the old pervert-ass dude that used to go with Suga Momma. You know that nigga been dead a long time—" I cut him off.

Starr had already told me the truth; she was brutally honest and didn't have to put herself out like that, so I didn't want to hear shit another nigga had to say because I trusted Starr. Her word meant more to me than any nigga on the street.

"Man, Starr went over Southside looking for cocaine. Not to apologize to that nigga Li'l Wayne. She ain't got shit to apologize for!" I snapped. "P, man. I can't believe you of all people, listening to rumors that them niggas from Southside putting out." I gave him a disappointed nod, then reached inside the fridge and grabbed me a grape soda. I popped open the can and continued my conversation with my righthand man.

"Besides, you know Starr ain't ever been with another nigga. She was a virgin until she got with me." I shared what I knew was the holy gospel. If I wasn't sure about anything else, I was sure 'bout that and that right there, I bet that on everything. Putt lowered his head, and then looked back up at me. He let out a slight chuckle.

"B, come on now. Malcolm?" he asked.

"Starr ain't ever fuck Malcolm. Malcolm is her boy, just like Baije is her girl." I defended her. "Putt, what the fuck is wrong with you? First you beat up a white man for no reason, now you come in here attacking Starr. P, don't bring me no shit from the street unless you got proof," I told him.

Putt cleared his throat. "All I'm saying is maybe there is some truth to the rumors and if Starr is hiding something, maybe we should know about it." Putt stood up from the table, obviously as agitated with me as I was with him.

"Yo, Jenny, are ya'll ready?" he hollered upstairs. Jenny and Amanda came down, ready to go. The baby was still asleep, so I took him from Jenny and held him in my arms real tight and kissed him on the forehead again.

"Love ya, man," I told him. Amanda kissed me on the cheek and grabbed her keys from the kitchen counter.

"You got enough money?" I asked her.

"Yes, Bilal. I do." She smiled back at me and followed Jenny out of the front door.

"Man, we still going fishing or what?" Putt asked. We had plans to go fishing later that day. I looked at him and thought about all the bullshit that he had repeated to me from the streets.

"Man, fuck a fish. I'm tired. I ain't going nowhere."

• • •

The next morning the phone rang, waking me up from my sleep. I snatched it from the cradle.

"Yeah," I answered.

"Bilal, is Pierre there with you?" Amanda wondered. Amanda and Jenny were back from Atlantic City and Putt was supposed to have picked them up. It wasn't like Putt to not be on time. Immediately, a red flag went off in my head.

"No, he ain't here. I haven't spoken to him since yesterday. Amanda, let me speak to Jenny." Amanda handed the phone to Jenny.

"Hello," Jenny answered, the worry in her voice so noticeable I could see it through the phone.

"Jenny, did you page him, did you call the house, the car phone?" I asked, running off a list of possibilities. I didn't want to think the worst, but the best was far from my mind. I had a gut feeling that something was wrong.

"Yeah, Black, I did all of that. It's not like Putt not to answer his pager or car phone. Something ain't right." Jenny said what we were both feeling.

"Okay, I'm on my way. I'll meet ya'll at the house. Call a taxi; take it all the way home. I'll pay for it," I said.

"Okay," Jenny agreed.

"Oh. Where is Head's mother, where's Ms. Cheryl?" I wondered.

"She got drunk and stayed in Atlantic City. She met some man there and decided to stay. She said she knew him, so we figured she was all right," Jenny said.

"Aight, I'm on my way."

I jumped up, called Frankie and Dread and told them to meet me at Putt's house. They said they had left Putt and the baby around nine o'clock. I told them that Putt hadn't showed up to pick up the ladies and that I was worried that something bad may have happened to him. We planned to check out the house first, and if he wasn't there, we planned on riding through the city until we found him.

I drove about eighty miles an hour trying to get to Putt and Jenny's house in Henrico County. When I pulled in the driveway, Frankie and Dread were standing outside waiting on me. A half minute later, a yellow taxicab pulled up and Jenny and Amanda jumped out. I ran up the sidewalk with my Glock by my side. Frankie and Dread followed me with their Glocks raised. Jenny had her keys out, but I snatched them from her hands.

"Get back. Let us check things out first," I told her.

As I attempted to put the key in the front door, the door opened right up. Jenny started crying right away.

"Oh, my God," she cried out to her higher power.

I pushed open the door, and me and the fellows ran inside. We checked upstairs. Nothing. We ran downstairs to the basement and that's when we spotted tiny droplets of blood, then puddles of it.

"Oh shit, man! Fuck!" Frankie screamed out. Jenny ran inside when she heard Frankie screaming; she went ballistic at the sight of the blood.

"Awhhhhh! Awhhhh! Putt! John Paul! Where's Putt and John Paul?!" she screamed.

"Get her out of here, Amanda!" I hollered at Amanda, who was standing there, not sure what to do.

There wasn't anything that Amanda could do to hold Jenny back, who had started running around the basement in circles, jumping up and down, screaming for her man and her baby. I ran over to the bathroom in the den and opened the door and that's when I found my man's body. He was sitting slumped over in a puddle of blood and the baby was sitting in it too. John Paul started crying when he saw me. I stepped over Putt and picked up the baby and handed him to his mother.

Then, I dropped down to the floor and grabbed Putt's head. Those niggas had shot my man in the face and blood was seeping through a bullet hole the size of a quarter. Putt was dead. Wasn't no coming back from that, but I tried to bring him back anyway.

I put my mouth over his mouth and began to blow air. I blew as much air into his mouth as I could muster, trying relentlessly to bring him back but I couldn't. I tried with every breath in my body to revive him but the mouth-to-mouth resuscitation wasn't working. Frankie and Dread tried to pull me off of him, but I struggled with them. I refused to let go of Putt. I just couldn't let him leave me.

Then the room started spinning around real fast, and everything and everybody seemed dark and transparent. I couldn't see anybody's face in the room but Putt's, so I figured I was hallucinating.

"Get up, man. Get up, Putt. Stop playing with me!" I smacked him in the face a few times, trying to wake him up. "Man, we can go fishing; I was just fucking with you when I said I wasn't going. Get up and go get your fishing rod and your hunting knife," I rambled. Frankie and Dread dragged me away from him.

"Black, he's *gone!*" they both shouted. The strength in their voices snapped me back to reality.

Then I heard my godson crying, and the reality that Putt wouldn't be able to see his children grow up hit me like a ton of bricks. I knew how much Putt loved his children. I looked over at Putt and saw all of the blood leaving his body and I lost it.

Two days later, I woke up in the psychiatric ward of Central State Hospital.

I stayed in the psych ward for two weeks. I didn't make it to Putt's funeral, but Head's mother, Ms. Cheryl, took care of everything for me. We buried Putt in the mausoleum next to Head. I had purchased an entire section at Fairlawn Cemetery for the Crew because we had decided as a team that we should all be buried together. We figured since we were living our lives as gangsters, then we would go out as gangsters. Being buried in a mausoleum was some classy shit, so Oakwood Cemetery was out of the question for the Crew.

Despite everything that the doctors were doing for Lucky, his condition hadn't improved that much; however, he was getting around a lot better in his wheelchair. I still had around-the-clock security on him and on Starr. Rumor was that the kingpin of Blackwell wanted to speak to me about the night we jumped out on his boys on Hull Street. He saw our invasion of his team as disrespect and he sought an apology from me. I wasn't about to apologize to the nigga for my actions. The way I saw it, he should've been thanking me for not dropping his dumb-ass unarmed men that night. I sent word back to him that I wasn't apologizing for shit and that if he wanted beef, that he could bring it too. I told the messenger to tell him that if he wanted beef, that it didn't make me no difference, because *Southside is Southside, now ain't it?*

Chapter 44

Around three a.m. we drove out to Li'l Wayne's crib in suburban Chesterfield County. Li'l Wayne's ranch house sat far back on a hill in a cul-de-sac. My paid informant, Detective Dotson, had mapped the house out for me and told me that the best way to enter would be through the back door. Dread was a master locksmith and security guy so we didn't have any problems getting into his house.

Once inside, we moved stealthily. We were geared up in our ski masks, bulletproof vests, and all-black army fatigues. I crept quickly into Li'l Wayne's bedroom. The volume on his TV was up as loud as it could go, so he never heard me enter his room.

"Raise up out that mufucking bed, nigga!" I stood over top of ̃m, pointing my Glock at his dome. Li'l Wayne rolled over on his ̃, his eyes full of surprise.

̃ck going on!" he screamed as if he didn't know what time it

"Nigga, turn that mutherfucking noise down!" I ordered him. "Fuck up out the bed, nigga!" I yelled again, then nudged him in the face with the barrel of the gun. Li'l Wayne rose up out of the bed, wearing nothing but his boxers.

"Can I get my jeans?" he asked me.

I gave him a look like the stupid nigga he was.

"Nigga, what the fuck do you think this is. Dress rehearsal? Nawh, nigga, you ain't getting dressed. Fuck wrong with you? I'm not here to play with your little ugly ass!"

Starr was right; Li'l Wayne was a ugly little dude. It was the very first time that I had actually seen him close up. He was about five foot three, 140 pounds. He had a smooth bald head and a lazy left eye. His left eye wandered all around in his head, so I didn't appreciate the little dude looking at me lopsided.

"Fuck you looking for nigga!" I shoved him in his back and pushed him down the hall with my gun.

"Where's my mom? Let her go. She ain't in this," he said.

For a little nigga, Li'l Wayne had big balls. He bopped down the hall like he was the shit; his cockiness made him a lot bigger than he truly was. I got a kick out of watching the little mutherfucker showboat. Li'l Wayne kept his hands up in the air, his head leaning to the side as he bopped to the living room.

"Yo, Ma, where you at?" he called out for his mother.

"Nigga, shut the fuck up and get in the living room," I ordered.

"Wayne, baby, you al'right?" his mother screamed from the next room. I met up in the living room with Frankie, who had already tied Li'l Wayne's mom to a chair.

I shoved Li'l Wayne over to Frankie.

I gave the order. "Tie his punk ass up!"

Frankie grabbed the rope and began to tie him up. Li'l Way' mother started crying.

"Please don't hurt him," she begged, tears rolling do'

face, mixing in with her black eyeliner. She reminded me of a clown at the circus.

Li'l Wayne's mother was a dark-skinned, heavyset woman. She was maybe five feet five and weighed every bit of three hundred pounds or more. Her hair extended past her shoulders, and her eyes were hazel. I couldn't help but notice, Li'l Wayne's mother was the spitting image of my mother; the two of them looked just alike.

"Please don't kill him. Let him go," she repeated herself. The more she cried, the angrier I became. I couldn't stand the sight of her or her son.

"Shut the fuck up! Tell your mother to shut up before I drop your ass now!" I nudged him again in the face with the barrel of my gun. "Frankie, cover her up! I don't want to have to look at her fat, naked ass."

Li'l Wayne's mother was half naked, and her stomach rolls and saggy breasts were laying all over the place. There was no way I was going to continue looking at that.

"Cover her up now!" I demanded. Frankie went into their hall closet and grabbed a blanket and threw it over her. Just then, Dread came out with a man walking in front of him. The man walked with his face damn near touching the floor. Dread smacked him upside the dome.

"Raise your fucking head, old man!" Dread screamed at him.

The man raised his head slowly and said to me, "You don't have to do this, son. It's not worth it."

I couldn't believe it was Coach, and I didn't waste any time jumping in his shit.

"So this is where you've been? Over here, living the life while your wife is out there strung out on dope! How could you walk out on Gurdy, Coach? Better yet, how could you walk out on me? Man, I loved you like a father and you abandoned me!" I told him.

Coach looked me in the eye and, in so many words, explained to me why he had been missing from my life.

"Son, I loved you too, but your mother wanted something from me that I couldn't give her. I'm sorry." He attempted to say more but I cut him off.

"How long have you known these people?" I pointed the gun around the room, back and forth between Li'l Wayne and his mom.

"I just met her a month ago. I don't know much about them, but you don't have to do this," he pleaded with me.

"Let him go. Let him get his shit and let him go!" I told Dread.

Coach gave me a surprised look and then opened his mouth as if he had something else to say, but I stopped him. "Coach, get your shit and get out of here now!" I said sternly. All the begging and pleading was getting on my nerves. There was nothing anybody could say or do to stop me from executing my plan. I just wanted everybody to shut the hell up.

Coach hurried to the back, and Dread followed him. He returned with a brown paper bag in one hand and a Jehovah's Witness *Watchtower* book in the other. He turned to the woman and said, "I'm sorry," then hauled ass to the front door.

"No looking back, Coach, no looking back. You ain't seen nothing or heard nothing. You hear me?"

Coach looked at me and nodded. "Yes, son, no looking back."

"Go get your wife, Coach, Gurdy needs you," I told him. Then Dread opened the front door and Coach disappeared into the night air.

I focused my attention back to Li'l Wayne and his mom.

"So, nigga, all I want to know is how you found out where my nigga Putt lived?" I quizzed him.

Li'l Wayne laughed before he answered. "The same way you found out where I lived," he said.

"Detective Dotson?" me and Dread said at the same time.

Li'l Wayne nodded his head. "Yep!" he answered with a smirk.

I had paid Detective Dotson fifty G's for information on Li'l Wayne and his crew. He had apparently played us all for cheap, selling information to both the Fairfield Wrecking Crew and the boys from Afton.

Li'l Wayne's mother began to sob even louder. She pleaded with her son.

"This violence has got to stop. Wayne, just tell him the truth and put an end to this violence!"

Li'l Wayne looked at his mom and said, "Mom, I ain't telling the nigga shit. He gone kill me anyway. Just promise me that you gone take care of yourself. Hold it down, know what I mean?" He tried to be cool even on his mutherfucking deathbed.

"But, Wayne, please tell him. My brother, your uncle didn't—" Wayne's fat mother began to say something but I cut her off.

"Shut up!" I snapped at her, getting up close in her face. Then I leaned over and looked her dead in the eye. "It ain't nothing he can tell me that I don't already know."

Li'l Wayne fought to get out of the chair and rope to protect his moms from me.

"And just where do you think you're going? First you roll through my hood, kill Lu and shoot my uncle Todd. You kill Head, shoot Luck, abduct my girl, then you kill my nigga Putt. Wayne, you ain't going nowhere so nigga stop fighting with that chair," I told him.

Li'l Wayne shot back at me, his face balled up in a tight frown.

"Nigga, you killed my cousin Dice over some bullshit. You killed Whiteboy over some bullshit. You tried gunning my niggas down at the mall over some bullshit and every . . . You know what, that's right; I killed your nigga Head and your nigga Putt, now what, nigga!" he boasted. Then he added, "But them niggas ain't go out like no punks, before I popped both of them niggas, they both said the exact same thing!" he spat.

"What did they say?" I asked.

"Both of them niggas yelled: 'Tell my niggas that I loved them. Fairfield Wrecking Crew for life. Now suck my dick!'

"So guess what, nigga. Since your boys ain't go out like chumps, I ain't going out like one either. Southside mutherfucker, now suck my dick!" Li'l Wayne screamed, then spit his chewing gum out on the carpet.

I laughed at him, because he was a comical little dude. He sat up straight in the chair like a death row inmate waiting for his deadly injection. Just as Li'l Wayne thought I was about to blast him, I raised my Glock from my side and tricked the little badass nigga.

"Nigga, you kill my dawg, I kill your cat. It's just business, nothing personal." *Boom, Boom.* I double-tapped his mother, hitting her twice in the center of her head. I split her dome open, and her fat ass flipped backward in the chair. Li'l Wayne started screaming and bumping around in the chair.

"Nooooh, you didn't have to shoot my moms," he cried. "Nooooo, nooo! Why you have to kill her? She ain't have nothing to do with this," he moaned.

"Nigga, shut the fuck up!" I smacked him upside his head a couple of times with my hand. "Keep this nigga quiet and make sure he looks at his momma until her fat ass stops breathing. Hold his fucking head still; nigga better not move his head or I'mma shoot her fat ass again," I told Frankie and Dread. Frankie grabbed Li'l Wayne by the back of his neck and gripped him tight and made him focus on his momma's lifeless body. I decided that I needed a break from all the drama.

"I'm going back into his room. He was watching *Scarface* when we came in, so I'mma go ahead and finish watching the rest of the movie," I told the fellows. "If he so much as blinks an eye, I want ya'll to shoot his momma's fat ass again," I said.

I returned to Li'l Wayne's bedroom and watched the ending of *Scarface*. The nigga had been watching *Scarface* like he was sho'nuff gangsta. Li'l Wayne wasn't no gangsta for real, he was just another perpetrating-ass dude, 'cause if shorty was gangsta, there shouldn't have been no way for me to roll up in his crib and pop him and his momma.

I grabbed the bag of sour cream and onion potato chips that was laying on his nightstand and finished them off. When I was done with the movie and my snack, I joined Frankie and Dread back in the living room. Li'l Wayne's mom was dead as a doorknob and he was still tied up to the chair, watching her as a puddle of blood formed around her body. I ordered my guys to clean up and wipe down for prints. Once we were done, we searched the house for money, drugs, and guns. Frankie came out with a bag full of all of the above.

"How much money?" I held the pillowcase full of money up to Li'l Wayne's face. Li'l Wayne whimpered. He was all cried out and his confidence level was at an all-time zero.

" That's the fifty G's I owe Detective Dotson," he told me.

"Leave the drugs and take the money," I told Frankie. .

We gathered up the money and the guns and headed for the back door. Li'l Wayne watched as we were leaving. Just when he thought I was gone let him live, I stepped back into the living room, snatched his head back in the chair, pulled Putt's hunting knife from my back pocket and in one quick move, I slit the nigga's throat.

Blood gushed from his neck like water from a faucet, and I politely stuck my finger in his blood and tasted it—just as I had been longing to do. Then I scribbled the initials GB on his forehead and walked away, leaving the punk-ass nigga and his momma to die in peace. Before we left, Dread walked over to Li'l Wayne, pulled out his handkerchief, and wiped the initials from his forehead. I strolled to the truck, jumped in and prepared for my happy ride home. *Justice,* I thought to myself.

• • •

On our way back to Churchill, we drove across the old penitentiary bridge. As we came up along side the Daily Planet Homeless Shelter, I spotted Floyd asleep on the side of the building.

"Stop the car! I see Floyd. Man, stop the truck!" I yelled at Frankie. Frankie slowed down and stopped as he was told to do. He and Dread begged me not to hurt Floyd.

I jumped out of the truck, ran over to the side of the building, and nudged Mr. Floyd on his arm, waking him up. He opened his eyes; at the sight of me, he damn near jumped out of his skin. He surrendered his hands as if I was going to hurt him. I leaned over and got up in his face. I could sense his body shaking with terror.

"Hey, Mr. Floyd, I'm sorry about disfiguring your nose. I want you to take this and get yourself together," I said, handing him the fifty G's I'd just taken from Li'l Wayne. Mr. Floyd sat up straight and accepted the bag from my hand. He opened it up and looked inside. His eyes almost popped out of his head.

"Oh thank you, son, thank you so much. I'm sorry for all the mean things I did to you when you were a child. Please forgive me too," he asked me, and stuck his hand out for me to shake it.

"No problem, Mr. Floyd, let bygones be bygones." I shook his hand real tight, then I jogged back to the truck.

I got back inside the truck and threw on my seat belt. Frankie and Dread looked at me like I had two heads.

"Did you just give your old enemy the bag full of money?" Frankie questioned.

"If your enemy is hungry, feed him. If he is thirsty, give him something to drink. In doing so, you will heap burning coals on his head. Do not be overcome by evil, but overcome evil with good," I answered him.

"Is that more Shakespeare?" Frankie wondered.

"No Frankie, that's from Romans, chapter twelve, verses nineteen to twenty-one," I told him. "You should read the Bible sometimes," I added.

We turned the corner and headed down Broad Street. Dread leaned over and I overheard him say to Frankie, "Man, I think Black is losing it."

Chapter 45

I started having nightmares. Whenever I laid down to rest, Li'l Wayne's mother's beautiful hazel eyes and at times her shoulder-length hair and jet-black skin haunted me in the shadows. The murder of Li'l Wayne and his mother was reported as a botched robbery. Coach didn't snitch, so nobody ever suspected that I was involved.

It was the Sunday before my wedding day when I received my wake-up call. I was sitting at church with a Bible in one hand and a gun in my waist. I knew then that I had to change my life because toting a gun and a Bible at the same time was blasphemy. I felt like a hypocrite and that was a new feeling for me. I was a lot of things, but a hypocrite wasn't one of them.

I sat attentively as Amanda's pastor told the congregation, "Let's open our Bibles to the book of Genesis. Today, we are reading from chapter nineteen, verses thirty to thirty-six." Everybody pulled their Bibles out and turned to the book of Genesis. Then the pastor began to read from the Scripture. "Lot had two daughters," he began. I read along with him and that's when I realized that I was reading the story of my life, of how and why I was conceived. I was reading what Grandma had been begging me to read. Suddenly, I became ill at what I had just learned. I jumped up from the pew and ran into the hallway of the church in order to get some air. Amanda ran after me, with her Bible in hand.

"Bilal, are you okay?" she asked me. I broke down crying hysterically. I couldn't take being a sinner anymore.

"I can't do this anymore. I'm tired of living like this. It's time to change, I've got to change my life," I sobbed. Amanda embraced me, holding me in her arms real tight.

"Yes, Bilal, it is time for a change. I've been waiting for you to make that decision. It's time that you leave this fast life behind you. You are so smart and have so much to offer the world. Bilal, I didn't want to tell you this, but I got accepted to Harvard Medical School. Leave with me. Come with me to Boston. We can make it there. There's no growth potential here in Richmond." Amanda pleaded with me, being as supportive and encouraging as she knew how.

"Yes, Amanda, I will come with you. After today, I'm giving this all up. This is it for real. I can't do this anymore. I can't live the life of a sinner. Thanks, Manda, for believing in me." I hugged her back real tight, then let go of her. I opened the doors of the church and when the pastor made a call for new members and for those who wanted to rededicate their lives to Christ to come forward, I was the only person to stand and make my way down the aisle. The small congregation stood to their feet as I headed toward the pulpit. When I arrived at the altar, I dropped to my knees. One of the elders of the church held my hand and prayed over me and my life.

Chapter 46

It was my wedding day and my private chauffeur picked up my groomsmen and me an hour early from the Jefferson Hotel. In order to kill time, I had him take the scenic route through Churchill before taking us to the church. We drove down Nine Mile Road, and the first person we spotted was Sneaky Pete. He was in the parking lot of Food Circus, selling a case of bean pies. We pulled the limousine over. We figured any old day was a good day to mess with Sneaky Pete. Pete walked over to the car, nodding with every step as usual.

"Man, every time I see ya'll niggas, ya'll riding limo. Damn, man, who dead now?" he asked.

"Nawh, man, ain't nobody dead. I'm getting married today," I told him. Pete's lip dropped to the ground.

"You what? Shorty, gangstas don't tie the knot," he said, talking slow as molasses. Sneaky Pete wiped his face with his dirty face-cloth, then raised his hand, showing us a bean pie. "Man, ya'll gone need any of these pies at the reception? They make a good appetizer, man, and I know you gone need plenty appetizers 'cause you know how niggas like to eat." He nodded all the way over, dropping the pie to the ground. Pete picked it up and wiped the dirt off the plastic covering.

"Nawh, man, we got enough food." I smiled at him.

"Pete, by any chance are those the pies that were stolen from the Muslims a long time ago?" Frankie asked.

"Man, those mufucking bean pies don't ever go bad. I'll cut you a deal if you want to get a few of them," Pete said, then pointed over to the curb where the box of missing bean pies was sitting.

"Nawh, man, I'm not asking because I doubt whether or not they are stale, but Pete, you shouldn't stole them pies from them Muslims. That's fucked up!" Frankie tried to reason with him. Figuring out that Sneaky Pete was the culprit who stole the bean pies was probably the smartest thing Frankie ever figured out. He took pride in that fact.

Pete nodded out for a second, then opened his eyes. "They shouldn't left the car door unlocked in the hood. What they think, they can leave a box full of bean pies in an unlocked car and ain't nobody gone take them? Man, them niggas crazy if they think that," Sneaky Pete said. "Anyway, can ya'll give me a ride? I'm trying to get down to Triangles Restaurant on Twenty-fifth Street. The owner might want to take this up off of me." He wiped his face again with his dirty face towel.

"Nawh, Pete, it ain't enough room," Dread lied.

"Aight then, I'm gone. Everytime I see them niggas they waste my time," he mumbled underneath his breath. Sneaky Pete spotted Dope Dick David from afar. He called out to him.

"Yo, David, come give me a ride to Twenty-fifth Street nucka!" Dope Dick David was chilling on a girl's ten-speed bicycle in the parking lot of Bill's Barbecue. Dope Dick David came flying across the street on the bicycle, one leg hanging off the bike as he drove it. David parked the bike and reasoned with Sneaky Pete before he agreed to give him a ride.

"Man, I know you gone look out for me if I take you down there? I'm trynna get my shot on too, man," David said, letting it be known that he needed a shot of heroin. Sneaky Pete looked David square in the eyes and sucked his teeth at him.

"Man, you know I got you!"

Then Pete picked up the box of bean pies, jumped on the handlebars, and Dope Dick David peddled away with Sneaky Pete, dropping beans pies all the way down Nine Mile Road.

Chapter 47

I made it to the church on time and was preparing myself mentally for my walk down the aisle. Ms. Cheryl knocked on the door, then stepped in to advise us that it was time for the wedding to start.

"Black, it's time," she announced to me and my groomsmen. I glanced down at my Rolex Yacht Master and thought to myself, *Yeah, right on time.* I turned to face the mirror once more. I needed just one more glimpse of myself as a single man. I checked myself up and down, making sure that my custom-made tuxedo pants that had been hand delivered from D.C. were lying perfectly at my shoes. Hell, I figured if the White House employed the famous Georges de Paris to dress the presidents of the United States, then why couldn't my staff hire him to dress me? I brushed at the jacket, merely out of habit, because I knew for a fact that there wasn't one lint ball or piece of filth near me or my suit. I was cleaner than the board of health. Nawh, fuck that, on the real, I was so clean that the Environmental Protection Agency couldn't touch me.

I stuck out my chest, and cleared my throat. "Let's do this." I gazed over at my crew and motioned for them to leave with Ms. Cheryl, the wedding planner. Before I exited the room, I thought of Putt, Head, and Keon and how they were all missing the most important day of my life. My stickman, Lucky, was right by my side in his wheelchair, which made things a little okay for me. However, I still missed my other niggas. I desperately tried to concentrate on the wedding and my bride, but then Starr intruded upon my mind. I worried about her and wondered what she may have been doing on this day, my wedding day, the day that she had initially planned for *us* to be married.

I left the dressing room and halfheartedly took my stand at the altar. As the organist began to play, I scoped the chapel, taking notice of those in attendance. It appeared that most of the people on my wedding list were present and accounted for. *That's what's up,* I thought to myself. Then I focused my attention on the aisle and watched as the wedding party fell beautifully into place. Finally, the big moment came. The organist began to play "The Wedding March," and Amanda began sashaying down the aisle. I was absolutely stunned as my bride headed toward me. I don't know if I was in awe of her beauty or more in shock that I was actually getting married to her. I glanced over at my moms; her head hung low, deep in her lap. Momma didn't care for Amanda any more than she cared for Starr, but in her words, Amanda was a better whore for me than Starr any day. Amanda sucked up to Momma, so Momma supported our union 100 percent. After checking Momma out, my eyes shot over to the pew where Amanda's mother and grandmother were sitting. They both wore the same solemn look on their faces. For a minute, I got lost in their eyes.

Suddenly, the doors of the church flew open, and Mousey came bursting in. "Blacckk!" he yelled down toward the altar, half covering his mouth with his left hand. "Come quick. Something has happened to Starr!" he screamed, motioning with his right hand. "Come on now!"

Before anyone could acknowledge his presence, he hauled ass out of the church. Murmurs echoed throughout the church. Some of the guests moaned, while others leaned to the side like a stack of dominoes, whispering in the ear of the person sitting next to them. The next thing I know, I hauled ass past Amanda and out of the church doors. My crew bolted after me. The crimson-colored, stretch Cadillac limousine that me and my groomsmen had arrived in awaited me outside the church. We jumped in.

"Everybody strapped?" I quizzed.

"Ready," all six of my men said in unison. We removed our burners from our tuxedo jackets.

"To Fairfield Projects now, and don't catch any traffic lights!" I ordered our chauffeur.

On our way to the pj's, there wasn't a sound in the limo, except for the grinding of my teeth, and the grinding of those mutherfuckers meant that I was just as pissed off as a sissy at a sissy camp with no sissies. My niggas knew that I was vexed and that some shit was about to hop off. I didn't know what was up with Starr, but one thing was for certain, and two things were for sure, if anybody had fucked with her, I swore on everything that I loved—it would be the day that the nigga's head would roll.

We made it to Fairfield in less than ten minutes. As the limo turned onto Rosetta Street, I noticed a bunch of niggas gathered around Starr's grandmother's house. Before the car could come to a complete stop, I kicked the door open with my gator and bailed out.

"Where she at? Where she at?" I shouted as I ran past the crowd and up the sidewalk with my Glock by my side.

"Starr, where you at?" I desperately called out to her, but didn't get an answer. I raced up the stairs, skipping two at a time. I wasn't prepared for what happened next.

Chapter 48

"Oh my God, Starr!" I yelled out to her. Starr was lying across her bed dressed in a wedding gown, her head dangling off the side of the bed. In her possession was the scroll that I had given her of my version of "The Last Supper." The Gorilla Black version. "Starr, what's wrong? Are you okay?" I asked her. I pulled her head up on the bed. Starr never looked at me. She kept her head turned away from me, then started crying.

"Boo, I'm so sorry. Please forgive me for what I've done," she moaned.

"Starr, what's the matter with you? Why do you look so pale?" Starr's face and lips looked dry and pale. I grabbed her by the hand, and her palms were sweaty.

"Starr, have you had anything?" I worried. "You've been getting high?"

"Black, I don't feel so good," she moaned again.

Suga Momma yelled from downstairs, "The paramedics are on

their way. There's a car accident on the bridge, that's what's taking them so long."

"Suga Momma, did she have anything to eat? What could be wrong with her? What happened?" I rambled.

Frankie stood by my side while Dread and the crew covered the front yard and controlled the crowd.

"Frankie, help me get her out of this dress; she is sweating real bad," I told him.

Starr sighed. She refused to take the dress off.

"No, don't take my dress off. Please don't take my dress off," she moaned.

"Okay, we'll let you leave it on." I didn't want to upset her any more than she already was. It was hot as hell, but if she wanted to keep it on, then it was fine with me.

I figured Starr had overheated and I needed to cool her down, so I sent Frankie downstairs to get a tray of ice and a cold glass of water. Frankie headed downstairs and as soon as Starr heard him leave, she turned to me and, for the first time since I had been in the room, looked me directly in the eye.

"Boo, I'm having trouble breathing," she said.

"Hold on, Starr, the ambulance is on the way. Did you have something bad to eat today? What have you been doing all day?" I questioned her again. Just then, Frankie returned with the ice and the water. I tried to get Starr to drink from the glass but she wouldn't. She started crying again.

"Boo, I am so sorry, please forgive me." She kept repeating that over and over again. I didn't understand why Starr was apologizing because she hadn't done anything crazy to me—lately.

"Sorry for what, Starr?" I asked.

Starr took a deep breath. *"I LIED,"* she moaned.

"You lied? You lied about what?" I hunched my shoulders at her because I had no idea what she was talking about.

"Everything. *I lied* about everything," she said.

Frankie looked at me. He shrugged his shoulders too.

"What are you talking about?" I asked her again. Then I remembered what Putt had been trying to tell me.

"Starr, are you saying you lied about Dice?" I asked. Starr nodded her head yes.

"So, you were messing around with him?"

"No, Boo, I never messed around with Dice or Li'l Wayne, and Dice did hit me in the face at the Showplace Arena. I didn't make any of that up," she said, her words slowly fading in and out.

"Then what did you lie about?" Starr was really starting to look weak and her eyes were opening and closing as she talked. I picked her up and held her in my arms.

"I *lied* about Mr. Wayne. Li'l Wayne's and Dice's uncle. I *lied* on Mr. Wayne. That man never touched me when I was a little girl. I made the whole thing up," she confessed.

"But Starr, I was there. Mr. Wayne did molest you. I remember the day clearly," I said as I grabbed a couple pieces of ice from the ice tray and rubbed her sweaty face with the cubes.

Starr shook her head lightly. "No, Boo, you didn't see anything. Nobody did. I made the whole thing up because I overheard him proposing to Suga Momma and I didn't want Suga Momma to marry him and end up with a no-good, abusive, cheating husband like my daddy." She sighed. Starr's rambling confused me. *This can't be possible,* I thought to myself. *Am I hearing what I think I'm hearing?* I needed to be sure, so I asked for clarification again.

"Starr, what on earth are you talking about?" I repeated myself.

"You see, when I was a little girl, my daddy use to beat my momma for breakfast, lunch, and dinner. Well, one day, on my birthday, June tenth to be exact, me and Mom went over to her girlfriend Trudy's house because Trudy had left her driver's license at our house when she and Chris was at my birthday party. Well, when we got to Trudy's house, Momma noticed Daddy's car parked out front. I guess Momma got suspicious, so she didn't knock on the door; she just pushed the door right on open. Well, to Momma's surprise, she found Daddy and Trudy in the bed together. Momma and Trudy started fighting and Trudy pushed Momma down a flight of stairs and Momma fell to her death. When Daddy realized that Momma was dead, he beat Trudy down until he killed her with his bare hands. Well, Chris came running with a butcher knife and stabbed my daddy in his back. Black, they all died at the bottom of the stairs. So Chris told me to go outside and get in the backseat of the car and pretend that it never happened. So, that's what I did. I buried the memories so far in the back of my mind that I forgot about it until years later when I started remembering bits and pieces. All of my life I grew up being told that my parents died in a car accident, when they didn't. The police found me in the back of the car, so that's the story Suga Momma decided to tell me. Suga Momma made up the whole car accident thing in case I remembered being found in the car. It just so happened that I started remembering way more than just that!"

Starr had given me a mouthful of information and it was all too overwhelming for me, yet I needed more.

"So what does any of this have to do with you lying on Mr. Wayne?" I asked.

"Well, when I walked up at the social and overheard Mr. Wayne telling Suga Momma how much he loved her, it freaked me out because Daddy used to tell Momma that he loved her all the time, then in the next breath, he would punch her and knock her to the floor. I didn't want that to happen to Suga Momma. I don't wish that on any woman. That's why I couldn't stand Head, because he was always beating up on Baije," she added. "Black, the only way I knew to break up Suga Momma and Mr. Wayne was to tell her that he touched me, so that's what I did," she told me.

Starr continued spilling the truth; it was time to come clean and she wasn't holding back anything.

"Black, I broke up with you for the same reason," Starr said, her voice getting weaker by the minute.

"Why did you break up with me?" I wanted to know. Starr let out a huge sigh, her eyes kicked back in her head.

"Boo, you are the only man that I have ever wanted, the only man that I have ever loved. But I was afraid. I was afraid of you becoming just like my father. I don't know, I guess I was afraid of love," she admitted. "Black, you were my first, my last, my everything, and I hurt you. When I saw Dice at the Showplace Arena, he only asked me why I lied on his uncle and I told him to kiss my ass, and that's why he hit me. Then, when Li'l Wayne abducted me, he told me to speak the truth. He said that his uncle had died a year after the beat-down and that his death was a result of the head injuries that he had sustained. Boo, all of these people have died because of me and I can't live with that," she said, breathing slowly.

"Starr, what do you mean you can't live with that? Starr, what did you do!" I screamed at her.

Starr moaned, "I cooked up some coke today and put it in a pipe."

"You what?" I jumped up and looked around her room. Sure enough, a pipe, a saucer, and other paraphernalia were on the windowsill. "Frankie, help me get her out of here. Starr's heart can't take this shit!" I lifted her and Frankie held her feet. "I'm taking her over to my mother's house; it's hot as hell in here. Moms got air conditioning." I panicked, trying to get my baby out of Suga Momma's place. The project walls were made out of cinder block, and it was hotter inside the apartment than it was outside.

Frankie and I hurried downstairs and I ran out the front door with Starr in my arms.

"Where's the ambulance?" I asked Suga Momma. "Are they on the way?"

"They said they're trying to get here as fast as they can, but that accident on the bridge has traffic backed up and they're stuck in it." The crowd looked on as we took Starr across the street.

"Dread, Frankie, keep everybody back, " I hollered at them.

I made it to Momma's house, but when I reached for her door keys I remembered that I didn't have them in my pockets.

"Where the fuck is the ambulance!" I spun around with Starr in my hands. Starr was burning hot, I could feel the heat through the wedding gown.

"Boo, I can't breathe. I think I'm dying." Starr sighed. If I could just get her to cool off, I knew she would be okay.

"Starr, why in the world would you be hitting the pipe? Don't you know that shit can kill you?" I asked, not really expecting a response to that question. I couldn't get her inside Momma's air-conditioned apartment so I sat down on the porch and laid her across my lap. I fanned her with my hand to keep her cool.

"Yeah, I figured it would kill me but I don't care, I just can't live with the guilt anymore," she answered me honestly. "Black, I'm tired. I don't know how much longer I can hold on," she sighed.

I stepped into Momma's garden, still holding Starr in my arms and my Glock in my hand. I turned on Momma's garden hose and began to splash water on my baby's face.

Just then, Momma and a lot of folk from the church pulled up. They all jumped out, leaving their cars parked in the middle of the street. They hurried over to see what was going on. Suga Momma ran over with an update on the paramedics.

"The paramedics are still having a hard time getting here but they said to keep her head propped up. I told them she has heart problems, and they are trying to get here as fast as they can." Suga Momma remained calm, her eyes still full of hope.

Momma walked up, with her hands on her hips. "Boy, what the hell are you doing in my garden?" she asked, words slurring 'cause she was drunk as a fish on my wedding day. Momma had the nerve to show up at the church drunk as hell.

The neighbors all started shouting at Momma 'cause they knew she was about to cause a scene.

"Joann, leave him alone. Starr is sick. Just leave them alone and let him help her!" people shouted.

Momma ignored them. She didn't give a damn about Starr, never had, and she sure as heck wasn't about to have her precious flower garden ruined because of her. Water had started building up in the flower garden because I had left the hose running.

"Boy, get your ass out of my garden!" Momma fumed.

Starr's breathing began to slow down.

"Boo, I'm tired. I can't hold on," she breathed in again.

"Starr, hold on, baby, the ambulance will be here any minute, " I said, trying to calm her down.

"I'm so sorry," she apologized again.

"Starr, we can fix this. Don't worry about it. We all do things that we aren't proud of. Starr, I have a confession, too." I decided to tell her one of my secrets so she wouldn't be the only one feeling guilty.

"What is it, Black?" she wondered.

"Well, since you're confessing, I might as well tell you that you were not the first girl I had sex with," I told her. Starr frowned. Of coure she was surprised to hear that.

"Whattt?" she grumbled.

"Okay, I never did tell you this, but before me and you hooked up, I had sex with Chelle. You know Chelle with all the gold teeth? Yeah, Starr, believe it or not, I hit that." I confessed to one of the worse sins known to man.

"Ooh, Boo, you nasty. Then again, Chelle's ass is phat so I don't blame you. If I was a dude, I would've hit that too." Starr laughed, so I assumed she was feeling better and coming down off of her cocaine high.

Momma was pacing back and forth arguing with the neighbors and the crowd about being too close to her yard. She focused her attention back on me and Starr and continued with her obsceni-ties.

"Boy, get your ass up!" Momma screamed again. I continued to ignore her because Starr needed my attention, not Momma.

"Boo, I can't breathe. I'm dying, " Starr predicted. I rocked back and forth with Starr in my arms. I tried to keep her up until the paramedics arrived but she kept opening and closing her eyes as if she was losing consciousness.

"Starr, don't you leave me girl. Starr, who gave you the coke? Where did you get it from?" I needed to know, because if Starr died I swore on everything that I would drop the nigga who had given her the cocaine.

Starr looked deep into my eyes and said,"Boo, I got the coke from you."

"Starr, that's impossible. How? Did one of my workers sell it to you?" I fumed.

Starr rubbed up and down her wedding gown, and at first I couldn't figure out why she was feeling all over herself and that's when I realized that she had something over the top of the wed-ding gown. It was a white apron. My old Church's Chicken apron. She patted around until her hand landed on the small pocket. She patted on it, trying to tell me something. That's when it all hit me.

"Oh my God, no!" I screamed.

"Yeah, Boo. I found your old apron way back in my closet, and I cooked up the rock that was in the apron pocket."

The last time I had seen that apron was the night that Skilow had given me the recompressed cocaine. It was the same night that I had taken the apron off over Starr's house right before she and I had made out.

Recompressed cocaine was more dangerous to your health because it had been mixed with God only knows how many different chemicals. Four years later, Starr had found the rock that Fat Tony had given me from Skilow. The cocaine was 89 percent pure. I remembered the day when Fat Tony handed it to me. He had said, *Man, get yourself a professional to test it out.*

"Starr, please tell me that you didn't cook up the coke from my apron?" I wanted her to deny it. Starr nodded her head.

"Yeah, Boo, I did and I also took some antidepressants that the doctor gave me. I just can't live with this guilt anymore," she cried out, her skin turning colors right before my eyes.

Starr's heart was failing her and there wasn't a damn thing I could do. At that moment I realized that no matter how big I was, or how much money I had, there wasn't enough money in the world that could buy Starr more time with me. Starr had suffered with heart problems her entire life and the doctors were always coming up with a different diagnosis for her. Her heart problem combined with the cocaine, antidepressants, stress, guilt, and shame was a deadly combination. I needed the paramedics to get the fuck there but those bastards were nowhere in sight.

"Hold on, baby, just hold on," I continued to say.

"Hold on, Starr, hold on," people in the crowd repeated.

Starr gazed into my eyes, and then one small tear strolled down her face. She took in three deep breaths. "I love you, Black," she sighed and, just like that, Starr was gone. I guess you could just say she died from a broken heart.

I jumped up from the ground and ran around in the yard.

"Noooh, noooh." I flipped out. "Help me, somebody help me." I ran in circles, not knowing what to do or who to turn to.

So I turned to my Momma. "Momma, please help me. Help me, Momma," I screamed for her.

Momma stood on the sidewalk, with her hands on her hips. "Boy, get your black ass out of my garden. She's dead now and ain't a damn thing you can do to bring her back, so stop acting stupid!" she yelled.

A few people tried to get into the garden with me. I pointed my gun at them.

"Get back," I threatened.

I wanted Momma to help me. I reached out for Momma again. "Help me, Momma, please help me." I was desperate for her help. Momma sucked her teeth and rolled her neck around at me.

"Boy, I'm not going to tell you again to get your black ass out of my garden!" she shouted.

"Leave him alone. Stop it, Joann!" her friends yelled, the neighbors yelled, everybody yelled at Momma. Momma ignored them all.

Just then, Amanda and her family walked up. Momma turned around and looked at them.

"You need to get your ass from out of that mud puddle and go on and marry this girl right here." She pointed to Amanda.

Amanda moved toward the flower garden. I raised my gun up and waved it around.

"Get back; I don't want anybody to come in here. Starr is resting," I said.

"Come on, Black, she's dead. Let us help you," my crew shouted.

"Bilal, let me help you," Amanda offered but there was nothing she could do to help me except leave me alone. I looked at Amanda. I figured I needed to tell her the truth.

"Listen, Amanda, you a nice girl and all but I can't marry you. Starr is my woman, the only woman that I have ever loved. Hell, Starr is the only chick that ever really made my dick get hard. Besides, Starr never tried to change me or make me out to be something that I'm not. She accepted me just the way I am, but you, you want to try and change a nigga. Let me give you one word of advice, Amanda, the next time you get a man, don't try and change him, just accept him the way he is," I told her straight to her face.

Amanda's father grabbed his daughter and carried her away.

"I told you he wasn't no good for you," her father said as he left with his daughter on his arm. Amanda cried on the way to their car.

"Oh, Daddy, I can't believe this. You were right," she whined.

"Yeah, get her out of here," I said, still waving the gun around. I squatted down and kissed Starr in the mouth, and that's when Grandma walked up.

"Bilal," she called my name. "Put the gun away and let me help you." She spoke calmly, her words caring and reassuring. I broke down crying at the sight of Grandma and Granddaddy, my daddy.

"Help me, Grandma. Starr is gone." I cried like a baby.

"Give me the gun, Bilal. I can help." Grandma held her hand out for the weapon. I was about to hand over the Glock when Momma opened her mouth.

"Who in the hell invited them to the wedding anyway? Did Cheryl's dumb ass invite them or did your dumb ass? Boy, stop acting stupid. You making a fool of yourself."

"Grandma, I'm so sorry. I should have listened to you. I read the story of Lot and now I know the whole truth," I told her. Momma stood behind her parents and smacked her lips.

"What truth?" she growled at their backs.

I began to recite the Scripture from the book of Genesis. "Lot had two daughters. He and his two daughters lived in a cave. One day the older daughter said to the younger daughter, 'Our father is old and there are no more men around here to lie with us, as is the custom all over the earth. Let's get him drunk and lie with him so that we can preserve our family line through our father.' So, the first night, the girls got their father to drink and the older daughter lay with her father. He was not aware of it when he lay down with his daughter. The next day, the older daughter said, 'Last night I lay with my father, let's get him drunk again, and you go in and lie with him so we can preserve our family line through him.' I recapped the story from the Bible.

I broke out laughing. "The only difference, Mom, is that you seduced your own father but your younger sister wouldn't go through with it," I said.

"What the fuck!" people in the crowd screamed.

I looked at the crowd and told them, "Yeah, Momma seduced her own daddy and got pregnant and that's how yours truly came to be," I said as I pointed to my chest with the Glock. "I'm my granddaddy's son!" I yelled.

My granddaddy/daddy looked me square in the eye. I saw fire in his eyes. The same fire that I suppose Keon had seen in mine the day we moved to Fairfield.

"Yeah, Momma, once again you lied to me. You told me your father molested you." Momma's eyes grew big, and she drew back like she was going to jump in the muddy flower garden and hit me.

"You black mutherfucker!" she shouted at me with her fist drawn. "I didn't tell you shit. I told you that my father slept with me. Your black ass assumed that he molested me," she shot back at me.

"Black, black, black. That's all you know. I'm sick and tired of you calling me Black. Yeah, I am a black man, Momma. But my skin is not black; I am two shades darker than Starr and four shades lighter than you. So stop calling me Black." I stood up to her once and for all.

It was true; I was not a dark-skinned brother at all. In fact, my complexion was light brown, but to Momma I was black mutherfucker, black boy, black ass, black punk, black, black, black. Momma wasn't the only person who used the term frequently or figuratively. It was common in the African-American culture, whether in the hood or the suburbs, for my own people to refer to each other as black mutherfuckers. The insult had absolutely nothing to do with skin color but rather ignorance and lack of pride in one's own race. I couldn't understand why as African Americans we would disrespect ourselves, calling each other black mutherfuckers, but if a person of another race so much as used the *term* we would be ready to chop them up and eat them for dinner.

I thought about how I was once a proud little black boy and how I had fucked up my life. I started tripping. I began to recite "Negro," the poem that I was reading the day when I first met Starr. *"I am Black as the night is Black, Black like the depths of my Africa."* I rambled the poem off, but Momma cut me short.

"I told ya'll that black mutherfucker was crazy," she spat.

• • •

Baije ran up out of nowhere. She starting screaming when she realized that her best friend was dead in the garden. She ran up to the yard, looked in, saw Starr and fainted right on the spot. A few of the guys picked her up and carried her into a neighbor's house. Next, Crazy Chris came running down the block. Mrs. Irene was running behind him, and they were both screaming.

"Come back, Chris," Mrs. Irene yelled after him. She was afraid that he was going after the crowd.

"Starrrr," Crazy Chris screamed. It was the first time since witnessing his parents' demise that anyone had heard him speak. I allowed Starr's half brother into the garden. He bent over, found one red rose in the mud, and stuck it into her hair. Then Crazy Chris kissed Starr on the lips and ran away.

"Starrrr," he screamed as he ran back up the block.

Momma started in on me again. "Boy, come out of that yard!" she yelled, caring about no one or nothing else except her prize-winning flower bed.

Finally, police sirens and the ambulance could be heard in the distance. We had waited a whole twenty minutes for help and those mutherfuckers were just getting there. Momma threatened me with the police presence.

"Yeah, they coming for your black ass. You better get up. Turn that goddamn water hose off. You're fucking up my flowers!" she badgered. The entire yard was muddy and water had spilled onto the sidewalks and into the street.

The realization that Starr was gone hit me like a ton of bricks. The realization that people had died because of a *lie* hit me even harder. My head started hurting, the earth started spinning and shaking, music started playing in my head and I couldn't shut it off. I heard Momma's favorite song, "When a Man Loves a Woman," then the song "Two People" by Tina Turner. Then I started seeing and hearing dead people. Keon, Dice, Lulu, Whiteboy, Head, Putt, Li'l Wayne, and Li'l Wayne's mother. They were gone! They were all dead because of a *lie*.

I looked over at Momma and she looked like Li'l Wayne's mother. I thought my mind was playing tricks on me, so I rubbed my eyes and sure enough, Momma's face kept changing. One minute she looked like Momma, next minute she looked like Li'l Wayne's momma. I flipped out.

"Oh my God, why did I kill Li'l Wayne's mother? Oh my God, I killed Starr too! Starr is dead because of me!" I realized that it was my product, the cocaine that was left in my possession, that had taken my baby's life. It was so irresponsible of me to hold onto it the night that the New York boys left it with me and it was just as irresponsible for me to be selling drugs on the street anyway. Not only had I killed Starr, I was killing people and destroying lives every time me or my Crew made a drug sale.

"Black, let us in, give us the gun, man. You ain't kill Starr, it's not your fault. Give us the gun." My crew reached for it but I pointed the gun at them, threatening them with it.

Suga Momma ran over with Starr's purse in her hand. She screamed. "Don't give up. Everybody pray! We got to pray! God can turn this thing around!" Momma laughed out loud, then sucked her teeth.

"That girl is gone. Bilal, I'm not going to say it again: Get your black, stupid ass up," Momma said one more time.

I couldn't take her insults anymore, so I began to tell her everything that I had been feeling and wanting her to know.

"Momma, all I ever wanted was for you to love me. But because you didn't love me, or believe in me, I didn't love or believe in myself. I spent my entire life trying to please you, trying to make you happy. You never once told me you loved me, so what did I do, I ended up latching on to the first girl I met—Starr. I wanted so badly to be loved by a woman because I never got love from you. Momma, if you would have believed in me, I could have been anything in life that I wanted to be. But because you beat my self-esteem down so bad, I settled for this life. I could have been a doctor, a lawyer, an astronaut, maybe even the first black president, but look at me. Just look at your son, I am a no-good-for-nothing drug dealer. A murderer. I've amounted to nothing but a foulmouth, egotistical fool. Everything out of my mouth is nigga this or nigga that; I use the word freely, like it's suppose to show some type of affection when my people have suffered and died for being *niggers,* and over the years my ego has grown bigger than my dick. Momma, this here ain't me, this is not who your son was designed to be. I've spent my whole life trying to fit in, trying to be somebody I'm not. I wanted to fit in with everybody else 'cause I never fit in with you," I cried, my heart hurting and my soul aching.

Momma just stood there, with her lips poked out and her eyebrows raised. I continued while I had her full attention; maybe something was sinking in, I thought. "I've been out here selling drugs, trying to provide for you because you told me that you was gone put my ass out of your house if I didn't make money. You even told me to sell my ass if I had to. Why, Momma? Why have you treated me this way my entire life? I didn't ask to be here," I cried.

Momma looked at me half crazy. "Well, if your ass didn't ask to be here, then why don't you just make yourself disappear," she taunted. I raised the gun up and pointed it.

"No, don't do it," someone in the crowd screamed.

"Bilal, don't do it. God can forgive you for anything except—" Grandma attempted to say, but Momma wouldn't allow her to finish her sentence.

"Go ahead, I got insurance." Momma dismissed me. I smiled at Momma.

"I know you got a million-dollar life insurance policy on me because I saw it in your shoe box, but guess what, you dumb ass? I bet you didn't know that there was a no-pay clause for suicide, now did you?"

Momma took a step back, her eyes full of surprise. You could have bought her cheap ass for a penny.

I leaned over and kissed Starr in the mouth one last time and then I recited two lines from one of my man Shakespeare's sonnets:

Love alters not with his brief hours and weeks,
But bears it out even to the edge of doom.

I thought about Adolf Hitler and all that I had learned about him. Historians to this day still don't know if Hitler or his ride-or-die chick Eva Braun ended it first. To me, it really didn't matter who made the first move. The most important thing to know is that the ruthless leader and his chick abandoned the world together. Whether it was planned or done on impulse is beside the point. All I know is the two of them went out together like true mutherfucking soldiers. I took in a deep breath, raised the Glock to my head, looked at Momma and then the crowd, and said, "I never liked the fat bitch anyway!" then *BOOM*. I blew my brains out. So much for the bitch's insurance money.

"God can forgive you for anything except self-murder," Grandma's voice trailed in the distance.

> "Half of ya'll brothers beefing, don't know
> what ya'll beefing about."
>
> —Seven

Acknowledgments

Writing acknowledgments is actually harder for me than writing a novel. Pondering and worrying about whom to thank and being careful not to leave anyone out can be quite taxing on an author. So at the last hour, I have decided to thank the people who have *always* been in my corner and the folks who were patient with me as I wrote and edited *Gorilla Black*.

Giving the highest praise to my Lord and Savior, for without him, I am nothing! To my mother, the strongest and bravest woman I know. I am but a reflection of you! I love you more than words can say. To my brother G, my strongest supporter and greatest fan. You've been in prison for nineteen years and not a day goes by that I do not think of you. I love you with all my heart and soul! To my dearest friends, LaShan Robinson, Elonda Dolly, Germaine Evans, Shonte Shelton, Traci Rollins-Johnson, Stefanie Lea, and Hope Murray. You all have seen me at my best and loved me at my worst. I truly thank God for each one of you! To my friend and personal assistant, Lakeisha Pitts, thank you for understanding the big picture and for being the eyes behind my back! To my cousins Gail Tinsley and Michael Pennick, thanks for hustling my books out of the trunk of your cars. I am forever grateful! To my nieces and nephews, I love you like my own! To Derrick Hardy, thank you for being a father to our son. To D.C.'s own businessman extraordinaire, D.J. Big John, your kindness, and true plutonic friendship, has meant the world to me. To Richard Brooks, Ph.D., thanks for treating me like a queen! Because of you, the bar has been raised! To my Starbucks Coffee Club of Largo, Maryland. On many occasions, our morning talks have kept me grounded! To Ditto and Four Sisters, with you I am free! To Dr. Evora Jones and Dr. Delores Hayes of Virginia Union University, thanks for demanding the best! You ladies prepared me for the real world. To Melody Guy and the staff at One World/Ballantine Books, thank you for believing in me and my work! I am truly honored to be a part of the team! To my literary agent, Marc Gerald, and Caroline Greevan of the Agency Group, thanks for sealing the deal! Marc, I still cannot believe you added little old me to your client roster!

To the Queen of Hip Hop Fiction, Ms. Nikki Turner. Who would have thought, four years later, we would be here? I remember first meeting you. A mutual friend referred me to you and within ten minutes of our conversing over the Internet, you invited me to submit a story for *Street Chronicles*. As we were typing back and forth, my crazy brain kicked out the first several lines to *Big Daddy*. You encouraged me to keep going and before the week was out, I had turned the complete story in to you. You cheered me on, every step of the way! Screaming at me on the phone, yelling at me on paper. "Bring it, Seven!" you shouted numerous times. There were many times I thought you would show up at my house in a cheerleader uniform, pom-poms and black-and-white bucks! Then, tons of submissions later, my story *Big*

Daddy was chosen to lead the *Street Chronicles* series, and now, I have been chosen as the lead author for the Nikki Turner Presents book line. Nikki, you wanted to see me win and I did! I must admit, if I must work with anyone, I'd rather work with a boss lady who doesn't mind getting excited and doing flips over someone else's work. So, for all of your flips and words of encouragement, I thank you from the bottom of my heart. You have truly been a blessing! To Travis Hill, words cannot begin to explain how grateful I am for you. Thank you for being the calm in the midst of my storm. I love you, I really do. And saving the best for last, I want to thank my children, LaDaryl and Isaiah, for giving me the strength and courage to live. You guys are the wind beneath my wings!

—Seven/The Urban Therapist

About the Author

Seven was born the seventh child to one of the most notorious hustlers in Richmond, Virginia. She was raised in the Whitcomb Court housing projects. She is also a poet and a graduate of Virginia Union University. She lives in the D.C. area with her children and is currently a graduate student, working on a master's in public administration.

Contact Seven at:
www.sevenspeaks.com (website)
Sevenspeaks@aol.com (e-mail)
or write
P.O. Box 6864
Largo, MD 20792-6864